I0554370

# The Psyop System

## Book One: Lights in the Sky

—Everett Hall—

This book is a work of fiction. The characters, incidents, and dialogue are drawn from the author's imagination and are not to be construed as real. Any resemblance to actual events or persons, living or dead, is entirely coincidental.

THE PSYOP SYSTEM. Copyright © 2016 by T. Everett Hall
NatureHouse Press
Philadelphia, PA
All rights reserved. This book or any portion thereof may not be reproduced or used in any manner whatsoever without the express written permission of the publisher, except for the use of brief quotations in a book review.

Printed in the United States of America


First Printing, 2016


ISBN-13: 978-0-9983875-0-5
ISBN-10: 0-9983875-0-9



www.everett-hall.com

*To my incredible wife, who always keeps me grounded whenever I start drifting off into space.*

The Major Realms of Planet Deaer

# Part 1

## 1 | The Voice Inside the Helm

—Landfall achieved—

—Landfall achieved, please confirm—

Consciousness returned to him in a torrent when he heard her commanding voice speak the directive, transmitted to him through his helmet. The voice of his Operator.

As she'd warned, Projection had been the strangest experience he could've ever imagined; the process by which his body had been vaulted through the fabric of space and set down, somewhere upon some unknown planet's surface. She'd said that, when Projection is executed properly, he ought to feel no more than a tickling or a numbing sensation, as when a limb temporarily loses circulation. Under more challenging conditions, it could feel quite like lying on a bed of needles. And when executed in significant error, Projection almost always resulted in fatality.

"Landfall confirmed," he reported quietly into the helmet's mouthpiece, grimacing from an assortment of aches and pains. A gray streamlined exosuit enveloped his body, snug but flexible. The humidity, dense and palpable, nearly overcame him, until sensors inside the suit assessed the climate and mercifully began cooling his skin with light jets of air. Presently, he knelt in a patch of mud beneath a canopy of looming trees, trying to revive his weakened senses.

—Complications?—

He stood up slowly, and though the suit and helmet were surprisingly light, he realized supporting their unnatural forms would take some getting used to, "Vision is blurry, balance is shaken, and my head feels like it's splitting from the inside out. Do those qualify as complications?"

—Senses are often impaired upon landfall. They will return to you momentarily—

"Fantastic," he cracked a woeful cringe, "any idea of the long-term health risks I'm taking for all of this?"

—Let's work on surviving this operation first, Mr. Spurlock—

"A brochure, or a pamphlet, or something I could skim through would be nice, if you can manage?"

An ominous hush followed his last remark, during which she offered no reply, forcing his derision to linger on the invisible tether that somehow connected his voice to hers. Sarcasm was really the only means available, at present, for coping with his circumstances, and he decided he'd employ it as often as needed.

The foliage about him was thick and laden with water, beaded and running into drops that fell from the leafy canopy above. There'd been recent rainfall here, but it was ended now, and a pale rainbow could be sighted far off through the tropical brush.

—Remember, Mr. Spurlock, you sought this mission out for yourself—

"Remember? If only I could," he scoffed. He didn't recall ever volunteering for this mission; or *any* mission, for that matter. Overhead, a colorful bird glided aloft, averting his attention. Its long beak clutched a fish that flailed helplessly; pathetically. A feeling of sympathy for the captured fish overcame him, for he too felt like a terribly helpless being, snatched up and squirming under the power of a predator far greater than he.

—What *do* you remember?—

"This morning. Waking up in a small room and your voice instructing me to put on this suit and prepare for this process you've called Projection; great flashes of light, numbness, pain. Then you asked me to confirm landfall in this… jungle where I'm standing now, waiting for further instruction."

—Is that all?—

"That's all… Is there more; *should there* be more? You didn't dissect me up there, or give me some other guy's brain, or neuter me, did you?"

—Such patterns of memory loss are troubling, indeed. Your condition may stand poorer than we've yet suspected. So let me declare to you anew as I did when you awoke this morning: I will assist you through completion of your mission. You will perform various operations, such as the one in which you find yourself engaged right now. If you cooperate, complications ought to be few. But if you do not, the most ultimate consequences are sure to follow close behind. Are we clear?—

"Is that a threat?"

—Not a threat, no. Quite the opposite. It is guidance, for your own protection—

"I see," he was detecting a hint of impatience in her tone now. "And what exactly is the purpose of this mission I'm on?"

—It is a mission of discovery. You will seek Coordinates on the planet's surface, and you will carry out objectives as they are assigned. In so doing, however, you must eliminate the most frivolous of chatter, such as we have exchanged thus far. Is that understood?—

"Yeah, sure. It doesn't seem like I have a choice."

—Now, if we're to get down to business, you must know you are at severe risk, even now where you stand, so please let us make up for lost time. Scale of operation: three Coordinates in sum. Scope of operation: strictly observational. All forms of sentient contact are prohibited; be they visual, verbal, physical, or other. Do you understand?—

"Avoid detection, yeah, I think I got it. Oh, and by the way, you don't have to ask for my understanding every single time you…"

—Do you *understand?*—

She cut him off with a sternness that made him straighten his stance in the elaborate suit.

"Yes… understood."

—Please proceed to your first Coordinate. Location: the tropical archipelago of Planet Deaer. Sightline thirty-two degrees—

His helmet's visor scanned the densely-forested incline ahead and registered a sort of waypoint, which appeared as a digital marker before his eyes. The visor maintained the Coordinate's plotted location despite his movements, eliminating any doubt over where he must proceed.

He said softly, "Bearings seem to have locked-in."

The incline proved steep enough in places to require nearly his most earnest of efforts. Mud burped underfoot with the breaking of suction at each emerging step, but at least it seemed his senses had returned to him in near-full capacity. *Or full enough that I'm not constantly face-planting in the muck, so that's good.*

There had been a room, indeed, where he'd awoken. A small room, that held within it only three personal items, which doubtlessly bore some measure of significance to him, but for which he regretfully, as in all other things, held no recollection. The first was a pair of eye glasses, which served an obvious purpose, but they remained behind now in the room, as his visor provided all the optical assistance he required. The second item was a framed photograph of a lovely young woman, smiling beneath a tree bursting with pink blossoms. A decidedly romantic setting, if he might have ventured a guess. And romantic their relationship must have been, at least to the extent that it had befitted the gifting of a photograph for keeps by his bedside. The third item was a key, which he'd hung around his neck by its chain. And that was where it remained, even now under his suit, while he trudged along, pushing through the foliage on Planet Deaer; though he questioned why he'd decided on wearing the key at all. *Considering I have no idea what it could possibly open.*

When he emerged from the mud and the jungle brush, brilliant rays broke through cotton-white clouds to bathe a grassy clearing in light, and the waypoint in his visor marked a modest wooden structure—*by all means a shack*—standing before him as his first Coordinate.

"Destination confirmed," he voiced, and the helmet made a hissing sound, like air escaping from a steam valve, when he lifted the visor up and away from his face to catch a breath of fresh air.

—Exercise extreme caution disengaging your visor! I repeat, exercise extreme caution—

"Geez," staggered Spurlock, "what's your deal? Do you know how stifling this thing is?"

—You do not want to find out what happens when Projection takes hold of you without full suit and helmet seal. It's not a pretty sight—

"Right…" he paused for a moment, considering the warning, "well I definitely don't wanna have my face sizzled off by the razor edges of some space continuum, if that's what you're saying could happen. But won't you at least give me a fair warning before warping me around again?"

—Circumstances aren't always so predictable. Bear in mind, your helmet and suit represent your life down there. Without them, you will have no way to communicate; nor will you have any safe means by which to engage Projection, and you'd be hopelessly and indefinitely stranded—

*You're just full of rules, aren't you madam dictator? At this point, I'm reluctant to ask how I'm supposed to relieve myself in this thing.* The mission parameters were stifling, but the pure breezes that blew across his face felt positively refreshing, justifying (if only in small measure) the hasty disengagement of his visor. He'd come upon the edge of a cliff, and down below, a coastline stretched along the reaches far beyond; a beach with waves lapping gently on white sand. A school of porpoises swam hurriedly through the aquamarine waters, the way a cluster of meteor might dart through an azure space-scape. He turned and looked back at the jungle. *Beautiful place, this Planet Deaer, but I wouldn't survive more than a few nights alone in this wild. At least not with this tinfoil voice constantly filling my ears.*

—Fortune also serves you well that Deaer's atmosphere stands supportive of human life, or else this would have been a very short mission, indeed, with your breaking of the pressure seal. I will repeat myself: follow my commands with all the strictness they are due, or the ultimate consequence will surely follow—

*Death. She means death. This arrangement just keeps getting better for me, doesn't it?*

He took her warnings to heart and lowered the visor back in place with a vacuum seal. Turning from the cliffside, he approached the shack with caution.

—Describe the contents of the Coordinate's structure—

He stepped inside.

"It's a mess." Shafts of light filtered through the gaps between the wall planks, illuminating bands of dust whenever the wind swirled, even but gently. "A stool, a small table, some dirty tools; all just thrown around and left here to be eaten up by cobwebs."

It all portrayed a bleak and dismal scene. Except, he noticed, for a machine, which was quite spectacular in form and size. It caught his attention standing in the center of the floor, pointing toward the ceiling and looking to assume every bit the function of an oversized cannon.

"But there's something else here; some kind of mechanized artillery," he continued, swiping his gloved fingertips along the machine's sooty barrel, and his suit assessed the residue. Data was displayed almost immediately in the corner of his visor, telling of the acquired properties. "Appears operational, but hardly ever used. If you ask me," he added, "it seems totally out of place for…"

—Prepare for Projection—

The voice cut him off again in all its perfect lucidity.

—Secure your position and prepare for Projection. Please stand by—

Sensing genuine urgency in her directive, he hurriedly withdrew from the structure and knelt down; compact and as still as possible, trying hard not to flex a muscle or inflate a lung. After all, he'd been told about the hazards of this surreal process. *And I'm not about to press my luck.*

Then the throes of Projection took him, and he disappeared where he knelt (into thin air) leaving behind the shack, its mysterious machine, and the broad-leafed trees blowing fervently in the wind.

\*\*\*

|Planet Deaer, The Realm of Maelnlock

—Projection in progress, please hold firm, Projection in progress—

Intense, abstract light stretched by Spurlock's face, seemingly *through* his face, and he was again immersed in this odd process, with which he imagined he'd never fully acclimate himself.

—Landfall achieved. Please be advised of hostile activity—

This time, his senses returned to him almost immediately. Stiff and lethargic, but entirely unharmed, he was placed in a rugged region of Planet Deaer marked by craggy landscapes in all directions. The ground was dry, but dense cloud cover threatened a forthcoming storm.

"I'm here," he said, "no complications."

—Your second Coordinate. Sightline, forty-seven degrees. Please be advised of hostile activity—

Her voice was calm in his ear, but again, the message was one of certain urgency.

—Please proceed to the Coordinate immediately—

Without another word, he was off setting a brisk pace in pursuit of a new waypoint plotted in his visor. *Hostiles. She mentioned hostiles.* Ahead, he saw nothing but escarpments and ridges with gnarled scrub growing everywhere in-between. And fog; like the cool clouds were rapidly dropping to combine with warm steam rising from the ground, filling each crack and crevice with a screen of mist. *But no sign of activity at all.*

"More information, please," he asked of her, while realizing just how unfit he was, laboring as he pressed on; anxiety starting to get the better of him, "you referenced hostiles?"

—Please proceed to your Coordinate with haste. Preparing oxygen feed—

Her indirect denial of additional guidance was unsettling, but he wouldn't refuse the offer she'd made in its place. A sudden dispersal of air filled his helmet; a supplemental boost of oxygen. *I guess when an Operator closes a door, she also opens a window. How generous...* He breathed the oxygen into his lungs with unabashed eagerness.

Fierce breezes greeted him, then, without warning, disrupting his footing in the rubble and nearly knocking him over. Ahead, a wall of rock seemed to make for a perfect shield, so he bore down and pursued its refuge. Gaining the heights finally at its upright face, he found cover, slumping himself down into a sitting position, his back flat against the solid formation.

"I hope there's a robust health insurance policy attached to this mission," he wheezed. "What's the co-pay on collapsed lung treatments these days? Are you near the internet right now? Can you pull that up for me real quick?"

When it became clear she wasn't going to respond, he exhaled slowly. Reluctantly, and with a desperate effort, he pulled himself atop the rock wall to have a look ahead for the waypoint.

*What a strange place.*

A craggy knoll was hidden neatly in the bedrock below. He watched while his visor automatically scanned the area. It revealed to him a small dwelling, camouflaged by the stone of its construction, somewhere amidst the rubble. It would sit nearly imperceptible, he imagined, to anyone lacking the benefit of such advanced technology. *The second Coordinate.*

"Destination confirmed," he whispered to her, "there's a stone dwelling of some kind, somewhere below my current location."

Abandoning his good sense, he attempted to vault himself over the crest of rock with legs dangling, one over each side, when a blast (hollow and tubular) abruptly sounded from the knoll below. He felt a pulse of energy ripple through the air and pound him in his suit's chest plate, knocking him back over the crest and down flat to the ground below, stunned.

"Object launched into the air," Spurlock trembled in horror.

—Get yourself up and recede, now—

He scrambled to rise and find cover, sliding helplessly in the effort atop a current of shifting rubble away from the crest. "Visibility is limited by heavy mist, clouds are low and thick as soup. A trail of fire and smoke... extremely loud... some kind of concussive forceful impact... hit me and I fell hard, but am searching for cover now!"

Then, activity stirred from somewhere nearby; movement and voices. *Hostiles.* And without risking so much as a cursory look around, he ducked into a crevice to conceal himself as best he may.

"Where was it?" barked a man's voice, deep and skeptical.

"As I've told you, just now, in the same place I'd seen it before," answered a smaller voice with hurried insistence, "Hadn't you seen it a moment ago, speeding through the clouds?"

"Neither of us caught sight of it," said a third voice, steely and direct, "Now lead us to the origin of its trajectory, and let us make haste about it. I should hope we haven't ventured all this way out here for naught."

With visor engaged and secure, Spurlock huddled in his hiding place, expecting the Operator to announce Projection sequencing, but she did not. *Can't she tell I'm compromised?* The sound of footsteps accompanied the hostile's voices. And soon, peeking through a fissure between two rock formations, he saw three sets of legs, outfitted in leather boots. Each figure carried a metal sword at the hip that swayed forward and back with every pace. He repositioned himself silently to better witness their passing. One had a bow and a quiver of arrows slung across his back and all three were armored in vests of boiled leather mesh. They mounted the rock shelf at the crest and slipped over to the other side.

"Men..." he muttered into the helmet's mouthpiece with a shaken voice, "Men observed. Three armed men, all of them looked like soldiers, heading toward the Coordinate site. Their weapons... are primitive, simple implements—like swords and bows and arrows."

When an announcement of Projection still did not come, he cursed silently, then gathered his wits and pursued the hostiles with caution, finding purchase behind the rock shelf and again peering over to have a look. The three men were searching the area below for signs of disturbance, stopping at the edge of a seemingly bottomless chasm that divided the knoll from dense woodland on its far end. *They don't see it; the camouflaged dwelling. It's right there, and they cannot see it.*

And for a time, the hostiles argued with one another, raising their voices. Until movement broke the stillness again.

"Over there," shouted the one with the bow, while a man emerged from the rock face and ran for his life across the knoll. An arrow was nocked and loosed in a whistle's time, and grazed the fleeing man's shin, bringing him down with pebbles careening across the ground and into the chasm. And the hostiles were on top of him a moment later.

"Fourth man observed; overtaken by these soldiers," Spurlock reported to his Operator, crouching behind the rock, hearing the voices rising from the knoll below, and finding he couldn't bear to witness any more of this scene, "I'm afraid to continue."

He waited for a moment's time without response before it crisply came upon him.

—Prepare for Projection, please stand by—

*She's pulling me out of here now.* He knelt to a crouched position again and held his breath.

—Projection in progress, please hold firm, Projection in progress—

\*\*\*

|Planet Deaer, The Southspur Mountain Peak

Spurlock was sunken deep in a berm of powdered snow this time. Drifts surrounded him everywhere, and more snow fell from the sky in distinctly generous proportion. Broad flakes swirled and clung to his suit, threatening to bury him in a fresh layer before he could recover his senses.

—Landfall achieved, please confirm—

It seemed he'd been set down at a point of severe elevation on Planet Deaer, upon a mountain peak plagued indefinitely by blizzard-like conditions. When he rose, he was panting, fogging his helmet's visor near completely before a built-in ventilation system automatically cleared it away. And his suit responded, in kind, feeding jets of warm air to his major pressure points. Even so, the bitter cold coursed through him in waves.

"Confirmed," he offered with a hint of terseness, disoriented and shaken by the whipsawing of his body from one location to another. *And the destinations are getting more hazardous, still, it seems.* A waypoint in his visor marked the operation's third and final Coordinate, and he was soon plodding through the snow to find it. Fighting the blizzard, he wondered what sort of meaningful Coordinate could possibly be located in such an inhospitable environment. But through the infinite dimensions of snowfall, he thought he saw an aberration—a faint plume of smoke not far ahead that billowed as it rose. *Fire? How can anything possibly survive here, much less produce fire?*

—Please be advised of your suit's advanced applications. Say now: Filters—

He obliged her command, saying, "Filters." Suddenly, a digital menu appeared within his visor, listing options: Optical Zoom, Chemical Signatures, Light Inversion, Thermal Image; and each option became highlighted when he aligned his pupils in their direction.

—Thermal Image. Say now: Select—

He looked at the option she suggested and said, "Select." A thermal imaging filter was then applied to his visor that blurred out elements registering cold temperatures, highlighting only those things in the environment that emitted warmth. Ahead, not far from where he stood, he saw an image formed in the outline of a shelter, buried near-completely in snow, and marked by the waypoint as his Coordinate.

"Smoke observed rising from a chimney, from some kind of dwelling built into a hill," he relayed, "third Coordinate confirmed."

The image revealed a scant array of furnishings in this small dwelling, but among them stood the unmistakable shape and form of a great device, identical to that which he'd discovered in the shack at the first Coordinate, and to that which, he presumed, had performed the launching event at the second Coordinate, in the knoll. Three separate locations; one warm, one in meteorological flux, and one ice cold. All of them deliberately remote, and all of them containing the same kind of large cannon. *What's the purpose of finding these machines if she's not going to command me to disable them?*

A wall of wind swept over the mountainside, forcing him to stabilize with one knee on the ground, and even the now-heated suit couldn't shield him entirely from the chill. But he held firm, and despite his struggles with the elements, he detected something else registering readings upon his visor. *A person?*

"Lifeform observed at the point of Coordinate. Looks like a man. Who would ever attempt to inhabit such a place?"

—Someone who wishes not to be found. Someone hiding. Or being hidden by another—

"Filters," he said, trying to acquire useful command of the equipment at his disposal. He looked toward the Zoom function this time, "Select."

Upon closer inspection, the man's movements betrayed a sense of futility, up to and including the moment when he emerged from the strange shelter with hunched shoulders, seemingly in an effort to catch a breath of fresh air. *You and me both, pal.*

"This guy seems somewhat young, but exhausted... Hold on, I'm seeing readings of some kind in my visor; of his vitals? Heart rate, blood pressure, lung capacity seem poor. Wouldn't be surprised if his health were compromised, living up here like this."

Spurlock kept the visor zoomed and watched his subject stand in the thick of the blizzard, seemingly unfazed by the extreme elements, breathing deeply of the cold, cold air; staring mindfully out at the layers upon layers of snowfall. He sensed something in the young man's stare. Something of a kinship that could certainly be felt, but not nearly defined. Something raw and true, yet elusive, like memories that lay behind a wall within his mind; just out of reach. But this contemplative spell was cut short once again by the Operator's stark and sterile voice.

—Deploying transceivers now; please hold firm. Repeat, deploying transceivers; please hold firm—

A compartment on the cuff of his suit slid open to reveal two small devices stored neatly within, and he raised his arm to have a closer look.

—I said hold firm—

"I was just curious to see..."

—Deploying transceivers. Please do not move a muscle—

He complied and the devices powered on, shifting their parts and connectors, and generating a force of propulsion that took them into the air. He watched them pursue a vector that, despite the wind gusts, carried them straight through the open door of the hidden domicile, unseen by the subject standing alone in the snowfall.

The cuff on Spurlock's suit closed and sealed its compartment shut again.

Already caught in a state of shock by this strange reality he found himself living in, this final curiosity tipped his scales of reasoning, and he could stomach no more ambiguity, "Ok, I'm gonna go ahead and ask, straight-up… Who are you, and exactly what am I doing out here? This is obviously some kind of game; someone's prank. Whose? It's all very funny, but I think I have a right to know, and I think I'm ready for it to end, if you don't mind. Immediately, please."

—I've asked that we dispense with frivolous chatter, and I was serious about that, Mr. Spurlock. Now allow me to bring you back up here before you are seen. This operation is complete—

He looked up at the flake-filled sky, and his visor flipped itself through its menus to activate the Light Inversion filter and a score of Optical Zoom progressions. And suddenly, an object of great mass became visible, orbiting this Planet Deaer with an ominous presence.

*The space station where I'd awoken.*

—I am sensing an appeal to various forms of emotion. Emotions are severe liabilities here, Mr. Spurlock. You must learn to suppress them if you hope to survive this perilous mission of yours. There is a puzzle to be solved here, a secret to be sought, and a conclusion to be reached; and as long as you remain subject to your emotions, you will lack the means to accomplish any of it. I advise you to remain wary of that—

"Eliminate my natural reactions to everything I experience?" He decided that if this were a joke, it was the most elaborate of its kind ever conceived, "What you're asking is impossible. You know that, right?"

—Prepare for Projection, please. Prepare for Projection—

The directive was sharp enough to split the hairs on the back of his neck in half, and immediately he knelt to the ground and stilled his movements.

—Prepare for Projection, please stand by—

The falling snow was already beginning to cover his footsteps and stumblings while he vanished in a blink, taken by Projection into the ether. And shortly thereafter, the area looked as if he'd never even truly been there in the first place.

## 2 | Waiting for the Bell to Ring

*"I wonder what a person could accomplish if given a singular focus. Would they bear down and leverage every last drop of ingenuity from the exquisite mind they've been given? Or would they grant all power over their potential for progress to invisible agents of fear, as to render themselves completely ineffectual? I cannot allow myself to be so assaulted by flurries of distraction or doubt, when the true singular purpose of my toils at this very moment rests unapologetically right before my very eyes."*
—excerpt from the personal journal of Steven Spurlock

|Planet Deaer, Southspur Mountain Peak

Layers of ice and snow were draped over Koryn Naylor's cottage like lead blankets, threatening to bury him alive. They would've likely succeeded if it weren't for the solid rock and frozen soil that virtually engulfed the sad, little structure. It was a veritable ice chest of wooden planks that, from the inside, looked as any typical dwelling might look. But, indeed, it sat securely within a blasted hollow; built at a time that well pre-dated Koryn's existence. Aided by the constant howls of violent wind gusts against the front door, it hadn't taken him long to determine why it'd been constructed in such a manner. Outside, the mountain niche was blanketed, too, as were the imposing peaks that stabbed the sky in all directions, like clusters of chisel-sharpened spearheads. The massif stretched as far as the eye could see; a jagged line of summits that eventually disappeared into a purple-gray haze.

Amenities in the cottage were scarce and comforts were few—a stack of firewood in one corner and a weapon or two upright in another. If any of Koryn's possessions could've been named luxury items at all, it was sure to be the kettle, which was warming over a bed of coals in the fireplace.

He'd pushed his cot nearly flat against the hearth stones for more warmth through recent storms. The blizzards had worsened, and the frigid cold seeped through the cottage walls straight into the current in his veins. If that weren't enough to ruin his sleep, the cot lacked support for the simplest of comforts as well. So small was it, that (at times) an arm or a leg would slip off in the middle of the night. This time, it was his arm that had fallen. It dangled at first, but now his hand landed straight in the hot coals stacked around the steaming kettle.

"Flames and ashes!" Koryn leapt out of his blankets to his feet, his knuckles burning with a pulsating pain. He kicked the kettle clear across the room, cursing and grumbling, "S'ppose that's one way to wake up, if not nearly the worst of all!"

Now he'd have no tea from the spilt kettle, and he had naught but a few burnt knuckles to show for it. He wrapped a thin strip of cloth around his hand, looking fleetingly at the broken skin, blistered and peeling. *Not so bad. Figure I'll be sorrier for missing my morning brew than for acquiring this trifling scratch.* He was lying to himself, of course; the burn was worse than he'd willingly admit, but even crises such as these seemed utterly insignificant in his grand scheme of misery.

He slid the cot aside and threw his blanket rolls on top before stoking the embers in the fireplace. It wasn't until he settled himself at the small table (with a heel of stale bread and a cupful of melted snow) that he drew a deep breath and stared blankly at the instrument standing directly in front of him.

A polished and refined machine; ominous and imposing. Cold to the touch, its presence made itself known to him at all times, dominating the small footprint of the cabin floor. Its surface reflected his tired, puffy eyes sunken in a long, sallow face that was cloaked by a bedraggled beard. *Quite strange to possess so little out here by way of luxury, let alone base nourishment, yet to be mocked at every turn by this… thing; this object of such high regard and such wasteful opulence. This flaming worthless machine, which so often, and so clearly, shows me the painful image of my own broken, decrepit face.* But he would not look away (nor stop looking, in the first place) upon waking each day.

It would be inaccurate to label this Koryn's morning routine, as he often (and quite simply) could not tell dawn from noon, nor noon from dusk, through the thick layers of snowfall. For this reason, he could not determine accurate estimates for each length of sleep, and he was largely and often hopelessly disoriented from any semblance of healthy, daily habit-making. *At least,* he thought, *there's a slight measure of sunlight peeking through the fray outside at the moment...*

He nibbled at the bread and lamented his fate a bit more, until he heard a sound from outside; a sort of buzzing or whirring. It was faint at first, but persistent, and when its intensity grew, he hurried to the cottage's window in a flash to have a proper look. Beyond a line of trees that stood like sentinels over the edge of a distant bluff, he saw movement. A small craft rose steadily until it came clear into sight above the trees now, passing through the rocky defiles.

*A buzzcraft.*

The window came open with a tilt, and he threw himself outside where he landed in a snow bank; then crouched down, in hiding. The craft's rounded cab gleamed with the reflection of the surrounding terrain, preventing his clear view of the pilot within. Sprouting from either side of the craft were the powerful flexor wings, flapping so rapidly as to be unseen, like those of an airborne insect. They dispersed the blizzard's flakes like a tornado would scatter feathers, and they brought the craft down to the ground. Someone disembarked, planting two boots firmly in the snow. Then, in quick succession, there came a swift, vigorous rapping at his cabin door.

From his concealment, Koryn risked a glimpse of the trespasser—a hooded figure, thin and of middling height. Flakes swirled everywhere, obscuring the view, but he was bent on remaining unseen; maneuvering himself silently around the yard and toward the drifts that'd been piled high by the forceful current from the craft's wings. When he'd gained the ground where the craft sat idle, a swift peek into the cab told of no other passengers inside, a revelation for which he was sincerely grateful. But the pilot was poking about the front of the cabin now, peering into the window in a huff then returning to the door. More poundings followed. A fist reached from a fur-lined leather cloak, and another pound, *pound, pound* suggested patience was fleeing the intruder, rapidly.

*Keep pounding,* he thought, *yes, that's it, keep pounding.*

He started toward the door, then, and with each loud pounding, he was able to take one and two and three more steps closer, and closer yet, upon the visitor's back; beyond detection. One deft motion saw his bandaged hand around the pilot's head to cover the mouth while the other hand forced them both through the cottage door and flush against the wall inside.

\*\*\*

"Thought you'd come out here and meddle with the cottage dweller, did ya?" Koryn Naylor rasped at the pilot who'd arrived by buzzcraft at his door, holding the other's form firmly against the wall, "It just so happens I'm not the sort to be taken so unawares." He released his grip, and pulled back the pilot's hood to find a young woman, near enough his age, with smart symmetrical facial features, deep blue crystalline eyes, and short-cropped hair.

"I've come to levy punishment upon a cottage-dwelling hermit of a man…" she declared with vitriol, "and it has been far too long." With her last syllable spoken, they embraced, kissing one another, her fingers upturned, pushing into his hair and grasping tightly. Gusts blew the cottage door wide open, banging and rattling it on its hinges; flakes surging into the cottage, completely unnoticed. Striding together across the room, he reached blindly (successfully) for the bed rolls and cast them over the floor in front of the fire, where their bodies collapsed together, beading sweat from the heat they'd conjured in the room.

Time slipped away, then, spent delighting in each other's company, and she'd settled her head into the crook of his arm. They laid there, hot and flushed despite the cold that surrounded them and the blizzard that still blew through the opened door.

They remained like this, together for a time, of a length indeterminable, and finally he asked, "Has it truly been thirty days since our last?"

"Truly it has," she answered in the affirmative.

"I've absolutely no sense of time here…" he sighed, "you have no idea of this place; what it can do to someone. Not until you've rotted here a good long while."

"Two years, today, it's been," she affirmed.

"Gods, two years?"

"I'm afraid so. Still, I don't know if the Settlement is much worth longing for these days, either," she shifted her body a bit and pulled the blankets up to her chin, "we're not freezing our skulls through like you are, here in this ice chest of a cottage, but many have met with a troubling malaise. Almost everyone."

"Well, if a particularly bored chap would like to come up here for a spot of adventure, I'll not turn down the chance to swap his place," a wry laugh hid behind each of his words, "and if it's a fever that plagues them, or a nasty turn with the mumps, you tell them the crisp air up here'll heal their belly aching in no time."

"You know they won't allow your return, Koryn," she pleaded, "not until enough time has passed…"

"I'd rather not talk about that, Haiyen," Koryn's voice was strained as he cut her off. He flexed his body, and attempted to sit up. She gathered his intent and moved away from him, taking up the blankets to cover herself.

"What would you prefer we talk about then?" she asked, "You know me, I've no shortage of topics."

"Actually, I'm not much for talking anymore," he propped his elbows on his knees and let his head slump down; his hands gripping his matted hair, "I'm surprised I even remember how."

"No curiosities about life back at the Settlement?" she suggested, "No interest in current affairs?"

"What's there to be curious about, Haiyen?" his voice acquired an edge but remained, in essence, a self-pitying sulk.

"You're saying there is nothing you want to ask about?" she persisted, "Nothing at all?"

"I truly don't see the point in it," he was hanging his head like it carried a burdensome weight he could no longer support, "really, truly I don't."

"You just don't get it, do you?" it was more a statement (born of conviction) than a question.

Without answering, he stood up and dressed himself with a certain dispassionate animation. *This same cycle every time. What does she expect me to say? Does she really think I care to hear news from the Settlement? Has she any idea what life has become for me—how irrelevant such petty news would truly seem to me?*

He walked to the window and looked outside upon a familiar sight. There, several paces into the yard stood a pole, rising from the snow drifts; a perch extending level at the top with a copper bell tethered to the end. The snow around it was disturbed from when he'd scrambled out the window in hiding, but when he saw the pole now, a light seemed to turn on within him.

"Oh gods!" he said, "I was so eager to free you of your blouses that I've plum forgotten to mention!"

"Mention what?" asked Haiyen. Her tone projected a severe bout of irritation that even Koryn, in his bleary-eyed, sleep deprived stupor, could detect. He looked at her, and she was standing, then, with the blankets wrapped full 'round her body and over her head, her crystalline eyes peering out from the dark folds.

"A message arrived," he said blankly.

"A message? Don't pull some half-wit lark, just to change the subject, Koryn"

"No lark," he said with certainty, "and actually there've been three. All in the past thirty days."

She covered her open mouth with her fingers in sincere astonishment, "Gods, how long has it been since the last?"

"I… I don't even remember; a year's time. Maybe more … Like I've said, Haiyen, time has plum lost its meaning for me."

"So a purpose still remains for your being here after all… beyond the punitive purpose, that is," her voice trailed off as she spoke, likely realizing she was delving right back into the subject he cared not to revisit. But Haiyen was right to mention purpose.

In fact, the purpose of his assignment in the snow-ridden mountains had seemed clear enough from the start. He'd no sooner been dropped off at the front door of the cottage on his first day of duty, before he'd noticed a roll of parchment pinned to the table by a knife. And it had articulated in no uncertain terms his greatest priority:

ABOVE ALL ELSE, MIND THE BELL. WHEN A
MESSAGE ARRIVES, TRANSMIT IMMEDIATELY.

Yet for the longest time thereafter, no messages had arrived; no messages in any form. Though his directive was vague, he'd simply assumed it was a homing fowl for which he waited. That such a bird would arrive bearing a message, land on the perch outside his window, and ring the bell under its weight. But time had passed slowly, and the bell did not ring. A fortnight had passed, then two and then three fortnights passed while he looked out the window for any sign of… anything. He'd been up early in the morning and down late at night for fear he would sleep through the ringing of the bell, and after a while, he began to succumb to sleep deprivation. When he did sleep, he dreamt of the pole and of the bell, and awoke often and in fits. His life had become a monotonous routine of meal preparation and mindless observation of the pole through the window. And still, the bell did not ring.

Then one day, a message had finally arrived by bird, and he had learned the fantastic method for securing its transmission, with the employ of the polished machine, which took for itself so much of his living space in the middle of the cottage floor. He was, at that time, flush with a cathartic sense of purpose. But then the pole stood frozen and neglected. No further messages had arrived, and—save for those moments when the wind gusts proved their impossible strength—the bell hung without ringing again for a long time.

Until the arrival of these three most recent messages.

"What did they say?" asked Haiyen.

"Oh, you don't think I'm crazy enough to open them and read what they say, do you? True enough, I'm quite crazy, Haiyen, but not *that* crazy. Don't you remember the warning that came with the first message?"

UNAUTHORIZED READING OF ANY MESSAGE IS
PUNISHABLE BY SEVERE CONSEQUENCE

"And if exile to a cottage atop a great spearhead isn't considered severe, I wish not to find out what is," he cast a look of exasperation her way.

Haiyen returned it with a look of displeasure all her own.

He peered out the window again, and stood for moments in silence, staring at the pole in all its dreadful familiarity. The bell swayed lightly in the wind, yet not enough for it to ring. His gaze shifted upon her buzzcraft sitting in the yard, its translucent cab gleaming shades of orange when the sun managed to peak faintly between the storm clouds.

"Probably best that I continue depriving myself of the knowledge the messages carry, despite how curious I truly am about them. We all know what happens when the rules of the Settlement are disobeyed, so I'll stick to my charge, clear and simple. I wouldn't want to bring more *shame* upon myself. Or upon you…"

He realized it had all come out so sarcastically, but even so, he held little regret for it.

A sapphire blue stone, hanging from a chain around Haiyen's neck, swung about while she pulled on her heavy jacket, boots, and a pair of gloves, and she gave him a glacial look with her piercing eyes in the process.

"What time of day is it, anyway?" he asked.

"It's approaching dusk," said Haiyen, "took me near twice as long as usual to get up here this time with the headwinds and strong evening gusts. And I'd gotten a late start." She grabbed the frame of his cot and pulled it (along with a clutch of blankets) against the far wall, behind the polished machine. "I'm going to take a rest now... Alone. There's no way I'll stay alert enough to make it all the way back through this storm."

"Be my guest," it seemed a strange thing for Haiyen to visit and stay, yet for the distance between them to feel as if she were still down in the Settlement; retracted and distant.

"You may want to retrieve the bottles, lest they burst open when they freeze," she muttered from beneath a blanket, facing the far wall, "They're in the cab."

Koryn strolled out to the buzzcraft amid the blizzard. The craft gave him an uneasy feeling, not unlike the disdain he'd always felt for the polished launching machine. The Settlement, he recalled, didn't exactly suffer for lack of advanced technology. In fact, they prided themselves on their ability to develop such things. But the buzzcraft took the prize as their crowning achievement, at least as far as he could recall from his youth, in that society so continually preoccupied with progress. He opened the cab enough to slide himself into the pilot's seat. The flight controls were far too sophisticated for someone to simply strap in and start piloting, and he had no idea how she activated those flexor wings the way she did. *There must be a power source somewhere, but I've no idea how to engage it.*

Sullenly, he reached into a compartment where three bottles of wine were stowed, and took them in hand, carrying them back into the cottage, and shutting the door tight this time. Removed long enough from the playful frolic at Haiyen's arrival, the extreme cold from the storms was even starting to affect him now, too.

"What took you so long?" said Haiyen, without breaking from the blankets upon his return, "I thought for a while you'd gone off again, in search of the flatlanders and their castles."

The reference was meant to boil his nerves.

"Believe me, there's no way off this mountain peak for me," he threw a new log on the fire and sat on the floor, "besides, we both know the flatlanders don't exist, Haiyen. Don't be so silly as that."

She offered no retort, and as the evening deepened, his body slumped into a sunken posture, and he felt every bit as alone as he'd grown accustom to feeling, those past two years through.

### 3 | Permissions and Warnings

*"I've been told human beings carry hundreds (maybe thousands) of strands of different personality traits, all twisted into one thick cord. That sometimes the strands can separate, and one can dominate the rest, as need dictates. Ambition, Confidence, Conceit. Apprehension, Cowardice, Humility—to name a few. Yet, even though these strands are always present, they are so deeply embedded within us that conscious control of them is not easily acquired, nor maintained. Patience, Generosity, Conviction. Frailty, Brutality, Remorse—a few more. They are behavioral archetypes that vastly affect our actions; even our thoughts. I've been shown this, and now I understand. I still cannot control them, but at least I finally understand."*
—excerpt from the personal journal of Steven Spurlock

|Planet Deaer, Castle Athyn

Night had fallen over Castle Athyn, dark and forbidding, yet Ethyn Solis strode along an upper rampart as though the world held within it nothing at all worth fearing. He'd completed a long days' worth of training in the yard, and his muscles were sore for the effort. But he took care that his strides betrayed no such weakness to the observant eyes of the Royal Guardsmen, who stood watch in the cool evening air. *How will these men perceive me once I've inherited the royal seat if I'm to limp and hobble about the fortifications like a flaming cripple?*

"How fares the night?" he asked one of the men.

"Free and clear, my lord." The soldier was clad in a deep blue cloak embroidered with the sigil of House Solis—the wings of a bird stretched toward the sky—and looked quite like a formidable statue hewn from stone in his stoic pose.

"Nothing suspicious by land, I presume?" Ethyn pressed.

"Nothing, my lord."

"And nothing from the sky, my good sir?" pressed the prince, looking southward at the great line of mountain peaks stretching far and wide.

"Nothing from the sky, my lord."

Ethyn would never tire of the manner in which a soldier must properly address him, nor the authority such formalities conveyed. Near as tall as the soldier, his face (longish and handsome) formed a smile, "Very well; let the good spirits hasten the return of the light, if we be so worthy."

"Thank you, my lord," replied the soldier.

The Ancillary Moon, hanging high in the night sky (silver and bold) lit the way for Ethyn's leave-making back into the towering keep. He had a task to complete this night, which he did not relish, but he'd resolved to dispense of it in due course, and he knew bandying about with the Royal Guard was nothing more than a delay tactic. The task took him through the castle's inner sanctum in places designed only for the royal family and its handlers, where the trimmings reached their peak of refinement. His pace quickened down a hall over woven rugs the color of red wine, leading to his father's study. And at the terminus, his hand closed tightly upon a doorknob etched in a most intricate scrollwork pattern.

The room within boasted a certain elegance, punctuated by a massive fireplace. Each of a number of chairs fronting the hearth sat vacant, and he took a seat in one of them, figuring to make himself comfortable. One never knew how long the man tending to the fire might keep a visitor in wait. *Father has always been patient with his handling of fires—a true master of fanning flames, even from the faintest of embers. Yet, when one flares erratically, he needs only provide a careful nudge here or there with the poker to set it straight.*

Patience, however, was one virtue that the son had failed to inherit from his father, and it eventually got the best of Ethyn, as was his proclivity in such situations.

"I've received word a coastal outpost has reached critical need for general provisions, father," he blurted out, "and I mean to lead the company that makes the delivery." He had already made up his mind he'd be the one to complete this simple task. Asking permissions of his father at this stage in life had (in his view) become a thoroughly unnecessary formality. *No, this is not a request, this is a proclamation of intent*, he declared to himself. Truly, he knew the shadow of a powerful man was a cold, forbidding place to loiter, and he was bent on stepping out of it, with or without the proper permissions.

The man remained focused for long moments on his doings by the fire before finally offering his response, though he did not turn his head to face his petitioner, "Commander Thorngrove is overwhelmed with the responsibilities of our Royal Legion. I've no doubt he would welcome any measure of assistance offered to him in aid of his auxiliary duties." Ethyn's father (forenamed Perwyn, surnamed Solis, and formally-titled the High Nhyle of Athyn) then paused in contemplation. It was a habit of his that vexed Ethyn to such an extent that he could hardly stand to bear its witness—the chin rubbing and sideways gazing into the distance—but shortly enough, the thoughtful spell had concluded. "Yes. So be it. You have my rightful permission to lead the effort. But take much care in this, Ethyn. It may seem a simple task, on its face, but I assure you it most certainly is not."

*Permissions and warnings. What need have I for those? He must yet take me for a babe in its blankets...*

"Be assured, father, I shall hold my most precautionary instincts close at hand, as ever I've been trained to do," he said, wisely abridging his full response to leave the less flattering portions unspoken. *The tenants of precaution, after all, most aptly embody the very reputation of our House, for all the weakness we project to the world.*

"As you should," his father bent down to straighten the remaining firewood in its bin before finally turning from the flames. The flickering light outlined his angular nose and flared eyebrows, and the wiry fringe of his silver-streaked beard, "In all honesty, the timing of this task could not have been more fortuitous."

"Fortuitous... how so?" asked Ethyn, straightening slightly, then, in his seat.

"I've given matters concerning your role in the High Council careful consideration, of late," said Perwyn, "This, insofar as your involvement in the diplomatic affairs of the royal seat."

*A rightful place for me in the High Council... is that what he just said?* Suddenly aware of his grin—the corners of which had almost spread clear to his earlobes at the thought of his finally acquiring an ounce of executive power—Ethyn made efforts to compose himself, "A seat on the council?"

"Indeed, a seat on the council," the man's even expression evidenced nothing of his inner thoughts on the matter, "though I've long wished to shield you from the dangers of this world, I think the time has duly arrived."

"Father, never have I asked for such protection."

"So you haven't, Ethyn, but the day may soon come when you will. You might discover darkness out there more insidious than you could have ever imagined."

"I know more of the world than you give me credit for."

"Perhaps. But as I was saying, in furtherance of your role in the council, I ask that when you're finished delivering those outpost supplies, that you ride along the coastline to Stief, the Harbor Town, where you will meet the Maelnlockian Ambassador and kindly escort him back here to Castle Athyn. We're to hold an assemblage upon his request."

"An escort," Ethyn delved excitedly into the idea of leading such a task; the responsibility it would place in his hands. "Have we any idea the nature of business the ambassador wishes to discuss?"

"No, our scholars haven't a clue what he may propose for debate this time around," Ethyn's father paced toward a stand of bookcases, "when last we convened, it was his displeasure with a minimal tax increase on grain shipments from the far north, which we've addressed quite generously to his liking. Before that, he wished to dispute amendments to minor tacking requirements of foreign vessels in Athynian harbors, to which we also conceded in his favor." He scanned a row of old books, running a finger across their bindings and pulled out a small volume titled *The Waters of Caddyr*. "All things considered, I suppose we ought to content ourselves with the relative triviality of those demands, but as always with Maelnlock, whatever it is he wishes to discuss, its impact could prove profound, indeed."

"Sounds like the man would complain of his own grand-mum's rules of dining etiquette, given the forum," scoffed Ethyn.

"Whatever it may be, we will do well to entertain his concerns," the Nhyle's tone was cautionary now. "Diplomatic relations, son, are thorny endeavors which, unfortunately, are compulsory in the lives of royal figureheads, no matter how aggravating these relationships may become. We must take pains to ensure the satisfaction of our influential Masters of Liaise. Even when they work their way 'neath our very skin."

"Might I suggest the virtues of a less conciliatory approach? Prompt punitive measures might well elicit more effective response when these ambassadors lose sight of the very privileged arrangements with which we've furnished them, here on our own pristine soil. Rather than dance to their every tune, why shan't we require they dance to ours? What is prying open our ears to their every petition? What exactly is forcing open our generous hands to act upon their every desire?"

Perwyn groaned and peered at Ethyn with a strained visage. "This is why I've elected to send you forth on this task, Ethyn; to learn by seeing and by doing. The appropriateness of our long-observed tactics of diplomacy will make themselves clear the moment you are beholden to the ambassador, face-to-face. And I should think it unnecessary for me to dissuade you from offending this man with derisive speech, but even so… son, please do not offend this man, if for no other reason, then in observance of the layers of influence that follow in his every footstep. Though Ambassador Salmen Fleurys may purposefully provoke you to anger, remember that your pride counts for nothing compared to the secure standing of our realm."

"I'm curious. How, exactly, might he attempt to provoke me?"

"Most ambassadors are masters of the art of conversational warfare; especially Fleurys of Maelnlock. Believe me, I've no love lost on the man. If I'd a gold piece for every audacious personal slight he's made upon me lo these past many years, our purses would run themselves over, bursting at the seams. But the latent tension underlying our diplomatic exchanges with Maelnlock is especially explosive; much more conspicuous and threatening than any we may carry with other realms. It is only natural to expect conflict may roil beneath such circumstances. So heed me well. Do not allow him claim upon the best of your good sense; your patience, your discretion. Consider this a training opportunity, and a most valuable one at that."

"Surely, other ambassadors grow weary of our constant counsel with Fleurys from Maelnlock. Especially under such frivolous pretenses, as are slight tax increases and minor sailing protocols. And more-so, I should think, if he treats us with disrespect in the meanwhile."

"Balance is indeed a valued virtue of diplomacy, and we cannot neglect our rightful dealings with other realms. But our frequent communications with Maelnlock are born strictly of necessity, and I needn't justify that to every fool who fancies himself a foreign emissary in these lands. Were that the case, there would remain little time for anything else."

In his mind, Ethyn shuffled through an index of notable ambassadors—there'd been the ceaseless paranoia of Byrin Osley from Nyrulia, and the baseless haughtiness from Farique Twyll of Turinguard, and he shouldn't ever forget Sorah Ghamshee, the eccentric delegate from Teluba who'd once sipped a bit too eagerly from her vintage, and had danced shoeless upon everyone's supper plate at feast. "What exactly is stopping us from ousting each and every one of these self-serving snakes from our land and letting them fend for themselves?"

"Credibility, for starters," his father paused again for a moment; apprehension and concern now apparent in his eyes. "Ethyn, if you've aims for some day presiding over this realm, and if you've wishes that I entertain those aims with a level of seriousness to which they are due, you mustn't carry such a vindictive temperament toward all things. I'll have you realize, it is unbecoming of the seat."

Ethyn ignored the warning outright, as if it hadn't been spoken at all, "Then it is settled, I will deliver provisions to the outpost in need," he rose from his chair, "and I will travel to Stief to collect the ambassador from Maelnlock for his assemblage." *If I don't take my leave soon, he's likely to rescind his permissions, and I'm likely to go mad if subjected to any further lecturing.*

"Yes, Ethyn, if it would so please you. You shall leave with a host of your choosing at sunrise," his father wearily took a seat for himself at his desk, "and as always, please make use of your very highest degree of discretion as you go."

*My highest degree of discretion, indeed.*

And the door to his father's study shut silently as he left.

*** 

The hall outside the study carried a chill, and Ethyn found needs to pull his cloak a bit tighter about his broad shoulders. He walked toward his bedchambers, considering what his father had said about the High

Council, and about this assignment of escort. *I wonder how long these new arrangements shall last.* This new-found inclusion in matters of state seemed like a wish that'd been granted all-too-easily, and so he couldn't help but wonder if he'd finally garnered enough trust from his father to deserve such considerations, or if he'd just been nudged artfully by the man's fire poker, like one of those many wooden logs upon the brazier.

All these trifling machinations left him weary; starved for a respite (no matter how brief it may need to be) and when he passed the last door before the one which led to his own quarters, he couldn't help but entertain the idea of visiting his younger brother, if only for a spell. *Tae. If ever there's a lad whose company remains blissfully free of dramatic foolery, it is he. And may the gods bless his tender soul for it, too.*

He turned down the penultimate corridor and passed through an antechamber decorated wall-to-ceiling in small mosaic tiles, deep blues mostly, with silver star shapes placed randomly overhead. His princeling brother sat in silence out on his private veranda, set determinedly at polishing a collection of ornamental glass globes. His wheat-colored hair swayed front to back when he looked up at Ethyn in frantic surprise.

"Be still, sweet Tae," said Ethyn. *It's quite remarkable to think only a handful of years separate us in age, and yet he still seems but a child to me.* Ethyn did not wait for a reply. He knew there wouldn't be one, for Tae was mute, "No cause for fear… it's only me."

And there was no reply. There had never been a reply, and Ethyn believed there never would. Tae was a tragic figure to most everyone else, but was such a precious one to Ethyn. He saw his brother's mutism as a gift unto the both of them, really. A gift to Tae because it had always ensured his comfort and protection within the safe castle walls. And a gift to himself because he'd cherished the ability to sit with his brother and revisit childhood whenever any such reassuring escape was needed—in fact, as it had been at that very moment.

So they sat. Ethyn took up a cloth and helped his brother polish one of the larger glass globes. A pale smoke swirled in their depths, evocative of the Ancillary Moon, which loomed above all on clear spring nights such as this. The celestial body was a marvel by all accord; attracting mythos and legends for its brilliance in the sky. The shine of the moon could light the world at night near a third as well as did the sun during the day. It was a luminescent silver light, prone to accentuating outlines and curves, rather than illuminating the whole of existence. And it had a way, at times, of lending certain objects an appearance as if they were glowing or radiating light from within. This was the precise effect they had on the globes, which is why their polishing was best done on the veranda.

Tae's veranda faced southward, providing not only clear exposure to the moon, but also an exquisite view of the snow-capped mountains that stood at great distances against the inky night sky. And after some time spent enjoying the silence of the evening with his brother (and the moon, and the stars), Ethyn ventured a subtle inquiry.

"Have you ever seen anything, Tae?" he asked, pointing toward the mountains, "Out there, soaring through the sky? Of course you've seen birds and clouds and the moon, but have you seen anything else? Anything peculiar, which you couldn't explain?"

Tae seemed to think for a moment, and then shook his head—*No.*

"No?" Though the negative response had been expected, Ethyn's posture still deflated a bit. A breeze picked up, and with it came a desire to change the subject, "You've a training session upon the morn with the Mystic Masters, have you not?"

Tae nodded his head this time, simply, absent any trace of enthusiasm.

"Well, just remember, you mustn't place any pressure upon yourself to do anything you wish not to do," Ethyn knew that Tae, while mute, was an extraordinarily smart boy. That Tae was a complex person, in possession of a great many sophisticated impressions and ideas. And these, to no lesser extent than any other person living in the castle, or elsewhere at all for that matter.

Ethyn also knew there were, at times, demands made of his little brother aimed at unlocking that powerful potential embedded within. But Ethyn never wanted Tae to feel overwhelmed, and so he was quick to provide calming reassurances whenever possible, "Only do that which makes you happy, brother, and care not for the desires of all those others around you. You can be or do anything at all in this world, but it won't be for any good if you don't truly want it for yourself."

Tae nodded his head again in simple recognition, and that was all that'd been said for the rest of the evening. And once all the globes had been polished to a shine, and once they'd drawn imaginary lines across the stars, marking all the constellations in the clear heavens above, Ethyn quit his brother's chambers, leaving Tae fast asleep on his veranda.

He thought it wise that he should retire to bed as well. A demanding few days lay ahead of him, and he would need to be good and well-rested to face them.

### 4 | A Troublesome Chemical Imbalance

*"The Station was a colossus, occupying a pocket within the Nycene Cluster for a time; the precise duration of which has officially been declared indeterminable. The broadness of its deck matched the diameter of a small moon. And of equal measure was the distance from the lowest tip of its keel to the masthead high above. Its design was no less a work of art than any piece displayed in a museum; a sculpted form, it was, that reflected gleams of light from distant stars in the darkness of space. Because of its sheer size, it was quite fortunate to find Planet Deaer nestled in a cluster with such gravitational stability, where random debris storms were a true rarity. Still, one would have to wonder, should a random meteoric impact have been made, which might have sustained greater damage; the massive Station or the speeding wayward meteor itself?"*

—excerpt from the personal journal of Steven Spurlock

|The Station

Projection had removed Spurlock from the bitter mountaintop on Planet Deaer and delivered him promptly to the floor of his solar, aboard the Station. He'd remained there for a while, inert, trying to re-establish his bearings, but this effort had proven insufficient as time had slogged along. At least to the extent he'd hoped for, which would've ideally included resuscitation of his life's memories as well as his senses. *Some better understanding of the predicament I'm in would be nice… Any idea at all would go a long way, really. I don't exactly feel like I'm positioned to drive negotiations here. Just… something.*

In time—knowing that progress was never granted unto those perpetually sitting idle—he'd summoned the energy to rise and disengage his suit; a process explained to him through animated instructions in his visor. And after removing his helmet, he'd looked around the place in wonder. He'd had so little time to investigate the premises, beforehand.

The solar was a streamlined box of a room with panels secured together by rivets making up the walls. Compartments were recessed therein, most of them empty, but upon one (adjacent to a small bed in the corner) stood the picture of a young woman standing beneath a flowering tree. Looking at it again, he still knew not who she was.

A dull ambient light glowed from the ceiling to cast everything in deep shadows and subdued shades of gray, apt for the most haunted of film noir.

*Appropriately so*, he considered, to suit his morose mood.

There was, of course, a small water closet with full utilities, but there were no windows to be found, and only one single exit door, which he could not presently open.

One wall panel (he discovered) slid aside to reveal an alcove, which served for his wardrobe. Within, he'd hung his suit and helmet on pegs designed purposefully for their careful storage, and he'd promptly slid the panel back shut, firm. Through the eerie white noise that *hummed* or *whirred* from some unknown source, he felt an odd sense of reality he couldn't quite define, but it seemed to drift in the air itself. *Maybe my mind's just scattered from that freakish Projection business. Or maybe I'm just totally losing my mind, altogether…*

There was a desktop, which seemed to have been folded out from the wall opposite his bed to expose a series of holoscreens embedded behind translucent panes. Quickly enough, he realized that the screens displayed running transcripts of some kind. When he approached the workstation, and took a seat for himself on its small stool, a sense pad illumined on the desk, and an audio feed began to emit from speakers in the wall.

> "What took you so long?" said a female voice, "I thought for a while you'd gone off again, in search of the flatlanders and their castles."
>
> "Believe me, there's no way off this mountain peak for me," replied a male voice, "besides, we both know the flatlanders don't exist."

After that, the feed went quiet, but the holoscreens indicated the location of its source down on Planet Deaer. It was the cottage buried in snow on the blustery mountain peak he'd visited on his operation. There was no doubting the equipment was highly impressive. *But what's the point of all this? I'm supposed to spy on the guy I saw down there, standing in the snow? Sounds like he's got someone with him now in that little cottage…Good for you, man!*

Fixed against the solar's far wall was a receptor chute, which gathered Spurlock's attention as it suddenly opened by a set of gears to lay flat, drawn level on its hinges bearing the weight of a tray holding an assortment of rations. He leaned over from his chair to have a look. *This must be how I'll get my meals… At least I won't be left to starve here, in this metal box they've locked me in.* His relief in seeing the food items was significant, but it was tempered by the looks of the simple offerings, which failed to appetize either by their looks or aroma. When he took the meal tray and placed it on the desktop, he noticed a small vial sitting upon it as well. And immediately thereafter, his Operator's voice came through to him from all directions, crisp and clear.

—Please be advised of the equipment you have received with your meal. Confirm receipt of equipment, now—

"Um, equipment is received," he answered, picking up the vial, "I think."

He opened the vial and spilled a collection of microscopic, semi-translucent devices into the palm of his hand. There were perhaps ten in all; it was difficult to tell, for how small they were.

—In simplest terms, they are listening devices. You will implant them within certain persons of interest, down on the surface of Planet Deaer—

"I'm sorry, I must've heard incorrectly," genuine doubt infected his impish tone, "for a second, it sounded like you're asking me to perform some kind of surgery with these things, but that can't be true."

—You are fully capable of this, Mr. Spurlock. Indeed, you are ideally conditioned. I will explain the procedure to you now, and will walk you through it once you have made contact with your subjects on the surface. The first two devices are meant for the brothers Solis of Athyn. They are the most integral subjects of all—

"I heard a recording here, that I'm guessing is coming from those little machines we released on the mountain. The ones that flew into the cottage buried in snow. If I'm supposed to spy on people's conversations, why not just release more of those things? They seem to be working just fine."

—That method simply will not work with these subjects. Now, Mr. Spurlock, please be advised your mission status has been elevated—

Then, despite his intense resistance to the very concept of this newly-assigned operation, she had pressed forward, briefing him first on the geopolitical landscape that existed on this planet called Deaer. Included was an overview of all known histories of the realm of Athyn, the principal members of House Solis, and the influence of power (such that it was) the royal seat exerted across their—by most relative means—primitive world. But the information, inclusive as it seemed, still fell short of explaining the rationale behind such intense interest in the planet, as a whole. And the briefing, much to his disfavor, also lacked any sliver of detail regarding his own personal identity.

*A supremely aggravating omission, at that,* he'd considered.

She'd then touched (all too briefly) upon the method by which he was going to perform the surgical procedures, to implant these miniscule devices within certain people on the planet's surface. When she was through, Spurlock remained dumbfounded by it all.

"I can't believe you're actually serious about this."

—You will find I'm a very serious person, Mr. Spurlock—

And thus, it had begun so quickly, his foray into advanced operations, which carried with them a distinct departure from the prior rules. Contact with sentient beings was prohibited through his first operation, and that arrangement had proven stressful enough. But these new demands—namely, hands-on work and the possibility of direct confrontation—were duties of a sort that would (by all estimates) lead him to ruin, and he was made remarkably anxious of mind.

Yet, it would all commence anew in the morning, she'd said, whether he felt comfortable with the assignment or not. *How can she possibly expect I'll succeed in this? As far as I know, I have an advanced degree in blank-headedness, here, and not much else. If anything, that should prove my complete uselessness for operations like these, but she makes it out to be some kind of strength...*

So, with his Operator's voice finally absent from the solar, and his decidedly unexciting meal consumed, Spurlock took the vial of devices into his hand and carried them to his wardrobe, as he was instructed to do. The panel slid away smoothly to permit access. But in-so-doing, a smaller compartment down below caught his eye; one he would swear had not been there a short while ago when he'd stashed away his suit. And therein, a single-handed sidearm was mounted tight and secure.

Above the compartment, a small screen displayed a message, which read:

FOR DEFENSIVE PURPOSES, ONLY

The sight of this newly-acquired weapon (and its apparent capacity for inflicting harm) made him positively nauseous, and so he placed the vial on a shelf, and slid the panel closed with unabated disgust. There was, apparently, no telling how complex or dangerous this mission would become.

And he had only just gotten started.

Settling down for his night's rest on the small bed, he thought he might have trouble calming his nerves enough to catch a bit of sleep, and he was right. Yet he discovered the method for dimming the lights in his solar, took another peek at the photo of the girl on his nightstand, and resolved to make an honest attempt at claiming a few winks of rest just the same.

\*\*\*

Spurlock had been told to expect commencement of his next operation come the morning, he just hadn't foreseen exactly how *early* in the morning it would turn out to be. Sleep had evaded him through the greater part of the evening, while he'd laid on his cot staring at the ceiling, wondering how he'd ever gotten himself into this mess. Nearly the remainder of the night was spent mulling over ways he might try to get himself *out* of it. And after only what seemed like a few moments' worth of actual rest, he received notice of his impending operation and an immediate requirement to prepare himself for Projection sequencing.

The Operator prodded him along with her verbal directives while he pulled on his suit and secured his helmet in place.

—Retrieve sidearm from your wardrobe and equip—

He saw there was a loop at the hip of his suit that might serve for a holster, and then he looked into the wardrobe at the weapon where it was mounted in its small compartment.

"But I haven't had any training with this thing, at all."

—Neither have you received training for your suit, yet it has proven user-friendly enough, has it not?—

"A weapon's a little different than a suit. I mean, c'mon. If you're gonna throw me into a den of wolves, at least gimme a chance to learn how to fight back."

—This is not a debate. Equip sidearm now—

"Give me a reason why I should comply with this mission at all," his exhaustion had made him irritable, there was no doubting that.

—Do you think you might want to remember who the female in your picture is, Mr. Spurlock? Or might you ever again want to remember anything at all about yourself?—

"I knew it…" he whispered as softly as he could, "you total wretch."

—I will inform you that your mouthpiece is quite sensitive; even to whispers, Mr. Spurlock—

"You know everything about me, don't you? So why don't you just tell me, already?"

—Be advised, though you will likely not believe it, I cannot tell you what you desire to know. Only *you* can tell yourself—

*Right. Because that makes perfect sense.*

Rolling his eyes, he opened the small compartment and took the sidearm into his hand. Its surface was a matte white composite. When he lowered it toward his hip, the loop opened itself up and accepted the sidearm, holding it snugly in-place in the precise spot where he'd most naturally attempt to access it, in a moment of dire need.

—This weapon is to be used solely for defensive purposes. Do you understand?—

"You mean I can't just go down there and start popping people off on a whim?" He was using recalcitrance again as his only available form of rebellion. "No, wait a minute," he continued, "I wouldn't do that, because I don't carry that kind of violent tendency, do I? And of course, you would know. You've somehow taken every sort of psychological profile you can possibly take of me. Isn't that right?"

—Your suit and the sidearm are linked, Mr. Spurlock, in such a highly intuitive way that to misuse either of them would require a most sophisticated level of technical expertise. Additionally, an earnest attempt to misuse the weapon would, indeed, suggest a troublesome chemical imbalance exists within its user, which, yes, we are entirely confident you lack. Now, please be advised that Projection will commence in thirty counts—

It was as if she'd completely disregarded his attempt to assert his protest. And what better way than to engage him in Projection? When he could either submit to the sequencing process properly, or risk the ultimate consequences.

He knelt down in perfect submission. And before he could think another devious thought, he was wrapped in Projection and removed entirely from the Station.

***

|Planet Deaer, Castle Athyn

A surface of stone, hard and abrasive, pressed against Spurlock's visor when he slowly opened his eyes. Something strange had occurred in the Projection process to reposition his body, now face-down on a dirty floor. Rolling onto his back, blurriness impaired his sight, slowing his comprehension of the small anti-chamber where he lay, with walls of tile painted richly in varying hues of blue. Focusing clearly now, he saw the ceiling was decorated with clever silver stars that mimicked the night sky. Voices came through to him from the other side of a solid wood door, presumably those of soldiers charged with safeguarding the room against intruders (and completely ignorant of his infiltration via Projection). It was all very strange. Very surreal. Very... terrifying. *I wonder what this Operator would do if I got caught sneaking around this place and thrown into some filth-ridden dungeon. She'd probably abandon me. Take off aboard that Station of hers and never look back.*

—Landfall achieved, please confirm—

"Landfall confirmed," he reported almost silently into the mouthpiece, "no complications. Unless of course you'd call a near-brush with messing my pants a complication."

—Gather yourself, Mr. Spurlock—

"Or should I say, 'messing my suit?'"

—Castle Athyn of House Solis is your current location—

"Messing my 'suit pants?' Does this thing technically have pants, or is it just one big suit? I couldn't tell when I took it off and put it back on…"

She continued to ignore the sarcasm.

—Pursue first subject now—

Spurlock rose and stalked silently along the antechamber, through a curtained entry and into the main chamber within, where broad stone walls gave a feeling of scale he hadn't expected. Long moonbeams filtered through expansive windows on the opposite end, cutting through the room, illuminating motes of dust that danced through the air. Beyond them, he saw the younger of the Solis offspring, fast asleep on a heap of cushions gathered on a covered veranda. The prince looked like the object of an exhibit out there—like some sort of relic from antiquity—just as she'd described him in the briefing. Spurlock stood and stared at the quiet form, covered to the shoulders in blankets, almost spirit-like; outlined by the slices of that radiant silver moonlight. Like a symbol unto him.

*But a symbol of what?*

Pacing to the veranda with such extreme caution cost Spurlock valuable time. The smallish figure remained oblivious and discreet, yet there seemed no leeway at all for a misstep, a jostle, or a juggle.

"Subject confirmed."

There was no doubt. This was the one named Tae—his first subject. The first of whom he must violate with an intrusive operation, made necessary by the terms of his mission. This was the moment he'd dreaded since receiving the devices the night prior, and he wished something—anything—would arise to justify his walking away, outright, from the responsibility. *I'd almost prefer the prospects of apprehension and imprisonment over this.*

"Filters," he whispered—thinking he might as well take advantage of the technology at his disposal to at least try and *see* what he was about to attempt, in the darkness of night—and he looked toward the Light Inversion option, "Select."

Drops of sweat fell from Spurlock's forehead, slow and irksome, while leaning over the prince's sleeping body. They landed on the inside of his visor and ran down into to the suit's collar. *What am I doing here?*

*This is insane.* His hands were shaking and his breathing, erratic. Indeed, it'd only been a verbal tutorial he'd received in his solar for completing the operation, and he'd doubted the legitimacy of the plan from the very beginning. *And now, a living and breathing person is lying right here, and I'm supposed to somehow summon the skill of a master physician from thin air?*

—Take out the vial of transponders and use the instrument as instructed—

*Deep breath...* He drew a specialized peripheral from a compartment in his suit and loaded one of the microscopic devices within it. When he lowered himself down to where his subject lay, a sense of strangeness overcame him, akin to onset fever and panic. *I'm not meant to be here; I'm an intruder. This is... just wrong.* He looked around and felt so very out of place.

—Perform surgical application now—

He stopped cold for about the time it takes a spinning coin to slow and settle flat, then continued as he was told.

But the hesitation was just enough to disrupt an unseen equilibrium, and the small prince began to rustle and rub his face.

Spurlock backed off and stepped away, retreating slowly to subdue a mode of panic he felt setting in. Yet, in doing so, his boot came down atop a stray wooden trinket, making an abundantly audible *snapping* sound. In a balancing act to stay afoot, the tiny listening device fell from the peripheral, landing somewhere on the floor with a *tink-tank-tank*. And seeing that the prince had been roused by all of this, Spurlock hastened to find cover behind a large, opened chest sitting in the middle of the room.

"Compromised," he whispered into his mouthpiece, moving his nervous fingers along the handle of his holstered new sidearm, leaning against the chest for concealment. He could hear the prince rising from his cushions and stumbling closer, and when he received no immediate reply from his Operator he huffed, with added urgency, "Do you hear me, *operation compromised!*"

—Hold firm. You *must not* be seen—

"Then get me out of here."

Absent her reply, he waited long spans of time—spans upon spans, it seemed—for the princeling to venture a few steps. It sounded as if the boy picked up the broken wooden trinket to lodge a sleepy inspection of its damage. Likely consumed by a cloud of confusion, the boy then padded his way closer, looking in all directions through the sluggishness in his eyes before thundering past Spurlock's hiding spot and heading for the opposite end of the room, entering the antechamber through its flowing curtains and was gone from sight.

"What am I supposed to do now? Projection, please?"

—Just hold firm—

The prince was gone for a twenty-count before returning and drawing the curtains closed tight. Spurlock hunched down behind the chest (in such a way to ensure the bulk of it remained as a shield for him) and eventually, the little guy made his staggered return to the veranda. Tae stretched for a moment, then flopped back down where he'd been, among his blankets out there in the pale moonlight, and resumed his rest, perhaps never having broken entirely from his sleeping state the whole while long.

—Re-engage operational posture, now—

Spurlock snarled softly at his Operator, but did as he was told, again approaching the place where the prince lay asleep. With the peripheral in hand, in mere moments, he loaded a new device, took a deep breath, and carefully (squeamishly) administered a successful application of one of the tiny listening pieces behind an ear, in the slight void where cartilage meets cranium, implanted by laser incision and flash-mend. A procedure barely discernible by a patient who is awake, let alone fast asleep. He had done it, and he'd turned and departed from the room back into the blue-tiled antechamber before the prince had breathed his next, serene breath; un-phased and un-shaken from sleep.

But in that time, Spurlock found the suit had become so hot that acute sensations of nausea quickly returned, and he began to lose control. Dizzied, he stumbled shoulder-first into a tiled wall and slumped to the floor, sucking air in fits. Hyperventilating. Rattled-through by a queasiness that suddenly wouldn't quit.

—Regain composure. Take a deep breath, Mr. Spurlock—

The suit displayed accelerating heart rate and blood pressure readings, and a warning tone sounded inside the helmet. He gasped, struggled, and fumbled around with his fingers to release the visor; to disengage the helmet completely, and when he had, he dropped it to the floor without regard. Sweat covered his face, stifling him like the suit that wrapped the rest of his body, tight and restricting. He wanted to strip the whole damn suit straight off.

—Lift the helmet now, and place it back upon your head—

Her voice came to him from the helmet, nearly muted compared to its typical clarity for his having taken it off.

—This is an order. Re-equip your helmet *immediately*. I repeat, this is a *direct order*—

In that moment, he hadn't cared where he was, or what the dangers were, or what his Operator was screaming about, or whether or not the guards outside the door could hear it all; he only felt that he was losing his wits, his composure, his good sense. And there was no helping him when he felt the bile rise through his system and up into his throat before vomiting with an utmost violence upon the stone floor, leaving traces over the edges of his mouth and down his chin.

Moments later, at the very least, he found he was still breathing. His chest rose and fell. His heart pounded, and his dizziness (the incessant spinning) slowed, but gradually.

—Equip your helmet *immediately*—

A cold sweat (as from the breaking of a fever he'd felt the whole operation through) washed over him. And, in time, seated in the silence of this castle antechamber, when he was good and ready, he finally lifted the helmet and placed it back over his sweat-soaked head.

—Do not *ever* disobey a direct order—

He let her fester for a moment without replying.

—Engage visor and prepare for Projection to next Coordinate—

Though it took some time to recover—to steady himself enough to assume a kneeling position—he'd found the strength to continue on. To endure Projection sequencing to the elder Prince Solis' bedchambers, and to perform the second procedure as he had the first, minus the excess wheezing and vomiting this time around. Then two more had followed with mirrored success, administered thusly upon the boys' parents (the Nhyle and the Nohnce of this realm of Athyn) within their bedchamber as they slept.

And when it was through, Projection had whisked him back to the Station, and he was loathe to discover what form of retribution the Operator would have in store for him.

\*\*\*

In a dark room, Haley Kenmore had come awake with a start and shortness of breath and switched on her small bedside lamp. She put on her plastic-rim glasses and looked at the digital clock display sitting on her nightstand, which showed an unseemly early hour of the morning.

She leaned over to turn on her phone, and promptly tapped open her messaging app to find there were no new messages.

*A full day now, and still... nothing.*

Out of bed and into the kitchen, she found a bottle of water in the refrigerator, which she twisted open, and from which she took several long sips while pacing her way back into the bedroom. A framed photograph stood on her dresser. She took it into her free hand and strode to a large window, which opened to a view of the city. In a swath of street light that intruded into her dark little apartment, her green eyes shone so brightly while she looked at the image she held.

"Why haven't you replied, Steven?" Her whispers were strained, "What's been going on with you lately?"

And moments later, in one of the thousands of windows that speckled the night's landscape in the District of Columbia, United States, Earth, a small light again went out.

### 5 | A Trick Common among Insignificant Lifeforms

*"Someone once suggested that, in our minds, we cannot compartmentalize the world in an orderly fashion, because the world is far too complex and unpredictable. But perhaps they were wrong. Perhaps the opposite is true—that it is the complexity and unpredictability of our own minds (themselves) that prevents us from understanding our world in simpler terms. And if we could just explore our innermost compartments and simplify our minds, might we simplify our world as well?"*
  —excerpt from the personal journal of Steven Spurlock

|Planet Deaer, Castle Athyn

Tae Solis awoke on his veranda to find brother Ethyn had placed each of his glass globes upon their proper stands, neatly aligned along a shelf in his bedchamber with care. He liked to display them in a line, largest to smallest, and it pleased him most when they were freshly polished and clean. And this was just how they were arranged before him in the gleaming light of Athyn's early morning.

His sleep had been wild as usual, wrought with dreams of a most colorful and frenetic sort, which he tried presently to recollect. *A maze which has no beginning and no end, and which contains within it a host of menacing beasts, on the hunt; stalking. Both behind me and up ahead; even hovering over me as I try to hide in peace. And I've not a hint which corridor of the hundreds that surround me will allow my escape.* It was from these dreams that (each morning) he would wake with a start. And each morning, he lay in silence beneath his coverlets until delivery of his morning meal by handmaid.

But this morning was different. His mother (her grace, Mailyn Solis, the Nohnce of Athyn) had arranged for Tae to join in the activities of the castle's own Mystics House. The resident Masters therein had been quick to request that the little prince fetch a wooden sparring sword from the weapons cellar to aid in his training. *'Bright and early,' they said. 'Fetch us that sword,' they commanded. I'd sooner disappear straight into thin air than subject myself to the servile activities of the Mystics House and its Masters of imperiousness.*

It wasn't exactly an empty threat, either, for Tae had actually (and quite famously) disappeared once. At least that's what brother Ethyn had always contested for as long as memory could serve. It had been many seasons ago, while the boys trolled creek beds for toads, northeast of the castle, where the fields' green grasses underfoot felt as soft as finely-spun cotton fibers.

"You vanished, didn't you?!" Ethyn had cried, while cool water had trickled around Tae's ankles, and a toad leapt just out of reach. Tae had wordlessly shaken his head while his older brother continued the emphatic plea, "Just now, yes you did. You vanished!"

The royal seat's faithful wet-nurse, Mistress Almetta, and five Royal Guard soldiers had accompanied the boys that day, and all of them had heard Ethyn's story onsite. A gray-eyed soldier claimed that, while turning his mount to ford the creek, he too had seen the little prince disappear. And it took little time at all for such talk of Tae's vanishing act to spread like wildfire amongst city and castle folk alike.

During feast time that evening, in honor of the season's harvest, the gossip had flared from every corner of Castle Athyn's great hall. "Vanished you say? And why not?" a nobleman had wailed, drunk as a horsefly drowning in a bottle of rum, "I'm given to believe the boy is downright peculiar enough to sprout a pair of wings and fly away to the land of faerie!"

Another man—*one of father's Lords of Land no less*—had boomed with laughter at the tale of Tae's disappearance, "Could he speak, surely he would tell us he only *seemed* to vanish; a trick common among small, insignificant lifeforms such as he!" And as the ale continued to flow, so too did the remarks and guffaws amongst the clatter of forks and plates and flagons throughout the night. And even the naiveté of his youth could not shield Tae from the hurt and embarrassment caused by such arrogant chiding.

"Do not listen to them," his mother had told him in the safe and quiet confines of his sleeping quarters, after the meals and music and pageantry were finally through. The Nohnce was a pretty woman; and had been exceedingly so in her youth, with a pleasant disposition nearly at all times. And her voice had a comforting effect on Tae, which had been unmatched by any rocking crib or teething toy they could find during his days as an infant. "Those bloated Lords of Land, ignorant such as they are…" she'd continued, "they're only jealous of you. They've no idea how it is that you've become such a special little boy. That's a secret I'll not tell a living soul. Except, perhaps, I'll tell you, Tae… someday. When you are ready to hear."

But it hadn't only been influential Lords of Land who'd taken certain pleasures in Tae's eccentric demeanor. Through adolescence, his peers—sons of nobles and liegemen—were quick to jest at his expense, mocking him disreputably in the fair fields and at court, often asking if he'd finally made up his mind to do them all the grand favor of disappearing for good. They learned quickly enough they could do so and suffer no penance for it. Tae would never tell a word of it to anyone.

Tae never really knew for sure what had happened that day. Perhaps he truly *had* disappeared; it wasn't so difficult to believe. There was, after all, record of a like occurrence, which was said to have involved none other than a sitting Nhyle of Athyn—Tymian Solis, who had, indeed, left the city one fateful day, never to return. No one had actually seen the great patriarch disappear. Or if they had, they'd apparently never come forth to claim as such. But Tae's witnessed disappearance had certainly rekindled speculation that it was possible. And it had become a dominant element of his very persona ever since.

Known far and wide: The Vanishing Mute Prince of House Solis, from the fair fields of Athyn.

Through his formative ages, the labels plagued him: mute, recluse, and craven among all the countless others. And although the frequency of such chiding had eventually diminished as he grew closer to adulthood, the experiences had made an indelible mark on him that resonated onward to present times.

Laying out in the openness of his veranda, with these thoughts swirling in and out of his mind as they usually did, he tried without success to recall the last occasion for which he'd left the royal seat's private castle grounds. Most of his time was spent alone in his bedchambers, or in the cloistered royal gardens. And so, the Masters' assignment, which would take him down into the cellars this very morning, constituted a most dreadful imposition, if not (at the same time) an entirely predictable ploy aimed at tearing him out of his beloved comfort zone.

*Well-played, mother and Mystics Masters. Well-played.*

With reluctance, he rose to find suitable clothes for the detestable undertaking. Crust fell from his puffy, irritated eyes while he rubbed them with his palms, trying to keep them from closing back up, again and again. And although he was just barely waking up, the castle's other tenants, no doubt, had been well roused and abuzz for quite some time—a prospect that colored this pending task all the more unenviable.

And it was with no measure of haste at all that he finally pulled on his tunic, breeches, and mocks, and laced them tight for this denigrating game of go-fetch.

\*\*\*

Tae Solis quit his bedchamber to set about retrieving a wooden practice sword at his own pace. He was in no hurry to fulfill what he considered a petty chore set upon him by his mother and the Mystics Masters, so he walked quite leisurely at the outset. The windows lining the royal family's private corridors offered an all-encompassing view of the city, and he peered across its expanse in passing.

From his vantage point, he saw thousands of stovepipe chimneys rise from slate-shingled roofs at varying heights. Beyond the castle's courtyards and inner wall, the city twisted and turned, fed by its broad avenues and narrow alleys, winding haphazardly around inns, shops, storehouses, stables, gardens, and private cottages. The districts were alive with the activity of people fluttering to and fro; throngs pouring through the streets wherever open space allowed. They carried their baskets and their sacks, their trinkets and their foodstuffs for market. He imagined they discussed thousands of different topics and lived thousands of different lives, and it was all a testament to the staggering complexity of Athyn Proper. *About near as complex as is my own mind, this city. This bizarre organism. Ever in motion, ever churning and always active, like so many thoughts whirling about my head. Like the mazes in my dreams.*

Leaving the windows behind, Tae silently wound his way down a knotted circuit of stairs, halls, and chambers, keeping austerely to himself. The simplest flash of human contact could break him from his make-believe cocoon; the mental device that allowed him courage enough to move through common spaces at all. The grounds were home to many folk who may innocently attempt such contact—a mere wave of hello, a nod of the head, or even a pat on the shoulder—men and women who kept the stronghold alive, feeding its many appetites. Legion ranks and castle workers were there; cooks and bakers, soothists and their potion clerks, handmaids, stable wards, tailors, weavers, and smithies. And in no time, he was thrust straight into the thick of the madness.

Immediately, a gaggle of young maids carrying neatly-folded bed trimmings pushed past on a narrow stair, falling over one another as they fussed and fettered and chirped like sparrows. "She told me my wit is more befitting the station of a mushroom picker in Dunlyn Forest than so much as a scullery maid in Castle Athyn; can you believe her nerve?" squealed one, who wore a handsome satin sash around her waist.

"Some folk haven't the slightest sense'a decency!!" replied her cohort, whose cheeks were of a light pinkish hue, "like my Faron, that dul-witted louse."

"What's he done this time?" asked a third sparrow.

"He oughta be sentenced to far worse'n mushroom pickin' for the way he treated me last night at the Dapper Duckling. It'll be a long time comin' afore I sneak out late'n the dark to see him for a drink in the districts again!"

Tae wondered how one maid managed to hear another over the layers of noise. He shirked away toward the wall and covered his ears as he sidled by. And like a near-riotous buzz, more bodies and more voices hurried on, threatening his personal space. It was enough to rattle his brain and shake it (in bits and pieces) straight out of his ears. *Should there be any wonder why I spend most my days alone in my chambers? If there is a benefit to leaving the comforts of our homes to bandy about the troubling discord of the outside world, I've yet to encounter it.*

It seemed like everywhere he turned, and through every corridor he traveled, there was a commotion. Yet Tae knew some castle conduits remained less traveled. Some, he suspected ever since he was a little boy, led to places which held things long forgotten; secret things perhaps. Deep down within the depths, in the cool sub-terrain. He had heard of such places. *The catacombs beneath the city, like those compartments within the mind that are so difficult to unlock; that we so rarely attempt to access.*

And so, it was his curiosity of the cellars and the prospect he might find a new place within the castle that offered such comforting and peaceful solitude (as only his bedchambers could provide) that had truly carried him in fulfillment of his task. Elsewise, he may have just spun himself right around and returned to his veranda for a bit more sleep at this awful hour of the morning.

\*\*\*

Beneath East Court, the cellars, which housed old surplus armory stores, laid a stairway's distance down into the ground. Torches lined the walls there, and Tae Solis stood on tip toes to take one into his hand. Dust covered most of the articles placed about the cavernous room, obscuring discernment of helmets from shields and staffs from spears, but the items were sorted and stacked in fine order, and his discovery of a wooden sparring sword (that would do nicely to fulfill his requirement) proved quite simple.

Its grip felt awfully good in his hand despite his disdain for the type of dangerous weapon it was made to mimic in training, and he wielded it, posing and gesturing like a fierce warrior. *Like brother Ethyn and his heroic friends!* Then he took a few gallant swipes at the air. *This one for Master Slynth, and this one for Master Hyon... For always telling me where to go and what to do! Manipulating me to their liking!!*

He was still sour about the assignment. Yet he knew the Masters were simply following orders from their Lady Nohnce, and Tae could never fault his kindly mother for her efforts to bring him along; to pry him from his bedchambers and prod him out into the world a bit. *I suppose I can only expect it of her.*

A score of unstrung bows stood upright in a corner, and quivers were hung upon a series of pegs, stuffed full of arrows fletched with beautiful feathers. Burlap dummy targets dressed with funny hats and painted with targets leaned against a wall, all with copious holes poked through and with the stuffing spilling out. There weren't many swords of iron or steel, but there were axes and hammers and pikes aplenty. Many of which bore a bit of rust; both from the dampness of the cellar and from a protracted time of relative peace enjoyed across the region. But as Tae had heard it often said, "Conflict on the field of battle is but a cyclical inevitability, and like the phases of the moon, it will surely return again, sharp and piercing as ever."

Tae hoped it wouldn't. He wanted only for the peoples of the world to mind their own business; Athynians included. He wanted all reasons for the very existence of dangerous weapons to dissolve. He quite despised all of these instruments of war, and looked around the room with an exasperated sigh. *I'd like nothing more than to return to my rooms now and leave these tools of brutality down here to rust full-through.*

It seemed quite perplexing, therefore, that he'd been prompted to train in the use of these weapons, and it only supported his suspicions that those around him lacked even the simplest understanding (or respect) for his desires. Standing there looking around, he could only hang his head in despair at the very notion of it all.

The Masters of the Mystics House and their pupils were likely already engaged in their morning exercises by the time he resolved to return the torch to its sconce in the cellar. The great house was close enough to his present location—just above ground, fronting East Court— to require only but a leisurely stroll to make his arrival. But he entirely misliked the idea of strutting through the door for all of them (at once) to turn and stare at him. Assembling the courage to report for his lesson, he knew, would be a calamitous business far more daunting than had been this act of collecting the sword.

On his toes, he reached up to drop the torch back into its rungs. Yet, in doing so, he suddenly felt a sensation wash over him that stayed his hand. It was piercing and heavy, but indefinable.

*Something truly distinct, but what?* He couldn't say.

He brought the torch back down, awkwardly enough that he stumbled a bit, and the wooden sword dropped from his grip to the floor with an impact that echoed, *echoed, echoed.* The sound, in fact, traveled in such a peculiar way that Tae couldn't explain its patterns, nor its reverberations. It was as if the sound continued to travel at lengths it ought not to have been able to travel. So he took the sword back in hand from the floor and began tapping it along the wall; along bins and baskets, and crates and shelves. He tapped it over floor stones and against the colonnades and the woven tapestries that hung in silence about the perimeter of the vaulted room.

One such tapestry stood apart from the others, woven in depiction of a great hunt; a man atop his mount blowing a twisted horn and dogs sniffing through the grasses; men with bow and arrow and spear and rope at the ready. Yet the scene lacked depiction of their quarry (whatever formidable beast it happened to have been). He tapped the sword against the wall there and the sound flew away, down into great depths unknown. And when he drew the tapestry aside, he found a small passageway in the wall; hidden by two crossbeams. But to look at the opening, it didn't seem too small for him to wiggle his way inside. *Perhaps my size may finally afford me an advantage.*

The passageway proved slight indeed (even for him), and he had to slide the sword into his belt to free both hands for climbing and for pulling himself through. But soon, the narrow shaft led to a tunnel, which opened to a proper corridor, freeing him to stand upright and walk, and it wound downward into the ground at such angles that made him skip-step with momentum. With torch in hand, shadows danced like specters, leaping at him from the walls.

It wasn't long before he met a fork in the tunnel, where the air became cool, producing goose prickles on his arms. *Something is calling to me.* Right and then left. Deeper yet he strayed into the labyrinth of tunnels. Drops of moisture fell from overhead, plunging (with more eerie echoes) into pools of water at his feet. Left and then right, he turned. *It's calling; reaching out...* Then the passage narrowed again and closed-in from above until he finally reached a disquieting impasse at which the wooden support beams (holding up the ceiling and walls) terminated, and so too did the tunnel. The way ahead, finally, seemed packed solid and closed off—a dead end. But there was a slight opening, lined only in raw soil and sediment; too small for him to fit through this time.

With murky puddles about his feet, he stared into the opening, wondering where it could possibly lead, and realized the sensation of summons had subsided. *This must be the source of whatever force was luring me along.* The torchlight revealed nothing further of the opening, save for its seemingly endless depths of darkness within. *Mother will scorn me for missing my training... and for what I've done to tatter my mocks and tunic.*

But shirking such concerns, in that moment, there came over him a feeling of peace; alone in that dark place. Away from everyone else. It was a sense of calm that seemed more restorative than any sort of training activity he'd ever been forced into. A feeling he would certainly never feel in front of an audience at the Mystics House. It was just what he thought he might find down there.

And for the first time since he was a little toddler hunting toads in the fields outside the castle, there in the depths of the catacombs that twisted beneath the city of Athyn Proper, Tae Solis disappeared into thin air.

## 6 | Beyond the Defiles

*"I became quite fascinated, for a time, with the basic principles of neuroscience, and I learned we have within our bodies a rather splendid network of micro-transponders. Neurons, they're called, or nerve cells. There are those neurons that respond to sensations of touch and taste and sound; in tune with the drum and hammer in the ear, the iris and retina in the eye, and the nerve endings beneath the skin. They signal one another by synapse, firing off pure data to the brain. Others travel the opposite direction, carrying intentions born of the brain back to the body, to the muscles, prompting movement. I've wondered what kinds of tricks these networks can play on us. How reliable this system can possibly be, and—if they should be unreliable in any way—what perversion of reality we must truly be living."*
—excerpt from the personal journal of Steven Spurlock

|Planet Deaer, The Southspur Mountain Peak

"Let's unload your provisions, shall we?"

Koryn Nailor heard the declaration from his curled-up position on the floor. He looked up and saw Haiyen Sün standing over him, bundled up and motivated to get on with the fulfillment of her task.

Outside the cottage on the mountain's peak, the blizzard continued unabated while they made their way to the buzzcraft, but it did little to numb the awkwardness that had clearly carried on between them from the previous night's quarrel.

"I still can't believe they trust you to fly this thing around," Koryn finally ventured to bark through a whipping wind that tossed the fur sewn within his collars in all directions, "and letting you come up *here* of all places, to see me? It boggles the mind." The remark bore shades of audaciousness; particularly considering Haiyen's present dissatisfaction with him.

She opened a hatch in the back of the cab to reveal three large wooden barrels.

"I've proven myself worthy of their trust."

The response, perhaps appropriately so, carried with it a twinge of judgment to Koryn's ear, for all of its potentially loaded meaning.

"Is that so?" he said as they unloaded one barrel after another in the snow-covered yard, "I suppose you've all but entered the Prima ranks by now then, huh? Have you given-in to the establishment, Haiyen, is that it?"

"I guess you wouldn't know anything about it, would you?"

"And what exactly is that supposed to mean?"

"Really Koryn?" she slammed the hatch of the cab closed, "you may have lost all track of time up here, but I haven't. It's been two years now since your exile. Two years exactly, and every thirty days, I fly up here to see you. To bring you these provisions so you don't starve to death on this frozen precipice. And here you are, just as self-absorbed as the day you tried absconding from the Settlement like some rogue wild child. Remember? You were going to 'leave the mountains behind and drift along,' you said. 'Come with me to the flatlands,' you said… But I had enough good sense to stay behind. Not you, though. You left in the dark of night with enough food to last you all of three days, if I recall, and by some miracle, they found you out there. You weren't even headed in the right direction, and you were so out of sorts you required resuscitation and transfusion when they brought you back. If you've lost track of all history up here as well, maybe that'll refresh things for you a little."

"I thought we agreed not to talk about all that," he said with furrowed brows.

"*You* demanded we not talk about it, and I've gone along with it," returned Haiyen, "for two years, in fact. But I'm through with that now. You wouldn't know anything about my life since then because you've been gone. You've been here, nothing short of a prisoner. And when I've come for you, you've asked but nothing of what I've been doing. How I've grown; the life I've made. Yes, Prima rank included."

"*Prima?!*" He gasped, stumbling over the implications of her confession, "So you've freedom then… from even the farthest Settlement limits?"

"As far as the tenants of Prima rank and my own prudent judgment will allow, yes, I've freedom of travel to go where I please," she ran her hand over a side panel on the craft, "I've flown to places of unimaginable beauty, Koryn. Of course the desolate southern regions mostly, where I'll not be seen or detected by those of the flatlands. Much of the arctic reaches, too. I've seen the seas."

"The seas?" He couldn't believe what he was hearing. Like the flatlands themselves, the seas were a myth known only to a select few in the Settlement—the Sages and the Prima rank—the protectors of all the others in the mountain dwelling just below the snow line; where they'd both been born and lived their whole lives, inseparably, until his punishment and subsequent exile for his attempted defection.

"It could have been us together in the ranks, had you not acted like such a fool and forced them to send you here on watch."

"When were you going to tell me all this?"

"As soon as you asked, but you never have. I thought I'd give you one last chance at it, this time... this visit, but you've failed again; failed to even feign interest in me beyond the purely physical. Instead, you make a game of it. You use me for your own devices without the simplest attempt to *talk* to me; to hear from me, or hear *about* me and the person I've become, and..." her voice caught in her throat for a moment, but she was able to recover, "and I'm moving on from this, Koryn. From us. Maybe it'll sink-in thirty days from now when you find it's Bartyl Gleon who delivers your provisions, because it won't ever... it *can't* ever be me again."

"*Gleon...*" he nearly choked on the snow flying in his face and down his throat, "gods, Haiyen, no!"

And it was then that her eyes reflected the sparkling blue light of the sky, following something soaring toward them at great speeds. The messenger fowl; its powerful spotted brown wings were spread wide overhead, and he heard the crisp ringing of the bell as the bird landed on its perch, knocking the accumulated ice free from the pole, and emitting a piercing call signaling its arrival.

He looked at Haiyen for a moment, then raced toward the pole, and she followed close behind.

The bird sat obediently on the perch, the bell swaying under its weight, and it looked straight at Koryn, its head darting left and right in uneven cadence. He held out his arm, and the bird flew to him, landing with grace. Inside the cottage, the bird stepped down to the table and waited obediently.

"He's beautiful," said Haiyen, who had followed them in.

Koryn took the bird's leg in hand and removed the message; a razor-thin strip of parchment, rolled tight and waxed together. "Watch this," he said, kneeling down and lifting a plank free from the floorboards. Hidden below was a case, which held a metal-handled crank, a polished cylindrical container, and a small leather pouch, cinched tight with a draw cord. "This is a capsule," he said, holding the container up for her to see, its components making a jostling sound. He carefully slid the rolled-up message inside. Then he paced the floor and fit the sealed capsule neatly into a loading chamber inside the reflective launching machine.

"Wait here."

Out the door he ran, pulling on a pair of gloves, and up the hill's slope to the roof he scrambled. Atop the cottage, a thin layer of ice cracked when he reached blindly into the snow to find an iron ring. It took much coaxing before he was able to lift free a hidden hatch. Its hinges groaned immensely until resting in place, wide open, to reveal Haiyen standing in the darkness of the cottage below, watching with intrigue.

"What exactly are you doing up there on the roof, Koryn?"

"You'll see," he said, slipping down through the hatch, back into the cottage, using the table as a landing pad before returning down beside her. He reached back into the case (which had come from beneath the floorboards) and pulled out the metal crank. It fit perfectly into the launching machine, and a hasp had been released when he began to turn it. A series of gears set at raising the bulk of the device through the hatch in the ceiling, and the higher it rose, the more the floor shook beneath their feet, grinding and wailing.

Until he stopped.

"Now comes the fun part," he said, with his eyes opened wide while he reached into the case, this time for the leather pouch.

\*\*\*

Koryn Naylor grabbed Haiyen Sün's hand and pulled her along with him, climbing again atop the hill. With hints of laughter the whole way up, snow flying every which way from their excited steps, she cried out, "Koryn, stop!"

When they reached the machine, which had emerged almost entirely from the cottage's roof, he turned to her with a smile.

"Remember when we were children, Haiyen, and the Sages would demonstrate the powers of the stones to us? And we would look on in amazement when they showed us fire and wind and the wonders of all the mystics?" He held up the small pouch for her to see, loosening its string to show her the contents within, "It's powder. Ground fine from the stones."

"Koryn," she said with a flat look, "every Prima rank knows about the powder."

"Shhhh," he interrupted, putting a finger to her soft lips, "don't ruin this for me. Besides, you don't know it like this." He knelt down next to the machine and opened a small compartment door, wherein he poured a very small amount of the powdery contents of the pouch. Then a wry grimace formed upon his face when, upon searching his pockets, he realized he lacked his spark-strike flint.

"Looking for this?" Haiyen asked, holding a small flame at the tip of her finger, blue and orange and steady, without even the slightest flicker. She leaned down beside him, and he could smell her. *Her hair. Her skin. Such familiar, fond, wonderful scents... Oh Haiyen, where did I go wrong by you? Have I taken you for granted?!*

She let him guide her fingertip to the fuse at the machine's base and, once it was lit, he took her by the waist and said, "Ok, now stand back!"

Something seemed to catch hold, some sort of bottled energy, and the bottom end of the machine began flaring with sparks. And without warning, like a shooting star, the loaded capsule was fired off, bursting forth, spitting a trail of flame in its wake, flaring and screaming; searing the air along its path into the heights. The eruption blew them to the ground, smattering their faces with soot and their bodies with debris, embedding them deep in a snow bank on the hilltop.

Koryn shook his head and smiled wide, laughing hysterically (maniacally) at the sight of the capsule disappearing far above its column of white smoke, "What'ya think about that?!"

When at first she didn't respond, he strained to catch a glimpse of her face, worried for an instant she might have been hurt in the fall. "Haiyen?" And finally, seeing her familiar smile, he could tell with relief that she'd slowly, almost reluctantly, begun laughing and reveling in the great launching display as well. Then she shouted and screamed and pointed at the capsule's tail of fire as it ascended into the strata of the atmosphere.

This reverie lasted a fine, blissful while. They stared into the sky, forgetting the chill of the snow and the wind. And so too, he could almost begin to forget her declaration of displeasure with him, and about her wanting to forget about him; wanting to put an end to what they had.

*Maybe she's forgotten, too?*

"You've simply got to teach me that fingertip flame aptitude," he said, lightly; playfully.

She let a few more gasps of laughter escape her lips as the capsule finally disappeared from view, and calmed herself before answering, "Koryn… you're right, I've seen the stones and their powder help lift and fly a buzzcraft, but I haven't before seen the likes of *this*, so I thank you for showing me. I needed a good laugh and a release from reality. This was fun; you've always had a flare for the dramatic."

They watched trails of smoke drift from the top of the launcher into the blue sky while she continued. "But, Koryn, this can't change what I've said… about wanting to move on. *Needing* to move on. And about Gleon making your next provision run, and everything else. It really can't."

He gave her a terribly sullen stare, in sharpest contrast to the broad smile it replaced.

"There is more to life for me now; there is responsibility," she continued. "Other people depend on me, and you and I; we're not the same as we used to be. We're seldom together anymore, and when we are, it's…" she let the sentence trail away. Instead of finishing it, she picked herself up from the hole they'd made in the snow bank and looked down at him. "… Look, I've said what I needed to say, and it was painful enough the first time, so I'm just going to leave it be."

"Gods… what's so wrong about wanting to see the world, anyway?" he plead; standing up and brushing the snow from his own cold, numbed body, "When I ran off from the Settlement, I just wanted to see the Beyond. The flatland they've always told us about. Is that such a deplorable offense, deserving of what they've done to me? To strip me of my freedom? To take everything from me, Haiyen? And now you'll be taken from me, too…"

"After the Sages undertook such painful measures to protect us from the evils of the world, Koryn? Yes. It was a serious, loathsome offense that you committed, and I don't blame them for leveraging their punishment," she said, "How did you expect them to react, after they'd done everything in their power to conceal us from the flatlanders and their treachery? You could have endangered the whole Settlement, doing what you did."

"I see. So you're telling me you don't ever take your buzzcraft to see these alleged flatlands?" he challenged, "You've never risked these fabled flatlanders seeing you at all, not even for a winking glimpse of the mysterious Beyond?"

"Not even for a glimpse," she answered, unflinchingly, "it isn't worth risking the lives of everyone in the Settlement over, and that's exactly what I'd be doing."

"You know, I would think twice about placing such blind faith in the Sages, Haiyen."

"Is that so? And what reason have they ever given me to doubt them? Their brilliance has provided everything we've ever needed; we should want for nothing more than the lives we have in the Settlement."

"You've changed, haven't you? Listen to you! The Sages have done a real number on you. You sound just like them."

"And I'm better off having learned under their influence. We were rogues when we were young. Foolish rogues. I thought your time up here would at least show you the truth in that, if nothing else."

"You look back at us and name us foolish, but I look back and I see two young people who were naught but curious and courageous. And that's a dangerous combination for the Sages. They wanted to repress our curiosity. That's why I'm up here, I am sure of it."

"Be serious, Koryn… repress us?"

"Don't you think there are a good many things about which they've never told us? About which they refuse to tell you, even now?"

"For instance?"

"These messages I'm receiving, for starters. You've already led on you don't know what they say. Wouldn't you like to know? More'n that, wouldn't you like to know who's sending them and what they're for? Because I'm sure *they* know," his tone was defiant and challenging. "Actually, besides everything else, how about telling us where, in the great blue Beyond, these messages *go* when I launch them? That's what I'd *really* like to know. I've got nothing but time up here to let my curiosity run wild about a great many things, but that one… that one reigns supreme."

She met his questions with a contemplative expression.

"I'm guessing they don't even inform the Prima rank of these details," he scoffed at the audacity behind it all. *And even more audacious, her willingness to accept it all with such resolute obedience!* He held the pouch of powder in his hand with the string still loosened, and he looked at it. Then he looked at her buzzcraft (idle in the yard below them) with a level of deviousness in his eyes. *She said she's seen the powder help lift a buzzcraft, didn't she? I wonder how much powder it would take to get a craft like that airborne and across the foothills?*

"Don't even think about it," she said looking at him as if she could read his thoughts.

"Think about what? I was just wondering…"

Before he could finish, she turned from him and began descending down the hill.

"Haiyen?" he called after her.

She moved slowly at first, until he started to follow. Then she quickly advanced her pace to a run; and then to a frantic sprint, as fast as the snow would allow, kicking and striding through the drifts.

But he was soon gaining on her.

"Haiyen, stop. You can't leave like this; I wasn't thinking of doing *anything*…"

She didn't answer, just kept pressing forward. He knew she wasn't used to plodding through the snow; not like he was, and especially not on foot at accelerated speeds, and he saw her struggle to stay ahead. He made up ground quickly, leaping and extending his long legs with each stride. Her steps were half the breadth of his, and her boots were not made for the slog. He continued to gain on her steadily until he was so close, he thought he might reach for her like he had at the front door when she'd arrived, to put his hand over her shoulder and subdue her... prevent her from leaving.

That was when she wheeled about and faced him with just enough time to pull off her necklace and the blue stone pendant. And no sooner did he see her clutch the stone tightly in her closed palm, then he felt a pulse ripple through the air and pound him square in the chest, blasting him back to the trampled and icy ground.

She recovered and finally reached the cab of her buzzcraft, leaping into the cockpit. The flexor wings animated and fluttered alive, and lifted the craft almost in an instant, swirling snow and pushing the coldest of air into Koryn's face while he struggled back to his feet. The craft lingered for a moment, hovering at treetop level while she looked at him with a deep and sorrowful face.

He shouted: "I am who I am, Haiyen. Do not forsake me!"

He thought she'd heard him, but the flexor wings accelerated, and turned the craft away. Moments later, she disappeared over the trees and beyond the defiles.

And she was gone completely from his sight.

## 7 | Harbinger of Evil

*"...Our powers of perception are tested each time we develop a hunch about something. Hunches are healthy occurrences; they force us to take stock of our instincts; our intuition. But the mere identification of a hunch is meaningless if we let it flutter away. It is how we act upon our hunches that defines our courage; our trust in our own understanding of the world around us. And like all other phenomena of human development, if we ignore our hunches, we fail to grow."*
—excerpt from the personal journal of Steven Spurlock

|Planet Deaer, Athyn

Dawn broke across the plains while a host of travelers emerged from Castle Athyn's West Gate at a purposeful pace. Rays of golden sunshine sliced through cotton-white clouds on the horizon like colossal swords of light, casting long abstract shadows of the riders' stately forms. Yet despite its majesty, Ethyn Solis ignored the view; even the countless droplets of dew that shone like opalescent orbs atop verdant blades of grass, speckling the vast countryside.

He sat straight-backed in his saddle, reins held waist-high, silently contemplating the previous night's conversation with his father. *Surely I haven't imagined this new-found willingness to entrust me with responsibilities more befitting an Heir Prince of my age and experience.* He'd been given a charge bearing no small measure of importance, to lead an escort of the Maelnlockian Ambassador to Athyn.

*Time to prove myself worthy.*

Two mounted soldiers accompanied the prince, along with a pair of supply wagons and a small retinue of Royal Legion soldiers, who followed in-tow. Legionnaires Aryk and Othys Frierstag were his choice of host; two soldiers with nothing in common save a family and its prevalent surname, made famous by an honored ancestral line, whose acts of bravery on the battlefield had long been sewn into the fabrics of lore and legend. Othys—senior soldier and uncle to Aryk—fancied the ornamental legion helmet for its attractive alternative to his balding, sun-reddened pate underneath, but it didn't serve well to keep what remained of his unkempt flame-orange hair from hanging out 'neath its edges, and in thick curls over his ears. And the regalia of the legion, lean-cut as it was, proved ill-fit for the elder's bulbous physique.

*If he could only see himself half-spilling from his raiment, perhaps he'd be more inclined to raise a shaving blade to that ridiculous hair, and less inclined to raise an extra mug of ale to his lips each night 'midst the taverns.* But the man had proven a trusted confidant to the seat through the years, and there wasn't ever a trait more desirable in a soldier than loyalty. Especially when it came to sensitive matters, like diplomatic escorts.

The broad-set trail ran like a ribbon thrown across the rolling fields beyond. It was this appearance that had inspired its namesake, the Ribbon Road, and it was the main conduit connecting the castle to all points north. Ethyn was outfitted in simple riding gear. Gauntlets that covered his wrists bore deep scratches marking the hardened leather in scores; the work of his companion fowl, for which he cared so fondly. From a hovel atop of the many towers rising above the city's heights, the Heron Bird emerged with wings spread wide—all elegance and grace—singing its mellifluous song. Slight, with smooth gray-blue and white feathers, a long pin-pointed beak, and a plume crest on its head; it would follow the prince in his travels whenever they took Ethyn from the city.

Gliding, the bird careened away from the course of the Ribbon Road, and Ethyn's gaze followed its path until it veered in the opposite direction, across the muted southern sky. The heavens hadn't yet bled orange-gold in that direction as they'd begun to do elsewhere, but instead, yet remained a morose purple-gray. The jagged line of the Southspur Mountains spanned far away; their peaks piercing the soft sky almost with an air of certain violence.

And there, above one such apex, he saw *it.*

It was something of an utmost peculiarity he'd noticed on two prior occasions, but had been inclined to dismiss as an anomaly of little significance—a fire-red plume painted anew over the mountain reaches. As before, he would swear the trail of glowing smoke was the product of something ascending from the ground up into the heavens above. *But what? Whatever could accomplish such an unnatural task? An aberration, or so I'd thought the first time; a curiosity the second, and now...*

He reigned his mount to a stop and called back to the younger of the two legion hosts, "Aryk, come here. Please tell them to halt the wagons."

The elder, Othys, shouted quite unceremoniously through his thick orange mustachios. "Halt the wagons!"

Aryk Frierstag, unlike his uncle, was thin and neatly groomed, well-spoken and thoroughly studied, and he wore the uniform of the legion in exactly the sort of way it was meant to be worn. He was a young soldier—of equal age to Ethyn—who carried books with him wherever he went; even managing to have tucked a few into his saddle bags for the morning's ride along the Ribbon Road. He'd been reading from a folio, which he hastily buried beneath the flap of his satchel when Ethyn called him forth.

"What do you see?" The prince pointed off into the distance south, toward the flaming trail for his friend to follow. The fiery wound was still quite fresh in the sky, "There, above the mountains. Anything?"

Aryk pulled his mount up beside Ethyn's and took a few measured breaths before studying the place in the sky where Ethyn had pointed; eyes squinting first, then opening wide with intense scrutiny, then back to squinting again. After long moments, he turned and looked at the prince with much chagrin, "...Nothing, Ethyn. I don't see a thing, I am very sad to admit. I feel perfectly foolish for having left my looking glass behind. I bring it with me often, for moments precisely such as these, and here I am without it. Is there something there? Something that I should see?"

Ethyn pointed at the shooting conflagration anew, and watched Aryk follow his gesture straight out to the mountains for another turn. But after extended moments spent staring and squinting, his friend sighed again in apparent failure.

"Nothing?" Ethyn asked, "Do you not see a line of flame making for the heavens, bleeding a trail of fire and smoke?"

"I wish for myself but a fraction of the keen eyesight you possess, Ethyn," admitted Aryk, "Ever since we were lads running the course of the castle together, you could spot a flying blinkbug clear across the court, and all I could ever see was but a faint shadow or a blurred abstraction, if that. In fact, for a time, I figured myself afflicted with exceedingly *poor* eyesight by comparison, but the soothists all agreed my vision was just fine. And so, as I've often said before, I'm convinced you've long been imbued with some kind of mystic-laden sense of sight, even if you will always deny it's so. If you say there is something there, Ethyn, for these reasons I've no doubt there is, but I'm ashamedly not to be counted among those who might corroborate it for you."

"It's quite alright, Aryk, pay it no further mind… It is perhaps nothing more than an aberration. And only a fool draws certain conclusions from evidence which he cannot confirm, much less understand. Still, I've seen it clear as day just now, plus two times prior."

"Two times prior, and this a third? Have you at least a theory for what it may be?"

"Sadly, I've not found the time to even begin such musings. But whatever it is, in my mind, I strongly suspect it's of a determinedly wicked persuasion; some sort of harbinger of great evil, and no less."

"That sounds bad!" Othys interjected without invitation, "Real bad; if you don't mind me saying so, my lord."

Aryk reddened, "Uncle, have you finally lost your wits in-full? This is an official procession of the Royal Legion, not a barkeep's consortium. You're not to bellow aloud your stray, ill-contrived ruminations." The young legionnaire turned back to the prince, "Please forgive him his indiscretion and me my inferior vision, Ethyn. It seems we are a sad entourage, at the moment, sorely deprived of our intended purpose."

"No forgiveness necessary. You're not the only one who's failed to see this flaming wound splitting the sky. Not nearly, in fact. Upon the occasions of both prior sightings, I've asked a number of those in the castle for their say, and none from the lot of them—not a single woman nor man—has been able to verify my description."

Thin, vaporous breath escaped from Ethyn's mouth as the words slipped reluctantly from his chilled lips, swirling about in front of them in the early spring air, then vanishing. Their mounts' nostrils produced the same melancholy effect with each bellowing snort and snicker, lending the exercise a distinct sense of pointlessness, and giving Ethyn no choice but to return to the task at hand.

"Let us continue on our way; we must set a strict pace if we're to make it to Stief before nightfall."

In the sky, Ethyn saw the Heron Bird aloft, seemingly weightless; its broad wings riding light thermal air currents like a spirit, lifting into the blue firmament, soaring now in the direction they were headed. *I'd wager she can see the rising flame on the mountains' horizon. If but only she could speak to let me know…*

And so, having commenced their conversation, they urged their animals into a trot, pressing forward unto the road without further delay.

\*\*\*

The Ribbon Road bisected Athyn's countryside; a landscape of vibrant foliage just starting to burst free from winter's frost-ridden entrapment, and it ran along open fields of fertile soil that bore the lifeblood of the realm. Ethyn saw the farmhouses and their barns; the sprawling acreage covered with orchards, vineyards, and gardens spanning leagues in the distance. And he saw that most fields lacking neatly-planted rows of crops instead bore livestock that grazed leisurely, nibbling at thick tufts of grass. *These folk work hard but live freely and choose for themselves what paths to take, what crops to sew and nurture, and what livestock to raise. And so it ought to be forever more. But I wonder if we're doing enough—if father's efforts and those of the council will prove sufficient to ensure it all remains this way.*

*Protected.* Ever since he'd been old enough to form impressions about the workings of the world, he'd feared it might only be a matter of time until the council's passive, defensive postures invited the aggressive attentions of ambitious foes.

While the sun rose toward its crest in the sky, the warmth settled down on Ethyn's shoulders, piercing an otherwise brisk morning, making for a comfortable ride by midday, and time passed quickly. Ethyn became pleased with the progress they'd made, past the reaches of the wooded Canterford Vale to the openness of the coastal flats and their views of the expansive sea. They had made good time, indeed; he and his Frierstag hosts, as well as the wagon master and their small retinue of soldiers. *This is a disciplined lot. Practiced at their craft and proud for it, too, and they deserve encouragement.* So it was with pleasure that Ethyn saw the old sea outpost, standing like a great beacon not far ahead beside an inlet lagoon on the coast. A perfect setting to consume a bit of sustenance, and to grant their mounts a moments' respite from the road while the wagon tenders delivered much-needed supplies to the men occupying the tower, within.

While the others crowded beside one of the wagons, each for a chunk of smoked tuna, a cusset root or two, a sun-sweetened nape of the hallow leaf, and a flagon of ale, Ethyn sat apart on the banks of the lagoon. The prince, who'd found he simply could not stay his mind from the vision he'd seen in the sky at morning's dawn, decided then to summon his bird, which glided down almost immediately and landed upon his leathered gauntlet. It waited patiently beside him while he scribed a private message:

> *To our fine Master Thurflyn, should you be so inclined to join my own company for a meal and a bit of conversation, you will meet us upon the second setting sun 'neath the roof of the commons at the Royal League House of Stief. I would be most honored to meet your acquaintance, should you choose to accept, and I trust preparing for travel will prove no challenge for someone bearing your credentials.*

> *–Prince Ethyn of House Solis*

The parchment fit snugly within the clip around the Heron Bird's leg. With but a few whispers into the bird's plumage, Ethyn released it to the skies, and it flew out of the trees and northward on its intended course. *If anyone can provide insight into these images of fire I'm seeing in the sky, it is Master Adrian Thurflyn.*

With the message on its way, Ethyn took a deep breath to rest his mind, if for only a short while. The sea outpost was a circular tower of stone that stood tall and strong at the head of the lagoon, indeed, but yet had seen better days from a superficial perspective. Its slate roof tiles were salted almost white, and its walls were pitted by blowing winds and debris and by the nesting habits of small coastal fowl. A blue pennant flapped vigorously from its risen peak, proud in marking the territory for House Solis and Athyn's people. The outpost was still in working order, and Ethyn noticed its Royal Guard residents had come down from its command deck to greet the retinue of soldiers, for conversation and to partake in their enjoyment of refreshments.

Waves crashed against the rocks below the prince, where swells churned, making deep baritone sounds of the sea, working together to emit a rich symphony that blocked out most of the other noises that might hinder Eythn's deep contemplation. All of this, save for a voice, which came to him so faintly behind the workings of the sea.

Out there in the depths of the lagoon, he saw an image of something in duress; something that ought not to have been there at all—a striking figure, to be certain.

\*\*\*

Ethyn removed his boots and leapt headlong over the rocks, into the lagoon with arms extended before him and dove not far below into the pristine waters with a great splash. The water hit him like a shockwave, cold and forbidding, but it enlivened him all the same. The lagoon remained warmer than the Great Sea, as the pools there were heated by the sun and turned over far less frequently by the tides. But even so, the season hadn't yet nearly arrived that would allow for comfortable swimming temperatures.

Surfacing, he saw the figure again. From his vantage point on land, the figure had seemed to be in some great peril. Now, though, she seemed to swim effortlessly as if she were a kite, gliding through the air on a steady breeze. He watched while she stopped to tread water, then tilted her head back and ran her fingers through her wet hair to clear it from her eyes. Then she squared her shoulders directly toward him, as if she sensed his attention. He caught his heart in his throat for a moment, embarrassed and enraptured at once. *How could she have come upon this place without the Royal Guard noticing from the tower?*

Then in a blink, she dove beneath the surface and out of sight.

As if drawn by impulse, he was diving in pursuit without a semblance of thought, and their motions and movements (in accordance with one-another) quickly progressed into a game akin to those played often between cat and mouse. Every time he'd thought he caught another glimpse of her form shifting ahead through the water, he surfaced only to realize she had vanished, seemingly right before his eyes. Again and again the trend continued, soon becoming a challenge that he simply *had* to conquer. With each failure to find her, the desire grew greater still, until it was nearly unbearable. *Such a seemingly simple task, swimming in clear, shallow water. She couldn't have gone anywhere, and yet she is nowhere to be seen!*

It was like reaching for a string that dangled just out of reach. And finally, he came to the surface again to breathe, quite exhausted by the effort.

"I'd like just a moment, if you don't mind," he voiced loudly to the empty, open waters. "Are you alright?" He remained still, waiting as long as he could bear, but nothing stirred for a long while. Until, as it happened, he sensed a disruption in the water behind him and turned to see gentle ripples rolling toward him. But he found no one there to claim responsibility for them.

"Have you a name?" he asked. And again, the water rippled behind, spinning him back around to find naught but a lonely sea, "My name is Ethyn, if it pleases you to know…"

He felt a tugging at his toe, then, which brought him down again, immediately. And beneath the roll of delicate waves, he was entirely mystified by what he saw only a few arm lengths before him. She was there; suspended in the water with endless depths of sea sprawling away behind. She looked like a being of another world, but thoroughly human; just inexplicably ethereal. Her long hair hung all about her face in the water, like strands of silk swaying in slow motion with the stir of the current, and her eyes (opened wide and the color of the brilliant sea) projected a nimble, yet cautious curiosity. Her body was wrapped tight in finely-stitched cloth, one arm raised and the other lowered, both slightly bent at the elbows. Her legs dangled, toes almost touching the smooth, white sand below them. And her movement was so subtle; almost too subtle for someone to stay in position underwater as she was. But all matters like these were lost on Ethyn, the prince who was holding his breath; only partly because he was submerged under water and partly for other reasons altogether.

The moments spent staring at her had a pulse all their own, drawn out with such incredible uncertainty. *But this could never last too long.* Reflections of the sun's golden shafts played off both their faces while bubbles seeped from their lips. She beckoned to him ever so slightly with her delicate hand, and an instant later, turned and began to swim away into deeper water. Immediately, he made his pursuit, swimming after her with conviction this time, as not to lose her again.

He hadn't noticed how far they'd strayed into the sea until she paused (at last) at the bottom and curled back to stare in his direction. He stopped to see her swim in a circle and turn her attention toward a growth on the sea floor, where he saw something peculiar was caught amongst a cluster of weeds and rocks. He dove closer to find a chain lying there, strung with an unusual stone, which he pulled from its place beneath the sand. Much like this mysterious figure, herself, the stone's visual appeal was magnificent; the color of honey and polished intricately in the shape of a tear drop.

*How could this have gotten here?* He looked to her for an explanation, but she only smiled and began to swim to the surface once again. And he followed.

At the surface, he breathed deeply. Their eyes met, and he held forth the mysterious piece of treasure. It glowed richly now in the sunlight, "I would like to give this to you."

But her reaction seemed strange. She held a hand up and backed away in the water as if she simply would not stand for receiving the gift.

He pressed, "Wouldn't you like to wear this?"

The ornament was not exactly spotless; it could have used a good polishing. In all likelihood, from the looks of it, the piece of jewelry had likely been lost on the sea floor for a considerable amount of time. It could very well have fallen astray from some matriarch's sea vessel, and the tides could have gradually brought it into the lagoons. But whatever its true story, Ethyn expected that this veritable siren had led him here so he could retrieve the necklace for her and present it to her as a gift.

*After all, I'd expect receiving a gift such as this from an Heir Prince ought to feel as something from a fantasy for a maid such as herself.* But her refusals continued, and it was made clear she wished not to receive the treasure as a gift. Instead, she pointed insistently to him.

"You wish for *me* to have it?" At this notion, she smiled again. So he reluctantly raised it over his head, strung it around his own neck, and once it was in place, with the stone resting upon his chest, she finally swam close to him. She slid her arms gently around his body and placed her cheek against his, whispering in a clever even-toned voice, "Never... take it off."

She stared into his eyes, then, and added, "I am going to need your help, but when I do... you will not be able to give the help that... only you can give, if ever... you lose this talisman." She placed her hand on the stone against his chest in a sort of ritualistic way that suggested a binding together of—something.

*But what? Our hearts, our souls… our trust?*

"I won't take it off," he said in reply, "I promise."

Then in an instant, she disappeared playfully back underwater. He submerged again and they swam for a short while, whirling around one another, and she remained just beyond his reach until she paused again and pointed toward the sand below. He swam toward the direction she indicated, and when he saw nothing there, he looked back inquisitively, and she was gone.

This time, seemingly for good.

The interaction had propelled him into a euphoric dream state. He was given over to this surreal feeling; this other-worldly aura that she had carried about her. It felt as though she had transferred, in some way, a bit of that ethereal essence to him. He was set quite adrift by it all, as well as by the waters of the sea, and he had lost all track of time.

When he came again to the surface of the water, on a course for the shore, not a further instant had passed before his environs took a decidedly severe turn. A great bell rang furiously in alarm from the outpost tower, and he could see his retinue of soldiers assembled in defensive posture. Before he could fully emerge from the waters, he saw Aryk Frierstag taking a longsword in hand.

Aryk shouted to him, "Ethyn, stay back. We've come under the threat of outlaws!"

### 8 | Just a Matter of When

*"We encounter such an accumulation of negative noise out there in the world, it's overwhelming. I've recognized, however, that this oppressive noise is completely immaterial to my actual meaningful life— that is, the parts of my life I truly care about. Navigating past the immaterial and focusing only on the meaningful involves strict dedication to a method of deep conditioning—i.e. mechanization of my human tendencies while in contact with the immaterial world; or 'humechanization'. Through this method, I'll troubleshoot immaterial problems by the most logical and efficient methods available. And I will not analyze them through an emotional lens, nor will I ever look back upon them in the future."*
  —excerpt from the personal journal of Steven Spurlock

|The Station

The efforts of Spurlock's advanced operation had proven a massive drain, and he was a wreck for it. He sat in his solar again now, his upper body stripped free of his suit; a victim of sleep deprivation and acute anxiety, conditions that were not (in the least) unrelated. His nervous system felt like a string of electric lights thrown into a tub of water, shocked and shorted out, and his chest ached with a numbness he'd never quite felt before, in all his life.

It was déjà vu; reluctantly animating his own aching body up from the floor to have-on with the inane charade he was living. He put away his suit and helmet—and the pulse beam firearm—in the wardrobe. While the panel slid shut, his attention then shifted to a corner of the solar where a peculiar object sat, which he hadn't noticed before. It was shaped like an obelisk with a pyramidal apex at the top, its corners rounded and smooth. Casting a sideways look, he approached it. Standing nearly to his knees, its surface wore a matte white finish, and the following characters were printed in black along one of its sides:

FHC.5

Though it seemed like a portable module of some kind, it lacked an opening where one might stash objects or discard waste, so he leaned over for a closer look. When he touched its surface, the thing powered up and suspended itself in the air, hovering a bit above the floor. Then the apex of the obelisk rose (detached) slightly from the rest of its form, and a blue light from its forward surface flickered on.

"Fabricated Human Companion; version five," it said. Its voice was grainy and child-like, "I am pleased to meet your acquaintance.

"Fabricated what-now?" Spurlock looked at the module, bewildered, "what are you, again?"

"I am the Fabricated Human Companion; version five."

"Right…" he studied the shape of the thing with interest, "do you have a name?"

"My codex suggests previous models have been known to carry the name *Giza*, however, the reason for this is unknown. Therefore, you may assign to me any name that you wish."

"Giza?" *Kind of a cute little thing.* "Interesting name, but I have no idea where it came from, either. I guess we share that in common, huh?"

The module made a blipping sound.

"Giza it is, then," Spurlock *almost* grinned despite himself.

"Confirmed. I am called Giza," the blue light from the apex softened, "I am at your service. What do you need?"

Spurlock had to smile in-full, then, for the sheer absurdity of it all; for speaking to a strange object such as this. *What I need is a one-way ticket out of this place, back home… wherever home is… a few headache pills, a warm shower, and a swift download of my memory, please. And then a signed and certified guarantee I won't ever be bothered again. How about it?* He wanted to voice all his demands aloud, but found he lacked the energy at the moment, even for sarcasm directed toward a robot.

"Hmm," he grumbled instead, looking around the room. He certainly didn't want to suggest he didn't need anything. *What a stupid question. I need everything!* "What's behind this?" he asked, finally pointing toward the door he'd noticed before, which was sealed shut.

"Let us find out, shall we?" replied Giza.

A small button by the door suddenly became illuminated. Figuring he had little enough to lose by playing along, he chose to push it. Powerful hydraulics slid the door aside in a blink, and a flood of bright light poured in. Spurlock motioned to take an inquisitive look outside before halting himself, "Why don't you come along with me for a while; can you do that?"

Giza's lower form made a quarter turn, but the apex remained still, with its blue luminescence pointing in Spurlock's direction: "Yes, I can do that."

"Good." They remained stagnant for a moment, tentative, "Well, what are you waiting for? Go ahead…"

The unit followed its cue and hovered along outside. Spurlock followed, advancing through the doorway to exit the solar. It took a moment for his eyes to adjust to the light, but when they did, he was taken aback by the sheer extent of the place.

*And she's had me holed up in that little box all this time?!*

Spurlock's tract of territory on the enormous Station was covered in many areas by organic vegetation. There were bushes, and even trees; many, many trees in some areas, in fact. But the metal-bound portions of the surface, which were absent such vegetation, seemed strangely hollow by the sound of his steps when he walked freely along them. He wondered how anything could possibly grow atop a construction of such solid material.

If the Station were a sail ship, his tract would be located in the forward prow, where the very tip of the bow cut through the fabric of space. It meant the entirety of the Station's deck (and all its mysteriousness) sprawled behind, stretching to the far-off limits of the stern. He made his way to a bluff that overlooked that view. The paneled floor plunged downward at a severe angle to adjoin with the rest of the deck below. There was a scattering of trees here that made for a sort of natural barrier, capable perhaps of lessening the likelihood someone might walk themselves (unawares) clear over the bluff and fall the considerable distance below.

Because his tract was elevated so high, the view was positively remarkable. He saw organic growth thriving across the territories of the massive deck as it did over parts of his own tract, but with greater variety, and in far greater expanses. Some areas hosted bodies of water. But beyond the green, oxygen-producing stretches of this mid-deck region, there stood a horizon of man-made construction—a kind of cityscape—at the stern. It was a territory of the Station he could but only vaguely see, and about which (like all other things here) he knew nothing at all. Only that a buzz of activity seemed to emanate from there. The rest, he could only presume.

Rising from the stern above any other height of the deck, in full, was a vaulted structure that seemed to act as a command bridge. It loomed over everything from the farthest point of visual perception; so far away, that it was ever-obfuscated by the haze hanging, perpetually, below the ocular dome above. The dome, cast blue in the day and gray at night, enclosed it all; the entirety of the Station—the deck and everything upon it. Including the life-sustaining atmosphere, of which he suspected the haze was an integral part.

*And here, somewhere under this dome, must be my Operator's dwelling. How can I find her? Confront her? Demand answers of her?*

He could have felt no greater desire.

\*\*\*

When Giza arrived at the bluff's edge, the hovering module emitted a machine-like warble sound. It almost seemed as if the unit was as much in awe of the view as was Spurlock.

"You've never seen the Station before, Giza?"

"I have not," the module made a quarter turn, hovering. "I have only just now been powered on. Not much unlike you."

"Powered on?" Spurlock looked at the unit with confusion, "Are you trying to say I'm some kind of robot, Giza?"

"Negative. You are human, and I have been furnished as your companion. I only allude to your recent embarkation upon this mission, which must feel somewhat empowering."

"Are you kidding? I feel the opposite of empowered."

"Discouraged? Weakened? These are the possible antonyms I have found for empowered. Is this what you mean?"

"Among others, I guess. I don't know how anyone could feel *empowered* after losing their identity," he frowned at the unit. "Is this why you've been assigned as my companion, to rub my own misery in my face?"

"To the contrary. It is proven that deprivation of thoughtful discourse over prolonged periods can exacerbate psychological dysfunction in humans. My purpose is to help you avoid such ailments."

"Okay," Spurlock rubbed his forehead, "but I have the Operator, too, don't I?"

"Yes. According to my systems codex, however, Operators are not commissioned as companions. They are administrators. Therefore, she is likely not a very skilled or helpful listener."

"Well, true, come to think of it, she shut down every attempt at conversation I made while I was down there on that planet's surface, trying not to die," Spurlock gazed across the deck to the cityscape, wondering again upon the prospects of venturing there, finding this *Operator* of his, and forcing her to tell him what he wanted to know. But again, his good sense (or perhaps, general fatigue) overcame him, and he turned to face Giza once more. "Thoughtful discourse, huh… So, are you saying you're able to think for yourself? Form opinions of your own? Somehow, I doubt you can."

"If it helps, you may consider it only a manner of speech. I have been programmed with sophisticated algorithms capable of developing responses that are highly intuitive to human thought patterns and concerns. I consider this a form of thinking. I won't take offense if you do not."

"I'm glad you won't take offense," he scoffed, then considered the notion for a moment, "What do your fancy programs say I'm thinking now?"

"Given your current status, newly arrived upon the Station, deficient in both situational awareness and memory core functionality, I would think… Or, rather, my programing would suggest your thoughts are governed largely by a great desire for information."

"You're good, Giza," Spurlock laughed. It was exactly what he was thinking, but instead of confirming this, he lied, "but I was actually thinking about food. Please tell me they make sandwiches on this Station. Greasy steak sandwiches with cheese, or roast-pork and slaw?"

For once, the module hovered silently, processing.

"You know nothing of hunger, I guess?" said Spurlock.

"No. I know nothing of what you call *hunger*. Though I am curious to acquire a better understanding of how it functions."

"Okay, forget about all that," Spurlock paused for a moment and shot forth a sardonic look, "You were right in the first place. I'm desperate for information. What do you know about *me*, specifically?"

"You are subject: Spurlock."

"Yeah, the Operator mentioned that name, too. You make it sound like I'm being studied."

"I know nothing of the nature of your mission, and can neither confirm nor deny the validity of such conjecture."

"Okay, then what else do you know about me?" *I'm failing to see the use in this stupid thing.*

"Very little, I am afraid," Giza's light blinked again, "only your given occupation, which lists the title of: Intelligence Analyst. Does this title mean anything to you?"

"Nothing," said Spurlock, "How exactly is someone supposed to analyze intelligence?"

"The term intelligence, as defined by my systems codex, refers to a person's innate aptitude for acquiring and applying knowledge and skills. Perhaps you are tasked with analyzing this concept; this aptitude for the acquisition of knowledge latent within sentient beings such as yourself."

"You're worsening my headache, Giza. I seem barely qualified to change my clothes here, much less undertake some mission to analyze… anything. They have the wrong guy if that's what I'm supposed to be doing." Spurlock turned away, "What about my personal life; do you have any details about that?"

"As is the case with your mission, I have not been programmed with any additional details regarding your personal identity."

"Then what are we supposed to talk about?" Spurlock's eyes turned intense, turning back. "Any recent gripes with your wife you'd like to share, Giza? Gone on any wildly successful fishing trips lately? What happened to those promises of *thoughtful discourse* you gave a minute ago?"

"Would you like to discuss matters of philosophy, for instance?"

"Philosophy?" Spurlock scowled at the module, staring at it straight-on now, "You can't be serious. What does a robot know about philosophy?"

"You might be surprised to find out," replied Giza.

The module's sentence was punctuated by sounds resonating across the tract from his solar, and Spurlock turned in discernment for a moment.

"Do you hear that?" he asked.

"Indeed," answered the unit, "it is likely your Operator."

Spurlock blinked twice in recognition before racing back to find out what was the matter; making clink-clanking noises over the hollow floor panels along his way.

\*\*\*

—Equipment infraction—

Spurlock re-entered the solar just in time to hear the Operator's chastisement.

—Please retrieve your equipment from the floor and secure it properly—

The vial containing his microscopic transponders sat at his feet. *Must've fallen out of my suit when I got changed.* He retrieved it and held it up to the glowing light from the solar's ceiling to stare at the five remaining listening devices within. The sight of them made him feel as if a virus were slowly infecting his soul and twisting itself around his vital organs to enhance the suffering. He wondered how he was going to muster enough courage to perform more of the same operation he'd administered upon this Solis Family. It was inevitable that he'd be called upon to do so; just a matter of when. *Somehow, I'm guessing the Operator's way too precise to give me ten of these things, if all I needed were four—plus the one I stupidly dropped in that kid's bedroom down there.*

He'd almost forgotten about that particular folly.

—You *must* develop discipline, Mr. Spurlock, or you will not survive much longer in this mission of yours—

Her voice came from the panels of the solar like a hammer, striking him (it seemed) from multiple, random directions.

"Lemme ask you a very simple question," Spurlock stood up and placed the vial on a shelf in his wardrobe, "If it's a robot you want for this mission, why not just send this little pack'n'stack here to monitor these people?" He gestured with arrogance toward Giza, who had just returned through the doorway, hovering.

—Such questions will not be entertained—

"I doubt he'd puke all over the floor, at least." Spurlock noted. "Think they've smelled it yet? The vomit? What're they gonna think… will they blame the kid for it? Should I feel bad?"

—Focus on your mission directives or you *will* feel bad, and worse, but for entirely different reasons; I promise—

"So I can't exhibit human reactions to any of this stuff? You're telling me that, if I *feel* anything down there, I'm a goner… That I'm to become a virtual robot in order to survive?"

—I am helping you see what you must see, and this is how you must do it—

She failed to elaborate any further.

The holoscreens above his desktop were displaying running transcripts, now, extracted immediately from his six sources; each person within whom he'd implanted a listening device: Tae, Ethyn, Mailyn, and Perwyn were their proper forenames, as he had understood; Solis their surnames. Plus, of course, the two in the mountains—the exile and his pilot. While he surveyed the screens, the Operator's voice returned from the solar's panels; a softer tone this time.

—You will monitor their behavior for anomalies; points of interest. When an anomaly is detected, you will save it and make note of it in a report, which you will furnish for me daily—

"How exactly am I supposed to distinguish between matters of importance in a world I still know next to nothing about?"

—Context. You will gather context—

As if on cue, one of the feeds then suddenly became active, so he isolated that particular dialogue and leaned forward to have a listen. A voice was playing from the eldest prince's device—Ethyn's:

> "Do you not see a line of flame making for the heavens?"
> "I wish for myself but a fraction of the keen eyesight you possess, Ethyn," responded a separate voice, as yet unidentified.

As Spurlock listened on, it seemed this source—Ethyn Solis—held suspicions over the cause of supposed *lines of flame* he'd seen in the sky on the mountainous horizon, in the southlands of Athyn. The description matched the launching Spurlock had witnessed in the rocky knoll during his first recognizance operation, and of that which he supposed the machine in the jungle's shack (and certainly the mountain's peak) were capable of producing as well. So he noted the tenuous connection as an anomaly for inclusion in the first report to his Operator. *Who knows what will come of it, or if any of these mindless details I'll gather from these feeds will amount to anything at all...*

In time, the other feeds became active, and it'd rapidly become clear these were important people—influential people in one way or another—and, accordingly, it'd also become clear why he'd been charged with their monitoring.

*Context, indeed.*

He listened and he recorded his notes, as he was told, while Giza descended to the floor to initiate a form of sleep mode. It seemed the feeds would continue playing (uninterrupted) all day long if he allowed them. Instead, and in the absence of any further input from his Operator, he tapped a button on the sense pad to quiet the audiblers once again. It was all becoming a bit overwhelming, and he'd had enough for the time-being. Plus, he'd discovered in his investigations of the screens and their many features, that the feed transcripts were recorded for the purpose of making reference to them at a later time. *I'm sure she'll scream at me the moment I neglect them too long.*

So with the console feeds muted, Spurlock stood up from his desk.

"Giza," he said, bringing the module back to life into its hovering posture.

"I am at your service," answered the unit, "what do you need?"

"About that *philosophy* you referenced earlier..." Spurlock was already walking casually back out the door, "Do you have time to talk? I need to study the way you think."

"I recall you rejected the notion of a machine's—or, as you have termed me, a *pack'n'stack's*—capacity for such things as cognitive thought."

"You heard that, huh?"

Giza emitted a melancholy warble.

"Well, it seems my stance on that issue is suddenly open for debate," Spurlock scratched his head, "I may not have a choice *but* to believe."

\*\*\*

Haley Kenmore hadn't gotten the greatest night's sleep, and she was paying for it now. So much so that she'd, for a moment, considered troubling her apartment building's convenience store clerk for a cup of coffee, a-feather with the flock of arabica addicts who were usually seen doing the same, with crazed spirals in their eyes and zombie-like movements possessing their bodies. But she resisted the unusual urge because, though it was quite early in the morning, it was also Friday, and that was all the incentive she needed to get moving. *Who needs a blast-infusion of caffeine when there's a four-thirty AM alarm blaring in your ear, the chill of a November morning to straighten your spine, and an all-merciful weekend right around the corner?*

Although the sobriety of the early hour had somewhat quelled her troubled thoughts about Steven, she expected her muse's extended lack of response over text would nag her all morning. Stepping outside, the cold air pushed a cluster of red leaves against her feet, and she pulled her scarf a bit tighter around her neck. Hope held strong she might see Steven on campus during this new day, lest she occupy her mind with troubled thoughts of him again come the afternoon.

It wasn't as if she needed additional sources of distress in her life. Hers was a nerve-wracking profession, which she'd stumbled into backwards, little over a year prior. After breezing through her graduate degree program, she'd hit the jobs scene hard in hopes of attracting interest from employers across a wide range of meaningful pursuits. Included, of course, were a select few federal government agencies. After all, when searching for work in the District, one could scarcely avoid letting an application or two find their way into the hands of the feds. At the very least, the assorted three-letter agencies strewn ubiquitously across town were useful aces stashed in almost every educated young professional's back pocket.

Her resume was finally shuffled into Homeland Security channels. Specifically, to the department's headquarters campus in the northwest corner of town, and she'd taken the offer for an entry-level position simply as a means to enter the ranks of the employed. To get her foot in the door—not knowing how quickly it would start slamming itself repeatedly against her toes.

The N4 bus was a monster of metal and tailpipe smoke, its innards typically packed tight with passengers sitting on tattered pleather seats or standing, clinging to handholds for dear life around sharp corners and traffic circles. It pulled up in a fuss, and she boarded. The large windows, which were like picture frames for the passing outside world, showed her views of Massachusetts Avenue in dim, pre-dawn shades of blue. A fluorescent light flickered off and on behind an advertisement panel for the Smithsonian Institute, with images of an upcoming Dead Sea Scroll exhibit. She seated herself, pondering the vagaries of life until the bus rumbled around Ward Circle and to a stop; the doors opening like great accordion panels, just long enough to let her shuffle herself out.

The headquarters grounds had long ago served as a college campus, but still boasted the character-laden, brick-walled and shingle-roofed architecture of its original design. It carried with it all the auspices of age and resistance to change that Haley once considered a near-perfect commentary of the federal government itself.

Stepping inside, however, showed an entirely different world—modern security features abounding. More than a year into the job, now, and she still wasn't exactly handling it all in perfect stride. For the hundredth time, she nearly card-swiped through the turnstiles while her personal cell phone remained in her bag; a violation of protocols for secured work areas. Catching herself, she pulled it out and chose a cubby from a few hundred of them, lining the lobby wall.

She took the opportunity to check her messages once more.

*Still no reply from Steven...* then locked the device up with a key.

Just inside the turnstiles, there hung the department's seal; large and softly lit by a fixture that came down from the ceiling. And mounted beside the seal were letters that read: *Office of International Affairs*.

She'd been hurried on her way to work early this morning because a delegation from Saudi Arabia was arriving to speak with her principals upon matters of mutual concern, and she was to play an important role in support of the event. Up the stairs to the second floor and around the corner, she came to the Assistant Secretary's door. The area where she'd found herself learning—on the fly, day in and day out—how to (barely) survive the pains and sufferings that assistantship of senior federal officials had in store for a young, well-intentioned soul.

"Good morning, ma'am," Haley said, with all the enlivened spirit she could muster.

The A/S, who was seated at her desk studying documents in an enormous binder, managed to lift a set of tired eyes above her reading glasses. It was an act of deference more generous than usual, but her message smacked of her typical disregard, "Please do not interrupt me, Miss Kenmore, when it is clear I'm trying to concentrate on my work. Must I continue to convey to you, again and again, my most basic preferences? It's going to be a long morning for me, and I'd rather not be hampered by nonsense, if you don't mind."

"Oh, of course, ma'am," Haley felt those pangs of workplace anxiety that had become all too familiar, "Your prep session begins at six. Ten minutes. I'll let you know when they're all ready."

"Please do," the A/S had already resumed her reading.

Haley spent the first five of those ten nervous minutes removing her coat, powering up her computer, and staging the conference room with printed materials, while members of the office's Mid-East Directorate started finding their seats.

One last check confirmed she'd covered all her bases, so she allowed herself a momentary breather back by her desk. The window beside her cubical provided a sightline across the commons to another building on campus—the one that Steven worked in; the Office of Intelligence. The view was normally obscured by a tree bearing broad leaves, but the leaves had since turned autumnal colors, shriveled, and many had fallen. She could see the entrance of his building quite clearly. Enough to discover no one was entering or exiting at that particular moment, as early as it was yet in the morning.

Not long ago in the summer, Steven had (on occasion) strolled by her window from the sidewalk down below and had looked up and whistled. She would hear his whistling—faintly, for the window could not be opened—and she would look out to see him. He did that, at times, when he wanted to see if she was free for lunch. They couldn't, after all, text one another on campus, with their phones locked up in cubbies as they were, and it was as good a method as any for coordinating their break times. Then they'd meet for lunch and talk about the weekend or other topics that might cross their minds.

*Here I am thinking of Steven and texts again... already!*

"Have they assembled?" The A/S's voice squealed with impatience. Haley had drifted off, and it was now five minutes past six.

She hastened to the A/S's door, "Yes. They've all found their seats. I'm sorry for the delay."

The scowl and grumble the A/S made while carrying herself toward the conference room caused Haley's cheeks to redden, and she followed along behind with notepad and pen in hand, and an enormous sense of discomfiture, as well.

\*\*\*

The Assistant Secretary's prep session was a typical one. Subject-matter experts reported on the topics that were likely to arise during the meeting with the Saudi delegation, and advised the proper responses the A/S ought to deliver; the diplomatic concessions the department might be willing to make; and, of course, the binding bilateral agreements she should expect to receive in return. Haley sat beside the A/S at the head of the table, taking down notations her principal deemed especially important, as signified by her frantic pointing at Haley's note pad.

This, until nearly an hour and a half had gone by, when Haley leaned in and whispered to the A/S, "The delegation is expected to arrive in fifteen."

"Then prepare yourself to escort them in five," answered the A/S, a prompt for Haley to excuse herself from the room. "You don't have to ask. Just, go!"

With hurried keystrokes, she typed up the most salient notations from the meeting, printed them, and left them on the A/S's desk. She straightened herself in her blazer and gathered her curly hair neatly behind her ears. It was a brisk walk without a coat (and a careful one in her heels) to the gatehouse, where guards operated x-ray machines and where the visitor badges were printed and issued. She'd already had badges made-up, registered, and in-hand for the Saudis, which had proven a blessing, as they'd already arrived and were causing quite a scene of confusion at the front desk when she stepped in.

"It's a pleasure to welcome you to our headquarters, Mr. Ambassador," she spoke to him through his interpreter, as she lacked even the vaguest trace of Arabic proficiency.

He responded directly, "The pleasure is all mine, Miss..."

"…Kenmore. Haley Kenmore, sir. Thank you." *I should've known an ambassador would speak English.* Indeed, it appeared the interpreter was intended for the benefit of one his fellow delegates, not the ambassador himself.

"I do not suppose you have been doing this very long, am I correct, Ms. Kenmore?" The ambassador had a way of maintaining his smile while speaking, even as he delivered a (perhaps unintentional) patronizing judgement upon his escort, "you seem awfully young for such a position."

"Only a year," Haley figured not to take offense to the comment, which was made in the spirit of small talk—a convention that seemed inherently awkward to begin with. She clearly hadn't yet gathered a firm sense of the etiquette required of these (quite official) moments of state, yet she wasn't ready to dismiss, out of hand, the possibility an ambassador might say something flippant, simply for the thrill of it. "I've found this work very interesting, so far. Especially when I'm given the opportunity to meet individuals of great distinction, like yourself."

"Indeed. Well, you are too kind, Miss Kenmore," the ambassador replied while his smile continued to remain in place, "and very easy on an old man's eyes, if you don't mind me saying."

Haley only smiled politely in response to that one.

When they had arrived at the entrance to the Secretary's suite, the A/S was waiting there, as well as the Under Secretary for Policy, and a number of policy and intelligence directors. The principals and the Saudis proceeded together into the Secretary's conference room, while Haley remained in the reception area. She found a seat, then, amongst a few junior advisors and analysts, with whom she exchanged a bit of whispered nothings while the meeting carried along.

"I hope my director can cogently spit out his talking points this time," said one of the policy advisors, a young male, perhaps as a means to impress Haley. "They should just let *me* do it. After all, I'm the one who wrote them. I'm the one who knows all this stuff."

"Man, I can't tell you how much message traffic I've read through for this one," an intel guy whispered. She thought he was someone Steven had mentioned before. One of his co-workers for whom he held little admiration, if she recalled correctly. *Glenn, was it I think?* "They're dumping a ton of resources into this threat stream. More than usual, at least," Glenn continued. Haley thought the analyst might be trying to impress himself as much as anyone else. She wished silently it'd been Steven who'd come along with the intelligence brass, instead.

Eventually, she felt pressure to pitch-in with banter of her own.

"The Ambassador said I looked too young to work here," she blushed so deeply she could almost feel the freckles on her face tingle, "think I should have been offended?" But the others just stared blankly ahead.

*Probably too wrapped up in their own self-absorbed worlds to care about mine. And that's probably just as well.*

At the conclusion of the negotiations, all principals exited the conference room, including the venerated Secretary of the Department, himself—a sighting that still carried a level of mystique for Haley, even despite the relative frequency of its occurrence, given her routine visitation of the cabinet official's suite. The expressions on the faces of her principals held a sense of satisfaction with the outcome, and yet (at the same time) a cautionary tinge of earnestness that suited the matters at hand. They made their respectful goodbyes with one another—the ambassador shaking hands and smiling effusively. Haley was acquitted of her remaining escort duties when a member of the Secretary's front office staff offered to show the Saudis back to the front gate, and so she was free to accompany her principals and their advisors for a well-earned break from the fray.

It was still early. Frost-capped dew still covered much of the ground on campus while they walked. In the cafeteria, over morning beverages, they found a corner table suitable for gathering around and discussed the outcome of the diplomatic assembly; the principals easing themselves down into their seats as if they'd just run double marathons.

"I'm surprised they agreed to all the levels of access we requested," said the A/S, who appeared satisfied, while taking a sip of her creamy (no-doubt caffeinated) drink. The steam rose from the top of the cup in bending tendrils.

"Not so surprising when you consider what they'll probably ask from us in return," said a senior director, "later on, of course, when favors are needed most."

"Whatever they ask for," opined the A/S, "and whenever they ask it of us, it'll be worth it if they can help us dig deeper into this mess we've caught on to. I'd rather pay a price later in diplomatic favors than pay one now in innocent lives."

Haley was barely listening; not for lack of interest, but for other reasons altogether. She turned her head and looked out the window again at Steven's building, this time from a closer vantage point than from her office window. She thought he may just happen to walk by at that very moment so she could at least verify he was well. Not lying in some ditch somewhere, completely unable to check his phone for important (or not-so-important, as it were) messages from his girlfriend.

But while she saw some of his fellow analysts reporting for work, she didn't see him.

On the way back into the lobby of their own building, she excused herself from her principals for a moment so that she might retrieve her phone for a personal call. The request earned her a slight scowl from the A/S, but the woman quickly plodded-on amidst her flock of senior advisors, which flew too high in the air to concern themselves with an assistant's trifling needs.

The cubby came open with the small key, and Haley dialed the number she was looking for from her contact list.

"Hello," said a hurried female voice after a number of rings.

"Nora, hi, it's Haley," she held her inflection quite steady despite a subtle fluttering of her nerves, "Steven's girlfriend."

"Haley," replied Nora, "it's good to hear from you, how are you? And before you respond, I'll apologize in advance for whatever pains my brother has caused lately. That's just him, I'm sure you've discovered. Quite committed, but a bit spacey at times, I'm afraid."

"I'm well, thanks for asking, and no need for an apology," Haley furrowed her brow. "I'm the one who's sorry… to be bothering you so early in the morning like this."

"Are you kidding? This is like mid-day for me," a slight laugh from Nora set Haley at ease. It sounded like she was walking somewhere while talking, breathing a bit heavily, "I wish someone had told me a doctorate degree required so much early-morning fuss, right?"

"Hey, so, I know you're busy, but the reason I called is—" Haley managed a final glance in the direction of Steven's building, still catching no sight of him, "I'm wondering if you'd be interested in grabbing lunch with me tomorrow."

"Oh," it would be their first one-on-one event together, but Nora didn't seem phased at all by the sudden invitation, "sure, that'd be nice. Noon on Georgetown campus sound good for you—meet me outside the library?"

"Great, sure," replied Haley, "I'll see you then."

Haley knew it might have been a small step out of bounds, cold-calling her boyfriend's sister like that, but he'd suggested on more than one occasion she ought to reach out to Nora so they might get to know each other better.

While they said their goodbyes, Haley locked her phone back up in its cubby, and she was beginning to consider it a fine idea, indeed.

## 9 | A Glimpse of the Beyond

*"If hearing voices in your head is a sign of mental instability, then count me among the unstable. Though I must clarify, I don't quite hear voices in the literal sense. They're messages, rather, that I'm subconsciously aware of; typically sentiments of a cautionary nature. And when I find it particularly difficult to shut them up, I know it might finally be time to provide them a proper opportunity to be heard."*
—excerpt from the personal journal of Steven Spurlock

|Planet Deaer, The Southspur Mountains

The buzzcraft's flexor wings fluttered and hummed with a power that exceeded any level Haiyen Sün had ever dared to push them. Mountain crests and spires sped past on either side, and snowflakes assaulted the cab while she leaned into her turns, zipping through the chasms and defiles. This was soon after she'd left Koryn Naylor's cottage of exile, her heart pounding and her mind so full of despair and regret (and hurt) from what had happened there. *Koryn...* She'd exclaimed to herself, recounting with bitter sadness the episode he'd put her through, and the multitude of emotional hazards he'd dragged her heart across, only to flash freeze and shatter it to pieces with his very immature nature, which was just so painfully and persistently deviant.

"KORYN!" She shouted aloud to the detriment of her vocal chords taking the craft through a craggy gorge, diving and swooping, blowing rubble and snow asunder in her wake. *His nerve is truly remarkable. As if some flame-ridden capsule launching into the sky was going to reverse my feelings... At least his environment matches his demeanor; ice-cold, dense, and hopelessly numb.*

If, at one time, she thought two years of solitary confinement might restore in him a fresh slate of good sense and reason, she knew now she'd been wrong. Such optimism may have always been a product of wishful thinking. She wanted desperately to believe he possessed the means to correct his ways, because, as it stood, *her* assessment of his progress was what mattered most.

It was nearly one year ago, exactly, when Fynian Arynel, the Sage of Judgment—standing tall and thin in his flowing robes—had presented to her a most troublesome quandary.

"My dear Haiyen," he'd said to her in the gardens of the Settlement, "you have ascended quickly the ranks of Prima, and I think it is time we confer upon you a responsibility befitting the great promise you've shown. This, with respect to the exile we've stationed on the mountain's peak. You alone shall determine this exile's fate; his term in banishment."

"I do not understand, Sage," she had answered.

"That is because you do not listen. Or because you listen, but do not truly wish to hear that which is being said."

"I heard well enough, Sage, yet I fear my ears betray me in this. Had you given me jurisdiction over Koryn Naylor's exile?"

"Indeed. It is for you to determine when he is ready to rejoin the Settlement. Though I hope your personal connection to him will not obscure your efforts in reaching a just adjudication." Then, with a suddenness that left her speechless and in a state of utter disbelief, the Sage had left her alone in the gardens to ponder the new charge.

And so it had come to pass that such a heavy burden was conferred upon her; that *she alone* would decide Koryn Naylor's fate. Her immediate inclination, of course, was to take this new-found authority and affect Koryn's release from exile without a moment's delay; to tell the Sages he was already reformed and ought to be returned to the Settlement at once. If she'd acted quickly, she could've flown to him and brought him back in her buzzcraft that very day, back to the shelter and warmth of the Settlement, which he so desperately needed. This, all before the sun went down.

But it hadn't taken long for her better reasoning to set in, and she'd realized the purpose of the Sage's assignment; that by placing Koryn's fate in her hands, they were likely testing her just as much as they were testing him. And they knew that in some complicated way, even with all of the emotional considerations attached to her relationship with Koryn (or perhaps *because* of them) she'd be the most capable of all to assess any progress he might make toward rehabilitation. So she resisted those immediate urges to bring him back and did her very best to pack them away, deep within, so that she might arrive upon a true and unbiased decision at some future time.

The Sages all commended her for her restraint, holding that her independent arrival upon these realizations was proof of her strong character. And despite how terribly difficult it had been for her, she had waited until the next scheduled delivery of provisions before visiting him again, up there in that snow-covered cottage. Yet it hadn't taken long before this burden truly began crushing her beneath its weight. *Crushing, crushing... crushing.* For she'd quickly realized, seeing him for the first time through the lens of judge and jury, that he'd (on the contrary) *not* yet been rehabilitated enough to return to the Settlement. That he hadn't earned it yet; hadn't yet learned the error of his ways. Not nearly, even. Instead, she'd found he all but lacked a single repentant bone in his body. And so, she'd delivered his supplies and had returned with a heavy heart back to the Settlement without him.

Soon thereafter, the consequences of this arrangement grew particularly difficult for Haiyen in new ways. Across the span of the year that followed, her life had grown increasingly miserable while she obsessed over Koryn's awful plight. All she needed to do was declare to the Sages his fitness for return. But she saw no growth in him that would allow her to make it so. Instead, he wallowed and suffered, and it was difficult for her to witness his regression. Over time, she realized the dream of sweeping him away from that place and bringing him back with her (fully rehabilitated) had become a mirage, dissipated nearly in-full by his unruly behavior. What remained was a heart-breaking scenario she was forced to relive every thirty turns of the moon when she brought to him his provisions.

Principal of all was the hurt caused by his dismissive posture toward her, which became more and more explicit over time. He had stopped asking about her life—her feelings, her needs—long ago. He'd ceased to exhibit any care for the effects his exile was having on her; lacked any hint of regret for having introduced such pain in her life, such humiliation. What's more, he showed no remorse for breaking the rules of the Settlement or a sincere desire to mend what he had broken.

He only seemed interested in one thing anymore: the purely physical aspects of her visits. Granted, she never regretted their passionate forays, in a heap rolling together on the floor of the cabin. Not even this last exchange they'd shared together. Because, after all, she longed for that kind of intimate contact as much as he did. But that was done with now. He had proven incapable of change, at least in the ways that mattered most. And when she fled from him in her buzzcraft this time, she'd finally decided—definitively, then and there—that she'd paid her very last visit to the cottage on the peak.

Enough had been enough.

But she knew not what it would mean for him; whether his exile would be continued indefinitely, or whether she'd ever look upon his face or hear his voice again. Yet it couldn't be saved, or changed. That much she knew now.

Those final thoughts were almost more than she could stand to wrestle with, so she gripped the throttle tight and urged the buzzcraft through the air even faster now, setting an arc across the mountain-scape. It rippling through space and sound barriers with the suction of her pilot's goggles pressing hard against her face and the cab bobbing and shaking in the turbulence. She weaved through valleys and jetted between outcroppings. And in those moments, she could almost hear Koryn's voice goading her on with such insistence:

*You're telling me you've never risked a glimpse of the Beyond??*

She was taking a turn around the broad side of one of the greatest of the Southspur Mountains when the final line of massifs separating her world from the flatlands came into view, like a menacing row of teeth, filed and sharpened to their peaks and immersed in strands of wispy clouds. The jagged line of crags marked the ultimate barrier over which the Sages had decreed pilots mustn't ever stray. And she'd been sincere when she told Koryn that a serious inkling to venture beyond them had never even crossed her mind. But it was crossing her mind now, and it made her ever so terribly uncomfortable.

*Never risked a glimpse?* His voice echoed again. *Not even once??*

Guided by a frightening impulse, Haiyen suddenly thrust her craft forward, not alongside that ridgeline of peaks (as usual) but toward it this time, instead. And the clouds started to come at her like all-consuming blankets of whiteness across the sky—across her field of vision—in no time at all swallowing her cab and blurring her view. But she pressed ahead with an ill-begotten assuredness, within a range she'd never before dared to fly. The air passed along the craft's body, nudging it and forcing it left and right, making the sound of an awful and fierce, turbulent wind.

The hatch in the rear began to rattle, and her grip on the throttle began to totter and slip. Yet she set her jaw tightly, determined. Her thoughts came to her then, like flashes of lightning, wrapped in a sense of momentary madness.

*Maybe I* do *want to see the flatlands! Maybe I* do *want to see the great Beyond!!*

Then the clouds parted for a wink's time and the sheer rock face of a mountain appeared right before her craft. Her eyes opened like saucers at the sight.

"Koryn!" she screamed, squeezing the throttle for her life. *"KORYN!!!"*

\*\*\*

Haiyen, a fair child of the Settlement in the Southspur Mountains and aspiring Second Rank of Prima, held tight to the throttle of her buzzcraft with one hand and clenched desperately at the blue stone hanging around her neck with the other, screaming with a visceral strain in her throat upon the sight of the mountain that had just appeared through the clouds in front of her. The craft careened and skewed itself at an angle so sharp that the transfer of centrifugal force nearly collapsed her lungs, and she felt the left tailfin rudder scrape across an outcropping of rock. But with the severe vector adjustment achieved, and in the split moment's time there was for her to react, she blasted into the thrusters all the energy she had left in reserve. The craft swayed and tilted in full propulsion away from the on-coming mountain, careening a whisker's width from the bulk of the great rock, and away.

Her heart pounded in her chest like a deep-barreled drum, and all she could do was focus her mind on bringing the buzzcraft steadily back into charted territory. Her speed dropped and her grip (with both hands now on the throttle) relaxed slowly, gradually, and calmly as her breathing returned to normal, and the beads of sweat began to dissipate from her forehead. Though shaken and distressed, she was back on her standard course for her return to the Settlement in due time, leaving the cloudy, craggy massif (and the mysterious Beyond, too) well behind.

*Koryn...* she thought again, scolding herself for her foolishness. *He just needles his way into my mind like a virus and spreads like an infection. He controls me, even from his place of captivity; even as I fly far away from him. How can I allow myself to succumb to such recklessness?!*

Haiyen had regained her composure quickly thereafter, and by the time she descended below the snow line and made her approach to the Settlement, she was in full possession of her reflexes and wits. A good thing, because a pilot, making for such a landing, had the aid of only a few discernable landmarks to make proper identification of the valley she called home. The Settlement was hidden neatly by the trees and boulders that characterized the landscape in this mountainous valley, and would assure any stranger that no such Settlement existed there to be seen at all, or visited, or paid any mind to whatsoever. *Unless, of course, they knew exactly what they were looking for...*

She slowly took the buzzcraft through the obstacles of extreme terrain. Inside the valley, she could see the sparkling waterfalls that spilled over the mountainous ridges all around it. Simple structures scattered about comprised the Settlement; the homes and the places meant for gatherings, and the gardens, too. She saw it all, now. The hangar stood along the outskirts, with its roof opened wide. She brought the craft within its confines and touched down gently for a perfect landing. The vibrations of the flexor wings slowed to a stop and then folded themselves together, tucking themselves in, and she stepped out from the cab, grateful for having arrived home; safely.

The perimeter of the open hangar was lined with mechanical work stations and equipment that Prima pilots needed for tending to their crafts. She tossed her coat over a bench and picked up a hammer while making for the rear of the buzzcraft to inspect for damage. But when she passed around the far side to have a look at the tailfin that had scraped against the rock of the mountainside, she noticed Bartyl Gleon standing in the next bay, polishing his craft. Gleon's craft was slightly larger than hers with an extra thruster and a sleek, more angular design. His presence was a nuisance. *Just what I need, someone to explain a dinged up tailfin to...*

"How'd it go?" Their eyes met through a mutual exchange of sideways glances. Gleon was a strapping sort, she had to admit, with a pleasant smile and a diligent work ethic that merited a certain level of admiration. And he was respectful to her; never one to join-in with the other Prima pilots, who often made conspicuous note of Haiyen's distinction as the only female among their ranks. But she'd always been a lone wolf of sorts; had always employed a strict practice of keeping to herself when amongst her Prima brethren, and (consequently) had never made more than a casual acquaintance of any one of them. Gleon included.

"Just fine," she replied, before promptly hammering at a dent in the damaged tailfin, attempting to return it to its true form. The sound of the hammering reverberated through the hangar with an unpleasant intensity—*banging-clanging-banging*—but soon she could tell she was getting nowhere with the repair, and she lowered the hammer in frustration.

"I won't venture to ask the cause of your tailfin's unfortunate plight…" Gleon remarked, yet not in a disparaging manner, for it seemed he was poised to continue, perhaps in offering his help. But she cut him short before he could finish.

"…Good idea. It's likely best that you do not." She took up the hammer and wailed on the fin again, in part to discourage any further conversation, until moments later when she sensed his presence, approaching with something in his hand.

When she again stopped her banging, he said, "Here, take this… please," and he offered her a small pouch with its strings loosened. She could see a stock of rare powder inside, which gave her slight pause, allowing him to continue, "I've found it the very best for reconstruction work like this. I've even heard this is the powder that helped the Engineers build the very first crafts, way back when... Can you imagine? But it's quite powerful, so be mindful, is all."

"There's a shortage," she said in refusal of his gift of the powder, pushing his hand away, "we're discouraged from sharing our allotments."

"I know," he said, but then raised the pouch closer to her, "but I insist. I'd like to help you. I deem it a very small price to pay, actually, in exchange for a few words of true conversation with you, if you wouldn't mind. In all honesty, I've sought your ear for some time now. Beyond the mere casual greetings we've shared, that is."

She looked up at him with a forced smile, then slowly (reluctantly) accepted the pouch from his extended hand, "Thank you." The powder felt the same in texture and granularity as did her usual reserve, but instead of a light citrine color, it was a deep blue; similar in hue to the stone she wore on the chain around her neck. She very carefully pinched a small portion between her fingertips and rubbed it along the affected area of the tailfin, placing her open hand flat against its surface, working the powder in circles until it became warm to the touch. Then, almost like wet malleable clay, she was able to reform the fin perfectly to her liking. And upon her release, it solidified like new in an instant.

"I doubt the Engineers could have done a better job themselves," said Gleon.

She tightened the strings on the pouch and handed it back to him.

"This was kind of you," she admitted. And now, she supposed, she would have to repay him with a bit of conversation, as he'd requested. She hated the very idea of such a thing; that he might attempt to pry into topics she wished desperately to avoid. Certainly, her relationship with the outcast of their society—the exile, Koryn Naylor—was a curiosity held not only by her fellow Prima Rank members, but by most everyone else across the Settlement, as well. It attached a stigma to her she could not escape. And yet she would not address the matter with anyone.

*Let them think what they will,* she often said silently to herself. It had become a mantra of sorts for her over the last couple of years.

Still, she had a favor to ask of Gleon, and there would be no way around referencing Koryn, no matter how she tried to phrase it. All in all, she supposed, this exchange had played into her hands better than she could have ever hoped it would. So she took a deep breath and started having out with it.

"I realize this may seem ill-timed… since you've just offered me a favor, which I have accepted. But I find that I must ask another of you."

Asking for favors was, indeed, well out of character for her, and she could tell her forthrightness was catching Gleon a bit off guard. But she pressed on. "Yet you've requested we engage in conversation, the subject of which, I presume, may be any of my choosing… And, you see, there is one particular matter with which I require a great deal of assistance. A matter that has weighed heavily on my mind, and I find myself in critical need. Do I presume too much in asking?"

"You speak in riddles," Gleon said as a smile crept upon his face, "but no, you do not presume too much. Please continue."

"You should know that this favor is of a most personal nature," she took a few paces around the hind side of her buzzcraft, marking her need to broaden the space between herself and Gleon for the defense mechanism that it was, but also to signal to him this was (for her) a very serious matter. "Although I'm aware we are no more than mere acquaintances, our discourse has always maintained a modicum of respect, which I have always appreciated. This is much more than I can say for our fellow Prima Rank members, within whom I am, in fact, reluctant to place any reliance or esteem at all. And so, if I may trust anyone in this, it would have to be you."

"I'm quite honored, I assure you, but if this matter is so personal, why not trust a family member with it?"

"Simply because it demands the kind of flight services only an active Prima pilot can provide," she coyly feigned an inspection of the body of her craft for additional bumps or scratches, finding none, then looked back at him, into his eyes, "I need someone to take a most painful responsibility off my hands. I need to relinquish my duties of provisioning the exile's cottage."

Gleon rubbed his chin for a moment, turning the request over in his mind. It was clear she was making herself vulnerable, and she figured he was calculating the limits of a proper response; one that wouldn't offend her, nor delve too deeply into the sensitive topics of relationships, feelings, and heartbreak (and things of that nature).

"I see..." he said, finally, "I can only imagine this must be a very difficult thing for you... For *anyone* to have to deal with, that is." He looked for a moment as if he had made up his mind, "But if I may be of assistance, it would please me to help release you from this burden. If the Sages approve, I will assume your responsibility for you. Besides, you ought to be free to devote your energies to more productive Prima pursuits. You've become a most talented pilot, Haiyen."

"Dinged tailfins and all... It's nice to hear someone say words like those, though. *He* hasn't taken notice of such things, nor bothered to ask," she said, then elaborated, "*Koryn* hasn't taken notice, that is. Notice of anything... for a long time."

"Well," said Gleon, and she saw in his eyes a look that seemed to tell of genuine warmth and caring, "I've certainly taken notice."

She exhaled and her shoulders seemed to relax from a tensed position they'd held for too long. Then she wondered if Gleon was merely being friendly, or if his forward complements were laced with flirtatious (even romantic) intentions. She feared she might be the most imperceptive woman in the world if she allowed herself to believe his actions, in no way, alluded to a certain level of interest in her. But she found that his manner in discourse, respectful as it was, did not offend her or cause her discomfort in the least.

Most of all, she was relieved he'd agreed to her request, no matter what his intentions might have been, "My thanks to you, Gleon. I will bring word as soon as I receive permissions from the Sages." She turned away from him to make final assurances her craft was secure and then gathered up her coat on her way out of the hangar.

"Until then, Haiyen," Gleon called after her.

She looked back and cast him an appreciative smile before taking her leave, and thought privately: *You have my thanks, Gleon, but you may soon discover, the last thing I need right now is another catastrophic romance.*

### 10 | Twisted Forms of Savagery

*"I've thought upon my dreams, at times; as if they could somehow reveal to me some hidden schematic of my inner subconscious, impossible to access while awake. I've found that the only dreams—of which I remember more than a mere fleeting notion—are commonly my most unsettling of nightmares. What does it say about me, then, that my subconscious seems only to reach out to me through dreams when there is something bad to say? If only I could find a way to reverse that tendency, I might find myself upon the cusp of deciphering the great secrets of happiness itself."*
—excerpt from the personal journal of Steven Spurlock

|Planet Deaer, Athyn

Prince Ethyn Solis emerged barefooted from the waters of the lagoon, north of the Canterford Vale, where his company had stopped to rest their mounts. A band of men had formed a line, marking a perimeter of the clearing, effectively cutting access from the outpost back to the Ribbon Road. They stood equipped with weapons at the ready; swords and staffs and spears. *Yet, what is this unusual quality to their appearance?* To Ethyn's eye, they portrayed an eerie weightlessness; as if fragments of light reflected off particles floating in the air to depict their lifelike forms. Smoky constructs resembled physical features that moved like true-to-life persons, but yet Ethyn was not convinced. *What I'm seeing cannot truly be persons of flesh and bone.* It was like nothing he'd ever encountered before. The soldiers in Ethyn's retinue stood in aggressive posture to meet the threat, as they'd been trained, but they seemed not to notice anything peculiar about their assailants.

Defying Legionnaire Aryk Frierstag's warning to take cover, Ethyn stepped forward, dripping wet from his swim in the lagoon.

"Who dares to contest a retinue of the Athynian Royal Legion on our own soil? I won't hear of it." Othys Frierstag had retrieved Ethyn's longsword for him from the gear on his mount and tossed it to the prince, who promptly unsheathed it and advanced toward the line of outlaws. He eyed their weapons, which also appeared to him (like their bearers) as strange immaterial constructs, and he wondered as to their effectiveness against iron and steel.

None among the threatening band had responded to his inquiry.

"Have you the capability to understand spoken word?" continued Ethyn. Aryk and several soldiers of the retinue stepped up to either side of the prince to join in his advance, "Or are you all as perfectly idiotic as you look?"

Again, none of them spoke. They simply mimicked his actions in drawing their weapons.

An archer from Ethyn's retinue nocked an arrow. All could hear the bowstring creak taut while a pervasive song of the cicada bug rose from the trees of the adjacent vale. Ethyn authorized the action with a nod of his head. Loosed, the arrow sang through the air, whistling in a tight spiral, and pierced through the chest of a challenger, who stood with his hand grasping the hilt of his sword. Ethyn saw the shaft pass clear through, shooting particle tendrils along its same trajectory, yet the man continued to stand firm, seemingly unfazed.

At once, an attacker burst forth from the line, fast and wild, and met a legion soldier sword to sword. As did the second and third attackers who charged. Then five came at once and slammed straight-forwardly into a line of legionnaires, whose longswords parried the blows of staffs and spears. The outlaws' weapons held strong against parrying and offensive strikes, alike, and they continued to push ahead, testing the limits of the retinue's resolve.

Othys Frierstag, in one fluid motion, disarmed an outlaw of his pike and smashed the side of the man's helmet with a one-handed hammer, which he'd favored for close-range combat. A few other attackers fell, either from a soldier's sword along the line or an arrow loosed from slits in the outpost tower behind them. But the attack surged when a score of outlaws broke from the trees of the vale, pushing the resistance back. One legionnaire was taken down by a flurry of multiple challengers, and the fray threatened to trample others, moving like a small mob into the clearing skirting the lagoon.

Ethyn absorbed and deflected slashings from a spear and responded with a swift combination of effortless longsword strokes. Though they hit their mark, each passed through the attackers with a similar ineffectiveness, disrupting smoke particles, which re-animated in place immediately thereafter. A staff came down on his wrist without warning from an unseen attacker, jarring free the longsword to the ground, while a second blow was delivered at his ribcage. He was quick enough to wrap his arm around the weapon and wrest it from the assailant's clutches. The staff was steel-banded, but light of weight, and his practiced hands took to it naturally. And he found that he was able to inflict damage upon the assailant, once disarmed, with blows landing firmly and repeatedly; knocking the man down and out.

The scene across the clearing was one of chaos and desperation, yet (at once) had developed a sense of slowed-motion to Ethyn's eyes when a wraith-like figure appeared; the very sight of which tempted to weaken the prince's trust in his own perceptive powers. *If not a wraith, then something else of a sort I've never quite encountered before.* It moved awkwardly, hunched and gaunt, in a soiled and tattered cloak, carrying a sack strung over its bony shoulder. It skulked as if injured, but when it took off running, it scampering up the side of the outpost tower with the dexterity of a spider, defying nearly every physical limitation of man.

*Incredible!* And without another thought, the prince dashed across the clearing in pursuit, staff in hand, while all had become bathed in a blanket of mist from the sea.

Ethyn burst through the tower door and raced up the steps for the observation deck, feeling the coarse stone against the soles of his feet. In reaching the room, he saw trails of smoke hanging in the air beyond extended, crooked fingers, as flames burned a circle in the planked wooden floor around a downed tower watchman. The cloaked figure stood there, looking (up close) like something that may have escaped from a grotesquerie; or worse, as if it'd just crawled from the grave. Its flesh appeared half stripped to the bone as it struggled to stand, bent over the floor in its ruined cloak, staring at the prince with a twisted form of savagery. The smell of scorched flesh flooded Ethyn's nostrils, and the penetrating stare of those beady eyes stopped him dead in his tracks.

It hissed at first, but did not move, and the two made as if they were appraising each other's strengths. *All I've got is this staff, which bears a size and weight to which I'm unaccustomed, and which I suppose is not impervious to projectile flame.* He furrowed his brows with determination, cursing his misfortune in dropping his longsword; likely being trampled upon now beneath the on-going fray outside.

"What sort of profane treachery have you born into this world?" he asked of the figure, in such a manner that conveyed a certain and utter disdain. But the thing just scowled in response. Then it began to move, stalking its way toward a line of knotwood desks. A bevy of notations and official letters lay there. It scooped up whatever it could of them and thrust it all into the sack slung over its shoulder.

Ethyn advanced, then, to strike the wraith flush in its side with the staff; pale ash reinforced with near-weightless bands of Athynian steel, making solid impact. *Constant motion; fluidity and brutal grace. Strike swiftly, then strike again and repeat; never stop moving. Always on offense; always dictating the flow; always my pace, not his.*

One flick of the wrist brought the staff up and against the side of the wraith's head, the fibers of the ash flexing on impact; a reverberation which fueled the momentum of a following strike back into the figure's mid-section. He could see vague features of its face within the dark shadows of the cowl it wore and he could feel the subtle resiliency of flesh in the contact of the weapon. *This is no apparition*, thought Ethyn, *this is a man. Unquestioningly human, but no doubt possessed of some dark mystical agent.* His strikes were substantial, sending the figure forcefully against a far wall, and smashing through wooden furniture pieces. But, at the last, it recovered quickly and leapt back.

Scrawny arms appeared from its cloak, and it began to summon energy for an offensive, but Ethyn was too quick; stinging its hands and disrupting its summons with two more lunging blows from the iron tip of the staff. Screaming, the cloaked figure shrank back and made frantically for the broad windows, jumping and landing upon a sill with such soft and swift dexterity. It crouched there with crooked fingers grasping at the window frame, and it seemed to Ethyn that (for a moment) the necklace hanging around his own neck caught the figure's full attention—the necklace given to him by the swimmer in the lagoon, just moments prior. The thing's battered head twisted with interest; its eyes struggled open in seeming awe, then it coughed in fits, like it might lose control of its every faculty, before turning and exiting; climbing down the side of the tower with as much dexterity as it had on its way up.

Ethyn ran to have a look from the window and saw the thing lope through the fray of men—legion soldiers and outlaws alike—across the clearing, spitting words in a tongue unknown to the prince. He saw Aryk Frierstag establish a firm foothold in its path, but the wraith screamed the shrillest of screams, and from its throat came a cloud of smoke that screened and stunned the legionnaire long enough to allow for escape. And (as if commanded by the shrill sound) its remaining band of followers chased after it, fleeing from the field of battle. They disappeared with the wraith back into the darkness of the trees, leaving Ethyn's men and outpost watchmen alike to swipe their swords at the air and shout their praises of seeming victory.

\*\*\*

The dust had settled north of the Canterford Vale and order was restored to the outpost there, overlooking the lagoon and the broad reaches of the Central Sea. The Heir Prince of Solis gathered together his equipment from the field and addressed his company with praises for their fearlessness. Two mounted soldiers of the retinue had pursued the cloaked wraith and its minions, but had lost them in a black tangle of branches and leaves. They had returned to the outpost tower with nothing more than reports of a full retreat, likely to the outlying archipelago in the South Seas, where such malefactors were known to reside.

"My lordship," said Outpost Captain Gael Riversong with a commanding voice, once Ethyn and Aryk Frierstag had time to collect their thoughts and assemble in the tower's observation deck. Riversong had an air about him that instilled a sense of authority, but it was obscured, in some measure, by more than a twinge of despondency. Ethyn could see it in his hard eyes, "Welcome to our post, it is an honor. Our men owe you and your company greatly for your valor here today."

"Indeed," said Ethyn, "have you any idea what may have incited this sort of attack, at this particular place and time? Such an occurrence is rare, I should hope; is it not?"

"We've considered the possibility of incursions by outlaws such as these," advised Riversong. The watchman who had been attacked by the wraith's fire had come-to and was being led down slowly to the lower levels of the tower for treatment and rest. "Brazen and senseless. Or so we've heard of them from sailors who brave the South Seas and come to anchor away from the storms and fierce winds here in the lagoon."

"What can you make of their speech?" asked Aryk; his words falling atop one another in eager succession as he busily scribbled details into his folio. "And how about their geographic origin? Can you suppose a *motive* for their incursion, captain?"

"Did I mention I brought along with me a most curious and inquisitive friend?" Ethyn smiled at the captain, who was staring blankly in the face of Aryk's avalanche of questions, "He's a very mindful type, especially for a legionnaire."

Aryk reddened, trying to dial down his level of enthusiasm a bit.

"Oh, I see. Yes." Riversong formed a polite smile upon his face, "Well, we're quite sure they've indeed come from the archipelago, off our western shores, by account of Athynian seafarers drawn there, perhaps by rumor of great treasure or some other perceived bounty to be gained. Their speech is no less foreign to mine ears than a seagull's cry or a mount's playful whinny. And as for a motive, I could not begin to conjecture, my lords."

"This cloaked wraith," pressed Ethyn, "he was after something."

"Our latest planned correspondence with the seat's High Council is what he took from the desks," answered the captain, examining the surroundings with a keen eye, "except I don't know what they could want with them."

"Whoever they are, they might well glean a good deal of information from that correspondence," offered Aryk.

"I've never taken these outlaws for the reading sort," said the captain, "and much less have I ever dreamed they could understand the meaning in such things."

"But what of the wraith?" asked Ethyn, "might he possess a more sophisticated, shall we say… appreciation for such things?"

"I'd not be the one to ask, my lord. This was the first we've seen of him in these parts, to my knowledge," answered Riversong, "though I'd wager it's not likely to be the last. If not again crossing steel in the field of battle, then surely in our nightmares to come, aye?"

"What exactly *was* the subject of your latest correspondence, captain?" asked Aryk, "If you don't mind my asking."

"We watch the coast from the outpost here and report our findings," said Riversong. "Trends from the tides and the winds, mostly; of rainfall and the like, and of rumors gathered at sea and shared with us by mariners moored here, time and again. Of course, on occasion, we shan't neglect mention of any other observations, such as we make by day or by night."

"Such as, captain?" asked Aryk, prodding.

"Well, we oughtn't assume outright importance of such things, nor jump to our own misguided conclusions, but I've beheld for myself peculiar sightings in the night's sky of late, which I've considered, at last, worthy of a notation or two…"

Ethyn could feel his ears perk up. *Peculiar sightings in the sky you say, captain?*

Intrigued by this thread of conversation, the prince ordered the retinue to make camp in the clearing for the evening; something they were always prepared to do when afield from the castle. Each of them saw to the tending of one another's wounds and, later, to the preparation of an evening meal with surplus provisions from the wagon master's stores.

Those in the observation deck spoke for a long time after, and it wasn't until the depths of the night had set in (when the light from the Ancillary Moon shone so sharp and so bright) that they had all finally made for their bedrolls to catch what precious little sleep might have been left to them. Until the sun would rise again.

## 11 | Wisdom in Details

*"Too often we are caught up in the big things, the grand spectacles that surround us, to take a meaningful account of the little things… the details. I ask you, is it the towering heights and the enormous reach of the great sequoia tree that ought to amaze us the most, or rather, the fact it was all grown from a seed the size of your smallest fingernail?"*
—excerpt from the personal journal of Steven Spurlock

|Planet Deaer, Castle Athyn

The mute prince of Athyn, Tae Solis, sat on a stool and looked upon a magnified image of the Ancillary Moon, glowing especially silver and bright in the night's sky. The device—which made such a view possible through a series of curved lenses—oscillated on a stand bearing gears and levers responsible for adjusting its angle of sight; a hair up or down, or a hair left or right. And it protruded from a notch cut from the very highest tower rising from Castle Athyn, built to such a height that on some nights, it was enveloped in the clouds, rendering a viewing of the moon (or any other such celestial bodies for that matter) impossible. But this was a clear evening, indeed, and Tae thought he could even see the accumulation of gasses in the moon's atmosphere, and land formations on its surface.

"Pay close attention," said a hoarse and wheezing voice belonging to a frail man who stood in bent posture close at hand. Idris Ansel was an honored member of the Nhyle's High Council by day and an avid stargazer by night, though one would think him more likely a homeless derelict, judging by his meager appearance alone. The truth could be no different, as the man had served two Nhyles of House Solis in his day, and had been afforded ample (and comfortable) space within the castle all those many cycles of season to pursue the fruits of his various occupations.

This tower contained not just a bedchamber and privy, but a full laboratory as well, outfitted with complex instrumentation, all constructed by the man himself from an endless supply of resources, furnished unto him in abundance by the royal seat. Yet, for all the attention the man paid to his crafts—his devices and models and charts strewn all about the room—he paid precious little mind to the virtues of personal grooming. His breath (at present) smelled quite strongly of onion soup, and his tunic was nearly as stained and tattered as a stableman's slop rag.

"The details..." the old man continued to say, coughing all the while as if he meant to expel a lung from his throat, "there is wisdom in the details, young Tae. Wisdom I say!"

Details, in fact, were precisely what the little prince had sought ever since he'd vanished from existence in the dank catacombs beneath the castle earlier that morning. In the thick of it, he knew not at all what was happening to him; only that a tingling sensation rippled across the nerve endings beneath his skin while he stood motionless in the torch lit sub-terrain, and that he'd seemingly been taken asunder, placed somewhere anew. He'd found the new place just as dark and just as damp as the one he'd left. But he was allowed to pass further along through the tunnel to a place where a brilliant band of light beamed down vertically from an opening high above.

In this new place, he'd experienced an overwhelming sense of calm and contentment that had cleared his mind; a powerful surge of joy, which cradled him and nurtured him like a newborn babe. He craved the sensation; reveled in it in such a way he'd never before thought possible. And then, an instant later (or so it seemed), and without warning, the sensation was gone. And he'd somehow been returned to the catacombs, standing at a dead end with torch and practice sword in hand as if naught had happened at all.

There seemed nothing left to do but return to the upper cellars from whence he came and perhaps make as if none of it had ever happened. Certainly, the notion of reporting for his training at the Mystics House had, by then, become a complete absurdity, and he gave it no more than a passing thought. *Mother will understand,* he'd dared to hope. Instead, he'd taken his leave back to his bedchambers for brunch. But while he ate from his platter of sliced fruit and finger sandwiches, he found it difficult to leave the strange experience behind, turning it around obsessively in his mind.

He considered how the world had often made him *feel* invisible, and that the experience had quite possibly been nothing more than a figment of his colorful imagination. After all, a person can only be told so many times they're insignificant before he or she begins to believe it for themselves. Perhaps the same could've been said for his vanishing, and it'd been nothing more than a self-fulfilling prophesy he'd simply forced himself to believe in.

*But no, this was different,* he kept telling himself, *this was distinct… palpable.* And throughout the rest of the day and evening, he'd determined (despite his firm penchant to avoid human contact) that he'd be willing to look *anywhere* and turn to *anyone* for answers. Luckily, he hadn't suffered needs to look very far.

Idris Ansel seemed just the man to ask for help. It was true Ansel had served three Nhyles at court; a phenomenon that prompted inquiring folks to perform a simple computation, which placed the man into an unnaturally extended age bracket. By Tae's determination, Ansel must have been at least seventy years of age, by service time alone. And, if the council's records held firm to fact, the man had lived fifty-some seasons before he'd even arrived upon the castle grounds to vow his loyal service; maybe more.

Such defiance of old age was not unheard of, certainly when compared to the veritable rarity of vanishing princes. In fact, even Tae had heard tell of men and women who'd lived to see beyond their two-hundredth harvest season. *The Ageless,* as they'd come to be called. But they were, indeed, very few in number, and most had grown weary and incoherent in their latter progressions of old (and older) age.

Ansel, however, suffered no such mental decline, instead displaying sharpness of mind, clearness of thought, and conciseness of reason. It gave the small prince certain pause: *Sure, his body has become frail, but no one can challenge his wisdom and wit; his knowledge of those many things unknown to others… the unusual, the mythos, and the legends. Even the heavens cannot escape his understanding!*

Tae certainly considered the night's sky one of Ansel's paramount interests, but he also knew the man's unrelenting thirst for knowledge was not limited to all things celestial. In fact, one topic always seemed to trump all others in the old man's catalog of curiosities, and it'd been (in itself) the bygone suggestion of Tae's very own act of disappearance as a child. Ansel had never ceased inquiring about the vanishing act, from the moment the story had spread throughout the great hall that evening of its occurrence. The old man had, in fact, taken a greater interest than anyone in the affair. *Even greater than mother's, and that's saying a fine deal's worth, indeed...*

Ansel had asked question upon question of the princeling after his disappearance so long ago, and he'd eagerly recorded his understanding of each of Tae's non-verbal responses. They came in a barrage at first; for weeks on end he'd sought the prince out, and each question had grown more prying than the last, until he'd eventually (and quite reluctantly) reduced his inquiries to a score here and a handful there. But the man had never *fully* given up investigating Tae's odd experience.

And so, it was this distinction that had ultimately led Tae up the steps to the stargazer's lair, for Tae so craved that feeling of joy he'd felt in those few strange moments in the catacombs. As crazy as it seemed, he thought that he may want to attempt a return there to experience that certain bliss again. *If anyone knows anything about this, anything at all, it must be Idris Ansel.*

"Do you see the bodies of water, Tae?" asked Ansel while Tae continued to look through the lenses at the moon's surface, "the water is vital; for without it, there can be no support for animate life."

Indeed, Tae *could* see the water upon the Ancillary Moon as he sat there, peering through the lenses of the great looking device, and it was quite a marvel to behold. It was difficult to glean much detail from the surface of the moon, but when he concentrated hard enough, he was able to identify blue traces behind the silvery glow that could only indicate the presence of a vast sea, though blurry and abstract as it may have seemed, from so far away.

Tae could never deny that looking at such beautiful sights through Ansel's many peculiar devices was a thrill. As was his proclivity with all people, he would surely have spurned all of Ansel's attempts at communication, had perks such as these not existed in the man's tower to pique his interest. But because the thrill of stargazing had been so appealing, the prince had put up with the anxiety of dealing with this most bothersome social arrangement.

When Tae was still but a toddler, Ansel had remedied the boy's mutism with a clever solution. He'd commissioned a painter from the Arts District to render a collection of images upon thick-stock parchment cards, one image to each card, each depicting a common subject in Tae's day-to-day life: one for the Nhyle (his father) and one for the Nohnce (his mother); one for his brother Ethyn, and one for Ansel himself. Another was made for the collective High Council, another for the castle, and yet another for the realm of Athyn. There was a separate image, not just for food, but for many different *kinds* of food, different types of flora, and different species of animals. And so on. The prince could present one or two cards, or any combination of others, to express thoughts and share ideas or stories with Ansel, and he'd become more comfortable with this method of communication than he had with any other.

So once he was through delaying the inevitable (by staring through the lenses at the moon's vibrant glow), it was this stack of cards that Tae took in hand from a nearby shelf. He placed them upon a desk within the laboratory, before sitting down on a chair and looking up at the stargazer with intent.

"I quite like it when you initiate a session with the cards, Tae," said Ansel in an astonished, yet overjoyed tone, "a very rare occurrence, indeed."

Tae took the deck in hand and shuffled through it past depictions of flowers, and foods, and family members. But when he came upon the *flame* card, he slid it out and placed it upon the desk. And immediately, a curious smile spread through the old man's coarse, untended beard.

"The flame?" said Idris while he raised his bushy eyebrows, "are you certain?"

Tae nodded.

"Do you remember what we said about presenting the flame on its lonesome?"

Tae nodded again.

"Then pray tell, where did this occur?" The man spoke now with mounting interest as he slid his stool closer and took the cards into his own hands. He held one up—the wheat stalks of the meadows of the Proper—and Tae shook his head in the negative. The arbor was revealed next, but Tae shook his head again, for it hadn't occurred in the gardens. Then the castle, and this time, Tae nodded.

"So you were in the castle..." Ansel squirmed with apparent excitement and blinked his eyes rapidly, suggesting his mind ran akimbo in penetrating thought. The prince then, again, took the set of cards back and placed another down, decisively: the cave. With this act, the stargazer's small, clever eyes twinkled like bejeweled treasures, and he asked, "A cave in the castle?"

Tae nodded, but also squinted a bit to show there was more to it than that.

"*Beneath* the castle?" Ansel offered.

The squinting went away, but Tae's nodding (in the affirmative) did not.

"And you disappeared, didn't you? Thus, your presentation of the flame card."

The nodding continued, still.

"This is most exciting, my boy. *Most* exciting, indeed." The stargazer asked hurriedly, anxiously, "Where do you suppose you went?"

Tae shrugged.

"Well you must've gone somewhere. A body does not simply exist, then cease to exist, and then exist again."

Tae shrugged once more, opening his eyes wide.

"Had the experience seemed the same as before? When you were but a wee lad?"

Tae gave a look that conveyed the equivalent of: *I suppose so...*

"Had you lost consciousness, my boy?"

Tae shook his head, *No*.

"Perhaps you'd been walking while asleep?"

*No*, again.

"Let me ask you, when this event occurred, had you the mere *impression* you'd vanished, or was there something... else? Had you seen or heard or even smelled anything of interest? Anything out of the ordinary?"

The prince thought for a moment, then nodded, and very deliberately took up all the cards from the table back into his hands and stacked them into a neat pile. The act was meant to confer that the prince had something more to share, but that the cards would not (could not) help in doing so, as the information he held was unique.

"You saw something, then?" asked Ansel, who was barely able to speak for all the excitement he seemed to conjure over Tae's revelation, "something for which there exists no common explanation?"

When Tae nodded, *yes*, the stargazer stood again from his stool, shaking so much Tae feared he might collapse. The old man's eyes began to bulge from their sockets, his grin widened to reveal the myriad of crooked teeth in his maw, and he wrung his hands together as if there was something on his mind he could not wait to discover. Then Ansel asked, "Was it, perchance, a brilliant band of light that you saw, Tae, cast straight down from someplace above?"

Again, Tae nodded, *yes*.

"Well this is quite interesting indeed, my young friend. I'm honored you've found it within yourself to share this with me," said Idris, so hurriedly that spittle began to pool on the man's lower lip. "You're confused, and perhaps a bit scared, is that right?" Ansel walked to an open window that provided a clear view of the countryside and all points east, "And you'd like to understand this event which, this very morning, has come back to haunt you from your burgeoning youth, wouldn't you?"

Ansel then paced excitedly across the room to another window, which afforded views of all points north and west. "These feelings... they are only natural," he swiftly shuffled his feet back to where Tae sat, and bent down, his face uncomfortably close to Tae's own, adding, "I will help you with this. The gods as my witness, I will work night and day to figure this out... yes, night and day. But I will require your assistance. You must promise to aid me in any way that you can; in any way that I ask. Is this agreed?"

When he was done, he let out a raucous cough and doubled over, feverishly sucking air back into his lungs.

If truth be told, the old man's speech made Tae feel uneasy, to the extent he'd regretted making the trek into the heights of the lofty tower at all, and he couldn't quit its confines rapidly enough after making his pleasant, yet silent, goodbyes. The tower was equipped with a wooden lift-chamber, counter balanced to allow a swift ascent to it's top (or in this case, descent to its bottom), and on his way down, it made him ill to think he'd promised anything of this sort—any kind of unconditional cooperation—to anyone. He'd rather disappear every day, with no trace or explanation at all, than remain beholden to someone else's requirements, even Idris Ansel's, whom he'd known all his life.

But it was done, and there was nothing he could do to reverse it now. *Except escape to my chambers and lock the door against any and all who might seek to enter; anyone who would place upon me a burden or a task, who would harass me, or would try to hold me accountable for any agreements I've made... or that they've claimed I've made, or that they'd try to impose upon me, despite my quite simple wish to be left to my very lonesome self!*

Yes, he regretted this decision to venture up to the tower and divulge his secret. He regretted it more and more with each step he took. It gnawed and gnawed at his mind, now, while he raced his way down the halls. *Away and away.*

When he finally reached the safety of his chambers, he slammed the doors tight, vaulted himself onto his bed, and squirmed under the blankets. And it would not nearly be the first of such times he'd locked himself away.

Nor would it likely be the last.

### 12 | Thoughts, Feelings, and Memory

*"Sometimes I wish I could bind an entire block of memories and vacuum-seal them within a container, then release that container from my hand into deep space to watch it drift, drift, drift away toward the darkest infinity. And I would then find myself under a new spell of such blissful ignorance; free evermore from whatever pollution those memories contained. Yet, the more I think about it, and after all I've been through, the more I wonder—maybe I can…"*
—excerpt from the personal journal of Steven Spurlock

|The Station

Spurlock sat with his legs crossed on the paneled surface of his tract at the bow end of the Station, where the view of Planet Deaer was displayed before him in all its magnificence. Giza, his assigned non-sentient companion, hovered next to him. They'd hunkered down and absorbed the sights of their resident galaxy for a while. Despite a nagging skepticism, Spurlock had expressed an interest in engaging the module in discourse of a philosophical nature. But they'd remained speechless, as yet, perhaps while Spurlock waited for the depths of deep space to inspire him, or to convince him this requested conversation might somehow prove worthwhile, after all.

"I am programmed to inquire of your needs," Giza finally said in his digital, childlike voice, breaking the silence.

Spurlock grimaced, reluctantly taking the module's declaration for a conversational prompt. He'd been enjoying the introspective calm imparted by the dark canvas draped before him and its millions of twinkling lights. Even Deaer seemed to emit an oddly peaceful luminescence at the moment.

"You ask me about my needs," said Spurlock, "but do you even understand what 'need' is, Giza?"

"I require a motherboard to process data inputs. I need actuators and sensors to move and to detect obstacles. Yes, I understand need."

"Okay, fine. Then to answer your question, what I *need* is my memory back," Spurlock smirked again, "and don't try telling me you understand what memory is. I'll accept some of the far-fetched explanations you've given me so far, like the mechanical 'thought processes' you mentioned before. Heck, at this point, I *want* to believe in a machine's potential for all of that kind of stuff, I really do. It'd make it a lot easier to deal with the conditions of this crap-stained mission I'm on. To think that while I'm warping around, running all these errands down there, I could maintain a little human dignity behind this cold, robotic façade I've been forced to adopt. But memory… I don't think I can convince myself you have the true makings of real memory in you."

"I can perform an array of sophisticated data recall functions. For instance, my internal drive stores the content of our prior conversations, which I can access at any time. Could this be what you refer to as, memory?"

"No, see, that's not the kind of memory I'm talking about," Spurlock peered intently at Deaer while he replied, squinting from its bright planet-shine; so vibrant, its edges seemed as if they were glowing. "Real memory is more than just a transcript of data. It carries things along with it. Important things."

"What sorts of important *things* does memory carry? Properties, perhaps, that determine how these memories ought to perform?"

"No, no. You're being too technical, Giza. You're being such a… *computer* right now. Memories carry things like sentimentalities or nostalgia. I don't know, I guess they make us *feel* certain ways inside."

"What certain ways, may I ask?"

"Some in comforting ways and some in troubling ways," the tract beneath him felt cold this far forward atop the Station's prow. *Not nearly as cold as dead space out there, though.* He shifted his gaze a bit and caught the faintest, glimmering reflection from the translucent dome that enclosed the Station, protecting against those extreme temperatures. The Station seemed to grumble and churn from some distant depth in the hull below, but this was a frequent occurrence so far as he could tell, and Spurlock wouldn't let it break his concentration. "Memories evoke emotions, which I guess you don't know anything about either. Some are good and some are bad; some bring pleasure and some sting, horribly."

"And you want these memories back? All of them?"

Spurlock's brows tightened at the question, "Of course I want them back, you twit."

"Even the bad memories?"

Now Spurlock stopped to think for a moment, but was resolute in his answer when he finally provided it, "Yeah, even the bad memories. They make us who we are—the good *and* the bad; they provide us wisdom and maturity, and... identity."

"Forgive me, but my logic protocols are continuing to suggest you will only want to recapture the good memories, and leave the bad aside. Algorithms unanimously disagree with your assertion that the bad possess any redeemable quality at all."

"Sorry to be the one to tell you, but your algorithms are wrong. We learn things from bad experiences. Sometimes, the bad stuff enhances the good; helps us appreciate things more, helps shape our identities. And no offense, but when a computer runs into a problem, it usually freezes or shuts down or does something else that's entirely frustrating to its human user. I can't take your advice on this one, Giza. Not yet, at least."

"I am programmed to troubleshoot malfunction and error," the module's apex rotated a bit, almost as if taking offense.

"But your past malfunctions don't continue to plague you, do they? They don't affect your future functioning."

"Once a system error is committed and corrected, there is no benefit to be gained in triggering its recapitulation. To do so would, in fact, prove counterproductive, under every circumstance. I am programmed to manage present circumstances as efficiently as possible, with provisional consideration for the future. No processing power is to be expended on the past."

"See, that's just it. It's not as easy for us to correct our errors as it is for you to correct yours, Giza, or to move on from them, for that matter. We think about them. We dwell on them. We let things fester within us," Spurlock ran his fingers into his hair and clenched them tight. "We get emotionally involved."

"I see. You mentioned emotions before. Troublesome viruses they must be. I would not risk the malfunction such infectious glitches would certainly impose upon my operating system, so I will henceforth block any programming language that might be so obliged to simulate their effects. Similarly, might there be a way for you, then, to retain the sense of identity you glean from bad memories, yet subdue your tendencies to react… *emotionally* to them?"

"I can't say for sure, but I think, somehow, that's exactly what the Operator is asking me to do in this mission of mine. But it's taking a lot of motivation and energy. More than I have to give."

"My algorithms, though flawed as you say, are preparing a conclusion based upon the data you have provided thus far, and it is this: that the path leading away from anguish and strife might lay right before your eyes, even as we speak, but your self-imposed limitations, your insistence upon attaching emotion to all that you encounter, keep you from taking a single step upon this path at all. This, in effect, seems to suggest you are your own worst enemy," Giza's blue light blinked slowly before he made another quarter turn in Spurlock's direction.

"But without emotion, I'd lose my purpose."

"A frightening notion, indeed. You are a complicated organism, Mr. Spurlock."

"Maybe you're starting to see what being human is all about, Giza."

"And perhaps you are starting to see the practicality in behaving, at times, more like a robot."

Suddenly, the Operator's voice could be heard all around them.

—Return to your solar and prepare for your next operation. Please return to your solar immediately and prepare for Projection—

Spurlock sighed heavily, standing up like a beleaguered old man.

"Alright, Giza, you heard her, I have to go. But I'll think about what you've said." Though dreading to discover what waited in store for him this time on Planet Deaer, he still proceeded toward his solar as he was told. He added over his shoulder to Giza, "If I make it back in one piece, maybe we'll continue this conversation where we left off."

\*\*\*

|Planet Earth, Washington, DC

Haley Kenmore's apartment building was a historic fixture in the northwest section of the District of Columbia, which offered not only a very short commute by bus to her place of employment, but also exceptional views of the Washington National Cathedral, standing tall and elegant in its gothic, medieval architectural design. Her unit on the fifth floor, while quite modest to most standards, was a costly one. Though her parents had surely desired to lend assistance, it was an expense she insisted on financing through her own means. Her master's degree had earned her a federal salary grade high enough to achieve such a lofty goal, but the rent had (in turn) allowed her very little expendable income at all by the end of the month.

When, in those rare instances, she determined a small allowance in her budget could be freed for recreational purposes, a modestly indulgent—yet thoroughly deliberative—procurement of her greatest guilty pleasure (shoes) had become a most trusted method of retail therapy. She justified this behavior by naming it a healthy exercise. Not only because the very act of buying shoes brought her immense gratification, but also because (though she purchased many different types of shoes, including those formal enough to be worn within her place of employment) a good many of them were athletic shoes designed specifically for the enhancement of her most arduous fitness activities.

It didn't hurt that she found them supremely cute and comfortable as well.

Her's was a particularly regimented fitness routine, which she adhered to without relent, and which—on Saturday mornings like this one, and no less than three workday mornings a week—found her form tightly outfitted in black training pants and a moisture-wicking top, and her feet laced firmly into one of those pairs of athletic shoes for a nice brisk run. She jogged down the building's stairs and through the lobby, along residential side streets and past community garden patches before hitting the earthen trail through Glover Park. The November chill flushed her cheeks pink, her hair (gathered in a headband and tie) tossed vigorously about, and her breath produced grand vaporous clouds with every exhale.

The trail always struck her fancy. For a metropolitan setting, it quite thoroughly enveloped its occupants within the wonders of the natural world; tall trees, crawling mosses, and clusters of colorful leaves that still held onto their branches in defiance of the approaching winter's cold. It was an ideal place to accelerate her endorphins and heart rate while breathing deeply of the cleansing cool air. Further-to, the serenity of the setting helped pin down her current distresses so as to prevent them from scurrying back into the recesses of her mind, where she admittedly too often permitted them to wallow.

At the moment, her foremost source of distress was, of course, Steven Spurlock's lack of communication with her these last few days gone by. In thinking upon the matter, she realized it'd caused more puzzlement in her than anger, a sensation that begged of her a greater desire to *solve* it than to wallow in despair over it. *But how to solve such a predicament?*

It certainly wouldn't seem appropriate for her to mandate a set of guidelines by which her relationship with Steven ought to abide, and she reminded herself that their union (though quite solid by her estimation) still remained well within its developmental stages. And so, it should not yet be held to the highest standards of co-dependent responsibility; her for him, nor he for her. But so too did she harbor a strong temptation to declare two and a half days well in-excess of a reasonable length of time for someone's significant other—however nascent the designation may be—to leave a question unanswered over text. *Too long for anyone in* any *kind of relationship to leave a question unanswered like that... Right?!*

There were more direct routes from her apartment to Georgetown University's campus, but the wooded Archbold Trail through Glover Park provided two miles of peaceful escape from the bustle of the streets. This was true at least during daylight hours, when an expectation of safety was, hopefully, still reasonably held by well-meaning folk in the District.

The cool air under the canopy of orange and yellow and red leaves staved off the worst of her perspiration, for which she was grateful. She didn't want to appear a soggy mess to Steven's sister when they sat together for lunch. And, in fact, when she broke from the trail to finally arrive upon the center of campus, she felt fresh and invigorated—if not a pinch nervous. She seemed to always become so in Nora's company (though she recognized no good reason for it). Nora was a proud and protective sister, no doubt, but equal parts kind and considerate, too.

After her stride had fallen into a more leisurely pace, and she'd been able to fully catch her breath, Haley found Nora talking amongst faculty members in the commons. Nora broke away from her group and offered a warm greeting when she saw Haley approach. "I'm sorry to confine our lunch outing to the limits of campus," she said, "all for the sake of an afternoon meeting I'm very much loathing, but also unfortunately required to attend."

"Oh, it's not a problem at all," said Haley, "it's been one of my favorite pit-stops for a while now, running the trails."

They talked lightly of the weather and of Nora's intense schedule of doctorate degree courses while making their way to the student center. They both selected hearty salads before finding a small table by a window. Having settled themselves a bit, their conversation turned, as it often did for Haley in *any* conversation, to hers and Steven's place of employment.

"That place seems crazy," said Nora, who had set her bag full of heavy texts on the seat beside her. "Whenever I feel overwhelmed by the blinding pace of my studies, I think about what he's doing all day long, and I'm grateful."

"Does he tell you much about his work?" Haley found herself eager to know.

"Well, not much. But what I know of it sounds pretty overwhelming. I imagine you can relate to him in that regard, with all that you're involved in, too. I don't know how you guys do it. I wouldn't be able to sleep at night, knowing the sordid details of all the plots hatched by the dark and evil forces that roam this planet."

"It's really not so bad, I guess," Haley could go on at length about the incredible reports she'd (on many occasion) read at work and the impression her job had made on her life, but she didn't want to talk about herself. Instead, and while hoping not to sound rude, she intended to direct the focus back upon Steven. She might as well cut directly to her secret reason for meeting with Nora, lest she wind up running out of time; an occurrence of vast frequency for people in this city, it seemed. "Have you heard from him recently?"

"Hmm, no, not recently," Nora looked off, thinking for a second, "it's probably been a couple of weeks, now, actually."

"It's been a few days since I've heard from him, which is unusual for us," Haley was only picking at her lunch. She wanted to pay particular attention to what Nora would have to say.

"Oh, well that's Steven. He'll zone out sometimes. But it doesn't mean he's drifting away, believe me on that."

"Drifting away? How do you mean?"

"From you," Nora took a bite of her salad and dabbed her lip with a napkin, "I recognize your tone. You're concerned he's losing interest."

"Is it that obvious?" Haley leaned forward.

"Don't worry. I'm telling you… He cares about you greatly, I'm sure of it. More than you know. I'd go so far as to say he's smitten, and I'm not breaking some kind of sibling code here by saying so. I'm sure he wants you to know."

"You're just about reading my mind here."

"Just a sister's intuition, but I see it," said Nora, "you're a grounding force for him, and he needs that."

"So then, why the disconnect for a few days, I wonder? How hard is it to reply to a text, you know?" Haley wondered, then, if she'd revealed a bit too much discontent; or that, perhaps, her persistence in the matter portended an unwillingness to listen to what she was being told. But Nora seemed unfazed.

"Maybe he's been sent abroad somewhere. Believe me, that's happened. I've gone weeks without talking to him, then he'll casually mention he'd gone to Cairo on a work trip or somewhere like that, and I'd never known. Another time it was New Delhi, I think. And he'll neglect to tell our mother, too. When he returns, he'll play it off as if it were a plan he'd concocted—with affection, mind you—to keep us from worrying. Which always makes me laugh, because no one in our family can worry like Steven can."

"It sounds like he's overthinking things a little too much."

"Oh, Haley, that's an understatement. Let me tell you, he takes a cerebral approach to all he does; I'm sure you've noticed. I think it's what makes him a good analyst. Someone who's so entrenched in his work like he is, locked in that sort of world where ideas have to blossom every day; contingencies must be considered, theories researched and debated; over and over. I think a person like that must spend a lot of time within their own mind, you know? Consumed by their thoughts. Constantly unraveling it all. All of the… mess, I suppose. He's always put a lot of thought into whatever he does, but it can get him into trouble sometimes when it comes to matters of practical decision-making. When it comes to his personal relationships, too. And he's just totally outside his comfort zone, here."

Haley knew well of Steven's tendency to overanalyze and worry, so the idea she might prove a calming force in his life was particularly satisfying, indeed. To think she might inspire a more laid back version of him to develop. In truth, she'd just as quickly welcome a more well-composed version of herself, as well, "I get outside and run off the steam when I need to."

"A little running might do him some good, if you could ever persuade him to join you, though that'd be quite a scene, now that I'm picturing it. Steven in tights and a head band," Nora laughed. "I say this with all due respect to my brother, but DC has chewed him up and spit him out a little. I think he needs you by his side to help him out. It's clear he needs the strength of your bond, which it seems the two of you share," she sat back then a bit and took a sip of green tea. "How long have you been together now?"

"We're coming up on a year," Haley had to smile at the memory of it; of their true start together, after a few months of casual lunches and walks around the headquarters campus together. It happened in Langley—their true start—during a holiday party thrown at the home of the Under Secretary. Steven had been so formal about it while they sat together in a corner study of the well-appointed craftsman house, tucked away in the trees of Northern Virginia. She could still hear Steven saying:

*So, this is for real, Haley; you and me, from this point forward, together.*

And she had said: *Yes and yes; a thousand times yes.*

"Christmas," she added, breaking out of her daydream of remembrance, "it'll be a year, come Christmas."

"Time just flies," Nora was shaking her head at the revelation. "Seems like I've been here six months, and it's actually been three years. Two and a half for Steven, who came when they started hiring analysts there at your headquarters. DC isn't like Philly. It's only a three hour drive south, true, but Steven, he's had a real difficult time adjusting. It's the work he's been doing; the politics of it all… the *strangle-hold* as he calls it. This place, it's… charged. Sorry, I know this is your home, but…"

"I grew up in Maryland, actually, but close enough that I always *felt* like I belonged to the District," Haley was starting to see the context of Steven's geographical upheaval perhaps for the first time, "And you're not off base. This place knocks me around, too." She hesitated, unwilling to suggest just *how much* it could rattle her, at times, "I know it's unique, in its own ways."

"Unique, yes. And I wouldn't question your pride in it, for a moment. Home is home. But to some outsiders, it seems so caught up in itself that sometimes it forgets the rest of the world; loses the meaning of good sense. It demands answers of you before it asks the questions. It writhes with an energy so hungry for power that its identity—its existence as a collection of human beings, entwined together—is obscured by something more relatable to a cold, hard *machine* than a collective of living organisms. And maybe for good reason. Maybe it has to be like that here, for all the responsibility it carries. But that's something Steven's had a difficult time reconciling; something that just doesn't jive with him. Until, of course, *you* came along and balanced things out a bit. Brought a much-needed human element back to his equation."

Haley didn't know exactly how to respond. Nora was effectively dismissing her concerns, in turn, before she even had to voice them. She knew Steven was flawed, as was everyone, but she was convinced he was flawed in all the right ways. That is, at least, for her own devices. And so, she said exactly what came to her mind—nothing more and nothing less, "He's balancing my equation, too."

They both took a breath for a moment, then Haley added, "You're going to make a great psychologist, Nora."

"I better. It's costing me enough," Nora pointed toward the massive texts in the bag by her side with a wry smile on her face, "but anyway, this was a great idea, Haley. We should do this more often. We're so close to each other, up here in the northwest of town. I don't know why he insists on making that commute from Arlington every morning, from so far out there."

"I've told him he'd alleviate half his stress just by moving across the Potomac," chided Haley, "the lesser commute alone would work wonders, I'd think."

"You might be right about that," Nora stood up and hefted the strap of her bag over her shoulder, "almost every book in here expounds upon the destructive nature of stress on the human body, in one way or another."

"If I can borrow one some time," Haley stood up, too, "I might leave it lying around the office for my co-workers' perusal." *And I might just leaf through it a bit myself, too.*

"Oh, I'm sure more than a few in that place could benefit from some serious stress relief!"

"Not the least of all, my boss, the Assistant Secretary," she hesitated a moment before adding, "She's maybe the most highly strung of them all."

"Just remember," Nora's eyes focused on Haley intently, "everyone carries their own sources of stress. We shouldn't let their poor coping mechanisms drag us down, but we shouldn't dismiss whatever personal battles they may be fighting in their own lives, either."

On that note, they made their goodbyes, recycling their lunch containers and vowing to one another they'd get back together, in like-fashion, before long. Then Haley found herself running the park trails again, still trying to evaporate the concerns for Steven from her mind, much like her breath that faded away in the cool air.

She thought upon the many insightful things Nora had said. And she only stopped twice along the way to check her phone to discover, anew, that Steven still hadn't texted her back.

## 13 | The Royal League House

*"What is hope but simple anticipation of a more blissful reality; or the belief that such a reality does or can, in fact, exist? And what, I ask, is hope that is finally realized? What does that look like? I'm given to believe—as I've gathered no suggestion to the contrary—that hope, yet unfulfilled, shall remain for me a permanent companion along life's journey. Life, therefore it seems, is a perpetual anticipation of pure contentment. But I'll not give up so easily my attempts to hasten its arrival, just the same."*
—excerpt from the personal journal of Steven Spurlock

|Planet Deaer, Athynian Countryside

Prince Ethyn Solis' company rode their mounts in the crisp morning air, north along the Ribbon Road of Athyn, back on track toward their initial destination. The night—which followed the ambush from unknown assailants on the banks of the lagoon—had afforded them little sound sleep, and they felt a bit fatigued for it, indeed. Anxious to get going, though, and with little time to spare, they'd set out on the road from Captain Gael Riversong's coastal outpost on a direct route for the Harbor Town of Stief. The retinue of soldiers and their pair of wagons followed behind at a slowed pace; afforded to them on account of the bruises many had acquired in the scuffle.

From the saddle, Aryk Frierstag was deciphering notes he'd scrupulously taken in the aftermath of their clashings. Riversong, during their talk the evening prior, had referenced sightings he'd recently made at night by the aid of a looking glass from his outpost's observation deck. Though intriguing, the gleamings of unusual light he'd portrayed, which allegedly occupied celestial space near that of the Ancillary Moon, hadn't quite matched the visions Ethyn held in mind, of his own experience. Aryk, who had scribed down almost every word of the exchange, would hardly quit searching for anecdotal evidence of the phenomena so easily.

"Well this is quite interesting, you might like to hear this, Ethyn," remarked Aryk, leafing through various texts, which he somehow balanced upon his saddle while he rode. "It seems the gnarled fellow— the cloaked wretch whom you'd confronted—may have provided a lead for us on the fiery apparition you believed you'd seen over the mountains in the south, upon our outset. In retreat, I'd heard him scream something in the foreign tongue of the archipelago, so I'd committed it to memory and had written it down phonetically last evening. It seems now I've come to assemble a crude translation through my philological texts here, which may help us understand its meaning. It's quite morbid, so prepare yourself. If my interpretations are accurate, he'd said something to the effect of the following."

Aryk read from his folio:

SOON WILL THE FIRE AND SMOKE THAT LIGHTS THE SKY RAIN DOWN UPON THE WORLD TO BURN THE OPPRESSORS AND THEIR CITIES. ALL HAIL ALAMERE.

"The fire and smoke that lights the sky…" Ethyn made aloud his mulling of the translation.

"Sounds a bit like what you had described," Aryk looked at Ethyn intently.

"Indeed, it sounds precisely akin to what I saw."

"I dunno what you two are talking about, but I agree nonetheless," said Othys with a clownish smile from his mount behind them.

Ethyn obliged the older man, "I'm glad you do, Othys, but in any event, I think your nephew is on to something. The timing and likenesses are too exact to allow a mutual exclusivity. These assailants must bear some linkage with the lights I've seen streaking the sky above the mountain ranges in the south."

"I trust the council will agree our discoveries meet threshold for action," said Aryk, "enough to endorse any and all recommendations you might make to your father for the deployment of a company to neutralize these traces of threats we've seemingly begun to uncover?"

"Perhaps it is a sign of arrogance that I should assume the issue will carry more weight when delivered from my lips than it ever has from Captain Riversong's quill, or any other outpost across our lands." Ethyn urged his mount along the hard-trodden path, "But I can't imagine anyone on the council would ignore outright what we will have to say about these strange assailants and their rogue, wraith-like leader of the archipelago. Or from whatever downtrodden region they come. Such would be, dare I say, an act of defiance against the offices they serve; which stand for, above all else, the protection of our peoples and lands. Isn't that so?"

"Perfectly so, I would say," agreed Aryk, his staid mood lightening a bit.

"Perfectly!" Othys, bringing up the rear of the small company of three, echoed along.

"No, if logic holds," Ethyn added, "I should not think we will encounter much resistance from the council.

"Unfortunately, I fear logic has made little difference at all in political matters such as these, lately," Aryk finally tucked the folio back into his saddlebags, hoping he hadn't overstepped his bounds, "if I may offer a humble observation..."

"Well said," offered Ethyn, taking no offense to his friend's opinion.

"In fact, I'd be hard-pressed to place bets on *any* matter of political significance," Aryk seemed to handle his mount's reigns more aggressively; his hands free of books and papers for once, "I do not, for a moment, envy your certain entrenchment in the sordid political affairs of the realm across these many seasons to come."

"Whether enviable or not, let us first hope the realm will *survive* into the future at all," Ethyn wrinkled his forehead, "what do you make of the last portion? What was it: *All hail* something?"

"Some*one*, I'd guess," said Aryk, "Alamere was the name. Or some close semblance thereof, if I'd remembered it clearly enough. Likely a leader or a symbolic figurehead in the least."

"I'm troubled to imagine anyone leading that *thing* I faced in the tower, for all it's erratic behavior and unnerving, penetrating stares," at that moment, Ethyn felt the small weight of the amber stone pendant resting against his chest; the one he'd obtained from the sea floor at the insistence of his mysterious acquaintance who had feigned her distress in the lagoon.

The company cut single-file through an offshoot of the pine-rich Dunlyn Forest Pass. Their mounts' hooves clapped over thick roots and kicked about bristled cones littering the ground. And there in the shade of the long branches, holding thick clusters of green needles, Ethyn turned his thoughts to a more scintillating topic; an attempt to digest the nuances he could recall from that most unexpected encounter in the water.

She had left him awestruck; quite firmly bewitched, in fact. *Only one night has passed since our meeting, and yet... an eternity.* He had already developed the nervous practice of groping at his tunic to feel the teardrop stone underneath, hanging by its weathered chain (just to make sure of its presence... safe and sound). *Surely the fulfillment of any promises I made to her out there whilst swimming about, will hinge upon my ability to keep this stone intact. But what ever for?*

He raced through countless possibilities, each one becoming more improbable than the last.

The thoughts occupied his mind to mid-day, which found the company out of the forest and across golden fields of wheat, where tall stalks swayed in calm, littoral breezes. And like the enormous bales of hay standing at intervals beside the road, and the hummingbirds that flittered from one blossoming flower to the next, time passed beyond Ethyn's notice.

*What exactly had I promised her again? Certainly* something *was promised, if not by my mere acceptance of this gift alone. I have entered into a pact... something I will have to honor upon her inevitable return.* He searched his memory in vain for a time when he had ever asked a favor of someone, whom he knew he would never meet again. *Scarcely would anyone do such a thing, meaning she's likely to return to me in some way, shape, or form. Wouldn't make much sense in the grand scheme of things if she didn't.*

Yet it seemed unlikely to Ethyn that the world was subject to a grand scheme where logic was law, with reality behaving in close accordance. *Aryk is right to doubt the presence of logic in this world. Not just in matters of politics, but in all things!* And so, the prospect of the fair maiden returning to him would have to remain a mystery, for at least a little while longer. He was forced to stash the diversion away, for evening was starting to set in, and the company had finally arrived upon the Harbor Town of Stief.

*And not a moment too soon.*

\*\*\*

|Athyn, The Harbor Town of Stief

Though Ethyn, the Heir Prince, had paid many visits to the realm's eminent Harbor Town, it'd been a good while since his last, and so, he led his Frierstag hosts (and his small retinue) toward its bustling center with the enthusiasm of a newcomer. The sights and sounds of the town could break anyone from a sleepy philosophical daydream, and Ethyn was no exception.

The sun was just starting to set when they approached Stief's provincial Royal League House. It stood as tall as any on the road, boasting a brand of architecture typical of Athyn's major settlements, but especially those of the coast, where thick beams, large windows, and flourished details were especially favored. Risen out of the ground by a foundation of stone, its façade was washed by sand, swept by the fluid air, and bleached pale by the vibrant sun. Its ornamented eaves were crowded by the whitest of gulls standing on their knobby, orange stilt legs. The deep blue hues of the evening sky met the blankness of the birds' white feathers with a contrast so stark in its beauty, it near as well caused Ethyn to stop and stare.

Tools of nautical trades dressed the benches and columns outside; not for decoration, but instead for quite practical purposes. Such was demonstrated by a young man collecting signal lanterns from the porch for posting above the docks to guide the return of Stief's many angling vessels. And a girl, likely yet to have aged beyond her twelfth season, gathered freshly-cut filets of sweetfish into a tin tray by the back entry and took them inside, surely for the house chef to throw over his grill for a fine searing.

These were the members of privileged families; confidants sworn to the throne, who tended to the property as a functional inn and enjoyed its luxuries for themselves in making of it their proud residence as well. Several such sanctuaries existed across the realm—and a score's count abroad, too—serving as places of refuge for Athynian brethren whilst on travel, across reaches far from home.

"Each of us will have our own room," informed Ethyn of his two Frierstag companions as they left their mounts in the able hands of the inn's stable master and made for the main house. The soldiers in their company continued apart, then, to assume space in a legion barracks, only a short ride further down the road. "They're large rooms, exceedingly well-kept, and intended for this very sort of purpose—matters concerning the affairs of the royal seat. And I have organized our meeting of three additional companions who will join us on escort tomorrow. As a matter of fact, they ought to be awaiting us within, as we speak."

They were; all three men (of whom Ethyn had spoken) had been seated in the common room at a comfortable corner table, but they had since risen upon the entrance of the prince. Adrian Thurflyn was a veteran of the Athynian Royal Guard, who (some many seasons past) had been assigned detail to Stief after a lengthy tenure in service to House Solis; a semi-retirement of sorts. Thurflyn's salt and pepper hair betrayed his age, but his was a handsome face that somehow told of wisdom without need of spoken word at all. The smile he wore, however, seemed to Ethyn only fractionally sincere. *Thurflyn's a good man,* Ethyn was willing to wager. *Stories in scores attest to at least that much, but something of a contentious nature churns behind that polite visage of his.*

Midre Donygal was next; from his looks, a handful of seasons older than Ethyn. He was a legion soldier scheduled to return to Castle Athyn from a year's assignment in Stief. His swarthy skin confirmed the time he'd spent, laboring in the fields of Bucklon Rowe during his up-bringing, as was noted in his papers. Ethyn didn't doubt the hardening experience had proven a useful preliminary to the designs of the demanding legionnaire lifestyle. Donygal offered a salute of the brow to both Aryk and Othys in acknowledgement of their shared station as servicemen. *Dedicated and responsible. We need more like Midre Donygal on our side.*

And last was Balyn Galdur, an especially youthful legion recruit from the eastern Athynian city of Mawr, who'd just finished touring the realm in training. Ethyn could see the tour hadn't completely wiped away the glassy look in Galdur's eyes; a look carried so often by new recruits, seeing larger masses of the world for the first time in life. A longbowman by trade, he stood at a modest height for an archer and was thin with light hair cut in a style resembling a mop. He held himself in a reserved posture. *Perhaps a pinch intimidated by my presence. I like that.*

"Good evening men," Ethyn greeted them firmly.

"Good evening your lordship," they said almost in unison, Adrian Thurflyn's older voice noticeably louder than the other two.

"I'm pleased the three of you will join us on our return to the city tomorrow, me and my companions Othys and Aryk Frierstag of the legion ranks." Othys and Aryk nodded. "I trust you were able to secure rooms without much trouble?"

"Indeed we were, Master Ethyn, each of us," answered Thurflyn, "the League House welcomes its own with open arms. We are well cared for by the royal seat. They're to bring us our keys after supper is through, so that we might get settled for the night."

"That is good to hear," said Ethyn, "Now do not let me keep you a moment longer from your mugs. Let us join you for a meal. I don't know about the rest of you, but I, for one, feel as though I could eat the day's catch of the Central Sea, in full."

The men volleyed light conversation around the table, and a particular detail or two about the escort duties they were to face in the morning, while waiting for their meals to be served. Ethyn spoke generally of the experiences at the outpost north of Canterford Vale, particularly the skirmish, but left out more sensitive bits like the appearance of the wraith figure and, of course, his encounter with the mysterious swimmer and her gift of the necklace from the lagoon. That detail, he was keeping exclusively to himself. Ethyn had no fear of outside parties infiltrating the League House and surveilling his conversations, but some details he'd rather not disclose to anyone without just cause; even trusted emissaries of his very own Royal Guard and Legion.

Each man had downed a pint of Seaspring Ale, a thick filet of tuna, a twiglet of grapes, a peppercorn roll, and a wedge of cheese by the time a sweet-faced, barefooted serving maid—dressed in short fringed skirts and a plunging neckline—came by, handing each man a key to their room upstairs. She saved Legionnaire Midre Donygal for last, pressing the key firmly into his palm and raising an eyebrow in (what seemed to Ethyn) a rousingly surreptitious fashion. Ethyn saw Donygal's free hand slip around the maid's waist and the fringes of her skirts. Then Donygal whispered something into her ear that made her close her eyes, while a devilish smile crept across her face, followed by a biting of her own lower lip and a soft giggle. *Either they know one another extremely well, or he's a greater flirt with the young maids than even I may claim to be.*

The serving maid disappeared into the kitchens, and conversation amongst the group began anew. Uncle Othys cracked a few jokes he'd undoubtedly picked up while training alongside the coarser men of the legion ranks—something or another about a mathematical correlation between the length of a maiden's skirts and the patience required of a man who'd seek to explore them. Midre Donygal hadn't laughed at that particular jape, but Ethyn (himself) had, and he realized how good it felt to be out of the castle, with men of the ranks, taking in a meal and a bit of revelry together.

\*\*\*

The bustle in the common room of the Royal League House in Stief had declined to a mere murmur, and Ethyn Solis was well satisfied with the tenor established among the members of his newly-formed company. But finally sensing the heaviness of the hour, he dismissed them for the night. When they each began to make for the stairs, Ethyn called upon one to stay behind.

"Thurflyn?"

"Master Ethyn," said the elder Royal Guardsman, who (in the muted candle light) began to resemble something like an aged mountain wolf with his silvered hair and keen eyes, along with his ears, always seeming on point and alert.

"Might I trouble you for a few moments longer before we turn in," the prince slid a chair out, which, until then, had been left vacant, "just the two of us?"

"For certain," said Thurflyn, taking the seat without hesitation, "I am at your service."

"And you have been at our service for a very long time, haven't you? The service of the royal seat of Athyn, that is. Your reputation, or should I say, your time-honored contributions to the realm precede you. I hope it is not your feeling that your efforts have been completely forgotten by those holding court these days in Athyn Proper. I'd have you know that some of us still celebrate your life's achievements."

"I am humbled, to be sure," said Thurflyn, while his face betrayed more than a hint of disbelief and, perhaps, a touch of resentment.

"You seem surprised; even doubtful," Ethyn meant to avoid all means of coyness in this conversation, "that saddens me, for it is I, of the pair of us, who ought to feel humbled. I was put to bed through all my early seasons of life, amused by imaginings conjured from the many stories of your famous exploits—your grandest of journeys the world-over. The old mistresses and castellans would tell me those tales whenever I couldn't sleep, and they would repeat them over and over again when I begged it of them. Every night, it seemed for a time."

Thurflyn's gaze slid past Ethyn, then, through the League's smoky-glassed windows and into the night beyond, as if he were taken to a different place and time, of a sudden.

"What we have before us is more than a simple diplomatic escort," continued Ethyn, getting to the point at hand. It caused Thurflyn to focus his eyes back on the prince's face, "You might have suspected as much when I sent for your company. You see, I require your assistance, your expertise, for a greater purpose altogether."

"I'll always provide the realm whatever benefits my knowledge and ability may yield," assured Thurflyn, "though I am obliged to stress I'm no longer the same man you recall from those fanciful bedtime tales in your youth. I am much older, much slower... much weaker now."

"I see. Well, you will find needs to tap into whatever reserve you have left, sir," urged Ethyn, "for we are destined to set a course for adventure. I've a mind for the western archipelago, or the Southspur Mountains. One or the other. Truthfully, I find great need to investigate both. I simply haven't yet made up my mind which it will be."

After turning the idea around for a moment, Thurflyn made a rumbling noise from deep in his chest, "A perilous journey, either."

Ethyn thought the man could have just as easily substituted *foolish* for *perilous*, given his tone and manner of speech. But the prince wasn't going to accept words of caution from a man who was made famous in his time for his daring exploits. "Even for a company led by the one who'd once begun the greatest Travelers Guild the world has ever known?"

"That guild is no more; it was disbanded and forgotten a generation ago," Thurflyn was freely revealing his true feelings of discontent now, a smidge more transparent than perhaps he intended. There could be no surer way to solicit honesty from a man than by striking an arterial nerve in him, and striking it hard. And honesty was precisely what Ethyn needed most from his chosen men. Thurflyn especially.

"As I said, your work, the guild included, is not forgotten by all; nor the countless maps you produced of nearly every remote region of this world," Ethyn knew this conversation would carry the utmost importance, and he was delivering the message he'd most scrupulously composed with cautious poise, "many of them hang about the walls in my living quarters as we speak."

"And what of the lessons of discovery and tolerance I worked so hard to instill?" barked Thurflyn, raising his voice, "I ask you, where do *they* hang?" It'd been loud enough that the barkeep and a handful of patrons, who still remained in the common room at this hour, looked over to see what was the matter, and Thurflyn seemed instantly ashamed.

"Please forgive me, your lordship," he continued; his voice now lowered. "For someone who'd spent his whole life traveling, always on the move, I've had much time—too much time, of late—to do little more than sit and *think*. A preponderance of thinking without the means to take action leads only to decline, and over-thinking leads to even worse ends. Doing is better. An active life suits me, and I've long been stripped of it. I do not know if you can fully understand."

"Oh, but I *do* understand. Precisely so, in fact. And that is why it will do you well to join me when I set out on this journey. You were a champion in your day, if I'm given to believe the stories. And your Travelers' Guild was a source of pride for Athynians everywhere. This, at a time when the Nhyle's High Council was occupied by men of action, not bogged down by speculators and theorists. With no slight to my father, I mean to restore that ideal of true initiative to the throne, when comes my time. In fact, I mean to restore a good *many* things, and I see no reason why your old Travelers' Guild shouldn't be counted among the first and foremost of them."

"A slight is a slight, even if you wish to avoid naming it as such," said Thurflyn, "and especially so when it is indemnified by the truth. He is not a bad man, your father; far from it. Nor has he been an exceptionally poor Nhyle. But an attempt to reverse these missteps of which you seem to speak—that were born of his time and from his edict—such an attempt…" for a moment, Thurflyn grasped for words, "…will require a tremendous uphill climb, the magnitude of which I am not sure one man can endure. I caution you, my lordship. You ask a lot of yourself in this task. Perhaps too much."

"A bit of irony here, isn't there? A man who once scaled the Southspur Mountains, among a host of other magnificent heights around the world by his lonesome, warns me against mounting an uphill climb?"

"Yes, except you fail to recognize that, with your climb come the burdens of familial ties, of politics, and the risk of catastrophic failure for the realm. You represent the future of Athyn, and so, by endangering yourself, you are playing with the lives of many. I played only with mine own, and upon a good many occasion, I was lucky to escape with it still intact."

"Perhaps you're right, but if indeed this errand carries with it as much risk as you say, you've done me a fine favor advancing my argument. In an endeavor where failure is no option, I will require the company of experienced advocates to help me succeed; because I'm determined to do this, one way or another. I need perspective and I need wisdom of the sort you've already granted me, here and now, in this very brief conversation. I need someone who's been there; someone who has stood atop the mountain and has looked down upon the path that led him there. A man who has circled the islands of the archipelago with naught but a skiff and a single oar, just to see all of its perspectives. After our escort to the city, we will stay there no more than three days forthcoming, and during that time, I shall send for you." Ethyn's stare was intense, "I share these plans—these sentiments—with you in strict confidence, Adrian. Speak naught of these matters until comes the time I, myself, speak freely of them again."

Thurflyn's countenance had changed since he had raised his voice, and it appeared his feelings of frustration had perhaps transformed mostly into skepticism. In the process, he had at least returned to a relative state of calm, "I can manage three days in the city, your lordship, if that be your wish."

"Very well. And I shall at least make things a bit more interesting for you. If such a timespan as equal to three days has expired, and I have yet failed to call upon you," assured Ethyn, "you have my approval on behalf of the royal seat *itself* to return here to Stief, or to venture anywhere else in this world that you please. And by this I mean to say that, after three days of silence, your tenure will be complete, and you may sever your ties to the royal host forever; retired in full, if that be your wish. But should I call for you before three days' time has elapsed, I will require your immediate response, and I cannot say how long we will be gone upon the road. Do you accept these conditions?"

"Accepted," said Thurflyn, who promptly extended a hand to shake Ethyn's own, affirming the pact. And as the man stood from his chair and made for the grand staircase, Ethyn could almost imagine Thurflyn, himself, in a seat of formative power—a Lord of Land or even a Nhyle, for that matter. *In another life, perhaps, though I suspect the man would never willingly submit to the kind of tethered life such a weighty title would require of him.*

"And Adrian," called Ethyn in addendum. Thurflyn turned to look back, and the prince added, "Thank you."

\*\*\*

It was late of hour in the Harbor Town of Stief when Ethyn Solis was awoken by voices. And although it was still night time, the silver shine of the Ancillary Moon reflected quite brilliantly off the water in the harbor, and did well to illuminate the inside of his room in the Royal League House. He gathered himself into a robe and passed by a hanger bearing formal raiment, set out by his wagon master's handlers for the morning's escort. And he pushed quietly through double doors that led to a small third-story balcony to have a look about, so that he might better understand the cause of commotion.

"I'm afraid I've not a choice in the matter," declared a man's voice from the yard below, "it's just the way it is."

"And you figured you'd take me to bed, and wait to tell me all of this until… after," said a maid's voice, squeaky and strained, "…after you've *had* me? As ever we've done since we've been together, like nothing in the least is the matter. And this, just so, the night before you're to leave me in the morning?"

"I told you, Emmy, I've no choice," repeated the man. Ethyn, squinting from his balcony, realized it was Legionnaire Midre Donygal, of his very own, newly-formed company.

The swarthy soldier continued, "I wanted to be *with* you again so badly, just once more. And I didn't want it to be any different than it's always been."

"*You* didn't want it to be any different? How very selfish of you! Gods, do you hear yourself, Midre?" Emmy—the serving maid with the blonde braids and revealing skirts, who'd handed out the keys for their rooms—began to sneer.

"I didn't mean—"

"—Then you felt it appropriate to remove yourself from my bed so casually," persisted Emmy. She was clutching tight to the collars of her night robes to keep them closed. It was apparent the pair had departed from the League House in a frazzled manner, she chasing after him (or, more likely, he after her). "You've removed yourself from my life as well, I suppose. For good, too, is that it? Was this how you'd always fixed it to be? All this time, did you *plan* to leave like this, or did this brilliant act of cruelty just occur to you *tonight*?" She was allowing her voice to shake and tremble, "I guess you've *always* known this was how you'd do it. You've always known you were leaving. How could you not have?"

"Emmy, yes, I'd known it was coming," admitted Donygal, bumbling, "but really only in the subconscious. It'd just sprung up on me, is all… I didn't want to believe the time had finally arrived, and I hated the idea of breaking it to you."

"I don't know what's worse, the way you're walking out on me now, so abrupt and so cold; or that you played me for a rotten fool from the very beginning… knowing this miserable end would come to pass. Such a fool!" Emmy hadn't indicated whether she meant Donygal or herself as the fool—quite possibly both.

"I'd never cared for anyone before," Donygal said as he watched her walk to the bulkhead and sit by the water, which still glimmered in the light of the Ancillary Moon, "I knew not the first thing about any of this—even the way I ought to act towards you when this all began. How was I supposed to figure out how it would, or *should*, eventually end? It was within but only a dream I believed this sort of thing could exist. I am hopeless in this, Emmy. Hopeless."

After long moments of staring out to sea, past the fishing and transport skiffs that bobbed and swayed on their anchor lines in the harbor's current, Emmy the serving maid finally forced herself to turn and look back at Donygal; her soldier and her muse. It occurred to Ethyn, as he bore witness from his balcony with mounting interest, that the girl must have felt she owed Donygal *something*, because to look someone in the eye (as she did now) in the midst of such discord, is to concede something of significance to that person. To concede that you're at least willing to acknowledge them. And maybe to listen. She was punishing him thoroughly with her silence, though, and Ethyn thought Donygal looked as a pathetic fool standing there in such misery. *But surely she sees something else entirely. Perhaps she sees a man she's grown to love, and nothing else…*

"What will I do, Midre? I cannot leave here, I am oath-bound to the League House, don't you know that?" The pain in her voice was unmistakable; it was pinching her vocal chords like worn-out strings on a fiddle, "Had I known all along that this would happen, perhaps I could have arranged something."

"Even if you *could* leave with me, we wouldn't be afforded the same kind of lives together," Donygal strained to say, "nothing like we've had here. If I could, Emmy, I would—"

"—No, Midre. I don't want to hear it," she interrupted, her pretty face turning cross as she stood and placed her index finger (without affection) across his mouth. And before he could say another word, she turned her back on him and stomped furiously back into the League House.

When she was gone, and Donygal was alone, Ethyn saw the man drop to his knees and bury his face in his hands. *Gods' sake, the man is a mess*, Ethyn thought. Despite having indulged in many escapades with members of the fairer gender, Ethyn could admit to himself that he'd never quite felt the ever-fabled sensation of heartbreak, at least not as Midre Donygal was surely experiencing it, in that moment. *Now, this is quite a dissimilar impression of the man than the one I'd gathered in the common room over supper. It seems soldiers are more than just men, but men with feelings. Men with lives exterior to the service. I suppose I'd do well to remember that.*

"Has something caught your attention, Ethyn?" a light voice emanated from the moonlit room, within.

Startled, Ethyn returned to his bedchamber to find the hallway door shut and locked, just as he'd left it. Yet, upon turning, he noticed there were the vaguest impressions of a silhouette standing in the corner; slight and alluring, with a flowing profile of hair. His hand instinctively rose to feel the amber stone necklace against his chest. And, just then, the Heron Bird landed on the railing of the balcony, outside; returned from its soaring and gliding, in patrol of the harbor.

"I've recalled your name correctly... haven't I, Ethyn?" the voice continued from the corner, in slow measures.

"Indeed," he finally managed to affirm.

"And I can tell... you have kept careful custody of my gift."

Though he couldn't see her, he could almost feel her eyes shifting their attention to the necklace.

"I have," he said, "per your request."

"Good," she whispered, stepping into a shadow, "good..."

Then she was gone from his presence. Again.

All too soon.

## 14 | To Be Afforded Sanctuary

*"It is perfectly common, as human nature would dictate, for a weak individual to be motivated by the sudden, unexpected weakness of another. This behavior is amplified when two subjects care for one another, and even more-so when, together, these persons face an implacable circumstance... When I am weak, you must needs be strong for me; and when you are weak, so strong shall I be for you. Force me and I will overcome, but coddle me and I will disintegrate."*
—excerpt from the personal journal of Steven Spurlock

|Planet Deaer, Castle Athyn

In the middle of the night, a dark and heavy band of clouds set in over the city, dropping heavy showers on thatched roofs with very little warning, when a girl had come upon the eastern-facing gates of Castle Athyn. By accounts, the guardsmen had known not (in the least) what to do with her when they saw her; rain-drenched and shivering as she was. So they did their best to encourage her to leave upon her own accord.

"Gated districts are closed to visitors at sundown," one watchman had told her gruffly, towering imposingly above her petite frame, "and closed to *vagrants* at all-times."

"I beg your pardon, sirs," the girl had said with measured timidity while cold raindrops splashed in volume on her forehead and shoulders, "but I believe Her Grace, the Nohnce, has made certain I am to be afforded sanctuary." She opened her right palm before them, and in it, conjured from thin air an orb of light that illuminated the silvery flecks in her emeraldine eyes.

Shocked, the watchmen stared in awe at the spherical apparition hovering over her little hand.

What the girl said held truth. Twelve years had turned since the Nohnce, Lady Mailyn Solis, had first sent word (the realm over) that anyone in possession of unnatural aptitudes was welcome to seek refuge within Castle Athyn. The Nohnce had only asked, in return, that respondents arrive willing to share their talents with the Masters of Athyn's famous Mystics House. And so, having determined this girl was no ordinary wayfarer, the guards granted her entry and the man who'd (moments before) so hastily refused her admittance wasted no time showing her the way to a well-kept, massive barn that stood proudly within the castle's east court.

"The least you could have done was leant the poor thing your cloak!" insisted a woman who had opened the barn door in answer to the watchman's incessant knocking and rapping.

Mistress Almetta was a slightly rotund, pleasant-looking woman of middling age with a cherubic face and an energetic quality. Her head was wrapped in a light blue, pointed night cap with a tassel at the peak that flipped with a certain innocence when she spoke. But even so, she seemed the sort who would suffer no fool, nor anyone's imprudent pranks, nor loud knockings and bangings in the middle of the night.

"Apologies, Lady Mistress," said the guard, "but to my understandin', we've not had a visitor of her kind for some time; countin' past since I can remember, anyways. She caught us unawares, is all, with what she'd shown she can do." He gestured with his hands as best he could to demonstrate the conjuring she had performed.

Almetta looked at the girl to assess for herself the man's claims. Before long, she turned her determined gaze back, "A watchman being caught unawares by a young girl? That's like a sea captain having been caught unawares by a guppyfish. I should have you properly scolded for that!" The tassel atop Almetta's cap spun around like a pinwheel. She put an arm around the girl and drew her in, patting her face lightly with a soft kerchief. "But 'tis well true, I suppose. Reckon five seasons or so it's been since we've made up a room for a new wieldling," she wound the kerchief up tight, and snapped it flush against the fleshy part of the guard's upper arm. "Now resume your post at the gate before I've another idea for you, which I promise you'll not favor half as much. And keep your wits about you this time, eh?!"

Almetta, who the girl gathered was the proud Keeper of the Mystics House, slammed the door behind the watchman, cursing his very existence. But once free of the gruff man's company, her countenance changed dramatically. She projected a welcoming and nurturing spirit, and showed the girl to a room at once, giving her a blanket and making up warm drinks for the both of them.

And she stayed at the girl's bedside nearly the entire night through, up in the garret space of the barn, where fussings and botherings would prove most unlikely for the newcomer.

*\*\*\**

In the morning—as soon as news of the visitor reached her ear—the Nohnce, Mailyn Solis of Athyn, had paid visitation upon the Mystics House to see the girl for herself. *How long have I hoped for something like this to happen? For someone like this to arrive?*

And she had not been disappointed.

Mailyn—outfitted in a traditional day dress bearing simple floral designs, a wool knit shawl for her shoulders, and soft leather boots—hurried to the garret space in the mystics barn. She did so with haste, indeed, but not in such an urgent fashion that her gait could have been taken for a scurry (or for heaven's sake, a *run*). Acts of haste, she believed, projected a certain lack of control over one's own business. *And if there is anything a Nohnce must project, it's control.*

Still, the anticipation she felt along the way was awfully difficult to quell.

Upon her eventual arrival to the girl's assigned dormitory in the garret, she casually let herself in through the door, in as non-threatening a manner as she could manage. The girl appeared awestruck, yet keen of mind enough (after a few moments of introduction) to express her profound gratitude for an invitation to join Athynian royalty behind the great walls of the castle. Something that proved a true comfort to the Nohnce.

"I've always known in my heart I would answer your call someday, to journey to the city," the girl confessed to Mailyn, grasping tightly to the quilted blanket covering her lap on the bed, "but I waited until I was old enough, so that when I did, I wouldn't disappoint my Lady Grace with a lack of will or confidence."

"You lack neither, child," Mailyn had answered, tilting her head affectionately, "this I can already sense in you."

"I feel as though I've been sent here," continued the girl, "in many ways, by forces greater than myself."

"Don't you worry, my dear," said Mailyn, "I know exactly what you mean."

The meeting was brief, but not so short-lived that Mailyn hadn't the opportunity to develop a strong connection to the girl, and before long, she had quit the Mystics House and hastened to her youngest son's quarters, hoping he would awaken with a pleasant (and tolerant) disposition.

She entered Tae's sleeping chamber much like she had the girl's dorm, slowly and quietly. Then, leaning over him and placing a delicate hand upon his forehead, she drew him from a deep sleep with a mild and measured account of the morning's happenings.

"...I've just come from her room in the garret of the barn," Mailyn was saying while she watched Tae tuck his head under a pillow, "she's a sweetling of a girl if ever there was one; come to us in the dark of night, soaked through and shuddering. Almetta has taken fine care of her though. And the mistress is right to call her shy, but I found her reticence only makes her more approachable... and while I know you will not care to speak to her, I insist that you visit her and welcome her in your very own unique manner."

Tae rolled away and squirmed beneath a goose-down patchwork comforter he'd had since he was a swaddled babe. Mailyn found the reaction most displeasing. "Do you hear me, Tae? Opportunities to interact with someone like her do not often come along," she persisted, "you may find that you and she have much in common."

Mailyn's youngest didn't so much as flex a muscle in response, and his stolid manner made her recoil while the silence between them filled the room.

"Taelysin Solis, you disappoint me," she said in a defeated tone, leaning back against his stone wall. She knew the quilt covering his head was muffling her voice, but she also knew he understood every word she was saying. "I haven't any idea what more I can do for you, son. I'm at a loss. You are accustomed to hearing soft words in soft tones from me, but lately I'm given to think those arrangements of ours simply must change. That *you* must change. Our approach to life *itself* must change. Surely you have noticed the Mystics House has been nothing short of a struggle for me... have you not?"

He lay quietly.

"Do you not care?"

Silence.

"Then perhaps it is time I treat you more like an adult, Tae, for my habits of babying you have gotten us nowhere... Did you know the Mystics House faced fervent opposition from your father's council from the moment I dared to propose it? That I was vehemently challenged at forum the instant I voiced the merits, the *potential* that the mystics may yield?" She said the last bit with an especially sarcastic twist of her lip. "But after thinking the notion through, and despite the unrest it had already engendered, your father ordered the Mystics House be brought to life. And, as expected, the council met his decision poorly, with loosely-veiled derision toward me, which continues to this day for my role. Councilmen are much like olyphants. They never allow themselves to forget a single thing. Don't you know that? And I've been reviled ever since."

She paused because, as was her habit, she had it in her mind to appeal to humor one last time to get through to him; one last attempt to avoid scolding him. This, in clear recognition that it had always been difficult for her to play the disciplinarian role. "Come to think upon it, there are but a few more similarities worth noting... between councilmen and olyphants, that is. Aren't there? They're big and slow... and gray," she was even speaking in playful tones; anything to elicit a response, "and don't forget the wrinkles!"

But despite her greatest attempts at getting through to him, Tae still made no reply. Not even a soft chuckle, and his unwillingness to concede to her gentle tactics finally touched (strangled) a nerve.

"You know... I've reached the limit of my patience with this, Tae. I've truly reached the limit. Have you any idea, or any appreciation for how it made me feel to oppose all those powerful ones?" she said with pain in her voice, "making myself the target of their scorn? So much drudgery and damaging discord... for what? Do you suppose I did it all for sport? That it was nothing but a twisted ruse designed for no purpose but to draw disdain from your father's council?

"Do you think I did it simply to loosen poor Enric Cursyo's miserly purse strings, just to leach gold pieces from his ledger of coin? Or maybe I did it to provoke dear old Mossa Zahyle and her scholars into some sort of competitive duel of Houses, grabbing for power... Would you believe I meant to frivolously steal resources from those who protect us;

Commander Thorngrove's Royal Legion and Orvyn Rothby's Seafaring Fleet? Or to grab attention from matters befitting the counsel of Idris Ansel?" her voice was straining to say the words. "No, Tae. It was for *you*. All of it… so that you might find your way in this world. So that you might find someone to connect with. Share something with. And I just suppose I've wished to see more from you in return than what you have given."

She waited for a moment, and when he still didn't respond, she sighed heavily and slumped down to the floor, burying her face in her hands; for her energy was simply depleted.

\*\*\*

Tae Solis remained silent beneath his covers, numbed by the disappointment he heard in his mother's voice during her lecture, which (if nothing else) strongly signaled the long-awaited arrival at her breaking point with him. It was as if he'd been struck by a lightning bolt from a clear sky. *I never knew she could grow so cross…* he thought. *And with such scant warning.*

"Sometimes I simply cannot understand you…" she said through the fingers that presently covered her mouth, from her position on the floor, "Truth be told, I don't understand much at *all* that goes on in this world." It seemed as if she were speaking private things she meant only to think to herself, but she continued on, aloud. "Sometimes I feel I cannot endure this sort of living; like I wasn't meant to encounter all of this in life…"

They were both still and silent for a few long moments. Then he heard her whimper and sniffle, and choke lightly on her own breath. She made one of those sobs that comes out sounding almost like a laugh, but is no laugh at all, then is nearly always followed by a full-bodied tear out the corner of an eye and down the side of a cheek. And slowly, he peeked out, over the top edge of the quilted coverlet and saw her there, distraught.

This was new. Tae had never seen weakness in his mother quite like this before, and he didn't know how to react. So often he had been the one to fold; the one whose face was buried in his hands. And as often, she had been the one making him feel better. She had been the one tirelessly devising ways to get through to him, to make him open up and feel better about himself any way she possibly could. He wondered if it'd been as painful for her to see him falter all those times as it was for him to finally see her, in that moment, do the same.

Slowly, he slipped out of bed and padded his way to the wardrobe to find a sleeved tunic, simple breeches, and a woolen cape to cover his shoulders with. Then he stepped into a pair of worn leather mocks and paced to the door, and he stopped to look back at her.

"Thank you," she said as if the words were drained from her, and she struggled to produce the slightest hint of a warm smile. The kind only a mother can make, despite the presence of severe anguish. And he saw her slink back against the wall with fatigue just before he quit the room.

The walk to the Mystics House took him along a private corridor to the East Wing. A foot bridge spanned the Gardens of Grace where enormous flower pedals and fern fronds burst forth below him like popcorn from their kernels in a heated pan. The bridge led to the loft level of the old barn where he imagined great heaps of hay were kept long ago, but which now held the wieldling dormitories. Some of the rooms within were closed, occupied by wieldlings currently in residence, but just as many (or more) were vacant; their doors ajar revealing tightly tucked beds that had not recently been used. *Perhaps never used... And that's just as well by me*, thought Tae. *These misfit wieldlings with their paltry aptitudes... they really have no business being here at all.*

Wieldlings had come to the castle for warm porridge and a bed fitted with clean linens, and more often than not had left within a fortnight, awash with the realization that castle life (of the order afforded them) wasn't going to be as glamorous as they'd expected. And House Solis had no grounds to force them to stay.

As such, only a handful of dedicated pupils remained, all possessing aptitudes that had failed to excite even the most eager of the Mystics Masters, and the House had ultimately fallen well short of achieving its intended goals. *Is it any wonder the House is considered a failure, with the likes of this sad lot of talentless beggars? Why should I believe this girl will prove any different?*

He thought he remembered his mother mention the girl was placed in the upper garret space, accessible only by a ladder leaning in the crux of the raftered ceiling. He figured Mistress Almetta must have placed her there because the garret was the coziest level of the barn in this season, trapping warm air that might've served best to thaw her after her chilled arrival.

Up the narrow rungs to the garret he climbed. There, he saw the pale beechwood thresholds and doors lining the hall, reflecting generous sunlight that passed through windows at either end. Most of the doors here were also ajar, revealing empty beds below dormered windows, through which he could see the hills and forests that stretched eastward for leagues on end from this height. There was a certain stillness in the silence that he found strangely inviting; like this might make for a suitable hiding place after all his current hiding spots run their course. *If only the likes of these wieldlings weren't here all the time...*

The third door on the right was closed. *This must be it,* he thought, dreading the uncomfortable interaction that was bound to follow. His pores began to flood with sweat, and his heart beat out of his chest. No matter how many times he attempted human interaction (of any kind), he could never conform to the routine conventions of conversation; could never quell his anxiety. *This is nothing more than a gleaming opportunity to make a marvelous fool of myself. What if I do something that offends her...? Most likely,* she *will do something that offends* me; *a flaming-well pleasant experience to be had, isn't it?*

*...I will regret this. I will regret this, sorely.*

He fidgeted with his cloak, loosened its collar about his neck, and tried to find a comfortable place to rest his hands. In his pockets. Arms crossed. Hands at his hips. *No! None of that will do!*

The garret suddenly felt as hot as Mistress Almetta's brick oven in the barn's kitchens below. *And about as spacious, too.* Then he thought he felt his throat swell up and a troublesome tremor lurch in his stomach. *No wonder it takes my mother's physical and emotional collapse to propel me into action. I am utterly insufferable.*

The door stood before him, a final barrier for which he was ever so grateful. It provided him one last opportunity to turn around and flee the scene. *I don't have to do this. I can bail myself out with mother later; she'll understand. She always does—*

"Come in, it's unlocked," said a soft voice from within, startling him. *Mortifying* him.

And now, he painfully supposed, he was committed to entering.

*\*\**

Tae faltered indecisively for a moment, then without much choice left, he turned the knob ever so slowly and pushed his way into the girl's room in the garret of the mystics barn. Everything in the room was bright: the linens on the bed, the white wash of the floorboards underfoot, and the plaster on the walls. All except for her curly, deep red-brown hair, which seemed to absorb the brightest of light in the space about her and produce from it a fine luster.

Her. The girl; of whom mother had spoken so highly. She sat with her back to him on a stool looking out her dormered window, her tresses cascading over her shoulders and down her back like a sparkling auburn waterfall.

"Athyn looks so beautiful from here," she said without turning from her view, "wouldn't you say?"

He stood in place silently.

When he didn't answer, she swiveled around to face him with a steely calmness; looking upon him with big doe eyes surrounded by light lashes. Hers was a delicate face of inordinate beauty—fair skin with light shades of pink upon her freckled cheeks, above generous dimples that framed her smile, pursed and polite. She appeared to have dried off suitably from the previous night's soaking, sitting barefooted and donning the plain colorless wear of the Wieldling Order; a tunic and simple drawstring breeches pulled tight at the waist and cinched at the calves to fit her smallish frame. "You must be the wordless one the Nohnce spoke of... her humble Prince Tae of Athyn," she said playfully in a formal manner of speech.

In the space of a moment, he was knocked asunder by the way her presence made him feel; her persona. Some ambient aura radiating about her. *Who is this stranger? Could this be some kind of manipulative effect of her aptitude?* He couldn't decide whether it was danger or something else altogether that he perceived, but he sensed an essence of remarkable strength residing within her. He smiled, then braided his fingers together over his chest and bowed to her in a manner one might interpret as a gesture of welcome, if a decidedly awkward one at that.

*You mean the 'Mute Prince' of Bryn Athyn*, he thought, abashed. *Yes, it is I...*

She accepted his greeting by smiling broadly, deepening her dimples. "Your Lady Mother is ever so pretty, and more kindly than I could have imagined. I never dreamed she would come visit me like she did," the girl seemed to look deeply into him with her emeraldine eyes while she spoke. "You are quite kind to visit me, as well. I owe you all my sincerest gratitude."

He stood in place and tried to work a smile, but it wasn't long before the two of them drifted into an uncomfortable pause.

"I heard you fidgeting outside the door..." she said after a bout of silence, "that's how I knew you were there. Keen hearing is one of my aptitudes, in case you were wondering." She shrugged, and suddenly her cool demeanor turned almost as shy as his, "I'm excited for the chance to join the Mystics House, but if I'm to be perfectly honest, I'm quite self-conscious about my aptitudes. I hope you will forgive me. It took every bit of resolve to conjure a demonstration for the guardsmen last night at the gatehouse. I can only imagine what performing for the Masters will be like."

*Enhanced hearing* and *conjuring, both?! She's already the most talented wieldling I know, and she's yet to even begin!*

"It would be nice to see *your* aptitudes on display sometime," she remarked, soft yet pointedly.

Before he could think to react to her subtle request, and thankfully so, Mistress Almetta whisked herself into the room from the hall. She was carrying a tray bearing three small muffins, a few apple slices, a modest wedge of cheese, and a glass of milk.

Tae's presence caught her by surprise.

"Oh dear!" she exclaimed when she saw him standing in the room, "Prince Tae, I must beg your pardon... I hadn't expected a visitor in the garret at this hour. Except of course for your fair Lady Mother, whom I called upon just as soon as the sun did rise. And wouldn't you know her to be full of such good grace; coming by to greet our talented little guest without delay." She took into her free hand a wooden stool that was sitting near the wall and moved it over to the bed, placing the tray on top. Then she turned to the girl and petted her on the top of her head, "You're quite the attraction, aren't you my little one? Our Lady the Nohnce, and now Prince Tae, both paying their visits... I should hope you have the energy for what lies ahead of you today… perhaps these morsels will help break your fast. Pray you slept well, child?"

"I did, but only for knowing I have a wonderful caretaker like you watching over me," the girl reached for the tray and took a muffin in hand, "thank you, Mistress Almetta."

"Aren't you a sweetheart?" Almetta turned to Tae displaying a grin from ear to ear, "Isn't she just a sweetheart?!"

Tae nodded his head in agreement (and meant it quite fervently).

"Now if you don't mind me going on for a bit," said the mistress, "there's something I'd always used to do on occasion of a new member's arrival. A spot of history concerning this-here barn and the Order of the Mystics, if you're willing to listen."

The girl moved to the bed so Almetta could take a seat on her the stool by the window. "That should please me very much," she said to the mistress with marked enthusiasm and a playful bounce on the mattress as she sat down and crossed her legs.

"Very well then," Almetta looked enthused. "The old histories tell it was an ancestor of the royal family Solis who'd first settled this hill we call Athyn Proper. They say he'd come to find high ground for protecting himself 'gainst looters from Mawr and others of the first settlements, like Stief and Wheatlyn and Bucklon Rowe, well before any Nhyles were fixing proper ordinances and assembling legions, and the like. Back when one's own two hands were his only protecting 'gainst harm, and each village *did* fend for itself."

Half listening to Almetta's history lesson, Tae watched the girl while she swallowed down a muffin easily enough, and then lifted an apple slice from the tray to her lips to take a delicate bite. Strangely, she seemed ill-prepared for the juice that the fruit produced, as it ran down her chin. She blotted at it, making quick, deliberate motions with a cloth napkin, and somehow Tae managed to look away before she could catch him staring. Next she took a nibble of the cheese, and the comparative saltiness made her grimace. *Has she never tasted apples or cheese before?*

"This man built a farmhouse and raised a barn," continued Almetta, "and he'd lived off the land finding the soil rich and fertile, the livestock hearty, and the weather favoring the pitch'n'sow. Then over the seasons and past his living days, his surviving kin felled the farmhouse to make way for greater structures. But the barn was built strong with stone and mortar, and survived the seasons that'd seen castle-building take over on all sides, and in every direction… Then Ages'd gone by, and the hill got looking more like a village than a farm, and the towers began rising. Then the walls and keeps had gone up."

Tae couldn't take his eyes from the girl. He saw she had eaten another small muffin and was working on a third. He doubted she had any intention of drinking the milk. She hadn't even so much as glanced at it.

"Mighty Nhyles came and went, but the barn still stood," Almetta was saying, "right here in the center of the city. Then some scoreful of years ago, our Lady Nohnce was arranging for us to make up this old place for the training of the mystics. Master Talyn Slynth's been leading us from the first, and yours truly, the Keeper of the House, making sure all things and everyone is staying clean, fed, and in order… Must'a been some reason this barn did survive all those hard times. I'd always said it'd make for a perfect spot for the mystics training, being darn near packed-full with the spirits of man and beast as it is, fixing to protect us from our enemies by all sorts of unnatural means!" When Almetta finished, she laughed hard, covering her mouth with her kerchief.

"It sounds like I have much to learn," said the girl, smiling along.

"Oh you do, sweetheart, you do," answered Almetta, "and they say there's naught a better time than the present. What say we make for the training hall downstairs and show you 'round a bit?" The mistress stood up and gathered the tray before heading out the door. The girl, who hadn't touched the milk, followed close behind.

"My name is Brychen, if you didn't already know," she said, turning to see if Tae intended to come along, "will you stay with me through the morning? I could use the company of a friend, I think."

Tae nodded ardently. *If that be your wish, then yes, of course I shall…*

## 15 | A Mutual Diplomatic Station

*"We do ourselves an enormous favor by developing a fundamentally sound formula for personal discretion. A whole world of anguish awaits those who ignore the consequences of momentary impulse. And so, if it is impulse upon which we, at times, must act, we ought to pray our instinctive reactions are strong, and prudent."*
—excerpt from the personal journal of Steven Spurlock


|Planet Deaer, Athyn, The Harbor Town of Stief

Each member of Prince Ethyn Solis' new company had found their way to the common room of the Royal League House for sugared muffins, poached eggs, fresh strawberries, and cups of warm tea before gathering outside in the brisk, salty air to load up their mounts in the yard. The aroma of the living sea filled the prince's nostrils. It was enough to rouse him from the lethargy of a restless night, and for that he was grateful. He would need to be alert in his dealings with the ambassador from the realm of Maelnlock, during what promised to be a rather lengthy escort. It would take no less than the course of the day (straight through to sundown) to make it back to the city. Escorts from Stief never progressed any faster than that.

It was yet early, and the streets were scarcely populated but for a small flock of children at play, and a mutt and a stray feline or two. Only a mere scattering of gulls glided on the breezes overhead, singing nothing more than short, faint calls between them. Ethyn took the point position, and the rest of his company followed behind, riding their mounts at a slow canter.

The prince had reached an impasse in thought, which was for him an uncommon condition. He was well trained in the discipline of nimble decision making, and so he did not often trouble himself with weighing gritty details, at length. That isn't to say he was a hasty arbiter of his thoughts; just that he was a young man who (quite determinedly) trusted his gut feelings. And yet, after witnessing a most passionate discord between two lovers, he'd spent a good portion of the previous night pondering what he ought to do in response.

"Company, halt," he then commanded, in abrupt fashion, with his right hand raised in the air. He drew a breath, and the sweet scent of the sea wafted through his nasal passages again, adding quite appropriately to his sentimental mood. Then he reined his mount around to face the men queued behind him, and said with stern resoluteness, "Legionnaire Midre Donygal... to me *at once*."

Donygal formed a perplexed look on his face, then spurred his mount toward the front of the column. The legionnaire's quizzical demeanor was shared in likeness by the rest of the assembled company, but Ethyn paid their expressions no mind. And while Donygal approached, the wind gusted for a moment, its edges carrying a hint of the past evening's chill that penetrated Ethyn's fine raiment; his twill-embellished gray cloak with gilded buttons, and his silken scarves. In the background, the Royal League House again stood boldly against the deepening blue sky, and (half hidden by a post draped with lobster traps and fishing poles) the prince's keen eyesight caught the long blonde hair of a serving maid named Emmy. *She's still sore at him, but she'd take him back at the drop of a spinner lure, that's for certain.*

"Master Ethyn," said Donygal, as if reporting for duty; halting his mount at Ethyn's proper attention, "your command, my lord?"

Ethyn raised his voice for all the company to hear, "Legionnaire Donygal, I hereby extend your term in Stief, indefinitely. You are to resume your assignment here this instant and carry on your duties in the same manner as they've demanded of you this past season through, with no deviation, until otherwise ordered by the royal seat. This means you will continue no further on this escort." Ethyn knew most guests of the League House had surely overheard portions (in the least) of last night's romantic drama by the docks, and so his companions would understand the motive behind his extension of Donygal's assignment in the Harbor Town. *Or at least they would* think *they understand.*

"You may take your leave, Midre," he said, making the dismissal final.

"As you command, my lordship," said Donygal with notes of unmistakable astonishment, relief, and joy evident in his eyes. The company watched as Donygal turned his mount back toward the League

House and leaned into a half gallop, shouting the good news to the porch upon his approach to the yard. And before Ethyn could turn his own steed around, Emmy the serving maid was leaping into the legionnaire's extended arms, and he pulled her up into the saddle, locking tight in a passionate exchange of intimacies.

Aryk Frierstag pulled up next to Ethyn and asked, plenty loud enough for the rest of the company to hear, "Have you the authority to dismiss a legionnaire from assignment, Ethyn?"

"It seems I have made it so, my dear Aryk," answered the prince, passing an intentional glance in Adrian Thurflyn's direction, as if to say: *And I shall make a good many things so, in due course.* "Besides," he continued (lowering his voice to a volume such that only Aryk could hear), "there may soon come a time I'll have needs for an honest-to-goodness, faithful strong-arm stationed here in Stief. I can already tell Donygal is a good man, and quite strong enough, indeed. I needed only implant an unwavering sense of faithfulness within him."

"But all men of the legion are faithful to the seat, by their duty," Aryk said with a terribly authentic flavor of naiveté.

Ethyn gave him a slanted look, "Even so, not many a deed can *ensure* such steadfast loyalty as can the gift of time with a significant other. As a matter of fact, I expect this pardon will pay off handsomely, in time. And if it doesn't, then who should care? This world could use a little more unfettered passion, could it not?"

Aryk almost seemed as if he had more to say, but decided not to venture another word, and instead, slowed his mount to rejoin with the others.

When it seemed to Ethyn that proper order had been restored to the mission at hand, and his remaining men had fallen in line behind him, he added for all to hear, "Onward we go to fetch the ambassador!"

\*\*\*

Not long after his dismissal of Midre Donygal from the escort, Prince Ethyn Solis and his company came upon a magnificent row of manor homes, where lived the ambassadors from foreign lands both near and far. A gaggle of mounted men waited about the center of the cobblestone road, in front of one particularly lavish house. They were 'Lockian helmsmen dressed in light uniform ensembles, and they were content enough to respond warmly to Ethyn and his companions' offerings of greeting.

Ever a paradox worth noting, despite the discordant history between the two realms, Ethyn had never met a forthrightly confrontational 'Lockian citizen. Perhaps their friendliness was a façade, but if so, 'twas a mighty fine façade at that, for the interaction always seemed quite genuine to Ethyn. Yet by that same token, Ethyn had learned confrontation was all but a certainty when dealing with the venerable Ambassador Salmen Fleurys. It made him wonder just how representative 'Lockian diplomats really were of the will of their own people. Then again, his only real interaction with 'Lockian leadership had been with Fleurys, himself. *So perhaps we're dealing with nothing but a single rotten apple in an otherwise healthy and flavorful harvest.*

It was following that very thought that, out of the elevated stately manor house (in front of which the companies were gathered), the Maelnlockian Ambassador to Athyn, Salmen Fleurys, emerged from an enormous door. Ordinarily, the ambassador from Maelnlock, ever pleased to garner attention, would have worn his finest raiment, adorned with the most garish of trappings, for a visit to Castle Athyn. It seemed, however, there was reason to forgo custom this time around, as his outfit was decidedly common. He bore a light vest over a cotton-woven chemise and riding pants tucked into scuffed boots, making Ethyn feel quite like a buffoon, outfitted in tip-top regalia as he was. And after taking a rather extended survey of the persons gathered, the ambassador acknowledged the prince with an undeniable air of austerity.

Sitting straight in his saddle, the prince chose to return the ambassador's frosty greeting with humility: "It has been too long since I last paid a visit to Stief," he announced, "I should thank you greatly, Mister Ambassador, for providing me an excellent excuse to return; if only for a night."

The introduction incited a mere moustache-muffled grunt from the ambassador; nothing more. Nothing so much as a word in spoken response.

"It's still just as beautiful as ever I remember it..." Ethyn concluded, blood rushing to his face at the recognition he'd just been snubbed; and blatantly so, at that. Fleurys was an older chap, no mistaking that, but he exuded a youthful arrogance, and when he descended the stairs to the roadway, Ethyn remembered something deceptive about the man's form and movement. Despite his near-elderly appearance, Fleurys' body was quite lithe; as physically fit as were his helmsmen, or even better so. Ethyn found the absurdity of it all entirely vexing, especially taken in tandem with the man's blatant slighting and overall snobbish demeanor. The combination molded the ambassador into a perfect object of disdain for the prince. *Acknowledge my greeting, you wretched, old whelp, or so help me...*

The ambassador took a moment beside his mount (which had been brushed thoroughly and saddled for him), pulled on his leather riding greaves, and then finally struck a response in brusque, lightly-accented tones, "So the dog sends his pup to execute his ill-favored chores any longer, is that it then?"

Ethyn was taken aback. *Power play right from the outset; not even a veiled attempt at false pleasantries...* So he deflected and parried, "I don't make a habit of wasting my time, Mister Ambassador, and neither does my father." He felt his temples flare with contempt, but he wouldn't allow himself to lose his temper so quickly. Not before the escort had even begun. "He has much to attend to this day. Of course, not least of which, his personal preparation for your highly-anticipated visit."

"Highly anticipated, am I?" said Fleurys with a chortle and a stroke of his little beard.

*Watch what you say,* Ethyn cautioned himself. *He'll read into every word if you let him, and he'll lure you to anger with his own.* "Indeed, as ever we anticipate visitation of all such prominent guests, I should say; and certainly no less for our friends from Maelnlock," he countered, biting back the words he truly wanted to say.

But the ambassador bellowed from deep within his chest. "Friends?" he said with an especially wry grin, turning to face a 'Lockian helmsman beside him. His laughter mounted as he continued, "Did he say *friends?!*" Outright laughter followed as he leaned forward and favored his stomach, as if it may burst from the effort, amused by the mere suggestion that a Solis of Athyn should ever claim friendship with a steward of Maelnlock.

Fleurys finally subdued himself, joining his five helmsmen by climbing atop his mount and placing a felted cap upon his undersized head. "Let us get on with this," he declared through fleeting chuckles and without the merest decline in his puckish manner, "you've arrived late enough as it is; I near as well left without you. Would have, had I'd known it were merely the pup and a sordid band of common soldiers coming to see me to the city." The dig against Ethyn's company of men was a low one, even for Fleurys.

"You know," said Ethyn, enflamed by the continued discourtesy. He looked back toward the manor house from which Fluerys had just departed, "The royal host has been on search for a new holiday home. Perhaps the high seat might well soon declare a suitable locale. And, if I may suggest, a certain luxurious manor house in this particularly affluent district of Stief would seem a mighty fine candidate. That is, if one should soon become available for any reason. I hear rent's cheap in the Mercantile District's *Mayfly Alehouse* this time of season, should you find yourself in need of a new roof over your head." Ethyn hadn't planned to speak with such vitriol so quickly, but Fleurys had left him no choice. *Parse my words now, and I'll be parsing much more than that by the time I'm sitting the throne.*

The subtle threat forced Fleurys (for the first time) to make eye contact with Ethyn as they began to ride, "I see the pup can bark, but has he a vicious bite to match? Pray we'll not find needs for a collar…"

Fleurys scanned the faces of Ethyn's companions more closely as they began to ride along. "Oh my, is that Sir Adrian Thurflyn I see amongst us, the traveling guildsman?!" he asked, and erupted full with laughter once again, "I can hardly wait to see the look on the Nhyle's face when he sees his pup's brought the banished guildsman back to the city for a triumphant homecoming. Oh this is too good. Too good, indeed!!"

"You dare insult a dignified member of my company?" Ethyn, for a moment, allowed his temper to overtake his speech craft.

"It is quite alright, Ethyn," interjected Thurflyn from behind, loud enough for both parties to hear. Then the guildsman rode astride Ethyn to share a private note, "Fleurys is not out of place to question my return to the city, though I surely would have been had I done the same last night. I will not challenge your decision to take me with you, to the castle or beyond—wherever it is you are planning to go—but you must know, what the ambassador has said bears truth. Your father will not favor my presence amongst your company, nor among any of his ranks within the castle. When last I departed from the Proper, it was by your father's edict, and it was not on the friendliest of terms. I believe it was only the memory of your grandfather's great affection for me that prompted my agreeable assignment in Stief. Elsewise, your father may have banished me outright."

"I'll have none of this," countered Ethyn in private to his honored guildsman, "you're nothing short of a champion to our realm."

"Perhaps I was, once, but it is sadly no longer so, no matter how much I may wish it otherwise," admitted Thurflyn. "In fact, I'm a bit relieved Fleurys has revealed this truth to you. You're better off leaving me behind; as you've dismissed Legionnaire Donygal. I've no forlorn lover agonizing o'er my departure, calling my name in dismay, but neither have I a rightful place in your company. I fear I would only weigh you down."

Ethyn internalized the new information while looking back at the ambassador with a sigh. Fleurys returned his gaze, smirking and whistling as he rode. *One more derisive comment like that, ambassador, and you'll find out what I have in store for you. Then we'll see who'll be smirking and whistling the long way home.*

Ethyn continued softly to Thurflyn, "I'll not idly dismiss the principle member of my company. Not for pride, nor for any other reason presumed by an old whelp in a felt cap. Fall in with the others, and let us assert ourselves properly."

Thurflyn did as he was commanded while Ethyn raised his voice for the rest to hear, "I've no misgivings about *your* company of helmsmen, ambassador. In fact, they seem as well-rounded and astute as any troupe, and we shall be honored to host them however long they wish to stay within the walls of our great city. In return, I will demand full respect for my own company, each and every member of it to the last, with no exception. In this, I trust I have made myself perfectly clear. Now, let us make for the city without further delay. After all, you still seek audience with my lord father, do you not?" And he urged his mount to the front of the procession with conviction. *Let's pray we make it there afore sunset. I doubt my patience will hold out any longer than will the daylight.*

\*\*\*

Ethyn Solis knew that ancient Athynian custom required the highest rank of any escort to ride beside their guests of distinction, while all members of subordinate companies should ride no less than two mount's lengths behind. By now, Ethyn's retinue of legion soldiers and their supply wagons had also gained their footing on the road, at a good distance. Separation from armed handlers was a sign of good faith and trust; a showing that was meant to polish off any ill tidings that may have lingered from past exchanges. It was also a personalized signal to any foreign dignitary that—unlike the once color-laden sails littering Stief's Harbor, turned pale by the sun over time—base courtesy and tradition had not yet faded on the shores of Athyn.

Given the present circumstances, however, the prince took a private moment to curse ancient Athynian custom.

He rode directly beside Ambassador Salmen Fleurys. The arrangement exacerbated the tension that had arisen upon the morning, only now it was broiling silently, as neither prince nor ambassador ventured a word since leaving the Harbor Town's limits. Fleurys had honored the traditional riding formation without resistance, though Ethyn sensed the act of compliance was tainted from the outset. *No doubt he's only biding his time until he might hurl the next barbarous insult in my direction, but I'll not grant him the satisfaction of letting it bother me.*

Ethyn had come prepared for a showdown with the ambassador; armed with an array of retorts designed to combat any degree of opposition Fleurys may throw at him. He wasn't about to let the old man upstage him on his own turf. His pride wouldn't allow it. So he'd leveraged the full capacity of the House of Scholars for whatever anecdotes they could uncover about the diplomat from Maelnlock. Something he could use in a pinch, if momentum needed to be equalized. And they had provided him with just the kind of morsel he needed.

*Identifying your adversary's motive is the first step to defeating him,* Scholars Master (and High Council member) Mossa Zahyle often said. *Understanding your adversary, himself—what makes him tick from within—is the first step to controlling him.*

The mounts of both parties had established a synchronized cadence as they traversed the causeway that bisected the Marshes of Mewth—the natural barrier between Athyn's northern coastline and the mainland. Waterlogged terrain laid low and spread (uninterrupted) for leagues to either side; grasses sprouting cat tails from the wetlands stood high against the fair firmament. At times, the tall swaying bulrush bowed over the path, quite like swords held up by soldiers forming an archway at a ceremonial procession. And, perhaps eased by the placidity of their surroundings, Ethyn finally broke the silence while the sun's rays were beginning to penetrate his cape with soothing warmth, "If you please, I ask that you pass my greatest wishes along to his lordship, Emperor Maeflewr, upon your next return to Maelnlock."

"Mmm-hmm," murmured Fleurys, minimally, in response.

"As well as his lovely daughter, Princess Irulan," added Ethyn with a reminiscent air. It was just a few seasons past that House Solis last visited the realm of Maelnlock for pleasure. Ethyn recalled sailing Athyn's Royal Schooner *The Swiftsail* across the vast Central Sea, and had taken a most inspired carriage ride from the 'Lockian shore to the Emperor's palace, known there as *The 'Lock*. That was where he had met the fair Irulan Maeflewr, princess of Maelnlock, and she had danced periodically about his dreams ever since.

It was shortly after his family's arrival, while dining in the Emperor's Hall, that their eyes—prince and princess—had first met across a table, set formally with wares of polished silver. There'd been a half dozen courses served of the finest of 'Lockian fare, which all proved delectable beyond reproach. But nothing served upon the dining table that night had been as desirable as were Irulan's immaculate eyes. Nor her hair, which was voluminous and wild, but set formally (artfully) by a talented handmaid to accentuate her positively flawless facial structure. She'd stared hauntingly in his direction for moments on end, and he was enchanted all the more by her distinct expression, which spoke of a genuine, prevailing distaste for him and his entire family. *Something forbidden lay within that stare; something so intriguingly wrong that it begs to be set right.*

It was a time of relative peace. The historic tension between families Solis and Maeflewr had been an abstraction then; present but not (in any tangible way) destructive. In fact, by its conclusion, the visit had proven quite a pleasurable affair, indeed. And by all accounts, the discourse over those several days had strengthened relations between the realms to new levels. For his part, however, Ethyn took but one thing home with him from that trip, and that was the indelible image of Princess Irulan's stare across the dining table—so very raw, so provocative, and so piercing as it was.

When his mind finally vaulted back into the present, he found himself riding beside the ambassador again; a regretful reminder of his current task, and of the souring of the relationship between families Solis and Maeflewr that had occurred over the last few years. One hand holding the reigns to his mount; the other felt through his tunic for the outline of the stone that hung by the necklace 'round his neck. *So many casual encounters I've had, like the one in my room last night; all too fleeting. The mere flirtations and the indulgent physical forays as well, yet I find myself in wonderment of how a truly meaningful relationship must feel.*

"The Emperor's fine host prepares a generous welcoming for his visitors, as I recall," continued Ethyn, "Not unlike those for which our own Athynian customs call. As ever, we will be handsomely rewarded for our day's worth of travel. I hope your men carry healthy appetites for High Athynian cuisine."

It was always customary for a visiting dignitary and his company to participate in the Athynian royal host's evening-time traditions; to eat from the table of House Solis upon nightfall and to sleep within the confines of Castle Athyn as honored guests. They would then wake the next morning, when they might be more refreshed and clear-minded, to eat a hearty breakfast before engaging in official dialogues. Though the customs were ill-fitting of the negative relationship Fleurys insisted on maintaining with Athynian leadership, both the Nhyle and Fleurys had always suspended their pride to uphold the image of a cohesive diplomatic (and inter-personal) bond. Departure from such an image would signal a critical breakdown. They both respected the fact that a serious wedge between their two realms could yield dire consequences, the world-over. It was all a farcical charade to be sure, but a departure from custom (by either party) could signal the beginning of the end... of many things.

"Mmm…" grumbled Fleurys again behind his moustache, exhibiting an apparent disinterest in the customs and fine cuisine that awaited them.

Ethyn turned around and saw his companions conversing merrily with Fleurys' helmsmen. *Why couldn't I have been born to a tailor, or an herbalist, or a worker of irons and steels? Aryk is right not to envy my attachment to a future of politicking… Gods, this is painful.*

"I fear we've gotten off on a sour note," said Ethyn in an attempt, again, to break through the conversational standoff, "a note both of us can ill-afford to carry for long, I'm afraid; given our mutual station."

Fleurys formed a look of exasperation, "Mutual station, you say? Is that the reason the Nhyle has sent his naïve pup to play diplomat on this little errand of escort… to suggest there exists a *mutual station* between myself and the likes of *you*?" His accent dripped with pretentiousness.

"You flatter yourself, Mister Ambassador," answered Ethyn, put off by the continuance of Fleurys' deliberately condescending tone. "A suggestion of mutual station between the two of us could only be considered a courtesy unto you. If one of us must reach down to the other's level, it is surely *I* to *yours*," he said, "collecting you and bringing you back to the castle was but one of many important purposes attached to this latest tour I've taken, about mine own realm."

"*Your* own realm?" Fleurys contested, "I should like to see the looks on the Athynian people's meager faces when they discover a tyrant intends to inherit their throne."

*Tyrant?!* Ethyn expected Fleurys to engage in aggressive discourse, but this seemed excessive. *There is something amiss here; he surely possesses some kind of agenda, but I'll not back down from a fight, if a fight is what he wants.* "I should like to see the look on your face the day I come into the throne. My people will love me as they've never loved a Nhyle before. Though it ought not surprise anyone, should some of my actions lead *you* to perceive me as a tyrant. No, I trust I shall carry little enough concern for that at all."

Fleurys simply laughed at Ethyn's threats, which he very clearly dismissed as such meaningless noise. And once he caught his breath from laughing, he said simply; cryptically:

"Your father shall die…"

The words shocked the prince into disbelief. *Did he just threaten my father?* And Ethyn cleared his throat, "I will ask you, Mister Ambassador, to explain the meaning and intent in what you have just said."

The ambassador paused extendedly, mumbling beneath his breath for a while and then finally said, "What I mean to say is, I doubt the Nhyle will surrender his realm to you before such a time as comes his death. For I ask myself whether I believe he would willingly bear witness to the destruction of his legacy that your obvious incompetence will inevitably cause. And that answer is, quite simply, *No.* I sincerely hope I am wrong, though. I might derive a certain amount of pleasure from watching it all fall asunder; sooner rather than later."

Ethyn knew it might come to this; that the ambassador may provoke him to such an extent as to measure the outer limits of his self-control. Fleurys was testing him; feeling out Ethyn's boundaries and searching for weaknesses, and the prince had simply had enough of it. *Time to call in the reserves...*

"It confounds me," remarked Ethyn with staged calmness, "how a man could wish such tragedy upon his very own land."

"And you suggest I wish harm upon Maelnlock?" Fleurys rasped, "You're even thicker-headed than I'd presumed."

"I suggest no such thing, ambassador," declared Ethyn, "not Maelnlock, but Athyn herself."

"Athyn is my very own land you say?" Fleurys smirked. "By what terms may an ambassador belong to a foreign land? You speak rabble."

"Do I?" countered Ethyn, "Please, I implore you to interrupt me when I reach an inconsistency. Your mother was born and raised in Mawr of Athyn. Your father was a 'Lockian soldier passing through this land during one of the many incursions of the previous century. He paid your mother a casual visit of a most promiscuous capacity and moved on, casting her aside like a used *rag*, perhaps never knowing he had planted the seeds of your existence within her eager self. Your fully-Maelnlockian appearance suggests his traits held severely dominant over your mother's, dismissing any superficial trace of Athynian blood, when looked straight in the eye. But you know the truth and have known your whole life-long. Your lineage bears strong holdings in our fair realm of Athyn, your early seasons of life even, and you've hidden the truth of those holdings deep within the recesses of your mind for fear of inevitable subjugation from your House of employ should the truth ever emerge into the light of day. Isn't that so, Mister Ambassador?"

*How's* that *for playing diplomat, you feted fool?*

With Ethyn's declaration, Fleurys became red-faced with fury, "*Eager?* You dare name my mother a whore, you princeling puissant?!" The ambassador snarled in a raucous and bitter tone and continued with like fervor, "From whence does this false and vile information pass? I demand to know!"

Behind them, the 'Lockian helmsmen stirred in their saddles at the sound of their dignitary's elevated voice, placing their hands near their hilts in cautioned confusion. Aryk and Othys, Thurflyn, and Balyn Galdur readied themselves as well, while the two escort companies broke awkwardly from their friendly discourse and parted to either side of the causeway, facing each other with sensory and adrenaline levels suddenly maximized.

The escort had come to an abrupt and complete halt.

Ethyn backed his mount away as one of the 'Lockian helmsmen, the captain (if Ethyn were forced to wager) sauntered his horse beside Fleurys for a private conversation. The two began speaking in hushed voices, their body language suggesting the swordsman was attempting to calm Fleurys down; but despite these efforts, Fleurys remained animated; irate.

Then Adrian Thurflyn again arrived at Ethyn's side: "It isn't the first time I've seen a haughty diplomat fall to pieces," he said quietly, "but I'm curious what it is you've said to make him react in such a way. What is there to make from this talk of mothers and whores?"

"Our Scholars have recently supposed Fleurys may be of Athynian descent," answered Ethyn, "so I've simply put him on the spot to test the assertion's accuracy. And I would have to say, based on his reaction, it seems quite accurate, indeed."

"Master Ethyn, if I may interject," said Thurflyn. "We'd learned much about the world by the time your grandfather vested in me his confidence to bring the Traveler's Guild into existence, and made me its Master," Thurflyn then readjusted himself in his saddle, "but perhaps the most important of those lessons was the realization that everything in this world is relative; that cultures differ… that our perceptions of the world often do not align with those held by peoples from other lands for a multitude of reasons: differences in belief systems, how the world came to exist, how we *ourselves* have come into existence; differences in communication, be it verbal or non-verbal; different emphases on values; and differences even in our diet or climate. But even despite all these differences, or perhaps *because* of them, when we tread beside those of separate cultures, we must do so lightly and with respect."

"That is a fine lesson, Master Thurflyn..." the prince sat silently for a moment before continuing, "...for traveling peddlers and juvenile pupils in tutor. Unfortunately, it is not so apt, nor welcome, in this circumstance. This is an earnest battle for power that we find ourselves locked in, and I've designed a future for myself devoid of consistent, submissive pandering to the likes of this, or *any* ambassador. Do you understand that?"

"Very well, your lordship," said Thurflyn, while shaking his head with a casual sense of disapproval and returning to the company.

Ethyn was in no mood for a critique. After all, there would come a day when his word would be law, and the people (the diplomats, the High Council, and everyone else) would have to act in accordance with his orders, without question. *They may as well start acclimating themselves to that reality, here and now.*

The helmsman (the presumed captain) who'd been speaking with Fleurys, appeared to have succeeded in calming the ambassador down a trifle and was presently guiding his mount toward Ethyn. He spoke, not in unfriendly tones, "The ambassador would like to continue on his way to the Proper of Athyn with civility and dignity," he said in an accented tongue, "and in doing so would prefer to ride privately among his own. He knows the way."

"I thank you for relaying this message, sir," answered Ethyn, "we shall continue along the road to the city as the ambassador requests." *In this case, a departure from custom is more than welcome, actually.* The 'Lockian nodded and returned to Fleurys, who spurred his mount and commanded his delegation onward, in the lead position.

And without paying the ambassador so much as a further glance, Ethyn waved his companions on to resume their pace to Athyn Proper, following tensely behind.

**16 | A Feather Caught in an Upward Draft**

*"Life is a performance. Our successes are based largely on our ability to perform to the satisfaction of others. And when it comes to performances, the difference between those that fail and those that succeed boils down to one thing: confidence in one's own ability. Confidence is the greatest cheat of all. Even those with poor abilities can succeed on the wings of false confidence, when it is persistent enough. Conversely, even those with superior abilities will fail miserably when confidence eludes them. And so, it should come as no surprise that the world is like play putty in the hands of the talented few with confidence to spare; in this life, and the next."*
—excerpt from the personal journal of Steven Spurlock

|Planet Deaer, Castle Athyn

Tae Solis saw Master Talyn Slynth standing on a mat before the resident wieldlings when he arrived with Mistress Almetta and the new girl, Brychen, on the training room floor of the Mystics House. The space was expansive, divided only by massive oak columns and raised beams supporting the ancient structure and the dormitories above. A set of immense barn doors stood open to allow a spring breeze to waft in, freshening the air, and making for a sensational view of the Gardens of Grace, which enveloped the courtyard just outside.

"Let's take a break," Slynth said to his group of wieldlings, who had been replicating his hyperextended poses and movements, "please take to your individual exercises for the rest of the morning through midday." His command seemed to gratify some of his pupils, but others cast glances laced with disdain toward the newly-arrived Tae. Strolling off, their assorted postures projected arrogance and resentment. *Either they see the new girl as a threat or they've found yet another reason to shun me. Perhaps it is both.*

"I leave you in the good hands of Master Slynth now, Brychen, and of course our dear Prince Tae," declared Mistress Almetta, "but remain assured, girl, that I'm never far away should you have needs for me, you hear?" Then she ambled off toward the kitchens.

"Rumor of your arrival has spread quickly," said Slynth, reaching a hand forward and placing it on Brychen's shoulder. Slynth was a tall, fit man, aged barely beyond his fortieth year. His light hair was short, and he wore a strong face with a squared jaw line that flexed when he spoke, "Welcome to the House of the Mystics. Come with me… both of you."

Tae and Brychen followed him to a corner of the barn where wooden desks sat in neat rows. "You will find everything you require for your development as a wieldling here," said Slynth, still focused on the girl. "If you discover a need for something you do not have, let me know immediately, and I will get it for you. For all matters of housekeeping, you may turn to Mistress Almetta." He gestured to a pair of desks for the two to have a seat, and they complied.

"Brychen; is that right?"

"Yes, sir," she answered.

"And where are you from, Brychen?"

"The Village of Kyrie, east of the Durnbeck Forest," she said.

"You're not terribly far from home here in Athyn Proper, but I still might not have expected someone of your size to travel here from Kyrie alone."

"Size is known to cloak strength, at times. I can well protect myself, sir."

"And of your parentages?" Slynth prodded, "Have they knowledge of your whereabouts?"

*Boy, he isn't wasting any time; lodging an interrogation on her first morning here,* thought Tae.

"Neither my father nor my mother know of where I am," she said. Tae thought he detected her nerves beginning to waver, "Unless they have some means to look upon me, from up above."

"I see…" Slynth cleared his throat, "I'm sorry for your loss. I shall not ask of them again, as I'm sure their passing is not a thing you wish to dwell upon."

"It is a thing I wish not to burden you or the House with. It is done, and it is past."

"You've quite a mature outlook on life. May I ask your age?"

"I am six years past ten but only a short time from seven past ten," she was regaining her cool disposition. *She is nearly of my same age,* thought Tae, who was, indeed, newly turned seven years past ten.

"What compelled you to bring yourself to the gates of the castle last night? Why not sooner?"

Brychen peered at Tae for a moment, then looked down at the desktop in front of her before replying. "Because… while I greatly respect their potential for aiding virtuous pursuits, I have never much favored the notion of displaying my aptitudes to the witness of others, sir."

Slynth looked at Tae and laughed, "You're not the only one, my dear. Our prince here has taken aptitude shyness to the very limits of my patience. Someone must have it in for me. If you're any bit as bad as he is, then between the two of you, I'm like to pull my hair out in-full by the end of spring's turn. I assure you, though, I'll do whatever it takes to draw forth the best in you."

"I'm grateful for your kindness, sir," she said, "and I promise to repay you with my finest efforts."

"Very well. Because I must remind you, our Lady Nohnce asks only one thing of her wieldlings when they join the House; that they share their talents, their aptitudes, with us," he said. "If even one wieldling withholds their talents, the House becomes a fraud, and the Nohnce would have no choice but to grant admittance to any homeless traveler seeking shelter and food for nothing in return. This cannot resemble a half-way house. Not in any manner. You must make efforts to improve upon your abilities, or you will be left to fend on your lonesome, returned to your place outside the castle limits. Does that make sense?"

"Perfect sense," she agreed, nodding her head while her big eyes gleamed and her chin furrowed with a certain resoluteness.

"Now, I would feel terribly inadequate as a Mystics Master if I didn't inspire you to display, at the very least, the aptitudes you'd shown the guardsmen last night. Please do not let it be said that Ulryk Gravesbane, the saw-toothed gate watchman, is a finer mystics tutor than I!" Slynth's challenge was delivered with a grin-infused chuckle.

Brychen looked at Tae again and back at Slynth.

"Yes, sir," she said, standing up from the desk and taking a few steps toward the center of the training room floor. She looked around to see if any of the other wieldlings were watching and saw no one but the prince and the Master sitting before her. Then she opened the palm of her hand, and closed her eyes, concentrating for long moments; focused and intense.

Yet, nothing happened.

The scene was all too familiar to the prince, only he was usually the one failing under the spotlight.

Standing on the tips of her toes, her hand began to shake and sweat beaded over her delicate face. But still nothing.

Tae wanted to walk to her and make it known she didn't have to do *anything* she didn't want to do. But she was shaking even more now, her whole body over, like she must've shaken while chilled to the bone the evening prior.

*No! You don't have to do this! I'll let you stay in the castle as my own honored guest!* Tae was cringing while he watched. *Without needs for aptitude displays or anything else!! With all the muffins you can possibly want and a wonderful view of the forests! And you won't have to drink any milk, either…*

She was shaking violently now, her face turning red, and her hair was beginning to float on end above her head, as if weightless. Then her body began to drift into the air, levitating like a feather caught in an upward draft, her feet lifting from the ground, dangling at the end of her legs.

"The gods… Tell me I'm not dreaming this," whispered Slynth, wide-eyed in disbelief.

*Tell her she can stop!!!* Tae was incensed Slynth would allow her to continue to push herself so hard, but he was too mystified by what he was seeing (and far too timid, besides) to act. *No one said a thing about her levitating last night; this is simply… unreal.* Then in an instant, they saw something else. An orb conjured from thin air in the palm of her hand. It cast a dull light against her slight form while she remained suspended, above the floor. She stared at its glow, and her hair spread out wildly on end now, as if gravity had reversed itself upon her, pulling her up from above.

Unawares of these goings on, at that moment, Mystics Master Rak Hyon walked into the training barn, letting the door shut behind him with a bang. Startled, Brychen twisted toward him (instinctively upon reflex) and lost control of the orb while it suddenly doubled, then quadrupled in size; and before she could compensate for her alarm, the orb was projected toward Hyon at blinding speed.

Hyon—just as tall as Slynth, yet more muscular and a few years younger—saw the projectile, and on sheer impulse weaved a ward with his hands to catch the orb a fist's width from his chest. It seemed to take all his strength to suspend it before himself, fighting to keep it from plowing into him. Sparks flew from the edges of the orb in contact with the ward's webbing, singeing nearby columns and rough-spun mats on the floor, forcing him backwards; the soles of his boots sliding, scraping, and digging ruts along the surface by sheer force.

Brychen's feet found the floor again, exhausted, but she pressed forward, running to Hyon to regain control of her orb. She cupped her hands around the orb and screamed as Hyon continued to keep it at bay. Her hair flew back as if she were standing in a wind storm at the edge of the world while she kept her firm hold on the construct she had made.

Yet it was no use.

When Slynth ran to join them, his attempts to relieve his fellow Master were equally helpless.

And apart from it all, Tae watched in terror underneath a desk.

Slowly, the orb began to shrink while Brychen toiled at its mass, and she finally (with an enormously strained effort) resumed control, emitting a high-pitched squeal from the exerted effort. She released the conjuration from Hyon's ward for a blink before it shot away from her again like a punctured balloon, careening across the barn and smashing through one of the massive barn doors. A shed in the Gardens of Grace collapsed in a pile of rubble outside, and the orb disintegrated completely from its multiple impacts.

Tae saw the rest of the wieldlings quickly return to the scene, led back into the barn by the cataclysmic sounds of splintered wood and tumbled stone; their jaws dropping in witness to the fallout.

Brychen lay on the floor breathing heavily while Rak Hyon stood with hands on his knees trying to recover from the shock and impact he'd felt, as well as the energy he'd lost weaving a ward of such strength and holding it for so long a period. Tae raced across the floor to kneel by Brychen's side, and Slynth leaned over the two of them.

"Is everyone alright?" asked Master Slynth.

"I'll be fine," said Hyon between gasps for air. His body was coated with sweat.

"And you, Brychen?" Slynth asked.

"I am... so sorry," she said, panting, "my aptitudes can be... unpredictable."

"Unstable and hazardous is more like it!" One of the wieldlings was hollering, walking toward the center of the floor, "This girl is nothing but an abomination, just as we'd supposed she was!"

"We would be wise to confine her," echoed another wieldling trainee, "this may only be the least of her destructive capabilities." Their verbal attacks against Brychen triggered something in Tae, and he wanted (with all his desire) to somehow teach them both a lesson about respect.

"Silence!" Slynth cast a stern scowl across everyone's face, "All of you, take leave of the House for the day. We'll resume our training at daybreak tomorrow." The directive was meant for the entire wieldling class, but was aimed especially at the two outspoken ones.

Everyone hesitated in place for a moment.

"You heard the Master," said Rak Hyon, firmly, and the wieldlings complied, exiting by the gaping hole left in the barn door and examining the splinters while they went. Hyon's breathing was still labored, but he was recovering. "This must be the one I've heard so much about this morning while cleaning the kitchens with Almetta. Will you be ok, child?"

"Yes," she answered meekly, sitting up, "I am sorry, sir. I haven't even met you, and I've attacked you—unintentionally, I promise... I suppose it goes without saying now, but you should all know I am easily startled. Especially while conjuring. Please do not throw me out of the House for this, Masters. I beg you to let me stay."

"We would be foolish to throw you out, my dear. I've never seen such a demonstration in all my life," said Slynth, "I only wish you'd given us proper warning, is all."

"You are adeptly attuned with the mystics," added Hyon, "you've great power within you, that much is clear."

"I promise to be more careful," she said.

"I think the two of you might benefit from a walk about the Royal Court," Slynth had begun examining the burn marks in one of the wooden support columns, "And please, make it a *quiet* walk."

"Yes," added Hyon, "I think it will do you well to breathe some fresh air, my girl. Prince Tae, why don't you show her around her new home?"

Tae nodded his head.

"Thank you, sirs, for your kindnesses," affirmed Brychen.

\*\*\*

The pair, Prince Tae Solis and wieldling greenhorn Brychen, made themselves scarce from the mystics barn and toured the Royal Court, as well as a few of the illustrious districts in the upper city. Tae was not the greatest of tour guides, given his apprehension toward all things remotely adventurous and (of course) his inability to speak; but for her sake, he challenged himself to turn the errand into something she might enjoy. And not long after they set out together, he'd surprisingly found *himself* delighting in the affair, which he took for a rather peculiar feeling, indeed.

He looked at her differently now than he had upon the early morning, for all of the power she'd exhibited in the barn, but the demonstrations certainly hadn't diminished his positive impressions. If anything, her aptitudes had intensified his admiration for her. *How does she do it?*

Along their imprecise tour path, they visited upon a score-fold of distinguished denizens and craftspeople; those who'd shown Tae kindness during times of gathering—fests and fairs and the like. Harlyn Rothspire in his Merchant Guild manor house, Quentyn Cynderlyn at his forge and smithy shop, and Equine Master Rossy Manhyme in the royal stables, to name a few.

But most of all, it seemed Brychen just wanted to experience the culture of the districts, and to walk amongst the crowds. She said she wanted to brush up against the life of the place; to hear the voices, see the faces, and feel the energy of the upper city.

Through the course of their escapade, Tae found himself doing things he'd never done before; had never even considered doing, and yet something within him found the means to navigate them, to survive the crowds and their noise. Tae's certainty that Rak Hyon and a few select Royal Guardsmen had swiftly taken to shadowing them along their way might have eased his nerves a bit. Hyon would ensure their safety, should any unlikely source of danger be found. But Tae was certain Brychen's presence also accounted for a significant portion of his courage, and he was content to let it be so.

*Especially* content, in fact.

Come the afternoon, while roaming the Arts District, they peeked into Irilio Pasca's famous glass-works boutique. It was a small shop nestled among many others on a main conduit running through the heart of town, and would have likely eluded the untrained eye of a casual tourist. Unfortunately, they saw it was closed for the day to patrons. Yet, just as they turned to leave, Brychen pulled him back to the window, "Is that not your fair mother, Tae? Speaking there, with that man?"

Tae took a closer look, and, indeed, it *was* mother, who upon seeing them had begun hastening the man—Tae knew for Pasca, himself—into a back room before making her way to the door and welcoming them inside, if only a tad surreptitiously in fashion.

"My Tae and our newest guest, Brychen. Goodness, how you've ventured yourselves out today!" Mailyn's pleasure in this encounter shown broadly across her face. Her eyes focused on the girl, "This is my most beloved shop in the district. It would please me to walk through it with the two of you, if you like."

Tae and the girl withdrew from the street and entered while Athynian Royal Guard soldiers, clad in polished helmets and boiled leather jerkins, appeared from their concealed locations and secured the door behind. Inside, Tae watched Brychen stare wide-eyed at glass spirals that hung in the hundreds from the beamed ceiling. Glass flowers were gathered in glass vases on the shelves, and glass animal figurines stood every place in-between. It was like a hidden cave resplendent with sparkling crystal sculptures of the finest detail.

"Welcome!" The voice of a man, who had quietly entered the room through an archway in the back, threaded its way to their ears in a charismatic tone. It was Pasca, returning. He wore a simply-woven tunic, baggy breeches, and leather sandals on his feet. Though slender and handsome, his hair was long and unkempt, and his dark, splotchy beard suggested he lacked possession of a proper shaving blade.

"My girl," said the Nohnce to Brychen, "let me introduce you to my dear friend, Irillio Pasca. He is the artisan who has created these lovely glass ornaments surrounding you."

"Warmest greetings my lady," Pasca said to Brychen, lifting and kissing her little hand, "aren't you simply cute as a button?" He pivoted delicately upon his heel, then added while bowing, "And hello to you my fair child, Tae. It has been too long since our last meeting. Are you enjoying your latest globe I'd made for your collection? I think it may have been my finest yet. Have you been polishing them regularly, as I've asked you to?"

Tae nodded politely.

"Our Grace flatters me with her praise for my work. I am humbled beyond measure to be sure. Please, please... allow me to invite you into my workshop." He walked back toward the arched doorway, and they followed in-step—Brychen still taking in the sights of the precious glass sculptures as they went.

Tae felt the warmth of her breath when she leaned to whisper in his ear, "How delightful!"

The workshop was a meticulously-kept space in the back of the boutique, with tools and materials hanging from hooks and lying on shelves. Works in progress lined a ledge on one wall, and detailed drawings of future works were pinned to another. But it seemed to Tae that the massive stonework furnace was what commanded most of Brychen's attention while they entered. The flames within pulsed and glowed and flickered, warming the room and filling it with a mineral scent.

"It isn't every day I'm afforded the opportunity to share my work with such noble visitants, I hope you will excuse my swollen enthusiasm," said the glassblower, Pasca. He slipped his feet from his sandals into plated boots and pulled on a pair of thick leather greaves, "Would you like to see how it works?"

With the Nohnce and the two apprentice wieldlings looking on, he drew a long blowpipe from the furnace, and Tae could see that a molten glass blob was spooled at the end, glowing. Placing the pipe firmly on the edge of an anvil, Pasca blew short puffs of air within, rotating evenly with his fingertips. The glass slowly began to expand into an asymmetric globe. "It is a very delicate business, this," Pasca said in-between puffs, "think of the glass as if it were a slight barrier between the air in this room and the air inside the globe, keeping the two apart from one another." He blew a few more puffs, before asking, "My girl, Brychen, what do you suppose might happen should I continue to expand this globe indefinitely?"

"I think that, perhaps it would burst," she answered.

"Cute *and* intelligent... quite a mystical combination," said Pasca, turning to glance at Tae with a wink, "I'd have been in a deal of trouble had a girl like this'd been summoned for me at that age..."

Tae deemed Pasca's mannerisms marginally inappropriate and noticed his mother's eyelids straining a bit, the way they were known to do at such moments.

"Carry on, Irillio," said the Nohnce with slight agitation.

In all, it seemed Brychen took his playful banter with good humor. "Luckily, then, sir Pasca," said Brychen, blushing through a sideways glance at Tae, "you'll be glad to know I've come to Castle Athyn upon my own accord without intent to stir any disturbances. Though, I've not been made to feel uncomfortable, for your suggestions."

The meaning of the exchange flew over Tae's head, but he noticed his mother replacing her flat stare with a smile. Perhaps *because* he hadn't picked up on a single thing they'd said. *Summoned for me? She hasn't been summoned for me...*

"I see! Then we are indebted to you for your wisdom *and* clemency, my girl," said Pasca with a deep grin of his own. "And so, too, is this globe, for your answer is correct! Prolonged expansion of the glass would eventually cause it to rupture, and I would find needs to cast it back into the furnace and try anew later. But a master glassblower knows his glass. He knows there are... weaknesses in the glass. Spots in the glass where fissures may grow; where the barrier may break and where the air inside may be permitted to pass through into this very room and mingle with us here."

Pasca continued to work the glass, rotating it with precision and (from time to time) lifting and extending it close in front of them so they might see where the glass rippled or strained. "It makes you wonder... if the air inside were ever to escape, would it prefer this world out here? Or would it simply desire a return to its comforting glass cocoon?" There was a twist of mystery about his voice.

The Nohnce gave him an uneasy look again, seemingly (this time) to quiet him from his meandering philosophies, before diverting the conversation altogether, "My dear Irillio is quite taken by his craft, as you can see. He's made all of those treasures you've seen out in the boutique."

"Your creations," said Brychen, "they're wonderful."

"I do cherish your kind words," Pasca bowed deeply to the girl.

"Well done, dear Irillio," the Nohnce's approval seemed a bit hastened, "now will you please excuse us while I see my Tae and his friend back to the door?"

"Without question or pause, Your Grace," Pasca placed the heated glass back into the furnace while the rest of them returned to the boutique's entrance.

"You've made for yourselves a little adventure into the upper city, I see," quite apparent was mother's approval, especially when they returned to the door and she peered outside to see Royal Guardsmen standing by to ensure their protection. "I'm quite glad, Brychen, you've found the means to acclimate yourself to your unfamiliar surroundings."

"I've suffered no spells of boredom thus far, that's for certain," said the girl, "for all the diversity here, and all there is to see and do. Though I'm afraid I've caused a bit of a scene in the House this morning, in summoning my aptitudes, which are still yet... rather unpredictable."

"I've heard of the affair," the Nohnce reassured, "please think no further upon it. As you can see, Rak Hyon is perfectly fine." She pointed out the window into a shadowed corner across the street where the Mystics Master leaned against the exterior façade of a carpenter's studio. "And I've been meaning to do away with that dilapidated garden shed for years. Really, they've already begun replacing the thing at my behest.

"Now, please do not allow me to delay you any further."

The Nohnce ushered Tae and his friend out of the store, bidding them a fond farewell before disappearing through the back toward Pasca's workshop and, again, out of sight.

\*\*\*

It was just around the start of evening time. Tae and Brychen were still making their way through the upper city districts, and if Irillio Pasca's glass boutique hadn't proven exciting enough—nor the countless other attractions clogging the streets—they, of a sudden, heard the Horns of Herald sounding from on high.

"The Heir Prince returns to the city!" shouted someone nearby, and a flock of people echoed the same as they emerged from their dwellings and shops, and headed for the main road.

"What is everyone doing?" asked Brychen, "Where are they going? I think I should very much like to see what this is all about!"

So Tae took her hand and guided her along with the crowd so that they might find a place to stand beside the cobblestoned main thoroughfare. He knew the Horns of Herald played to welcome Athynian royal companies back to the city after extended departures of any sort, and that it was nearly certain to be brother Ethyn who was making his return this time around.

Brychen remarked upon the spectacular view of the castle from where they settled, finding a wooden crate to stand upon for a better look. She reveled in the pageantry that had seemed to materialize all around them, right up from almost nowhere at all. *Thank the gods I keep myself well away from the public eye,* thought Tae, *else I too, like Ethyn, might have to suffer the nightmares of such feverish fawning and groping at the hands of these people. They don't know me from any other commoner my age, walking the city, and I'd just as soon like to keep it that way.*

But the pleasure was his just the same as it was Brychen's, to stand there in anonymity and welcome home his brother. He looked at her and felt something well within. He knew not exactly what it was, but he knew he enjoyed it. And, after brother Ethyn's procession would pass, he'd be content to walk with her up and down each and every street of the upper city until nightfall, if that was what she truly wanted to do.

### 17 | For the Dream of Halcyon

*"It is at the same time a necessity and a tragedy that our collective fates so often balance on something as woefully fickle as human interaction. As a result, conventions of diplomacy are catastrophically flawed across most civilized worlds. In the end, I suppose we shall all suffer for the collective imperfection of the human race and its persistent inability to cooperate."*
—excerpt from the personal journal of Steven Spurlock

|Planet Deaer, Athyn Proper

The Horns of Herald (and their tune that pierced the air above North Gate) had always reminded Heir Prince Ethyn Solis of splendid homecomings following magnificent childhood travels overseas. Their song would evoke memories of exotic realms, where the royal family was oft treated to the finest accommodations. He'd usually been buried within the cushions of a spacious carriage in return to the city when the horns would awaken him from a deep slumber. They would interrupt his dreams of the breathtaking sights he'd seen while away—sea vessel cabins with decks for viewing leviathans leaping from the ocean's depths, enormous felines with saddles for riding, and cliff-side pagodas overlooking pristine mountain vistas...

But this occasion was quite separate, in nature. This time, the horns signaled his return home from a bothersome mission. An escort turned sour and the promise of repercussions, the breadth of which he'd turned about in his head continuously ever since the incident with Ambassador Salmen Fleurys of Maelnlock had erupted in the Marshes of Mewth. *Surely, he will not be pleased this evening; to sit down at supper and cavort as if our confrontation had never occurred. And he should make no mistake that I am equally displeased as he.*

Peasantry had gathered in front of their humble lodgings along the roadside, waving emphatically to Ethyn as he passed. Further on, gate masters tending to the outer wall bowed before both Athynian and

'Lockian companies, allowing them to enter the city unfettered. Folk swarmed within the city limits, clustering five or six bodies deep along certain stretches of the main thoroughfare. They stood shoulder-to-shoulder to glimpse their prevalent heir, and suddenly his flustered disposition began to soften a touch.

Young ladies of his age were assembled in groups singing songs of adoration, while others simply shouted out his name, calling praises to the heavens for his safe return. On the second floor balcony of an inn, a less penitent troupe of ladies, self-assured and provocatively clad, posed and blew kisses in his direction. One young lady broke from the roadside crowd, grabbed at his boot buckle, and reached for his arm as he passed, until Othys Frierstag grunted so loud that she leapt away in alarm.

"Now-now, Othys," said Ethyn with a grin, "use some discretion. You need only frighten away those who threaten me. Leave the beautiful maidens to their own devices."

It was funny what a casual saunter through Athyn Proper, brimming with an adoring populace, could do to overturn a bitter mood. But it wouldn't last. He knew the pomp and circumstance in the streets would do nothing to simplify the stuffy, complicated matters of diplomacy awaiting him tomorrow morning upon assemblage, when Fleurys would undoubtedly renounce his behavior to his father and to the council.

Orders had seen to the clearing of all merchant carts and other clutter that might otherwise clog the road, and passage forward continued brisk and unimpeded, until the towers of Castle Athyn loomed over them. Approaching North Gate, Ambassador Fleurys and his company finally drew their mounts to a stop to allow Ethyn command of entry.

It had been an insult Fleurys hadn't given way as soon as they reached the city limits, but the beautiful young ladies of Athyn Proper seemed not to notice, and thusly, Prince Ethyn seemed not to care. Yet that didn't stop him from making a point of the matter. Before entering the keep, he turned his mount to face the crowd. They had rushed up the road and pushed against a gatehouse fence to find adequate positioning and to view the procession's entry into the castle. People leaned out of windows and pushed down alleyways to see Ethyn, calling his name again in admiring tones. *Now tell me, Ambassador... where in the world might you receive such an outpouring of feverish affection?*

*Nowhere, you say? I thought not...*

He raised his hand in salute for all to see, noting a few familiar faces here and there. *There is fair Celestyn, standing about the Baker's Ovenry—oh the sweet smell of her flaxen hair like that of a fresh loaf of bread! And Alleryn, there in the window above the Fainting Flower—I should not soon forget her delicate whispers like rose pedals softly tickling my ear... And there, Matalyn, with wool and needles in hand, outside the Crocheted Crane—her woven scarves as cozy as her warm self 'neath the sheets.*

Yet as they all smiled, or curtsied, or winked, Ethyn's eyes dropped, and the sounds of the crowd lessened in his head as he looked down to where the amber-colored stone hung from its chain, beneath his tunic. His fingers found the teardrop outline.

*Still there... still safe.*

"Are you yet prepared to enter, Ethyn?" asked Aryk, "We mustn't tarry much longer."

Ethyn looked back up at the people. "Yes, of course," he answered, then glanced at Fleurys, whose temper seemed tested to its limits over the needless delay. The ambassador's eyes almost spoke aloud: *Are we quite through with this irksome display of pretention?!*

Both companies entered and dismounted. Young legion archer Balyn Galdur (who had never before stepped foot inside the inner walls) gaped at the sheer size of the castle. Towers rose above them like mammoth stone trees grown from the rock-hard earth—the bulwarks, hall houses, and fortress keeps playing the role of their root systems and foundation, formidable in size in their own right. And every nook spilt attractively with flora of the most brilliant greens and flowers of every assorted color. Castle Athyn was a marvel, indeed.

Almost instantly, handlers appeared to tend the mounts, leading the magnificent beasts along the gatehouse pathways toward a stable, capable of accommodating perhaps a five hundred count of the animals at any given time. Curiously, Ambassador Fleurys signaled two of his guardsmen to follow along, presumably to supervise the effort.

"Your animals... they're in good hands," assured Ethyn while they started across North Court for the keep's main entry. It was the first thing he'd said to the ambassador since the incident in the marshes, "You needn't send your men to watch over them."

"Now the pup figures to tell me how to command my own men," Fleurys lashed out, speaking to his remaining guard company, of which there were three, "Does this one's impudence know no bounds?" The ambassador trampled unceremoniously, then, into the castle entry and led himself down the West Hall corridor to a chamber where Ethyn's father held a great share of his diplomatic assemblages.

*This man finds offense in everything!*

"Ambassador," Ethyn exclaimed, hurrying his gait to follow them inside, realizing Fleurys had made a wrong turn—not toward the guests' quarters to settle himself (as per custom), but toward the council chambers instead. "As you know, your quarters await you in the Visitors' Keep," he said, pointing down East Hall.

"Neither I nor my men shall require sleeping chambers this night, *prince,*" responded Fleurys, tersely—his accent twisting the royal title as if (in Ethyn's case) he deemed it a dubious application of an otherwise distinguished moniker. "Inform the Nhyle I require his presence immediately," and he commanded his three remaining guardsmen to stand watch in the hall before turning and entering the assemblage chamber door, and closing it firmly behind.

\*\*\*

A dark figure waited at the table, seated still as a headstone, when Ambassador Salmen Fleurys entered the assemblage chamber off Castle Athyn's West Hall corridor. "We haven't much time," proclaimed its voice, strained yet concise, while the ambassador squinted to hasten his eyes' adjustment to the dim light.

"Idris?" Fleurys spoke expectantly. Fleurys and Idris Ansel were accustomed to meeting in secret, but never in the Nhyle's own assemblage chamber; not like this.

"Yes, it's me," said the astronomer, "sit."

Fleurys sat, grateful for the opportunity to rest his legs, "Thank goodness you've received my message. I pray the bird arrived unmolested?"

"Unmolested it was," Ansel's face, barely visible within the shadows of his dark cowl, shown stern and cold. The silence of the room permeated its atmosphere; no natural light within, just one lit candle in a sconce on the wall. There were two doors leading into the chamber; the first feeding from West Hall where Fleurys' men stood guard. The second was a back door, where Ansel had entered from a private corridor that fed from the High Council's sitting room. "There were neither eyes nor ears outside when I slipped in, but that is a fleeting condition, at best. I expect we have but a precious few moments before I must take myself away from here."

"Indeed," answered Fleurys, "the princeling is fetching his father as we speak."

"We shall make as usual, like foes readying to clash across this table in their presence. Any other manner would, of course, raise suspicion. We are in no way prepared to reveal our surreptitious liaison, understood?"

"Of course I understand," Fleurys pleaded with a smirk, "do you take me for a fool?"

With the formalities addressed, Ansel's disposition calmed. "I assume from the language in your message you have urgent news to pass, but I must preempt you, for I can scarcely prolong the disclosure of pressing news all my own," he whispered. "The boy has disappeared; in an underground pass deep 'neath the castle. At the mouth of a cave, if I've read his cues true."

"A cave?" blurted Fleurys, "disappeared, you say?!"

"*Shhh...* yes," hushed the astronomer, "and he'd returned without a clear notion of where he'd gone. In my laboratory, he conveyed the event to me with picture cards and signal cues." Ansel was not ordinarily an excitable man; this was a side of him he hadn't shown to Fleurys in ages, and they had known one another for several ages now, indeed. "Salmen, my suspicions have finally come to fruition. The boy... this castle..."

"And to think, after all these ages," Fleurys squeaked, flushed with enthusiasm, holding his hands out and examining the lines in his palms as if to recount all the hardship he'd endured in his life. "It is time, my old friend, to put the wheels in motion. Let me now share my own news, which is nearly equal to yours in consequence. A catalyst for conflict between these great realms has been thrust upon us. If you sensed urgency in my note, it was for good reason," the ambassador pulled a kerchief from his pocket, and his hand quivered while he dabbed his face. "A small 'Lockian sentry troupe discovered Launch-station North not three days past, and suspicions are mounting."

"The northerly station, discovered?" Ansel wheezed, for a moment defying his own directive to whisper, "The one in the 'Lockian chasms?"

"Yes. It would seem so," the ambassador nodded his head in confirmation. "The 'Lockian High House is desperate to find an explanation for its existence, and for the instrumentation they found inside. I've busied myself planting seeds, fanning flames of rumor and hearsay by message fowl to the 'Lock. Emperor Maeflewr and his House are all but convinced the station and its machine are assets of Athynian origin; some sort of weapon in hiding, and he is labeling it a militaristic incursion of unprecedented proportion."

Idris was quiet for a moment; calculating.

"At first blush, it's quite shocking to hear a station has been discovered," he said at last, "given all the effort we've put into secreting them away. Yet I suppose I oughtn't be taken by such surprise. Indeed, Launch-station South has generated attention of late as well, despite its remotest of locations in the snowcapped mountains. There've been rumors throughout the castle of sightings; of *our* launchings, if my instincts are correct. I cannot imagine the means by which anyone has seen such things from such great distances. And yet they have—or *someone* has—by means all their own. I would've known if my viewing scopes had been tampered with," Ansel paused. "Might it only be a matter of time until the stations are, all three of them, discovered?"

"Especially now that one station has been so thoroughly exposed by the 'Lock," agreed Fleurys.

"And what news of the station's machinist?"

"Held captive by 'Lockian sentrymen in the station itself."

"Seems odd," posited Ansel, "but I won't question their methods."

"They hope to force a demonstration of the launching instrument; its targeting capabilities. That's why we must act quickly," urged Fleurys. "It won't take Maeflewr's best advisors long to discover what is really going on; that the apparatus bears a sophistication far exceeding anything these Athynian half-wits might ever develop."

"I suppose we should count ourselves fortunate Maeflewr yet prohibits torture as a means to gather information, elsewise they might have already solved the station's mysteries, and our cover would've already been blown." Ansel was considering the implications of Fleurys' news, even as he spoke; weighing one urgent question against a multitude of others, "Any mention of the powder supply?"

"None. The machinist must have been able to somehow jettison his small pouch. There is a particularly large chasm, as you recall, along the knoll where the station resides. I expect he threw the supply into its depths once it became clear he was compromised."

"That will buy us some time at least," considered Ansel, "even if they find a way to coax the machinist into compliance, no demonstration of the instrument will ever prove successful without the powder. Heard you any other whispers about this machinist? It eases my concern a bit that he's proven at least a shrewd lad, in his judgment-making with the powder."

"Just one. I understand he bears strong Athynian features, which has only strengthened suspicion he's an agent of the Nhyle."

"Remarkable…" Ansel turned his head from side to side, "After all this time, Alamere has left no stone unturned. So meticulous… so thorough."

"Have we been any less devoted to this cause than he?"

"No." Ansel's reply was deep and solemn. The candle on the wall flickered. *Flickering candles betray movement; a swinging door, an occupied hallway. We must quit this conversation.* "It's a convenient thing *your* bloodline isn't nearly so readily identifiable," he whispered, beginning to stand up and take his leave.

"Indeed," said Fleurys, grabbing the astronomer's arm to keep him within earshot, "but you remind me of one last item I ought to disclose…"

"I must be gone from here, Salmen, make haste," Ansel's urgency was renewed, looking toward the candle's flame, which had stilled, then toward the back door, which remained firmly closed.

"This is important," Fleurys insisted, "there was an incident today with the cursed, trifling prince on escort. Somehow he knew of my lineage; somehow he learned of my Athynian ancestry and he used it against me, like… like some kind of verbal offensive."

"Impressive, that… and troubling," said Ansel, "the boy posesses some nerve after all, I'll give him his due credit. But how could he have come to possess such information?"

"I don't know, but he has. And if I were you, I wouldn't take for granted immunity from an investigation of like proportion into your own past. You, yourself, have garnered the prince's sharp disapproval in recent years, have you not?"

"I mislike this…" croaked Idris, gravely, "the meddlesome heir becomes increasingly dangerous every day. How did you react to all of this?"

"Like a madman, of course; you know my temper, Idris," Fleurys was quite flustered, even by the mere recollection of the event, "But I figure to use it to our advantage. Let the Nhyle come away from this dialogue blaming his own son for agitating a powerful adversary and instigating a disastrous assemblage. You need only sit back and enjoy the hysterics."

"They will be but a mere prelude to all that will soon follow."

"Indeed," Fleurys grinned.

Ansel's mind was abuzz. There was so much to accomplish, and so little time. "Now I really must take my leave." And he made for the back door, then paused and turned once again before exiting, "For the dream of Halcyon."

"For the dream of Halcyon," echoed Fleurys.

\*\*\*

The assemblage chamber was quiet when Prince Ethyn and the Nhyle, Perwyn Solis, arrived. Two young pages (assigned to the High Council's sitting room) had dutifully risen from their desks to light all the remaining candles within. Ambassador Fleurys' spare frame was illuminated, sitting silently in wait for the royal audience. The Nhyle sat himself at the end of the table closest to the back door, while Ethyn took a seat directly across from Fleurys.

The pages closed the door shut as they departed

"The Honorable Ambassador Fleurys, it is a pleasure to receive you this evening," said Lord Perwyn, breaking the silence, "but surely we do ourselves a disservice by hastening ourselves to the assemblage table, when we could instead enjoy a fine meal and bottles of vintage at the dining table, with mirthful music and a good night's sleep in tow. Let us postpone these impersonal formalities of diplomacy until comes the morn, when we are suitably fresh and able-minded."

"Your Lordship," answered Fleurys curtly, yet with a requisite nod of his head, "I am pleased that by finding me in your assemblage chamber you have, at the very least, grasped my desire to dispense with our common supper rituals. Given the gravity of the matters before us, I trust you will recognize the degree of imprudence those pretenses have finally achieved. It is my intention to talk now, and perhaps to listen a trifle, but mostly to talk, so that you understand the condition we find ourselves in. And it must be done without delay."

It was a vexing feeling for his father, Ethyn was sure, to be subjected to the dictates of a visitor in his own assemblage chamber. *At least I should hope it is. I simply wouldn't stand for it. I'd tell Fleurys he has a choice. He can either observe the sacred traditions of the House he's intruding upon, or he can saddle up and ride back to Stief right now without stealing so much as a single moment further from the royal seat with his childish nonsense.*

"Very well, if you insist," the Nhyle—much to Ethyn's displeasure—appeared resigned to the idea that this dialogue was going to transpire absent typical traditions of hospitality, whether he wished it to or not. "I have sent for my High Counsel, Idris Ansel. We will at least await his arrival before we begin."

"Ansel… you speak of the *stargazer*. Am I correct in this?" asked the ambassador, with a hint of condescension.

"Yes, that is he," confirmed the Nhyle, "and I would invite you to ask him whatever you please about matters of the night's sky over a warm bowl of vegetable broth and a steaming plate of suckling pork, should you be assuaged to observe tradition and retire with us to our great hall. Our discourse can surely stand adjournment for an evening's time, no?" He was making one last ploy for the deferral of this assemblage, "But for proper diplomatic purposes and under these conditions, Idris Ansel ought to be recognized as my High Council, so long as we remain here in this assemblage chamber."

Fleurys grumbled into his moustache and said, "Perhaps Athyn would find itself in better standing with its fellow realms in this world if its Nhyle would surround himself with advisors suitable for the offices they hold. I say your page boys would befit the title of High Council truer than the stargazing lack-wit, whom, you should know, is no more a compelling conversationalist over supper than he is a negotiator at assemblage."

The back door swung open, and Ansel stepped into the room. His cowl was pulled back now, and he had replaced it with a simple gray cloth cap. Taking a seat beside Ethyn and across from the ambassador, he greeted Fleurys with perfect indifference, then braided his fingers together and rested his hands casually upon the table.

"Do your ears tickle, Idris?" asked the Nhyle, "because Ambassador Fleurys was just speaking of you, and not fondly I will add."

"Is that so?" said Ansel, smiling, while he shot Fleurys a look of discernment, "Well, they say you should scarcely expect the mouse to speak praises of the owl."

"So too they say, you shan't ever rebuff a kindly invitation to feast," added the Nhyle. "Yet that is what the good ambassador has done, and so I believe we must oblige his demands to address us outright, with no undue deferment."

"I see," said Ansel, adding, "So it shall be, then."

"If you are both well through amusing yourselves, I will aim to keep this short," Fleurys interjected. "I trust you are cognizant, your Lordship, of our Agreement of Territories and the prohibition of a House's placement of offensive assets within the borders of another realm."

"Of course I am; that goes without saying," responded the Nhyle, visibly caught off guard by the mention of offensive assets.

"And you are keenly aware such placement of offensive assets is justification for a realm, as infringed upon, to declare war against the House responsible?" The Ambassador's tone was challenging.

"Naturally so, as the dark pages of history have shown, there is much precedent for conventions of war precipitated upon unprovoked acts of aggression," said the Nhyle, adding, "provided, that is, a proper investigation into the act in question has been conducted by a neutral commission. What, may I ask, brings us to this particular topic of conversation?"

"You will soon see. Being the splendid historian that you are, Lord Nhyle, I'm sure you will concede there have been times, across ages long-passed, when conditions disallowed the development of a proper neutral investigation," led Fleurys, "when two realms involved in longstanding disputes both possessed the strength-in-arms to wipe entire regions off the map with the pointing of a finger. That is to say, Lord Nhyle, that you might have greater luck convincing a lesser realm to volunteer their land for mass waste containment than to serve on such an investigative committee. The findings, whatever they may be, would surely anger either your House or ours, and if you haven't noticed, the lesser realms have exhibited no such intention to provoke either one of us for quite some time. I deem it evidence of a calculated effort on their parts to avoid wholesale extermination. And would you blame them?"

"Then we ought to form our own commission," suggested the Nhyle, "It would cause no strain unto me to meet with your Emperor again. In fact, I'd quite enjoy the opportunity, if he is amenable. For every barrier, there is a ladder or bridge to be built to overcome it, is there not?"

"I'm afraid recent Athynian intrusions have pushed the patience of House Maeflewr beyond such limits."

"If you mean to suggest House Solis has committed some kind of infringement of 'Lockian territory, you are mistaken, ambassador," the Nhyle countered, "and an accusation of such wild proportion would not stand on mere, empty suspicion. I'll grant you that a commission of lesser realms might fear our reprisal, but they simply would not stand for such hastening of conflict."

"However unfortunate it may be, my lord, Fleurys is right," posited Ansel. "Of the lesser realms, who would be so foolish to intervene in a dispute between Athyn and the 'Lock?"

"In accordance with your understanding of these ordinances…" interjected Fleurys in rehearsed speech, tipping everyone off in the room as to what was coming next.

"Hold on here, you have no basis for this," pled the Nhyle, interrupting the ambassador's statement.

"…And in my capacity as the Maelnlockian Ambassador to Athyn," continued Fleurys, his phrasing precise, down to each individual syllable.

"What does House Maeflewr hope to gain by this?" Perwyn Solis' expression was becoming strained.

Fleurys continued on, "…Emperor Maeflewr of Maelnlock, on behalf of his arms and his peoples, hereby passes to House Solis, and the realm of Athyn, a formal declaration of war."

"This is madness!" Ethyn stood up and struck the table with his fists. The stark interruption stopped Fleurys' speech cold, "I'll not allow this nonsense to continue any further—"

"Madness, my little pup, is a more adequate classification of the gross impropriety you exhibited on escort, of which I am certain even the likes of your treacherous father would not have taken kindly to, had he been there to witness it," Fleurys seemed to be enjoying himself now, in some twisted way, rousing the tempers of all the others in the room, "and which I certainly did not appreciate, in the least."

"Your declarations in this assemblage," rejoined Ethyn, "have only *vindicated* my behavior on escort. Without a neutral investigation, you've no basis upon which to declare anything." The prince was gesticulating wildly as he spoke. Leaning forward to punctuate his statements, he pounded a fist into his open hand so hard that the teardrop amber stone flipped free from his tunic and swung high, reflecting candle light from around the room as it rose and fell on its chain, dangling over the tabletop.

When Fleurys saw the stone, he flung himself backward in his chair and landed upon the floor with a crash. A look of horror marred the ambassador's face while he fumbled and struggled to pull himself up. He wheezed hard as if the wind had been knocked from his lungs. "This assemblage is over! Take me from this accursed city!" Trembling, Fleurys darted in a hastened scamper out of the chamber and back into West Hall to join his soldiers, slamming the door shut behind as he went.

The Nhyle stood up from his seat, dumbfounded.

"My Lord, let him go," urged Ansel, who had (as well) recoiled at the sight of Ethyn's stone, and had made for the back door on reflex. "We must retire, lest more be torn asunder. The man is unstable; it would do no good to provoke him any further. Let us rouse the council and share with them these grave developments."

"I suppose we've no alternative," the Nhyle turned toward Ethyn. "Son, see that the Ambassador and his men are shadowed. I want confirmation of their whereabouts… assurances they all depart the city, if that is indeed what they intend to do."

"I shall," Ethyn watched his father and Ansel quit the room with anxious urgency before moving, then, with haste to West Hall, thinking that (should they lose track of this lunatic Fleurys) the day's calamity might compound even further.

And at once, the assemblage chamber sat empty, somber, and quiet yet again.

**Part 2**

## 18 | One Turn of the Gear

*"Emotion is a very difficult force to suppress. Everything within our innate makeup as human beings prompts us to levy responses in accordance with our emotions. But emotion has no rightful place in a professional environment. Sometimes we have a job to do, which will consume us if we invest on too personal a level. When we violate that rule, and we entertain our emotional urges in the course of fulfilling our professional duties, we complicate our lives and make ourselves unhealthy. We must save our emotions for those things in life that truly deserve them."*
—excerpt from the personal journal of Steven Spurlock

|The Station

Spurlock awoke in his solar with a start, sitting up quickly in his cramped bed, gasping for air. Whatever it was that occupied his dreams must have whipped him into quite a frenzy, for his cube-like dwelling (lined with its panels and lights and screens) seemed as if it was closing-in on him from every direction. Voices cried out to him, or to *someone*, with great urgency, and the chaos of it all had disoriented him into near hysterics.

*"This is madness!"* He heard a voice shout, followed by a great pounding and rustling and heavy breathing. Then more aggravated discourse continued, thereafter.

The clamor sent him reeling, groping for relief; covering his ears and shielding his eyes. He rose out of bed with a stammer in his legs and a dizzying thunder-clap in his head. And when, from deep within, he finally found the wherewithal to search about his room for the source of this great disturbance, he discovered that he'd simply forgotten to power down the feed audiblers on his console before he'd taken to sleep. The oversight meant that, all night, the running broadcasts from his sources on Planet Deaer had been repeating themselves aloud—several of them at once. And now upon waking, he could only stand and stare, wearing a look of sheer exhaustion upon his face. *No wonder my dreams have been so completely messed up tonight.*

"Audiblers off," he commanded, and the voices faded mercifully into silence.

Normally, his transition from bed to workstation proved far less jarring, allowing him adequate time to emerge from sleep and shake loose his lethargy before plunging headlong into the ceaseless reading and logging of each day's collected feeds. But then again, most evenings lacked the kind of spirited exchanges that'd been transmitted to him this particular night. It made him wonder what sort of business had roused such dissention among the subjects of his acute surveillance.

He hadn't recently perceived any such evidence that might suggest a boiling over of their collective froth down there on Deaer, so it was a near certainty that his work was going to be cut out for him. *And oh,* he thought, *I can barely contain my excitement!*

He was yet only one day removed from his latest operation on Planet Deaer, which had begun when his Operator called upon him with a degree of urgency. He'd been engaged in a complex, philosophical conversation with his module companion Giza out on the deck, when she demanded he return to his solar, throw on his suit, and (again, as he'd dreaded) equip not only the sidearm, but his vial of transponders as well.

She'd Projected him back to Planet Deaer to perform two *more* implants of the tiny listening devices within two new sources. One was a man with salt and pepper hair, who slept in a large inn by the sea, and who had remained unwise to the incisions, implantings, and flash mends of the surgical procedure, completely.

The second subject was an aged wizard of sorts, taking residence in the uppermost tower in Castle Athyn, which was populated by instruments of all kinds; including a particularly sophisticated telescope. It seemed that both subjects were native to this supreme Athynian region, to which he'd apparently been assigned, and which he had come to embrace as a sort of second home away from his little solar, throughout this mission of horrors and nightmares he was living.

The wizard's operation proved perilous in both Spurlock's hunt to find the subject and the implantation, itself. In holding the suit's incision peripheral no more than a fingertip's width above the subject's face, Spurlock watched the wizard all but awaken to see what was happening.

But, while grimacing behind the helmet's blast-proof visor, Spurlock had resisted the urge to turn and run, and the wizard had eventually settled himself into a new position of repose without incident. By the end, Spurlock was convinced the wizard had remained oblivious to his presence, right through successful completion of the operation, and he had returned to his solar via Projection; a man in complete fulfillment of this latest operation's requirements.

*And that's all that matters, right?*

He had to at least *try* and convince himself there was truth in that sentiment.

*It's certainly all that would matter for a robot—which I'm still convinced is exactly what this Operator is bent on turning me into.*

But, indeed, he had fulfilled the latest tasks she'd set upon him, and in the most basic sense of things, it was a measure—albeit a very twisted measure—of success. At this juncture, he resolved to take what positives he could from the quandary he was in, or he'd go completely mad.

Covered in sweat, he'd stripped the suit and helmet off and shoved them back into their compartment along with the sidearm. Then he had looked carefully at the vial, within which remained only three more of the micro listening devices he'd originally been given. And before placing them on their shelf in the wardrobe, he had said the names of his subjects silently to himself, then and there: *Naylor and Sün. Tae, Ethyn, Mailyn, and Perwyn... all of surname Solis. And now, Thurflyn and Ansel.*

The Operator had made no further communication with him the whole day that followed, for which he was beyond grateful. He used the time to adjust to the frenetic process of monitoring eight sources now—versus only six—which he'd found exceedingly difficult from the very start; for the new sources (like the old) all seemed very active sorts, engaged in a vast array of meaningful pursuits. This was especially the case when some (or all) of his sources interacted simultaneously, yet within separate contexts apart from one another. It made for a mass of competing dialogue and often forced him to quiet the audiblers of all his feeds but one at a time. And then, when opportunity arose, he could backtrack and reference the transcripts of the rest to see if he'd missed anything of interest.

That was, in essence, what he resolved to do now, having arisen so abruptly. Standing there staring at his console, he was too shaken to even consider returning to his bed and the land of knotted-up dreams. So he took to his seat and began scrolling through the transcripts displayed on his holoscreens, to see if he might find an explanation for all the latest ruckus. All the *madness*.

It seemed as though higher ranks of the planet's most influential realms were assembling under pretenses of great importance. And even despite the occasional grittiness of the feed translations (applied instantly to his transmissions), there could be no mistaking the declaration of war that was made, quite distinctly, which (paired with a rather tense confrontation during escort between prince and ambassador) seemed to be the greatest source of malcontent revealed within all the feeds he scoured throughout the night. He frowned when he considered what it might mean for his future operations down on the planet's surface. *Outright warfare. As if it wasn't perilous enough for me down there already.*

He expected developments of such significance would surely meet threshold for inclusion in the latest daily report to his Operator. And along with the contextual clues that arose during the wizard Ansel's private conversation with this visiting ambassador, who had (himself) provided the fearsome declaration of war, it seemed clear that his tight Athynian union of confidants had within its midst a sinister member possessed of traitorous intent.

"Giza," he said, prompting the module to power up, "Why is she showing me these things; making me track these people? Come on, let's hear it. I know you're smarter about all this than you've admitted."

The unit took a moment to light up and assume its hovering posture before speaking. "Do you question the value in studying such destructive pretenses of war? And how to, perhaps, solve it once it has begun?"

"C'mon, seriously, knock it off. I'm asking... why *me?*"

"You are an analyzer of intelligence," Giza asserted, "are you not?"

"So you say," rebuked Spurlock.

"Then who better?"

"Anyone, Giza," he threw his hands up, "literally, *anyone* would be better than me."

"You are juggling many things," plead the module, "perhaps she is teaching you the value of balance. I can certainly see a bit of self-confidence training wouldn't hurt here, either. And how are your efforts detaching yourself from *emotion* coming along? Are you feeling more *robotic* yet?"

"Giza, power down," said Spurlock, frustrated. The module winked out and settled back to the floor.

As a matter of fact, detachment from emotions was coming along almost too well for Spurlock. He'd performed that last operation without so much as a whimper within his helmet, or even a slight wave of anxiety, and it was frightening him. *What'll happen to me if I really* do *lose touch with the essence of being human?*

He didn't want to know the answer; even if this roboticization was the very thing that was keeping him alive during this cruel, freakish mission of his.

And so the holoscreens glowed, and the atmosphere in the solar hung dark and oppressive.

His mind spun.

For a while, the Station itself seemed to spin, and he was filled with anger over his predicament; one of the more salient of all human emotions. But shortly, even without thinking, he packed it away, defeating it with the precision of a sophisticated anti-virus program.

And he turned back to his work, obediently grinding himself along.

One turn of the gear after another.

\*\*\*

|Planet Earth, Washington DC

It was Sunday night, and Haley Kenmore was sitting alone at the *Cactus Cantina* on Wisconsin Avenue, eating flautas and sipping a frozen margarita. Lime. She preferred more exotic flavors, but Steven liked the boring standard. He also liked flautas. It was she who'd introduced his palate to the delights of Mexican cuisine. From then on, she could seldom convince him to patronize any other style restaurant. She couldn't deny the satisfaction her influence had on him, though. Maybe that's why she'd ordered his favorites this time, to remind her of how well the two of them seemed to fit together. *Or maybe I thought it'd make him magically show up, somehow...*

In reality, she'd settle for a mere text response.

Just then, her phone lit up beside her plate on the table. It was a message from her mom:

> 7:12pm: Busy next weekend? Your dad and sister
> and I would like to see you. Been a
> while… love you, mom.
> 7:12pm: ps. I'll make pasta.

Haley entered a prompt response:

> 7:13pm: Thx mom, love you too. Pass along to dad
> and Brea for me. I'll let you know.

She sighed. It was beginning to seem to her a fool's occupation—this business of obsessing over her phone—good only for supplying frustration and misery. So she threw the phone into her purse and took a few more sips from her straw, looking across the dining room. She heard, then, a familiar voice speaking in conversational tones. It was her boss, the Assistant Secretary, following a hostess into the restaurant while talking on her cell. It didn't seem to bother her that everyone in the place could hear what she was saying.

"I just left my office," she explained to whoever was on the other line, "I was there all day today."

The A/S took a seat at the table directly opposite a glass partition from Haley, who promptly slid down the back of her chair in hiding.

"Ok, I gotta go, I'm having dinner now," said the A/S into her phone, "bye." She closed out the call and sat the device on the table top, where it could be monitored.

The hostess smiled, waiting patiently for her to get settled.

"That was my mother; our usual Sunday evening call. It's difficult to get her off the phone sometimes. I'm so sorry about that."

*'So sorry'?* Haley was mesmerized. *Boy, how polite of her!*

"Can I get you anything to drink?" asked the hostess.

"I'd like a bottle of seltzer water, if you have it," said the A/S.

*Bleh!* A sour look formed across Haley's face.

"Sure, I'll bring it right out," and the hostess departed the dining room for the kitchens.

Haley dared to sit more upright in her chair, then, to sneak a peek through the wavy glass. The A/S was putting on her reading glasses—at the tip of her nose—to read the menu. Then her phone buzzed to indicate a new email had arrived, and she checked it right away; shaking her head a bit in the process, as if the message were written by a complete moron and made no sense at all. It was a familiar expression she often cast upon Haley.

"Here's your drink ma'am," the hostess returned with a bottle of seltzer water, "And, I'll give you some time to decide on the menu."

*Everyone she knows calls her ma'am...* thought Haley.

"Thank you very much," said the A/S, without taking her eyes from the phone.

"And, will you have someone joining you this evening?" asked the hostess.

The A/S looked up, "No. It'll just be me."

"Very well," said the hostess, who promptly removed the other table settings, and set off again.

*You and me both, ma'am.* Haley slid back down in her chair thinking of how she might go about squaring her check and departing without being noticed.

*You and me, both...*

\*\*\*

|The Station

"Who do you think she is?" said Spurlock, picking up the picture from his bedside in the solar.

"Someone of importance, I would presume," replied Giza. Spurlock had allowed the unit to power back on, so long as it promised to withhold its mischievous little barbs.

"It's starting to bother me, looking at her and not knowing. Not being able to remember. I mean, it's *really* starting to bother me... She's beautiful."

"Do you recognize any clues in the background?" the module blipped.

"I don't recognize *anything*," Spurlock squinted, lifting his glasses off to look at the photograph without them, "though that tree is interesting, isn't it? That's a lot of blossoms. Hundreds on every branch." He placed the picture back on its ledge and his glasses back over the bridge of his nose. "In any case, something tells me I better remember soon if I want to remember at all."

"Why do you say that?" asked Giza.

"Why?" scoffed Spurlock, "Because we're doomed, that's why. The people down on this planet I'm watching, it sounds like they're getting ready to obliterate each other. And I think some of them have ridiculous magical powers. Some *definitely* have flight technology. Oh, and most of them are talking about seeing mysterious lights up in the sky."

"Is that all?"

"Is that *all??*" stressed Spurlock. "I've been down there looking up into the sky, and I've seen this station. *We* are a light up in their sky. Get it?"

"Remember, you have a highly advanced suit and helmet to aid you. It is unlikely they can see this far beyond their own atmosphere."

"I don't know, man. It's dirty and ancient down there, but they have stuff… some magnifiers and telescopes. I wouldn't put it past them." Spurlock began typing a new report for his Operator. He'd already submitted his formal report for the day, but suddenly felt compelled to author an addendum, under the circumstances. It wasn't a lengthy one.

> Daily Report—part 2:
> Pretty sure they know we're up here.
> We = screwed.
> Time to go yet?
> -Spurlock
> ps. come on already, who am i? and who's the girl in
> my photo?!

He sent the message, knowing it wouldn't be well-received. Daily reports weren't supposed to raise questions; they were supposed to answer them. And they were supposed to be formal; formatted neatly with all the proper conventions of analytic writing.

The voice came quickly to his solar.

—We are quite safe here, Mr. Spurlock. You needn't worry about that—

"Wow, you must read these things immediately."

—Time is always of the essence—

"Hey, so how's about it? Mind telling me now, who I am?"

—What makes you think I can tell you anything of what you want to know?—

"Oh, seriously? You're really gonna keep playing it like that? C'mon… I'm one hundred percent sure you can tell me everything. This whole 'mission' would be totally useless if you didn't know every last thing about me before it even began. I know I'm nothing more than a test subject for you. Your little robot, Giza here, told me all about it."

The module lit up brightly at this suggestion, "I have done no such thing."

She ignored their bickering.

Spurlock made a face at Giza; sticking out his tongue.

—Have faith, Mr. Spurlock. It might serve you well in the end—

## 19 | Truth to be Found

*"Oh, the mess of it all. If only the power to instill peace and tolerance in these worlds t'were granted unto the nurturing hands of peaceful, tolerant people, we might eventually stand to make some degree of progress. It only takes but one bad actor within the drama troupe to sully a play. When they're all bad, I suppose it takes at least one miracle star to come along and save it from widespread critical ruin. My heart truly goes out to that one star, brave enough to try."*
—excerpt from the personal journal of Steven Spurlock

|Planet Deaer, Castle Athyn

Heir Prince Ethyn Solis had witnessed the complete withdrawal of Ambassador Salmen Fleurys and his helmsmen from the city atop their mounts, following the rushed and discordant assemblage with his father. Fleurys had delivered his message of war and had made off, much like a coward, for the harbor town; likely to board a ship bound straight for the 'Lock without delay. Ethyn was confident that if he'd ever meet the ambassador again, it'd be on a battlefield somewhere, either to discuss the terms of some hard-fought truce, or to sink a sharpened blade into one-another's vital organs.

*I'd much prefer a shot at the latter.*

Now, the prince sat at forum in an old council chamber—under its massive wood beams and vaulted ceilings—amid a sorry lot of grumblers and brawlers who called themselves High Council members. The diminutive Enric Cursyo, Master of Coin, spoke (through a particularly sour twist of his lips) of the kingdom's fiduciary holdings, compared against the economic strain that war would surely place them under. In the meanwhile, Marilyn Enswall, Chief Bastion of Labor, sat scowling at anyone and everyone around her. Commander Ryce Thorngrove of the Royal Legion grumbled audibly every few moments or so; stubborn remonstrations of something or another. A huddle of council members—

whose faces were more familiar to Ethyn than were their names—remained thus far quiet, though their expressions screamed of discontent. And there was Idris Ansel, of course, who sat close beside the Nhyle to provide his commentary upon all things said and done, at all times. *Why should he enjoy a position of such prominence? That should be me beside father, voicing my opinions whenever I wish.*

Next to Ethyn, toward the back of the chamber, sat the Master of Scholars Mossa Zahyle; in stark contrast to the others, revered by Ethyn for her wisdom and solid temperament. He could think of no better person to shadow during his first official council forum than she. "You are certainly the most dignified of all the councilors gathered here this evening, Mossa," he whispered, leaning toward her ear.

"You've not yet observed me at forum long enough, Ethyn," said Mossa in her kindly tones. For her own part, Zahyle was tall and thin, and bore deep wrinkles around her eyes, but she carried an aura of strength about her. Not physical strength, but a thoroughly-toned intellect and a flexible disposition that had helped her cultivate the utmost kernels of respect, not just from Ethyn, but all her peers. "You'll find that sometimes in this chamber, we are forced to speak the kind of language these others will understand. Less dignified than you might expect, I assure you."

"A nature of discourse consistent with my latest enquiries, it seems."

"So I've come to understand," said Zahyle. "By all accounts, the assemblage with Fleurys seems not to have gone by way of a docile mid-summer's picnic among friends."

"If only the assemblage were our lone sample—and ruinous, it certainly was—I may find myself less exhausted by the trend, as I fear the life of the escort proceeded, from its very inception, rather contentiously as well. Your Scholar's anecdotal whisperings of Ambassador Fleurys' true heritage certainly lit its proper fuse. Well-beyond intended breadths of conflagration, I may add."

"I see," Zahyle's face contorted, "I've only very reserved confidence in the veracity of such claims. It was reckless of my Scholars to share such information with you, short of its ever being corroborated."

"It is surely not my intention to fault, in any way, the integrity of your analyst's service to me. It was furnished, I assure you, in a manner attentive to my own utmost and particular request," said Ethyn. "Either way, the information has been very well corroborated, indeed, by Fleurys' unrestrained emotional reaction, wrought entirely with guilt, when I'd hit him with it; somewhere along the road 'mongst the towering reeds of the Marshes of Mewth. There's no better way to procure precious minerals that to mine directly at their source, yes? Fleurys, a turncoat Athynian. Never in a lifetime should I have guessed; yet now knowing, I cannot deny the good sense it imparts."

"Neither should I have guessed," very little ever evaded the understanding of Master M. Zahyle. Ethyn thought she seemed troubled, perhaps, by the fact that he'd confirmed the secret through such cavalier means. "It isn't an analyst's nature to confront their subjects of surveillance quite so directly. I shall have to consider closely the implications of all this. Upon the matter of good sense, which you've referenced, one may be hard-pressed to ever find such a rare commodity here at forum. Rarer even than your purest of precious minerals, I'm afraid."

"I must confess," Ethyn recalled, "that on the road—not two moons past—I held confidently in my ability to convey the importance of our realm's security to these councilors; that convincing them to take action against imminent threats to our very livelihood would come with great ease, for such is—or ought to be—their foremost concern. The irrefutable logic—and good sense—inherent in such arguments seemed to me, then, undeniable. Yet, my friend Aryk, who is wise like you, was swift to point out the devious nature of politics and the vexatious scarcity of logic found therein," Ethyn scanned the faces of the councilors seated around the chamber with a glare and listened again to the nonsense spoken between them. "Flames and ashes, it hasn't taken them long to prove him right."

"I wonder," said Zahyle, "why someone might be invited into the fold of a forum, if not for the very purpose of bringing their insight to the fore. Whilst harboring such contradictory understandings of our present circumstances, should you be so content to let them prattle on as they may?"

That was all Ethyn truly needed to hear. If sweet-natured Mossa Zahyle approved of his jumping into the fray, he saw little reason to hold himself back. It was the careless talk of a few, which had finally frenzied his temper to a boil. Talk, specifically, that supposed the council ought not match Athyn's assailants with aggression of its own, but rather, that further confirmation of imminent danger was needed before mounting any sort of active (and costly) resistance at all.

*Why is it, again, that I'd been so enthused to join this dust-ridden troupe of dim-wits?*

He stood up and at last began to speak his mind.

"These long few days gone by, I've come to find our very own lands have fallen under siege by outlaws, and it has brought me, in all earnestness, quite unto the edge of a most dreadful concern." Some fellow councilmen and women turned their heads to see who had spoken. His was an unfamiliar voice—at least at forum—and they did little to conceal their surprise at his commandeering of the room's attention, in a manner that was quite out of turn.

Poor Enric Cursyo was forced by Ethyn's declaration to cut short his lecturings upon the thrift management of coin, and he yielded his hold of the floor, in deference.

Ethyn continued, "I've witnessed an attack at one of our sea outposts, north of the Canterford Vale, that would raise the hairs upon each of our own necks, to a man and woman in this chamber, and I cannot conceive of a reality in which this threat, and those like them, might diminish; absent our firm, resolute, and immediate intervention. Certainly now, in the face of impending war."

"With finest respects to the prince, my lord," Legion Commander Thorngrove broke in, speaking directly in an authoritative tone to Ethyn's father, the Nhyle. Thorngrove was a large man with broad shoulders and muscled arms that served him well on the field of battle, but so too did he possess a fitness for complex political sparring, "As concerns the state of our lands, I assure you that *'under siege'* is an overstatement of vast proportion. Master Ethyn's alarm in these matters is doubtlessly fed by his ignorance of our affairs, which concern the Athynian Royal Legion. This foray of his along the coast to the Harbor Town of Stief was the first of an official sort he's ever made. I'm afraid he lacks a certain... refined perspective typically required to cast such judgments. I assure you all, we are well appointed to absorb any sort of 'Lockian assault that might threaten us, let alone any threat some flea-ridden band of outlaws may endeavor by the sea."

Ethyn scowled, his mind conjuring a vivid image of the wraith figure that had stolen its way into the outpost tower and had pilfered *documents*, of all things. He recalled, as well, the manner with which the assailants had resisted certain methods of attack with undue ease, and he hardened his resolve anew. "Let me make it crystal clear to all who sit in this chamber," he pressed, "that we've now encountered a new threat, altogether. There was a near-spectral form of a man, of bones and rotted flesh. Supremely cunning and in possession of dark aptitudes never before seen by anyone in these lands, I assure you. And I do not know if he acts alone, or as a proxy for a greater foe like Maelnlock, but for the moment, it makes no matter. He was seeking not our blood alone, but, foremost, our formal correspondence. Perhaps he was seeking information to use against us. Perhaps we're sailing this realm through the shallows in the dark, without the slightest clue how close we are to hitting bottom. We've just this evening been placed under notice of war, by our most powerful adversary in these lands, and we cannot but rid our own immediate premises of thieves and cutthroats? Perhaps we haven't a notion, in the least, what enemies lurk in wait 'round the corner—wraiths, and outlaws, and the gods know what else. And I hesitate to illuminate the obvious, as you are all surely perceptive enough to conclude for yourselves, but it certainly bodes unwell for our chances against the 'Lock, despite the commander's assurances otherwise." Many of the room's occupants emitted gasps of shock and repulsion at the generalized accusation leveraged against their Royal Legion (of all regencies!), and certainly too at the notion that Ethyn would paint for them a false image of some half-dead being possessed of dark mystics roaming the countryside, just to prove his point.

At this juncture, Chief Counsel Idris Ansel spoke up, his voice strained, "Are you suggesting, my Lord Prince, that we as a council lack a certain urgency in the manner of securing our lands and our people? That we fail in our most basic duty?" It was a calculated remark, aimed at making an enemy of Ethyn in the eyes of each member gathered within the chamber, just in case any among them hadn't already been turning as such in the wake of his declarations.

The prince had long despised Idris Ansel. The man carried an utmost peculiar air of wickedness about him, which (it seemed) only Ethyn could rightly detect. Ethyn had tried many times-over to convince his father to put the man out of the castle. But without sound evidence of Ansel's corruption, which Ethyn could never quite produce, the Nhyle would never part with his chief counsel. Yet, in any case, it was more than all that. Much more. Ethyn reviled the man's attempts to placate everyone around him in a manner so blatantly replete with insincerity; and for his exceedingly feeble council, whispered endlessly into the Nhyle's ear, which, to Ethyn, reeked of a soporific negligence the realm could ill afford to perpetrate any longer.

"I believe," Ethyn was staring at him judgingly, "in the very least, our spectacles have needs for a good polishing, is all. I *know* what I saw, and my tale bares no inflation of severity. We often understand little of what we see, and more often still, we fail to look hard enough in the first place. We've become complacent in our ways; our methods. We piddle far too long over what ought to be done and seldom ever take action bearing any real consequence. Do we not possess great responsibility here?"

"Most of us here surely realize, my Nhyle," Ansel said to Ethyn's father for all to hear, "as did the commander, moments ago, that the prince finds himself yet a wee bit out of his league amidst this council. Did I not warn you he isn't nearly yet ready?"

That was the last straw for Ethyn.

"At assemblage with the ambassador from Maelnlock; I ask, where was your *fire,* Ansel? Where was your insistence for *truth?* Why should you have waited for *me* to confront the ambassador and his false accusations, when it is *you* who are chief caretaker and arbiter of such matters? I cannot speak to specifics, but something in your demeanor during that exchange isn't sitting well with me. Not in the very least. And to be completely honest, your very essence has never sat well with me, and it frees me now to admit before all who gather here, so there will be no mistaking my true feelings."

"Ethyn, *enough!*" The Nhyle's interjection carried with it more than a hint of agitation, "I'll not allow for slander of our own principal council members. That is not the purpose of this forum. We do not cast accusations upon one another here. Not now and not ever. We've a declaration of war placed before us, if you'll kindly recall, and this is hardly the proper manner of facing it. Now, please be seated."

Commander Thorngrove was flush with contempt for Ethyn's outburst. Idris Ansel stared antagonistically at the prince, as well, then shifted his attention to the folds in Ethyn's tunic, as if trying to peer through them to find the stone that hung from its chain beneath.

"Forgive him, my lord," said Ansel with a sneer, "in times like these, it is within one's nature to assign blame, especially over matters that may escape one's own understanding. I am sure he will employ a more earnest approach, next time around." He was doing his very best to belittle Ethyn as much as he may; to embarrass him in the company of the council, and it was working. *This man has remained father's chief counsel all my life-long, and as yet, I cannot determine an adequate reason why. We ought to blast him off to one of those stars he's so fond of looking at from his tower, and leave father to follow his own counsel… or better yet, mine.*

Ethyn looked, then, across the breadth of the room; first at his father, who peered at him disapprovingly, and then at the other council members, who'd formed expressions telling of shock and disgust (of apprehension as well) at the accusations he'd made; as if they all feared he might turn against each of them next, right down the line—all except, of course, for Mossa Zahyle.

Slowly and reluctantly he found his seat again, and spoke not another word the rest of the session through.

\*\*\*

Ethyn Solis was, at present, wrapped in a most bitter mood after the High Council forum had drained the last vestiges of patience from his soul—not to mention the escort and assemblage, and everything else he'd put himself through of late.

Without registering a great deal of thought for where he was headed, he found himself opening a heavy set of double doors. The Nhyle's Court (and its perfectly-manicured gardens) spread out before him, then, like an open manse; its walls covered in ivy and flowering vines. He strode between two Royal Guardsmen who held spears at their sides, while a soft bong emanated from the tower abbey's bell house, high overhead. And though the evening had fallen dark, the labyrinth-like court remained plentifully lit by hanging lanterns and torches, spaced aesthetically throughout.

His boots hit the plush turf of the hallowed grounds, falling into a leisurely pace. In stark contrast to the hard realities he was facing at the present time, he had often romped about here in blissful play as a child.

He'd often run circles with brother Tae around the old statues of long-past Nhyles; each sculpture weathered slightly more than the next, standing in straight lines flanking the slatestone promenade. The brothers had skipped to and fro without much thought for the statues' significance, but the figures had since taken on new meaning for Ethyn. They came to embody the essence of Nhyledom, of rulership and power; their faces, their posture, the weapons of choice clenched within their hands of stone. And so, it was this place that he'd grown to favor most of all for contemplative thought as a young man, where he could turn to these historic figures for assurance, especially at times when great clarity of thought was so desperately needed.

*As is quite certainly the case right now.*

He stopped still where he stood, exhausted, and silently asked of the stone statues: *Is this my path, this burden of Nhyledom? Is there truth to be found in such a charge? Is there purpose? Validation?*

The questions were meant to encompass a broader context than just the prospect of someday inheriting the royal seat. He was asking, also, about life and the world around him—about the future that was (or was not) yet ahead of him. The statues' presence leant these questions more poignancy, while the flowering greenery, all around, alleviated some of the foulness and impropriety inherent in such musings. He knew not whether he expected to hear an answer. But to date, the Nhyles and their stone faces hadn't ever offered a response.

*Yet I shall keep asking, nonetheless.*

In lodging his inquiries, Ethyn meant to explore the virtues of something more, as well, something in the here-and-now; this prospective journey, which his intuition begged of him to undertake in short order. Lights in the sky over the Southspur Mountains hadn't simply piqued his curiosity over nights and days of late, they had challenged his very conception of reality. *Yet, might a journey of such improbability and peril prove even feasible? Might the source of those lights even be reached by the likes of mortal men like me and like those I would choose to accompany me?* Then this business of outlaws had arisen, and thoughts of their native archipelago had taken precedent in his mind. This, certainly given the imminent threat their tactics of wanton attack might pose to Athynian peoples and lands; the mystics-bearing wraith he'd encountered and its band of resilient assailants.

And finally, of course, was the latest concern thrust upon them by the foolish ambassador from Maelnlock, which had blown nearly all other matters out of the water. The declaration delivered at assemblage made Ethyn wonder whether embarking on a journey *anywhere* away from Castle Athyn, at a time like this, could possibly prove a beneficial (or responsible) undertaking at all.

*And then, and then, and then...*

It was all, without a doubt, a great deal to consider. He only wished the statues *could* respond to him, because he would very much like to hear what they might have to say. Not unlike his frequent desire to communicate with his Heron Bird, which circled now in the night sky, high above the court.

Despite all that had happened, though, in his heart of hearts, Ethyn was indeed leaning toward journeying somewhere. Where, precisely, he wasn't yet sure—whether it be the mountains for their streaks of flame or the archipelago for its wraith. Or elsewhere entirely. *Perhaps straight into the 'Lock itself!* He only knew of his burning desire to affect a positive outcome for the realm, and that sitting around and arguing pointless matters was never going to achieve meaningful results of any kind. And he'd become more satisfied, by the moment, in his decision to share these sentiments with the former guildsman of travel, Adrian Thurflyn, who would undoubtedly prove an invaluable asset.

*The man doubts many a great thing about my fitness for this pursuit, but he'll come around. He will fall in place, like the others.*

The prince strolled down the promenade for a time, looking along the line of those statues before him; the line of his ancestry. Nhyles of Athyn from the early Houses of Solis, their faces so worn he could barely make out the shape of their eyes and the curvature of their noses. But their weapons would surely still draw blood, given a proper sharpening. They held iron-tipped staffs, the primitive harbinger of the spear used even now by select Royal Guard footmen like those patrolling this very garden.

A finely-trimmed topiary divided the first grouping of Nhyles from the next, whose faces ranged from barely distinguishable to vaguely lifelike. They held, all of them, longswords of steel; blades of slightly finer workmanship than their predecessors' spears.

A few more toed the line, and Ethyn scanned their faces, too. More Solis men holding longswords. All except for one figure, which was always his favorite. A woman; Nohnce Marin Solis, who held a longbow and wore a quiver of arrows at her hip. He could remember looking up at her figure as a boy; the form of her face relatively well-preserved. Enough so that he could form an almost tangible image of her appearance when she'd sat the throne. Her strong features were said to have mirrored the makeup of her resolve.

One last topiary divided those figures from the remaining statues of Nhyles; four more men whose sculpted features all remained reasonably well-defined; including those of Tymian Solis, who held a twisted hunting horn in one hand, and a greatsword in the other. It was the legend of Tymian Solis, Ethyn knew, that carried with it a rather unusual tale.

"Tymian," said Ethyn, this time aloud as he scrutinized the sculpted visage before him. By blood, Tymian was Ethyn's great grandfather, but the two had never met. "If the tales are true, early in your reign, you were seen about the castle one day busying yourself over your practical duties as Nhyle, and then you were simply gone the next, without a witness and without a trace. Disappeared, like smoke in the air."

It was a mystery that engulfed Athynian lands and peoples during its time, to be sure, and one that still remained hopelessly unresolved. Even now, while Ethyn gazed upon the statue, he knew the grave beneath was filled with naught but soil, roots, and worms. Many believed Tymian had simply run away, overwhelmed by the toils the royal seat had (at every waking moment) thrust upon him. Others had their own theories; one for every imaginable scenario, and even some that were quite *unimaginable*, by common-sense standards.

"Do tell, great-grandfather; where had you gone? Wouldn't we all like to simply run away sometimes, as you did? Perhaps, before all is said and done, I shall follow in your footsteps; running away to some unknown destination as well."

*Perhaps sooner, rather than later.*

And so, lacking the desire to take himself through the castle to his private quarters, and in consideration of the especially mild temperatures this night, he decided to hunker down right there in the Nhyle's Court. A particularly plush bed of silk-grass was there, akin to that which he'd always favored walking through, barefooted in the fields just beyond the city's outer wall, where he and Tae used to troll the creek beds for toads in their youth.

And he nestled his head against an outstretched arm, and was taken by sleep before he could make even one guess upon the true whereabouts of his great-grandfather, the once-departed Nhyle of Athyn, Tymian Solis.

## 20 | A Loose End

*"Loose ends are irritants in our minds that dangle like wires disconnected; trying to surge somehow and reconnect themselves once again. We are so inclined to investigate our loose ends that they affect us beyond our cognitive function. Even after they are long forgotten, they subconsciously tickle and vex us, like an itch we cannot reach to scratch. But some loose ends miraculously return to us, to our awareness. And rarer still, we are (at long last) provided an opportunity to tie them up. Tie them up. Tie them up."*
—excerpt from the personal journal of Steven Spurlock

|Planet Deaer, Castle Athyn, North Court

The manor house was still an architectural beauty like its many twin structures lining the castle's inner wall, but it looked shamefully unkempt to Adrian Thurflyn's eye as he made his approach. The former guildmaster had made directly for the old building after the escort of the 'Lockian Ambassador had come to a merciful, if not tumultuous, end. *I'm getting far too old for these inane conventions of bureaucracy,* he'd lamented. *The sooner I'm on my way back to Stief, the better.*

Thurflyn thought his days of such highfalutin nonsense were far behind him, but it'd only taken a few moments in the midst of two political hackneys before he was thrust right back into the fray. *Why send a boy to wrangle a bull? Whatever comes of it, as usual, the Nhyle has only himself to blame.*

The front gate made an industrial yowl when he swung it open; familiar and strangely soothing, like the voice of an old friend from a previous life. But the prideful man looked with shame upon his former residence, in such disrepair as it was. The weathered shield bearing the sigil of the Traveler's Guild—a gnarled walking stick over a cardinal rose, lettered in flaking gold leaf—hung cracked and crooked above the front door. *This is why Stief suits me now; there is a reason the memories of the past are sweeter than the past itself... or sweeter at least than what has become of its physical remains.*

Inside, the house was just as he'd left it. The walls of the main floor rose three stories high; deep shelves lining each, from hand-hewn chestnut floorboards to coffered ceilings, all stocked with artifacts plucked from the most distant corners of the world. The air was musty. His nose filled with scented traces of the collected articles: insect specimens, idols carved from unknown petrified substances, barnacle-laced relics raised from the sea... and it was all blanketed in a thick layer of dust.

He stepped inside and shut the door, breathing deeply the stale aromas of his past. A globe was cradled atop a marble plinth in the center of the floor. With his finger, he drew a line in the dust on its surface from Athyn across the Central Sea to the Realm of Maelnlock. *Doesn't seem so far when you look at it from this vantage point,* he thought, then rotated the globe a quarter turn. To him, no point on the globe ever seemed too far away from where he stood. His travels had filled-in many uncharted regions of the world's map for Athyn's royal seat, and he was exalted for it in his time. *The places I've been,* he reflected, *the faces I've seen...*

He breathed a sigh of relief, then, knowing now that his beloved collection of artifacts remained intact. He'd curated it with care, as only one with a personal connection to each item could. But in short time, the subtle grin faded, and (as he looked around the cob-webbed quarters) it turned into a frown. It was the kind of frown that stirs from deep within and shows itself on one's face the only way it knows how, with a tender feeling of remorse and regret.

For he knew the days of the Traveler's Guild were long gone.

The dust certainly stood in evidence to that. Grand stairs leading to the upper sleeping chambers (once frequented in volume by fellow excursionists both young and old) looked as if they hadn't been climbed since the day of his leave. And as he hung his pack on a hook and eased into an armchair, he peered around the place with a true sense of loss. *I don't know exactly what I expected to find here. I only suppose the pain I feel looking around this place confirms the fears I've held for it, for so long. All has been abandoned; all hope has been lost.*

Thurflyn's tenure in the Royal Guard had lasted a storied forty-cycle of seasons. He was a natural-born talent from the start; an expert tracker by ten, an accomplished rider by thirteen, and he enrolled shortly thereafter, fueled by a desire to serve his realm. By twenty he'd solidified his position in the guard as a captain, responsible for the castle's South Gate pavilion and surrounding keeps. But his true passion was discovered some seasons later, when he was assigned temporary duty overseas.

He traveled first to the realm of Teluba, where the native peoples knew naught of weapons; only primitive tools and an unquenchable desire for mirth. Upon his return, he lobbied hard for another assignment abroad; this time in the ancient lands of Nyrulia, where magnificent structures stood of untold age and beauty. Thurflyn was certain they'd predated the Gilded Age; each building mended and fortified a thousand times over. There, he'd seen the peoples had grown so skilled at their crafts that he no longer wondered why Nyrulian textiles were the softest, nor their steel the strongest, yet lightest of weight.

Dozens of like assignments to foreign realms followed quickly behind, because the royal House valued the knowledge he brought back with him, time and again. "Perspective," the sitting Nhyle (Perwyn's father) had once said in a ceremony honoring the guildsman, "His contribution to Athyn is the invaluable gift of *perspective* in this world."

And so Adrian was gone from Athyn more than he was home. Travel became his mistress; his refreshment; his necessity. Halfway through his career, the royal seat advocated expansion of his enterprise and awarded him the manor house, so that he might host pupils; and soon, a small order of travelers was begun. They learned the skills of wayfinding, archeological excavation, and most importantly, the art of map making. The group would eventually be known as the Traveler's Guild. His life's work. His legacy.

There was a time he was certain his work represented the future of the realm—of the world, even; a gateway to peace and prosperity. An awakening from the quicksand ages of constant soldiering and war-making. *As I meant to instill in Prince Ethyn, we need only recognize that, should disparate cultures simply take the time to explore, to travel, to understand... there would be no desire for bloodletting or the breaking of a neighbor's home.* It'd been those very precepts that so inspired the royal seat in Thurflyn's day, and for a very long time, the need for the Traveler's Guild went unchallenged.

Yet now, he could see it was all withering away, and he had nothing left but the memories of what had once been.

\*\*\*

Adrian Thurflyn sat in his old armchair in the manor house that once hosted the teeming activity of the Traveler's Guild. He'd immersed himself in thought until the setting sun cast its rays through the westward-facing windows and crawled across the room where they faded indefinitely. Finally, he rose, lit a few candles, and set a small kettle to boiling in the kitchens for a cup of tea. *At least the pump still draws water, the kettle doesn't leak, and logs cast into the oven still carry a pure flame.*

The tea was fresh from a canister in his satchel; a mineral, smoky blend he'd always favored from the blue mountains of Turinguard. He'd sought the rare leaf while trekking the farm-laden realm on assignment. There, too, had been sugarcane known to grow in the fields of Turin, a perfect complement to the tea. The fibrous stalks produced perhaps the richest saccharine juice he'd ever tasted. *What I wouldn't give for a sweet nibble of Turinian sugarcane right about now and a few drops in the brew.*

Thurflyn's daydreams of journeys gone-by were admittedly far too frequent, but daydreams were nearly all he had anymore. Indeed, he couldn't deny his body was aging, his muscles and ligaments travel-worn. And they were less fit to endure the physical demands required of the kind of excursions he'd taken as a virulent youth; which was but one of the many reasons why Prince Ethyn's proposition for travel was so very troubling.

*The archipelago may not require a great deal of a strenuous travel, depending upon our mode of conveyance, but the Southspur Mountains? Should it come to pass I make one last taxing journey, I would scarcely select such a forsaken destination, with its blizzards and woeful gusts.* The thought made him morose of mind. *And such a journey would no doubt prove pointless. There's nothing up there at all. Nothing but...* He stopped mid-thought, pausing for a moment with tea cup in hand, and recalled something queer from long ago.

*An unlikely discovery and a journey potentially left incomplete.*

He set the cup down and strode to a shelf in the main gathering hall. Pulling out an especially worn book, he then recalled the story that told of its strange acquisition:

It was a mercifully mild night near the end of a long expedition when he'd found himself dining at the Olive Branch Inn of Elklyn, a remote Athynian village tucked into the foothills of the Southspur Mountains. He never forgot the warmth of the fire in the common room that night, for he'd just spent many frigid turns of the moon traipsing through the snow-covered heights of the dastardly mountain range to map the uninhabited, arctic frontier beyond its southern base. All of this, only to return suffering of dry mouth, brutally windswept of the face, and famished.

He'd dropped his gear in the common room and wasted no time acquiring a tankard of ale in one hand, a greasy leg of game fowl in the other, and a table by the blazing fire to thaw the chill from his bones. It was shortly thereafter that a woman had entered the inn carrying a burlap sack full of trinkets and other personal effects, and asked the barkeep if she may solicit his patrons for sale of her wares. She was a tiny thing with a pointy nose and dark hair cropped just above her shoulders.

"Might be you'll have more luck in the mornin' when folk ain't half sunk in their mugs," the barkeep had said, motioning for her to heft the sack onto the countertop for inspection. He'd pulled it open to have a look inside, "But it don't matter nothin' neither way to me, so long as you're fixin' to pay for a room."

The woman had nodded in agreement and dropped a copper piece on the bar before finding a table to spread out her items. Thurflyn couldn't remember the nature of all the things she'd had, only that they were of superior quality. Perhaps a silver belt buckle and a fine chiffon or hauberk—mostly men's items—but the unusual-looking book had been one of them.

"Excuse me, ma'am," he'd said when she pulled it out and placed it among the other items, "I'm traveling back to the city in the morning and could make use of a good tale to read while I rest 'neath a tree or two on my way."

She looked at him closely, and for all the travel-hardened effects he'd suffered, she still must have taken him for a wealthy sort. "The book'll cost you two silver pieces," she'd said, tersely.

"*Two silvers?*" He'd protested, "That may well fetch me an anthology's worth from any proper book merchant."

"Won't find many books for sale here'n Elklyn," the barkeep interjected. The grin he wore suggested meddling in the private affairs of his patrons was a special treat he quite enjoyed. "Not much use for readin' out here, as it is."

"Take it or leave it," she countered, "two silver pieces."

Truth was, with precious few settlements bearing merchant trade between Athyn Proper and the arctic hinterlands, he'd spent so little coin on his journey that he'd had surplus left over. He paid two silvers in return for the book and the small woman peddler threw in a forced smile for good measure.

The following day on the trail home to Castle Athyn, with his pack strapped on his back, he pulled out the book, searched its pages, and in short time cursed the tiny woman for a flaming crook. The script within was drawn in strange hand; provocative, with flourishes so exaggerated it more closely resembled a work of art than a narrative or historical sketch of any sort. Frustrated, he'd taken it for a foreign text and had almost given up trying to translate it altogether, when at last, he recognized a very ancient word scribed in the middle of a page: *Halcyon.*

The capital H, with quill strokes so broad their tendrils twisted into the swirling forms of other words above and below. The A and the L intertwined together like parsippany vines; the C and the Y so stylized they appeared as an illustration of a beast (or serpent) linking itself to the O, a lady's ring encrusted with gems, and the N resembled that of a great wave crashing onto a beach.

He loosened the straps of his pack, found a tree on the side of the road, and began to read. It'd taken some time, but once accustomed to the hand—drawn so carefully by the author 'Syrus'—he'd trained himself to find the words hidden in the artful script and soon marked the volume for its fantastically lucid prose, stylistically unlike any other he'd ever read. He sat 'neath the tree for the afternoon, slept through the night, and read straight through the following morning, forsaking his prior urgencies to return home. It was a stunning portrayal of a young woman's life, heartbreakingly beautiful in its simplicity. And, as he read on, he thought that if her tale were true, she'd have been perhaps the loveliest, most unassuming person to have ever lived.

As he'd continued to read on, unexpectedly he'd found—pressed between the young woman's last moments living alone on one page and meeting the love of her life on the next—a small, hand-drawn map. It'd been apparently slid into the book and forgotten, causing him to pause in his reading of the tale. He'd held the scrap of paper up and studied it with intense interest until his curiosity inspired him to pull out his own maps—those he'd just drafted of the Southspur Moutain regions. He found the sketch was nearly a precise duplicate of one of his own, in particular, of a valley in the mountains. Except the sketch found inside the book also seemed to depict a small village, and it bore a distinctive X, marking a spot in the valley's northern face.

He thought that at first, perhaps, the tiny woman who'd sold him the book had drawn the little map herself, but somehow (in the end) decided she hadn't, for reasons he could not pinpoint. *Intuition,* he supposed.

*But if not her, then who?*

*And how could I have missed an entire village in the mountains?? If I missed a village, what else might I have missed up there?* It was a frustrating proposition, but he'd been through the region—to the south-arctic and back—documenting the natural passes and valleys, not once but twice-over, and at no point had he encountered a village of any sort at all.

He'd considered turning around and hiking straight back into the mountains for one last survey of the terrain. *Just to confirm this sketch is a ruse.* He was, of course, never one to cut a corner or run from danger, but in the end of it, he realized he was so fatigued that he dared not risk extending the voyage, for fear he might very possibly never return. And he believed to do so for the sake of a simple sketch (which was left stashed and forgotten in a book) was folly of such great proportion that his peers might never allow him to forget it.

*Look at me,* he'd thought, when he finally stood up from 'neath the tree and resumed the trail back home. *I'm so frostbit of the mind that I've conjured this doodle into some sort of treasure map!!* And he'd become so resolute in his decision to disregard the sketch, that he'd hollered across the wide-open wheat fields that had surrounded him on the road, "Is it not a far better virtue to hold faith in one's own work than to constantly call into question its value and validity?!"

No sooner had he returned to the castle, than was he commissioned to design an itinerary for his next voyage. The High Council declared the greater southern regions desolate (and of no interest whatsoever) when his maps confirmed no habitation in the Southspur Mountains and the arctic frontier beyond. And the odd sketch's very existence had withered away from his consciousness. Time passed, and the book stayed on his shelves, the small drawing secured within, while countless other journeys were embarked upon, and countless other maps were dawn.

Now, presently—so many years later, standing by the bookshelf in the old dusty manor house and holding the volume in his hands, he thinly breathed aloud, "Ellessa," which had been the lead character's name from the story. But alas, this time, it wasn't a calming cross-meadow frolic with the spirited young woman that he meant to revisit by cracking open the book (though he did, for a moment, think upon how nice it would be to lie back and read the tale once again). What he sought instead was that very same small map, secreted between two pages toward the back of the volume.

*It once seemed so improbable that I would ever again consider the Southspur Mountains a suitable travel destination at all.* But here he was, looking at the small sketch again, and now, a prince was asking him to return to those mountains; a prince convinced there is something strange going on up there.

*High Councils, Nhyles, and princes... A fool's company, if you ask me.*

He brought the tea cup back to his lips and drew a long sip of his artisanal brew. *Three days,* he thought. *I promised him three days in the Proper to settle his mind over this journey. Three days only. After that, with his promised leave, I'll return back to Stief, and I'll not be seen around these haunts ever again.*

*And this time, the gods willing, free from the ties that have bound me to this place for far too long.*

### 21 | Strict Adherents to the Law

*"The bindings we sew for ourselves along life's journey
are unavoidable, I presume. I only wish we weren't
inclined to knot them so tightly at every pass, for a
good many of them are bound to deliver undesirable
results. Though, truly, if we ever hope to engage
meaningfully in life, at all, we ought to tie ourselves
with conviction around those things we value most.
Because unto the most ardent and faithful of investors
are the most satisfying returns granted. Or at least
that's how things ought to be... right?"*
    —excerpt from the personal journal of Steven Spurlock


|Planet Deaer, The Southspur Mountain Settlement

The public gardens in the Settlement sustained a tranquil ambiance
that always served to calm Haiyen Sün's nerves. The aspiring Second
Rank of Prima strode by a blooming crystalis shrub—in such fine fettle
and so fragrant—and breathed deeply of the clean air. She looked up at
the lofty stark-white pillars that circled the secluded Settlement. Far
above, they held their enormous convex lenses, designed to catch warmth
from the sun's rays and beam them down to basins set evenly throughout
the valley. The heat energy harnessed therein produced a perfect
microclimate for all those living in the tight-knit community, which
Haiyen called her own. Standing beside one such basin in the garden's
center, she closed her eyes and let the warm light fall generously upon her
face.

The gardens lay in a straight line from the Prima residences to the
Sages' Court, where the elder figureheads could always be found in their
various states of contemplation. Long before she'd moved into a room in
the dormitories, she'd often visited the gardens with her father, who'd
helped tend them in those days with his most greenest of thumbs. While
waiting for him to finish with his plantings and prunings—which
sometimes seemed to last the whole day through—she'd wandered into

the Sages' pavilions to tumble about their floors in play, or lay upon their cushions for rest.

It'd been, at first, no more than a tolerable means for passing the time, for satisfying childish curiosities; but eventually, it became a routine she relied upon for guidance and for lessons on morality, strength, and purpose as she grew older. The Sages welcomed her visitations with open arms, and it'd been a solid foundation for her life's bond with the place, indeed. But she never spoke of these early beginnings anymore, at least not with her fellow Prima rank members, and certainly not ever with the exile Koryn Naylor, who would have sorely disapproved.

Despite her familiarity with the Sages and the gardens, Haiyen held a tightness deep within her stomach on this particular occasion, departing from the solar basin and walking the paths through the manicured lawns. Begging for leave from her most undesirable duty, she knew, wasn't going to be an enjoyable task, and it was knotting her up inside, in no small sense. Yet she knew she oughtn't delay the resolution of this matter by tarrying about in fear. She must face her predicament head-on.

She would have it no other way.

All too easily, she found the Sage of Judgment, Fynian Arynel, sitting alone—legs crossed—on the immaculate wood floor of his private portico. She peered in, tapping lightly on the door casing.

"Enter," he said with a most serene voice.

His eyes were closed, and he sat as unmoving as the stone statues that occupied alcoves throughout the compound. Before him was a natural spring, which bubbled with crystalline water and flowed peacefully over rocks in a channel that ran the length of the gardens, feeding the flower beds. Haiyen took a seat on the planks across from him, and awaited his attention.

The wait wasn't long.

"Remember, my dear, when we took you in as a fledgling, when you needed help finding your way?" Arynel spoke without so much as opening his eyes, barely moving his lips.

"I do, Sage, very clearly," she replied, bowing her head, listening to the calming sounds of the running water. She had arrived with a troublesome matter strangling her mind, but already, she felt a renewed sense of peacefulness breaking loose within. "I shall not forget it. I was looking so desperately to dispense with my time, to hasten its passing, and you showed me that time, itself, was life's most precious resource; a thing never to be wasted."

"Such progress you have made since then," he offered, "because of your inner strength; your inner light, your will to succeed. Your mother's virtues endure within you. This is truth. You are every bit the Prima pilot she was. And your father's virtues, they reside within you as well. They've both passed the best of themselves on to you." Haiyen knew well of her mum's tenure as a pilot, which was said to have been a major breakthrough for all young women in the Settlement who may ever dream of joining Prima, as she had been the first. But her service had ended earlier than most, when Haiyen was born.

"I've heard mum's stories. They may be the source of inspiration I've leaned on the most so far, in all my time serving the ranks."

"I have no doubt they are."

"But she is a home-keeper now. And pa, I know him only as a gardener."

"Everyone has a role to play in their own time. Flying a craft in the sky in her youth, your mother helped protect us from the harm the flatlanders would bring upon us. Now, she cares for her home so she and your pa, and little sis might live in comfort. Of equal importance are these two duties, in their own ways. Do not think otherwise. And your father has taken to his life's calling for the benefit of us all, the beautification of our surroundings and the raising of nourishing foods. This, you must see, is also of equal importance."

"Yes, Sage, I am proud to follow in their footsteps; to make a contribution. It is… good to hear these things every once in a while, and I thank you." Her words faded, dissipating like smoke in the air, until once again, nothing but the sound of the spring's trickling water remained between them.

"But now you come to me with a nervous energy I've seldom sensed in you since those times long-passed, when you were a child," Arynel's declaration was all-too-perceptive, "and I desire to know of its source."

She nodded her head slowly, and looked up to him, seeing his eyes were still closed, but sensing he remained quite receptive. Somehow his inquiry had relieved a bit of her mounting anxiety; his perception of a lingering stain upon her mind, and this offer (to help wipe it clean) emboldened her enough to divulge her thoughts without pretense. "I have come to realize there is no use trying to hide my feelings from you, Sage, in these or any other such matters..."

Yet, in the midst of offering her overdue confession, Haiyen's attention was stolen by the sudden and graceful arrival of a magnificent bird, which swooped like a flash into the portico. It flapped its wings and landed with such feathered grace upon a balustrade between two support columns. And it folded its spotted brown wings, just so, standing there, silent and patient. Haiyen could only sit, unmoving, while her eyes glazed over at the sight.

She tried to ignore the fact this bird carried a remarkable, if not identical, resemblance to the messenger fowl Koryn had handled in his cottage. But the exile's voice began buzzing, unyieldingly, in her head trying to reaffirm her suspicion:

*I would think twice about placing such blind faith in the Sages,* it croaked. *Wouldn't you like to know who's sending these messages I'm receiving, and what they're for? What they say, and where in the great Beyond they go from here?? Because I'm sure* they *know. But they don't even find needs to inform the Prima rank, do they?*

Perhaps prompted by her extended pause, Arynel opened one of his eyes and peeked at her expectantly, as if the arrival of the bird were no irregular event at all.

Haiyen chased the exile's voice away and resumed, "What I mean to say, Sage, is that there is no sense in keeping my feelings from you, for I know you have our best interests at heart in all that you do." While she spoke, he closed his eyes again to resume his effortless meditation, but she was certain he was still listening. "It is nearly one year ago that you conferred upon me a great duty, and a great burden all the same; this jurisdiction over the fate of our Settlement's exile in the mountain's reach. I have just returned from there, and I must confess, this duty of mine has proven a most painful chore. I feel as though I cannot continue to fulfill it, Sage; to visit him thusly and to remind myself of his failure to care for me the way I have tried so dearly to care for him, and also his failure to care for the good of the Settlement, which is, moreover, his greatest wrong in all of this. And so I ask you, with my sincerest regrets for my own failures in this endeavor, to relieve me of this responsibility and allow me to confer it upon another, who is more willing and able." She felt so relieved, having put her feelings into words, and in such a way that she could only expect would resonate with Arynel—would convince him to release her from her burdens.

Now it was her turn to look upon *him* with an expectant eye.

But her relief was short lived, as she saw the Sage's brows furrow in disappointment and doubt. And after long moments, laced with tension, he answered, "We Sages have seen these matters in a different light. Where you have perceived failure, we have found success, though we understand it may be difficult for you to do the same. You have acquitted yourself admirably. And so, for these reasons, this duty of which you speak must only be fulfilled by you. You alone. Your request is, therefore, unequivocally denied."

Her heart sank at his words, and she was, all at once, flushed with shame and embarrassment and frustration; and to her great dismay, Koryn Naylor's voice wasted no time infiltrating her mind again, with full impact:

*The Sages have done a real number on you, haven't they, Haiyen? Haven't they?!*

It was all she could do to draw a deep breath, push the voice away again, and spit out a few words of acceptance, and apology, "Forgive me, Sage, for bowing to my own weakness in this. I see the wisdom in your decision, and will continue to pursue, with determination, the fulfillment of my duties." She rose from the floor trying in earnest to mask her deepest regret and made haste to exit.

"Child," called Arynel, beckoning her to halt.

*Please tell me you've changed your mind... oh, please*, she thought in desperation. But his next words dashed her hopes yet again.

"Make us proud out there," he said.

"I will," she replied.

"And child…"

"Yes, Sage?"

"Please shut my door for me. I will require my privacy for a time."

She looked at the back of his head, bowed stoically as it always was, and then shifted her gaze to the bird standing atop the balustrade; its head bobbing left and right in uneven cadence.

"As you wish," she said and slid the door shut with emphasis.

\*\*\*

It wasn't until the intrepid member of Prima rank had paced her way through the dormitories and into her private rooms that she realized just how exhausted she was, both physically and mentally. She tossed her flight satchel on a chair and prepped the boiler system for a warm shower. Located apart from the rest of the facilities in the compound, and having been designed exclusively for her private use, her residence, though modest, was the envy of her fellow male ranksmen, and she knew well of the childish resentment they harbored for her as a result. This, presumably, as if to suggest life in Prima rank were made easier for her as a female, for her so-called *special treatment*. She wished so badly she could tell them just how misguided those notions truly were.

*Just one of the many reasons I may never feel wholly at ease in this lug-headed fraternity.*

Large windows facing the open court of the gardens stood floor to ceiling, but could be frosted upon her command to preserve privacy. Once, half-asleep and clouded of mind, she had partaken in a shower nearly full-through before realizing the windows remained clear. She'd given passers-by a real show that time, including some of her embittered fellow Prima ranksmen, and she was still receiving sarcastic cat calls in remembrance of the embarrassing event. She'd presumed the source of their immaturity at the time: *Repressed desires must surely give way to the basest forms of primordial behavior. Despite their desperate wishes otherwise, they know they can't have me, so they give me their worst, instead.* She truly doubted it was an accurate assessment of the situation, but it had helped her cope, nonetheless.

This time, with the windows properly frosted, she stepped into the soothing stream of water; nearly scalding hot, just as she liked it. It comforted her, if only a trifle, to imagine the pain she felt in her heart might be washed away like such insignificant dust and dirt from her skin. To visualize the steam that enveloped her body melt away the chill from the ice and snow of that wretched mountain's peak, and the frostbitten memories that'd been made there. To presume that the lavender soap compound she cleansed herself with could disinfect the nooks and hollows of her spirit and her conscience. That the water could comb her mind's tattered mess into a fine flow of silken strands as it did her short but lustrous locks of hair. Or that the warmth itself could somehow lift the burdens that remained so heavily upon her shoulders with the Sage's denial of her seemingly most reasonable request. To dispatch of these duties that made her beholden to the wayward Koryn Naylor and to her haunted past, of which he was such a major part.

*Yet, can I resent the Sage for his decision? I've accepted my duties, and I've committed myself to seeing them through, no matter what personal cost they may exact. And I have no right to complain.*

She stood beneath the hot flow of water to let it fall upon her head and roll down her face for a time. And eventually, with near-pickled fingers, she pulled a catch to stay the boiler, and stepped from the basin to dry off with a plush cloth. Then she dressed herself quickly in casual Prima wears. She didn't want to consider the forthcoming consequences of the Sage's denial just yet. She most certainly lacked the patience (and energies) to engage in such a draining exercise at the moment. *But gods, how am I going to face Koryn again, after everything I said? After I'd run from him and forced him to the ground in such a panic?*

It occurred to her that she might implore the Sage to change his mind by telling him she felt threatened by the exile, but she knew that to be a falsehood. She'd never for a moment feared Koryn's intent; not even when she'd fled from him for the buzzcraft in taking her hurried leave. She only wanted to escape the emotional tension he was causing her. And so, she figured lying about such things now might only compound her sticky predicament.

*And things are good and well sticky enough as they are.*

Then there had been the arrival of the homing fowl in Fynian Arynel's portico, which most certainly was the same animal that had honed itself in on Koryn's icy perch, bearing its secret message. *Sage must have perceived my recognition of it, the way I paused and stared. He's always found ways to search me for my honest truth. Thank the gods Koryn didn't open the message and read it to me, or I'd have had some real explaining to do. Arynel would have perceived that as well. And it makes me wonder... Perhaps Koryn's paranoia is warranted.*

It went against everything she ever believed; that the Sages, in all their brilliance and compassion, were the perfect servants of the Settlement. But alas, it was there—this burgeoning measure of doubt.

*Perhaps the Sages are keeping things from us, after all.*

*No!* She told herself. *I will not wallow in this. I will not let Koryn's voice overtake my own judgment and reason.* When she lifted the frosting effect from her windows, the light came into the room, blood orange from the setting sun and of a most placid consistency.

Her thoughts turned, then, to what the Sage had said about her mum and pa. She looked at her neatly-made bed with such a burning desire to lie down and drift away into a well-deserved nap, but there was something she felt she must do first.

Something she hadn't done in quite a long while.

\*\*\*

The Sage's Court and its gardens were, by far, the most beautified grounds in the whole Settlement. This was a fact made apparent to anyone setting off for a walk through the surrounding streets, which were populated by dwellings of minimalist and utilitarian design. But that wasn't to say they weren't comfortable. In fact, the Settlement's Engineers had made progress—leaps and bounds-worth—through research and experimentation, improving nearly every facet of civilized life over nearly a century's time here. They'd devised tools to maximize the efficiency of basic utilities in the valley, and they had broadened the horizons of the elsewhere world, as evidenced by their flight craft designs docked in their hangar bays. But despite such advancements, it just seemed that most of her fellow peoples found success in their pursuit of happiness, not through an indulgence in opulence, but through a more simplified approach to life.

In this way, the Settlement was a modest one, indeed; small and tucked away in the great valley. She looked at the mortared buildings, white and box-like. Some stood vacant, and had done so for as long as she could remember, while others housed families; most frequently with children, parents, grandparents, nephews, and nieces (and the like) all in one living space. She passed the engineer's laboratory, which was equally practical in design, but its scale dwarfed that of the other buildings; standing larger, even, than the Sage's Court and Prima compound. It bore great double doors, through which entry was strictly prohibited, and supported two enormous climate basins on its roof.

Shadows had lengthened across the terrain when Haiyen broke through the outskirts and climbed a small ridge to a home that sat apart from most of the rest, at the northern foot of the valley's mountainous incline. The front entry was an open portal with a simple drape hanging down to make for a door. The greater microclimate extended its reach here, so she felt quite comfortable, despite sensing a slight drop in temperature; perhaps a pinch or so from that of the inner Settlement confines.

She peeked inside.

"Mum? Rhyn? Is anyone home?"

Before long, a woman came 'round the corner from the next room and smiled deeply when she saw Haiyen standing there.

"Mum!" Haiyen exclaimed.

"My dear," said the woman, and they embraced.

Then a girl favoring Haiyen's smart facial features and bright eyes came running to join in the greeting. "Haiyen!" she exclaimed.

"Rhyn. How've you been, sis?"

"As well as can be, I suppose."

"And you?" Mum seemed enthused, her gratified expression broadening to form familiar compassionate dimple lines, which had only become more defined with age, "It's been a long while since we've last seen you."

"So it has," confessed Haiyen, "I am… doing well. Where's pa?"

"Where else? He's tending his garden. If you take these, you might get there before darkness falls. He won't leave for home until it does." Haiyen's mum reached into a cubby and collected for her a small pouch filled with powder and a set of propulsion jet forms.

"Mum, please, I can't use this," she said, lifting the pouch, suddenly reminded of Bartyl Gleon's similar display of generosity. "It's in low supply, and it's yours. You need it."

"Take it," mum insisted, "He'll want to show you his latest growings, and you'll never get there in time without it."

Haiyen exhaled and gave in, "Well, alright then…"

With a pleased look, mum swung 'round to peer into the kitchen as if to check on something that required tending. "I'll add one more portion for supper," she said, then paused and made to look past Haiyen for a moment, "Unless you've brought another along with you?"

"No. It's just me."

And at that, mum and Rhyn both smiled, even more deeply than before.

*\*\**

The jet forms held tight while strapped to one's calf muscles and, when supplied with a bit of powder, allowed for a significant boost in the wearer's strides along solid ground, greatly reducing travel time over significant distances compared to unaided walking. Haiyen glided gracefully up the ridge embankment, thusly, and through a narrow pass in the valley's edge that'd been carved by a stream, which flowed quickly and abundantly through. She could match the rushing water's speed; even surpass it with particularly vigorous strides. And it became apparent that mum was right. It was certainly a distance that would have taken too long to cover under her own power alone. She'd forgotten just how far pa's secret garden lay from the homestead.

The rocky pass glowed in shades of burnt amber, and, once she'd glided through, her destination spread out before her, taking her a bit by surprise for how beautiful it was, especially as the sun shone with such intensity from its present, severe angle. The stream flowed over a fall, sparkling and shimmering on its way down to the planted meadow, and coursed straight through, feeding the neatly-plotted growings in such abundance. There was so much to see; so many new and different varieties of plants compared to her memory's image of the place while she descended.

Bent over, heaving a spaded tool overhead, then pitching it down into the soil, was pa. One strike after another, working and shaping the ground at his feet. He stopped for a moment to collect his energies, and in turning to dry a brow with his sleeve, he caught sight of her over the leaves of the taller crops that stood between them. A brilliant smile, hinting shades of disbelief, spread across his face as the realization set in. She smiled, too, emitting small bursts of joyful laughter, and when they came together, she effortlessly hopped the banks of the stream by virtue of the jet forms, and they embraced.

"Am I really seeing you, my girl, out here at this moment? Or have I indulged in the sour tabac leaf too much this day?"

The dirt smudges on his forehead made her chuckle some more, "You're seeing me, pa. Though these enormous blossoms did their best to hide us from one another. The garden has really become quite marvelous."

"It has, hasn't it? And yet, you and your sis shall always remain my two most prized flowers I'll ever have the pleasure of raising," they held to each other's forearms for a moment before separating, and he took up his spade again. "To what do I owe this wonderful visit?"

"I was just thinking about you and mum a bit today, is all. Thought it was about time I paid a visit."

"Well, we're always thinking about *you*," he'd never said anything to make her feel bad about living her own life, and she figured he never would, but she knew they missed her dearly. "You're busy out there, protecting us all. Just like your mum did when she was your age. We understand." He was leaning on the handle of his spade with a fond look in his eyes, illuminated wildly by the orange light of the setting sun, "It's uncanny, Haiyen, how you've grown into quite the image of her."

She looked down to the ground, "I've been thinking about her lately. How I've come to follow in her footsteps," she removed the jet forms from her legs and, at pa's prompting, they started strolling leisurely along a row of fruit trees together. "I wanted to ask, did mum enjoy her flying days? I mean, was she content in the Prima rank while she served?"

"As far enough as I could tell, sure; though you might want to ask it of her directly, if you really want to know."

"No, I intended especially to ask you. You were on the outside. You would have noticed things about her she may not have noticed about herself."

"If you're asking whether the Prima rank changed her, then yes, I'm sure it did. I'm sure it had a profound effect on her in many ways, as I'm sure it's having on you, too. She carried a lot of responsibility on her shoulders. There were times she was overcome by it all; there were times of weakness. But she pressed on. *We* pressed on. We persevered, together."

"She was lucky to have you, helping her through it all," they both smiled with sincerity in their eyes. At the same time, Haiyen wondered if her pa was making a connection in all of this to her own life. Specifically, she wondered how informed he'd been when it came to Koryn Naylor.

Certainly pa had always known of Koryn's crime and the exile piece of it, but she'd always wondered how much her family knew about the romantic side, which continued to drag her into the mire, even now. Her dalliances with Koryn had always been very secretive, per her own design, perhaps for this very reason. Perhaps because she'd seen things going terribly awry from the very start. Yet despite those efforts, folks across the Settlement (informed by whisperings and rumors) had presumed much of Koryn's life after the exile. And some of those details—most of them—had pointed indefinitely to Haiyen. To her assignment to deliver to him his essential provisions.

Her fellow Prima ranksmen seemed to know all but the most intimate details of her relationship with the exile, as well. But when it came to her own family, she knew not exactly the extent of their understanding of things. Of course, her mum and Rhyn had practically strained their necks trying to see if she'd arrived at the homestead with a guest—perhaps the exile himself—and had not hid their great relief when they realized she'd come alone. In any case, she wasn't about to start confessing her romantic missteps to her father at this stage; there was little sense in that. So she figured, instead, to investigate her newest curiosity, while she may.

"What about the Sages. Did mum ever seem to question their guidance?"

"The Sages... yes," her father then wore a face that suggested he'd moved his mind into a deeper level of thought. "Haiyen, you may have already taken note through the years, so this may come as no real surprise, but your mum and I," he began scratching the back of his head guiltily, "we've never been what you might call *strict adherents* to the law. We sort of do our own thing out here, you know? The homestead's off the beaten path. Heck, this garden of mine is *way* beyond Settlement boundaries. Some days, I think I might catch the sun with my spade just so, and signal a flatlander way off on the horizon. Who knows?"

They both shielded the evening light with a hand above their eyes and looked across the vast mountainous landscapes that sprawled northward, far and away. It was a spectacular view, comparable to any Haiyen could achieve in her buzzcraft, but nothing of the flatlands could ever be made out through the majestic peaks and layers of mist. No matter how brightly the sun would shine. Then her father continued: "I just can't get these plantings to grow this vibrantly anywhere else. Maybe it's the creek bed, or the northern exposure; but the point is, I'm not worrying too much about the Sage's boundaries whenever I'm out here, looking at these beautiful growings all lined up, and watered, and healthy as they are. And your mum, I know there'd been some element of friction in her day, maybe even distrust with the Sages. I always attributed it to our particular philosophies of life, but maybe there was more to it than that."

"So it wouldn't surprise you to find she'd had misgivings about the Sages' judgement? Perhaps even in their sincerity toward certain things?"

"Let's put it this way. She wasn't heartbroken over leaving the Prima rank when you were born, and she's never shown any inclination to go back. But I don't think she'd stand to let her beloved daughter serve in a rank led by folks she flatly distrusts either." He laughed a bit, "I don't know if I've quite answered your question, my girl. It all seems a bit complicated, I'll admit."

"Your efforts are most appreciated, pa. But, as in many things, my outlook on the matter is, as yet, perfectly murky, indeed," she laughed along.

"Such is life, I'm afraid," he looked down at their feet. They'd come upon a narrow channel carrying the stream water from its main conduit to feed a line of hearty stalks of some colorful, blooming species. The water was brown and the ground was turned mostly to mud, "I suppose it's what we *do* with the murkiness that matters most, huh?"

The lesson was well-taken, and there'd been just enough daylight left for pa to show her a good number of his finest plants. She helped him store his implements in a shed nearby, and strapped a satchel across her back to help him carry the load over the long walk back home. No jet forms to hasten the effort this time; just welcoming, restorative conversation, and a home-cooked meal of warm broth, noodles, vegetables, and spices with mum and Rhyn into the later evening hours.

## 22 | A Series of Weighted Bellows

*"Should we allow ourselves to indulge in the ecstasies
of passing fads, even when doing so may threaten our
long-term wellbeing? The pragmatist will advise
against taking risks bearing consequences you cannot
afford to face. Yet, the opportunist urges that one can
ill afford to suffer the ignorance of having never taken
risks at all, asking: When might you ever again feel this
excited about anything? Meanwhile, the man from the
future would likely say, forget the fads and the risks,
lock the door to your room, and find a nice, quiet place
under the bed in which to hide…"*
—excerpt from the personal journal of Steven Spurlock

|Planet Deaer, Castle Athyn

Little Tae Solis was trapped in a maze again. He looked back and saw Mystics Masters Talyn Slynth and Rak Hyon advancing briskly in his direction, carrying wooden practice swords; calling out that he was late for his training. He turned away from them and pressed forward, noticing then that he, too, carried a sword in his hand. But this one was made from steel and bore sharpened edges, and he used it to slice a passage in the hedges that lined his path. He stepped through, and on the other side there were people—many people—gathered together, cheering in anticipation of something.

Riders came into view. It was brother Ethyn, who rode in an upright posture leading a small company of soldiers with a foreign delegation into the city. The elder prince acknowledged the crowd with waves and gestures, and seemed to look in Tae's direction. But Ethyn's attention was averted by a young woman's desperate attempt to break from the crowd and reach for him, grazing his boot and nearly fainting under the spell that such proximity to the Heir Prince had cast upon her. And by the time the maiden had gathered herself up from the scene and had suffered admonishment by one of Ethyn's soldiers, Tae saw that the whole delegation had passed without anyone taking notice of him at all.

And he was glad for the anonymity.

Except someone *had* noticed him. But it wasn't anyone from the procession. Instead, it was the newly-arrived girl from the Mystics House, Brychen, who had found him in the crowd. He reached for her hand, then, and walked her away from the frenzy, catching a passing glimpse of Slynth and Hyon, both of whom were eyeing him closely. Brychen could not mask her excitement; she'd been enthralled by the festivities; the Horns of Herald, the singing, the dancing. And she'd begged him to continue with the tour he'd been giving her, if he would be so kind, and if he didn't quite mind her company. Then she'd advanced upon him slowly, until he felt the branches of the hedge maze touch his back and the greenery folded about him again. She pressed up closer, putting her lips against his cheek, and—

—To come awake at that particular moment was a cruel and twisted jape, but it couldn't have been helped. He was surprised the discomfort of his most awkward position on the floor had allowed him any sleep at all. *Much less these dreams I've dreamt, in such great detail.* He wondered how much of the content of them had been imaginary, and how much had been actual memory of the prior evening's events. *More likely than not a muddled combination of both, I suppose.*

But the most shocking revelations of the morning hadn't truly ceased until he'd surveyed the room through sleepy eyes, and had seen, curled up in a heap of sheets and blankets, the girl's smallish form— Brychen, herself—peacefully at rest upon his very own bed. And his nerves pulsed at the sight.

He rose and padded on bare feet to the bedside, his wheat-colored hair shooting out in a tangle every which way, and he stopped to have a closer look. He'd been gentlemanly enough, it seemed, to offer her his most comfortable accommodations, and that had to garner him *some* credit. He supposed it wouldn't do much to endear himself to her most tender heart, however, if she should find him standing over her, staring at her like this. *Breathing from my open mouth, nearly drooling as I am…*

But it was thusly that he *did* stand there and stare—for a few moments at least—enthralled by her form and features, which were just so exquisitely well-suited to each and every one of his tastes, including those he never knew he had.

It was only when he saw the glass globe nestled within her clutches that he'd been wrested from his voyeuristic trance. *Is that one of my globes she's holding there? One from Irillio Pasca's shop?* His head swiveled sharply to see that one of his globes was, indeed, missing from its set, perched upon the shelf on the far wall—the smallest globe in the series; its stand sitting empty at the end of the row.

Then he remembered, at last, another scrap of detail from the previous evening.

When their whirlwind tour of the upper city's greater districts concluded, Brychen had begged his approval to join him in his chambers, saying she simply wasn't yet prepared for the evening to come to an end. And well, neither had he been, for the truth of it. The small hand-holding piece of the affair, alone, had lifted him to heights he'd never known. And a precipitous release from her presence, he expected, would certainly have initiated a most treacherous emotional collapse. So he had obliged without much (or any) extended convincing required.

She had, when they arrived, taken an almost immediate, keen interest in the globes. In fact, as he recalled as well, she'd spoken continuously of Pasca's curiosity shop upon their passing through the rest of the upper city, and had been regretful of the fact their visitation had been so brief; that they were deprived of the opportunity to explore more of its wonders inside. So he hadn't discouraged her when she reached for the globes in his room. She'd taken them, one-by-one, into her hands and looked deeply into them—their pale silver, smoky depths—and she'd said she couldn't quite explain it, but that they'd given her the feeling of something terribly familiar.

His reluctance to allow her to not only handle the globes, but to *remove* one from the shelf and clutch it within her possession on the bed, had been strong. But it had worn off quickly enough when he realized the extent of the joy it was giving her. And now he saw that the effect had lasted, indeed, the whole night through, seeing that a smile of peace and contentment remained upon her face, even as she began to wake. She stretched her arms and opened her eyes to see him there, hovering as he was, but she made no expression of offense. She just emitted a little yawn and gathered her voluminous amber-colored curls away from her face.

"Is it morning, Tae?" she asked, rhetorically—both because evidence of dawn had clearly begun to show from outside the windows, and because she could not have truly expected a verbal response, besides.

He nodded, then walked deliberately to a large chest at the foot of the bed and opened it with purpose, tossing through its contents until he found a small leather satchel. It took only a moment more to return to her side, where he held it open for her to drop the globe inside. She lifted the curiosity up between their faces and stared in awe while it captured sunlight that filtered through the windows, brilliantly. Then she placed it inside the satchel, and Tae buckled it tight before handing it to her, making a gift of it, for her to keep.

"You're giving this to me?" she swung her legs over the side of the bed and stood up, still dressed in her simple mystics wear, and she accepted the satchel from him, lifting it up and over her head and hanging its strap over her shoulder. "I can't tell you how much I do love it, Tae. Oh, it's just magnificent!"

Then she leaned in and graced his cheek with a swift and light kiss.

*The dreamstory predicts the waking world... how terrifying.* He considered the thought for a moment, and almost turned around to see if there stood a maze of hedges behind him. There was no hedge, of course. This time, he was more awake than he'd ever been before. *How wonderful!*

"Oh, but I fear I must return to the Mystics House now," there was suddenly worry in her big, deep green eyes, "if the mistress might be looking for me. If she might be worried…"

He nodded in agreement, knowing this was undoubtedly the case, and made for his wardrobe, pulling out his favorite cloak and leaping into his mocks to hasten their departure. She joined him, and they were on their way to the Mystics House in moments; the barn that housed the wieldling dormitories. He found himself walking with such a lightness in his step that he'd never (in all his life) allowed himself before; with such carelessness for all matters beyond his singular, current focus of this girl. He'd previously believed only fools would carry themselves in such a way; that to do so was to make oneself ignorant of all the dangers that could befall anyone at any given moment. But with Brychen by his side, something had changed.

*And well then, I say, I have promptly and without regret joined this preeminent Society of the Foolish; for this life's worth the living, and I'll not feel ashamed of it.*

*Not in the least!*

\*\*\*

"Tae, is that you?" called a familiar voice coming toward them from down the hall, startling him from his whimsy, "Fancy seeing you here of all people, out and about in this early light, but what great fortune!" The broken voice belonged to the High Counsel himself, Idris Ansel. The astronomer's wispy eyebrows carried upon them strands of spider webs that swayed and drifted from side to side as he moved closer. He appeared to Tae like he'd just awoken from a crypt.

When the three of them finally met in the hall, Ansel anointed Brychen with a particularly curious stare.

"Well hello," he murmured, "I hadn't seen you there at first, girl."

"Hello," she'd replied, simply, staring back at him with an equally curious aspect, and Tae could almost feel a nervous tension emanating from her; from both of them.

The beleaguered councilman seemed as if he'd been derailed from his purpose, but for only a count or two, before recalling his motive, "Tae, as I was saying, it is good fortune that I've found you. I've a map here that is begging your interpretation."

The Ageless unfolded a shock of cloth bearing schematic drawings and held it up to a nearby window so Tae could clearly see its markings in the dawning light. "You know what this is, hmm? This is a map of the warren of pathways beneath the castle. I've just been down there through the night after a most jarring council forum, let me tell you—but that is a separate concern altogether. And it seems I've run into a bit of a dilemma. Do you recall telling me of your assignment to retrieve the practice swords?" Dust sprinkled down from the man's hair and beard while he spoke, "Might I trouble you to identify where, exactly, you were when the *event* occurred? And precisely how you might have found your way there?"

All Tae wanted to do was continue onward to the garret in the mystics barn with Brychen. His nerves were mounting, thinking she might be scolded for her extended absence, and this unforeseen delay wasn't doing them any favors. *If he prattles on much longer, Brychen's likely to think I've no concern for her reputation with the Keeper of the House at all... or the Masters, either.*

Tae looked at Ansel; expressionless and without a motion or gesture, somehow in hopes the old man would simply go away. But he didn't.

"You know that of which I speak, Tae, no? You played the flame card..." Ansel's eyes were twitching. His frail body and robes were bathed in sweat and sprinkled with soot, and for a time, he was shaking so much he could barely hold the map still enough for Tae to see its particulars. Tae took the man's display of physical distress for signs of desperation. It was all in keeping with his peculiar behavior ever since their exchange in his tower; after the playing of the flame card, which Tae now ruefully regretted. *But what is it about my recent disappearance that could have possibly driven him to such limits so quickly?*

"My boy, you do recall, yes?" His speech was ill-measured and his breathing was labored. "I would shudder to think I may be forced to inform your dear mother that, in addition to prolonged stints of self-isolation, you've begun to exhibit forgetfulness of a most troublesome nature. That would not make her glad in the least, I should think... No, not glad at all."

It was a threat, Tae could intuit as much, and it made him angry that Ansel had chosen this moment to belittle him so; in the company of Brychen, no less. He formed a scowl on his face and raised a finger, pointing to a few indeterminable clusters of lines on the map. Then he drew his finger along one, through intersecting strokes in the armory until he finally rested on a spot where he believed his disappearance had occurred. Right in front of the mysterious cave he'd found down there in the catacombs. But he was not particularly concerned with the accuracy of those locations, or with the nonchalance he figured he was exuding in the process.

"There? Are you *sure*?" Ansel huffed through a crack in his voice.

Tae nodded in the affirmative. *Now will you leave us be??*

"Very well, Master Tae," the astronomer was grinning from ear to ear, content as a bee in a field of flowers dusted over with pollen. And his demeanor changed from frazzled and threatening to a sort of coddling display of positive reinforcement. "Your insights, though limited, are more significant than you can possibly understand. Your mother will be pleased to hear of your continued communicative proficiencies. Perhaps someday we will have a true breakthrough. Perhaps we will even have a proper conversation, you and I, over mugs of ale. But you know, my little prince, it is quite true that the absence of progress still trumps the very dark bleakness of regression," he looked again at Brychen with an eye of keen interest and said: "Now carry on with your most vital quest, whatever it may be. And please, my boy, feel free to make like this conversation never occurred!"

Tae was happy to do just that, as he watched Ansel make haste in the direction of his personal tower chambers. Tae had to focus his attention now on more pressing matters—like how, exactly, they were going to pacify Mistress Almetta over Brychen's absence. Accordingly, as Ansel walked away, a preponderance of anxiety began to festoon around him like a stole woven of poisonous snakes, and he simply could not permit his thoughts to linger upon such insignificant rabble as was just coughed up by the flaky astronomer.

*Focus*, he told himself. *Focus on the task at hand.*

After climbing the barn's second story ladder, they found, to their great relief, the garret hall was empty of visitors, or Masters, or nosey Keepers, too, for that matter. But the girl's door was open a crack, casting a band of bright light in their path. And inside, they heard the pacing of worried feet; back and forth, and back and forth across the floor. When Tae slowly pushed open the door, they saw the footsteps belonged, indeed, to the stout Mistress Almetta.

"Oh, for mercy's sake!" The woman exclaimed to him when the door swung open, "The two of you cannot begin to imagine how worried I've been. Master Hyon said you'd returned to the inner sanctum safely last evening, but when I'd come up to the room this morning, you were nowhere to be found!"

Tae had made plans to offer a combination of pantomime gestures to convey Brychen's innocence, but Almetta hadn't allowed time for any such appeal. She grabbed the girl by the wrist and pulled her into the room, while simultaneously rebuffing Tae's attempts at excuse-making.

And she promptly shut the door, leaving him in the hall.

"We have rules around here, my little girl, important rules, and you'll do well to learn them," her chastisements were muffled, but he could still make out the majority of their meaning, "I'm not sure what sort of unruly, fly-by lifestyle you're accustomed to, but inside these castle walls, we abide by House standards. Do you understand? And I'll not—"

"The girl has returned, then?" Master Talyn Slynth had somehow made his way into the garret without Tae noticing. Tae looked up at him. The Master was too tall. He had to lean his head to the side in order to stand upright beneath the low-peaked ceiling.

Tae nodded.

"Well it's a good thing, then," continued Slynth. "And how about you?"

Tae shrugged. He could still hear the muffled lecture continue from behind the door.

"There's no use in standing out here," said Slynth. "They're going to be in there for a while. Almetta's life lessons are, as you know, not often brief affairs. But since you're here at this hour, might I interest you in a bit of training? You've fallen so hopelessly behind the rest, Tae."

Without a response, the smallish prince simply walked past Slynth to the ladder, and began climbing down. And when he arrived on the second story, instead of descending to the training level, he made for the foot bridge that led over the Gardens of Grace to the castle proper, and his personal chambers.

Slynth came down the ladder, too, and watched him go.

And Tae figured that was answer enough.

***

|Planet Deaer, Castle Athyn, The Nhyle's Court

Elder Prince Ethyn Solis awoke in a bed of grass at the end of the promenade, along which stood the statues of Nhyles, who had ruled Athyn through the ages. Absently at first, he gathered himself up and made his way through the gardens; their twisting and turning pathways. He climbed the stairs of the battlements, and strode more briskly along the wall-walks that skirted the castle's southern face. Thoughts born from prickly encounters the previous day still scurried through his mind; he had met adversity on escort and at assemblage, and during the high council forum as well. In the end, he'd decided firmly he must respect his own intuition as applied to matters of great importance, even when such feelings are at odds with others—ambassadors, council members, and his own father, alike.

At the parapet's height, he found that a lifeless prelude to dawn had fallen eerily silent about the castle grounds, where (upon a light breeze) not a single leaf rustled nor did a morning dove's gentle cooing sound. Even the locusts' constant whirring from the wooded groves tapered off and away. And just as he was about to label the simultaneous convergence of these strange effects a coincidence, and cast them aside— for he really oughtn't delay his preparations for leave-taking on this proposed journey of his any longer—he believed he saw from the corner of his eye a dark form move through the very stillness of the court below. Like a long-legged insect darting over the surface of a serene pool, a man bolted on foot through the yard, heading for South Gate with an urgency, which was impossible to deny.

*Who is this man that flees the Royal Court like his life depends upon it? And why?*

In the instant that followed, like the crashing of a giant wave against the hull of a ship, the sound of an explosion pierced the air and rocked the castle to its core, shaking Ethyn's footing where he stood. He felt the foundation of the great structure buckle and creak. And the explosion was followed immediately by a series of weighted bellows and scrapes, as if an entire fore-keep had begun to collapse and fall to the ground.

He ran as fast as his feet would carry him. Down a battlement stair to South Hall (past its leaded glass windows) and through hidden passageways scarcely wider than his lean frame would allow. Along concourse and arcade; into the kitchens—steam in his face, and the rattle tat-tat of pots and pans shaking from the blast—chopped fruits spilt upon the floor, an aroma of succulent meats beginning to burn, and the simmering of breakfast omelets in oil as he passed the untended stoves.

*The cooks have all fled in fear of the blast...*

Across a hall, down a case of stairs, and to an open court he pressed, where he saw castle folk (most as yet in their night clothes) pushing toward the doors leading out and away from the chaos. Block and mortar was crumbling and falling in great masses from the Servants' Keep. Slabs slid off from above and smashed into the tiled yard, splitting into thousands of pieces, scattering people who tried desperately to avoid the next impact. And a great billowing of dust followed in thick clouds close behind.

From the court, he charged down a hall and into a broad doorway that opened to a room walled and capped with glass panels—the solarium—where the Nohnce's garden of lush flora burst forth from every angle. But the structure here was shaking, too. Some of the panels overhead shattered with the concussive blast, leaving glass and roots and leaves strewn all over the stone footpaths, threatening to trip him up as he ran. He entered an atrium and came at last upon a thick, arched door, which he burst through with a lowered shoulder, out into the morning's haze beyond South Court. It was there that the Royal Guardsmen had (in the frenzy) abandoned their posts at the gate to lend aid to those in peril. And it was very well, for people swarmed everywhere in hysterics, desperately in need of guidance.

South Gate, however, stood open and swaying on its hinges as a result. *The fleeing coward must've had free passage for escape!*

Beyond the grounds, Ethyn well knew that the roots and low-hanging branches posed dangers to any such absconder, often reaching out and catching someone around the ankle, or across the chin in the muted grayness at this hour. He had, in fact, stolen away from his bedchamber many nights in his youth to go adventuring in the dense woods south of the castle—absent his father's permission, of course. It had only cost him a trip to the royal kitchens to swipe a freshly-baked slice of pumpkin bread or a cup of cinnamon ale, which he'd always given to the Royal Guardsmen on duty in return for their absolute silence on the matter.

If the roots and branches weren't barriers enough, he knew the brush became a tangled web of vegetation only a few paces ahead. It would take a trailblazer in possession of the finest hand axe in the world to make short enough work of the undergrowth, as would be needed to make a clean escape without taking the time to follow each and every twist and turn of the narrow trail there-through. And so, his pursuit lasted only a few moments further before he happened upon the man, who was so hopelessly ensnared in vines and thorny thickets, that his every move (his every attempt at escape) only embedded him more and more within nature's trap.

"A curious thing," Ethyn was speaking so loudly it bordered on shouting, and the words were harried by an effort to catch his breath, but he continued, "A very curious thing, to think that a man could anticipate the cataclysmic destruction of the sort, which has just befallen Castle Athyn, even *before* it should occur. Tell me, sir, are you possessed of some oracular mystic? Or can it be *you yourself* were the perpetrator of this foulness?"

The man started speaking in a frantic tongue, not unlike the vernacular he and Aryk had heard from the assailants at the outpost, and he squirmed and fought against his leafy restraints. Ethyn couldn't understand a word of it, but the theatrics were wrought plainly enough with guilt that the prince had a mind to strike the man where he lay, for all the unfettered anger that poured through him. *Innocent people have undoubtedly lost their lives by this act, and someone is going to have to answer for it.*

It was then that the wings of a wick-feathered redbird suddenly batted and fluttered against the air, landing upon a branch so very close at hand, and Ethyn noticed (at once) a clip fastened to both of the fowl's legs, taking it for none other than a messenger fowl. One clip held a message while the other was empty, meaning it was yet in need of a second—*Which this perpetrator undoubtedly holds secure, somewhere within his possession.*

"I will have it now!" Ethyn shouted. When the man did not answer, Ethyn repeated, "I will have the message now. Show me where it is, or I'll find it myself."

The suspect refused, or simply did not understand, but in either case he was so thoroughly tangled in the brush (the thorns and the thistles) at this point, that despite his greatest efforts to fight the prince off, he could barely move. Ethyn muscled his way into the man's pockets and sashes, finding nothing (and nothing more) for his efforts. Then a search of the man's cloak yielded a scant few coins and a hair brush, but little else as well. Finally, with no recourse left, Ethyn stripped the man of his boots, and in the toe of one, found a small, razor-thin scroll, rolled tightly and waxed. And upon Ethyn's unraveling of it, the man bellowed and bristled, again in that same, foreign tongue.

The prince's patience was spent, allowing for only a brief pause before slugging the man flush across his cheek bone, at last leaving him unconscious and limp in the bramble. And it was a relief for Ethyn to have silenced such brackish nonsense, despite the throbbing in his hand from the impact. But as the prince held the message up to a golden beam of dawn's light—newly projected through the dense leaf cover overhead—his attentions were averted, in full. The script was, again, foreign, yet there was a hint of familiarity at the end, for which he could venture a translation, himself.

*All hail Alamere.*

## 23 | Falling to Pieces, Hard and Fast

*"What defines a person's identity? Is it one's own perception of 'self' that reigns supreme, or is it the outside world's perception that matters most? Or, rather, is it a clever combination of the two? Can it be? I've wondered whether the two might ever be in concert with one another. Are we truly seen by others the same way we see ourselves, or are we all just hopeless, hopeless delusionoids?? Perhaps we might only hope to identify the forces of good and bad within ourselves, and let the chips fall where they may..."*

—excerpt from the personal journal of Steven Spurlock

|Planet Deaer, Castle Athyn, North Court

Athyn's very own Master of Travel, Adrian Thurflyn, had chased the dust from a bed in the upper dormitories of his old guild's manor house. He'd enjoyed a surprisingly restful night's sleep, thus far, despite—against his greater desires—having partaken in a particularly bothersome diplomatic escort the day prior. But it was in the lingering stillness of the morning that he was roused from 'neath the coverlets by the sound of an enormous *thud-clapping bang* and a series of ground-shaking *crackings and poundings* that followed. And after rising in a jolted frenzy, hurrying to peer through a small dormered window, a most dreadful source of it all was revealed to him.

He took up his travel clothes from a bedside chair, slipped into them recklessly, and scrambled (as fast as his sore joints would allow) down the grand staircase to the front door; out onto the lawn, and through the creaky iron gate to have a closer look. What he saw halted him in place. He found the Servants Keep (part and parcel to the great Castle Athyn itself) had, indeed, collapsed to the ground nearly in full, with stone blocks and roof slates and objects of all various sorts strewn far across the court. Shouts and screams pierced the air, as did the commands of Royal Guardsmen who swarmed the yards in an effort to secure the scene.

*Flames and ashes... what ever could have happened here?*

Thurflyn was not a man of combat, having never trained as such, but he was full of compassion for others and his heart was composed of great courage as well, and those two qualities (such that he *did* possess) forced him, many times throughout his life, into conditions of peril. And likewise, they had done so again, as he took off and ran alongside guardsmen toward the fray, watching pieces of the keep continue to wobble and fall from the upper reaches and roofs. On his way, a woman had lost her footing and had fallen in her attempt to flee from the keep, and he stopped to help her up, seeing she carried a newborn baby in a sling across her body.

"Head for the Travelers Guild for shelter," he told her amid the madness.

"Beggin' your pardon?" She seemed in tremendous dismay.

*Mercy me, I can see the guild has already passed from the memory of our people...*

"The manor house of the Travelers Guild," he repeated, pointing, "first in line beside North Gate. You'll be safe there... Go!"

She seemed to understand, nodding her head, limping her way toward the house, and Thurflyn immediately turned back toward the fallen keep. Clusters of people stood around the yard, not sure what to do with themselves; many of them watching as he pushed past the debris and the crowds. He leapt onto the piles of rubble, trying to dislodge larger fragments in hopes that survivors might be found beneath them. Heavy masonry stones were laid asunder that he could budge aside, but merely, and thick wooden support beams barely yielded to his quitting strength. Piles of linens, a wash basin, and a scattering of different-sized bars of soap; a cupboard smashed to pieces, spilling spools of yarn and bolts of fabric. He hefted a mattress aside, finding an exterior window of the keep underneath, its frame buckling and glass shattered, and heard a voice (perhaps two) strained with heavy breathing inside.

He kicked the window open and thrust himself into the failing structure, finding two boys—squires or pages likely still in training—pinned beneath an overturned armoire. With little room to spare, he winched the piece free from the ground, clearing them by the narrowest of margins for escape, which they did, and they followed him from 'neath the structure back down the rubble slopes and out into the open yard. This, only moments before watching their portion of the keep collapse under increasing weight from above, where the facades were still crumbling and falling, with smoke rising from a score of fires that had taken to flame.

A group of hysterical bystanders gaped in witness to Thurflyn's heroics while a grateful Head Mistress came forth with tears in her eyes to claim custody of the two boys, kissing their heads and holding them close to her as if they were toddlers. And it was then that a murmur began to stir around him amid the sobbing and the screams. It was a curious prattle, or so it seemed to his ears, and he thought he heard his name *'Thurflyn!'* float upon the air more than once… more than twice.

Mere paces away, he saw a castellan pointing in his direction while speaking to a Royal Guardsman. The soldier appeared to take notice, and attentiveness flickered brightly in his eyes while he approached. At the soldier's arrival, the Head Mistress pulled the two boys over, interrupting his advance.

"Please, reward this man who has saved these two boys, right before my eyes," she said, "when I was too overcome with fear to save them myself!"

The guardsman gave Thurflyn an inquiring look that seemed to reveal a bevy of suspicious thoughts running through his mind, but the woman grabbed at his cuffs, diverting his attention for a moment, pleading, "He is a champion in our midst… a champion!"

And without a moment's hesitation, Thurflyn integrated back into the press of gathered people, making himself scarce from the curious throng. *Men of exile do themselves no favors returning to their forbidden places, let alone making themselves material parties to great catastrophes therein. I can only imagine Perwyn Solis' thoughts, were he to find me here, all-of-a-sudden, in the midst of such an awful scene as this. Yet it pains me to flee, without recourse to provide more aid.*

Though flee he did, among castle folk and guardsmen, and others of a great many station still pushing and shoving their way to (and from) the destruction; some trying in earnest to lend a hand, and some fleeing wherever and however they could. And in looking over his shoulder at the scene one more time, he fell upon despair.

*Blast it all. Only one night returned to this accursed city, and my fears are confirmed. Athyn is falling to pieces… hard and fast.*

\*\*\*

Former Guildsmaster Adrian Thurflyn made a swift entry back into his old manor house, and looked up to see, sitting in the expansive living room before him, the woman he'd helped earlier in the yard. She held her baby in her arms, rocking it slowly back and forth while it slept, and she looked at him when he entered the room, greeting him with a warm smile.

"M'lord, you're back. I'm grateful for havin' run into you, and I'm glad you've returned to keep us comp'ny with all that's go'in on out there. My name is Hattie. I don't think I'd had the chance to tell you b'fore."

"Pleased, Hattie," he said, nodding, "I'm Adrian."

"I'd never seen anythin' quite like what I'd seen this mornin', and I was scared for my baby. But when you'd helped me, and showed me where I could go, it'd given me such strength. Thank you for your kindest hospitality."

"It's no burden on me," he offered, looking at the neglected furniture, "sorry about the dust…"

"We're payin' it no mind, m'lord," she was rocking the baby in her arms gently.

"You were quite fortunate to escape the keep before it collapsed."

"When the loud noises started, we were already well awake," she looked down at the infant, "he was cryin' the whole night through, it seemed. I was worried he'd kept most everyone else awake, too. Now I'm hopin' he did. I thought that if he did, then maybe a few more'd been able to escape before gettin' themselves hurt."

"Indeed, his crying may have saved more than a few lives this day," Thurflyn wasn't the most comfortable man around infants (or children at all, for that matter). Usually sharp and insightful, he found himself strangely at a loss for something meaningful to say, "I didn't know handmaids were permitted pregnancy during their term of service in the keep."

Immediately, he regretted lodging such a personal observation.

"T'was mis-gotten, m'lord, I'd had no intentions for it, truly," she was patting the baby's head ever so gently. Her vast affection for the child was unmistakable, "but our mistress cares 'bout us too much to have put us out. She's always made for certain we've everything we need.

Hasn't she Aaryn?" She was talking to the infant through a broad, flattering smile that spread across her face.

Thurflyn smiled, too. "Speaking of needs, have you an appetite?" His stomach grumbled then, signaling a hunger he'd felt ever since waking, and he couldn't free it from his mind any longer, "I know *I* certainly do."

"I don't wish to impose any more'n we already have," she said.

"Again, it's no imposition, I assure you," he answered, "I'm quite accustomed to hosting gatherings in this house, though it's been a great deal of time since the last. You'd be most surprised to learn the half of it. Please, make yourself comfortable. I'm off to see what I can do to find us some supper."

Hattie smiled graciously.

In the corner of the room, against the splendid bookcases that lined the walls, there leaned a knotted walking stick, which he retrieved with a swipe and a gleeful grin. Holding the stick tightly and using it as a sort of cane, he made his way down into the cellars, taking in-hand a lantern as he went. The stacked-stone walls of the subterranean chamber surrounded him like a cave. He made pokings and jabbings swiftly along the walls with the stick, then did the same in a recess between two stones; and then two others.

"No, that's not it," he said in doing so, more than once. More pokings and proddings into the wall, and again he said, "No, no... wrong spot, wrong rhythm." Then one final poke into the wall and twist of the stick had produced a clicking sound, like an iron pin sliding and settling into an encasement, and a portion of the stone foundation began to creep slowly aside, leaving an opening scarcely wide enough for a small child to walk through.

"Ah yes, there it is."

Kneeling down, he stole his way along a tight corridor where cobwebs had draped about in such thickness that he was forced to use the walking stick as a tool to clear them from his path, and it'd been an effort. Eventually *(finally!)* he'd found his way to a grated culvert made for collecting rainwater from the back alleys of a residential district, within the crowded upper city. There, he'd left the lantern, but kept the walking stick before making his way 'round a few cobblestoned corners.

The air was damp, and it reminded him of the queer ambience the districts of the Proper held—different from that of the immaculate castle grounds. The street led him out of the culvert and down a lane, past affluent dwellings not entirely unlike his guild's manor home, but smaller and less ornate in design. It terminated at the entrance to a tavern donning a sign that swung back and forth ever so slowly, which read: The Dapper Duckling.

*That's good... a new name, which may mean new faces, too, apart from those who might possibly remember me. The gods know I've spent enough long nights drawing drafts from this particular tap house.*

He pulled his hood down a bit farther to hide his face and walked inside, convincing himself that no one would still be around at all who would remember the disgraced Master Adrian Thurflyn, of the dishonored and disbanded Traveler's Guild.

\*\*\*

|Athyn Proper, Upper City Residential District

The Dapper Duckling Tavern was teeming with action; a stark difference from the quiet back streets outside, to be sure. *When there's gossip about town, the tap house is the place you're likely to hear the best and worst of it,* thought Adrian Thurflyn, making his way through the crowd. His hood was drawn over his head, and he searched himself for his pipe, finding it in a breast pocket of his tunic. A cluster of five men were huddled 'round a table, smoking like chimneys, and he ventured to approach one of them.

"Trouble you for a spark?"

The man standing closest was a tall, dark chap with a long face and thick sideburns, and he scowled at the request, but obliged just the same with a quick strike of flint when Thurflyn extended his pipe. The spark caught well, and Adrian took a slow drag of the tabac, held it in for a while with a stern look from the shadows of his cowl, and released a plume of smoke to the ceiling overhead before moving along.

*Even the affluent gated districts are getting rough these days.*

Thurflyn could act tough when needed. Truth was, he could blend-in just about anywhere, and (for that matter) he practically had. It'd kept him alive, he was sure, on many occasions. More often yet, it had helped him obtain what he needed—most of all, information. It had helped him thrive, even in the strangest of locales.

*Which, I would observe, Athyn Proper itself has quite thoroughly become.*

Passing another group of men, all with their caps drawn low and their scarves tied tightly about their necks, he heard someone say, "I'd been told few night's past some little girl been taken into the castle, and she'd turned right around thanking the Nohnce by conjuring some freakish force that'd blown out half the Mystics House right to pieces."

Rumors often proved useful, but even Thurflyn (gone from the city as long as he'd been) knew *that* one stood little chance of bearing truth; and he continued on.

"It's that flaming 'Lock!" A drunken fool was howling from a small booth toward the back of the tavern. He held a mug to his mouth and guzzled more ale, dribbling streams down his discolored beard, "I'd seen the adv'rsary—hiccup!—the *emissary*… ridin' up our street. He'd come to visit, an' we'd been attacked, right next! No surprise ta' me. No surprise with them dirty 'Lockeenes!"

It seemed rumors surrounding the attack had permeated through the city quickly, and conclusions were already being drawn by the scoreful. Thurflyn thought the drunkard must have been among those who bore witness to the escort of Ambassador Fleurys the evening prior; a gathering which, to most estimates, had included a vast share of the city's population. *It seems everyone will have a theory, and even the most inebriated among them is proving especially insightful.*

"What'll it be?" The barkeep—a large, bald fellow in obvious possession of significant upper body strength—greeted Thurflyn when he finally took a seat.

A few puffs of the pipe later, Adrian responded, "Are you still drawing Allyrian amber from these taps?"

"Indeed, we are," despite its coarse delivery, the barkeep's voice seemed friendly enough. Not so much as old Petyr Neuss' had been in the time this place went by the name *The Greatlyn's Galley* some thirty years past, but it would have to do.

"One mug for starters," he said, slipping a silver crown from his cuffs and placing it on the bar top while casting a serious gaze from beneath his hood, "and two hearty meals well-suited for the road."

The barkeep called a scullery maid over to fill the order. Then he drew a mugful of ale to the brim with an air of suspicion about his movements, and placed it down on the counter, "I'd gather someone'd be looking for more than a simple drink and meal in exchange for that type'a coin."

"Just a few moments of your time, if you don't mind," Thurflyn took the pipe out of his mouth, "I can see you're busy…"

"I've always time for good coin, my friend."

"They say, long ago, this bartop rivaled the Scholars House for its collection of secrets. Pray tell, might that tradition still live-on today?"

"The stewards of this tavern have changed, that may be so," the barkeep cast a devious smile, "but the old rumor mill… it remains intact. Lookin' for a helping of the local chatter, I s'ppose?"

"Standard fare for a man who finds himself alone in a city turned strange from his memories. What's been said in these parts of the Prince of Solis?" Thurflyn paused and rubbed his chin, "If you don't mind me asking."

The barkeep took a drying rag in hand and leaned forward, placing his elbows on the bar, pretending to wipe down a few mugs, and he lowered his voice, "Looks every bit the wordly gentl'man to see him saunter through the Proper on his great mount, he does. But word tells of a mighty temper b'hind closed doors, quick with the venom whenst provoked. At odds with the big daddy Nhyle, they say. Takin' measurements of the throne; already makin' designs for change… All this supposin' he's to take the seat outright; though I say it's no more'n wishful thinkin' for those hopin' he takes it sooner than later, which is most everyone 'round the city these days; all lookin' for a change'a sorts. And he's their prince in his strappin', shinin' armor." He picked up another mug and ran it through with his rag.

"If it's the little one you're askin' about, there in't much to tell. It's said all the coin in that pointless Mystics House a'been dropped for hissake. Some great potential in him lyin' in wait 'neath the surface they say, but near no one's believin' it, and even less are thinkin' he's worth all'em efforts to begin with. Boy can't even speak his own name." The barkeep then pounded his fist on the bar top, causing all the mugs to hop and land with a clatter, and he turned his attention to the old drunk who was still crying about 'Lockeenes in the back end of the tavern, "Time for shuttin' up, Mad Solly, or for gettin' tossed out on your arse! Your choice. You're drivin' business away with your rantin' and rootin'!'"

Thurflyn was too lost in his thoughts to notice the clanging mugs. *So Ethyn has truly grown as popular with the people as it seems. And brother Tae... only a babe when I was dismissed from this city like a mad man tossed from the Dapper Duckling without regard... The little one's established a trail of whispers all his own, too.*

More pressing, however, was the state of Prince Ethyn's progress to the throne. Apparently, there were those who doubted Ethyn's rise to the royal seat might occur with any measure of expediency at all. That, in fact, the realm may spend a great deal of time, yet, locked in anticipation of his rule. And unfortunately for Thurflyn, without such bearing behind Ethyn's name, none of the Heir Prince's promises could truly be made formal.

*Official pardons of old guildmasters from service, included.*

It seemed old Mad Solly had chosen to shut up rather than have himself tossed on his arse into the street, and the barkeep had returned his attention to the conversation at hand.

"Ever heard of a man named Idris Ansel?" asked Thurflyn next, "Is he still around?"

"Strange wizard?" asked the barkeep.

"That's him," verified Thurflyn. *So the old soothsayer Ansel's still kicking. Amazing... and terrifying, all the same.*

"Loner, they say. Coops himself up in that high tower'a his—flashes'a color been seen up there late at night, on occasion. Never leaves the castle. That's 'bout all I got on him, I'm 'fraid. Got'ny more curiosities, good sir?"

"Aye. In fact I've many," Thurflyn looked to either side this time, ensuring there weren't any casual eaves droppers nearby before speaking, "but my time is slim."

The scullery maid came from the kitchens with a hearty stock of provisions, wrapped and ready to go, smelling delectable to the famished Thurflyn, and laid them on the counter. The barkeep took up the bundle and handed it over, grinning again at his hooded customer. "Go on, then. I won't have it said the Dapper Duckling isn't livin' up to its traditions'a secret passin'."

"Indeed," answered Thurflyn with a slight strain of hesitation. "Another before I go, then. What have you heard of the attack on the castle this morn?"

The barkeep emitted a throaty chuckle. "That's the big one today, of course. Most word floatin' 'round tells the Servants' Keep been felled to rubble and stone. Figures. They're always postin' all the heavy guard 'round the royals' keeps, and seems no one's ever watchin' out for the workin' folk, even inside their own castle." The barkeep coughed then, perhaps to punctuate his disgust. "As for who dunnit? We've heard recent tellin'a questionable sorts comin' into the Proper; their names and life stories a myst'ry—criminals, thieves, and the like. Always figured it only a matter'a time before one of 'em with an axe to grind did somethin' unreal like this."

"Common outlaws, you suspect?"

"Somethin' strange 'bout them," the barkeep nodded, "but I've not yet made up my mind for certain what it is. 'Course the easy explanation is the 'Lock, itself, been the ones behind the attack; keepin' with whispers'a war this early dawn."

"War?" Thurflyn was taken slightly aback.

"Supposin' by declaration'a that Ambassador sort, come thru here yesterday. Drunken Mad Solly's been preachin' his disdain'a the 'Lockeenes for ages, and he in't the only one. But I can't be so sure 'bout all that, m'self. Met many'a 'Lockeenes in my day, and never had they given me any trouble. Nice folks, if you're havin' the truth of it from me. After this, though, I'm bettin' I'll not see their sort 'round here for a while, and it's a shame. I'm puttin' my money on the chances one'a them wayward crooks had done the deed instead. I'd seen, couple days back, a group'a suspicious fellas, pulling a wagon full'a who-knows-what. Didn't recognize them, and I flamin' well recognize every man 'round here, who by all their rights belong," he slung the drying rag over his shoulder, ran a palm over his shaven-bald head, and looked discerningly into Thurflyn's eyes.

"Interesting theory, but for all you know, I don't belong here either," said Thurflyn, taking his pipe in hand and blowing a few puffs of smoke out the bowl, "Maybe *I'm* one of these criminals of which you speak."

The barkeep grumbled deeply and grinned again in the manner he'd grinned their whole conversation through. "Way I'd been told, you're not any such criminal," he said, and he took his index finger and slowly (deliberately) slid the silver crown back across the bar top, refusing to accept the payment. And he leaned over, close, to ensure no one else could hear, "No sir… way I understand it, you're a hard and true hero 'round here, if you don't mind me sayin'… Master Thurflyn."

### 24 | Whistles in the Air Require No Pity

*"The sea: its color, its texture, its sound. I've looked into it; into its depths. It speaks of a certain personality and character as it swirls around the planet. I need to stand beside it, often. I need to feel its power and fear its wrath. Because whenever I dare start believing I have any control whatsoever in this life, it is the one thing that instantly reminds me of my station, my insignificance; my smallness and lack of true power. Yet despite all this, I know that it will never refuse me when I require its cleansing, its healing, and its unmatched perspective."*
—excerpt from the personal journal of Steven Spurlock

|The Station

Translucent streamers of cold space skimmed off the smooth curves of the great Station's atmospheric dome, drawing a wispy outline against the darkest of backdrops, while the behemoth lurched through Planet Deaer's thermosphere.

The Operator announced Projection early in the morning's cycle, but her directive had, for once, lacked its usual bite of urgency. Pulling on the suit and helmet had become an especially familiar act, though, and Spurlock roused himself from sleep and prepared himself in short order for whatever operation she had in store. This, despite resounding fatigue, which had been the result of a long night of transcript reading and report writing. He couldn't say how many dialogue streams he'd reviewed, nor sound bites he'd listened to, but he *could* say how much sleep he'd gotten.

*Not nearly enough.*

And so, his approach did not lack its usual cast of reluctance.

"I'll be back," he informed Giza in a morose tone that well-fit his mood, "Look after things, will you?"

Giza's blue light illumined, "If that is what you need, that is what I will do."

When Spurlock reached into his wardrobe for his sidearm, the Operator stayed his hand; her voice emanating softly around his solar.

—Leave your weapon. You won't need it—

"Sure thing, Madam Operator," he said, mechanically.

*Fine by me.* He'd never felt comfortable wielding the thing in the first place.

Moments later, after kneeling himself down and passing through the ether, he felt himself break out of the discomforts of Projection, sensing contact with some location on Planet Deaer materializing beneath him. The sounds of the surf came to him first. He opened his eyes to see white sands and aquamarine waves curling and breaking upon one another, crashing on the beach; the water rushing up before sliding back into an expansive sea. Behind him, he saw a sheer rock cliff face. But no waypoint was established in his visor, and he received no immediate directive.

He surveyed his open surroundings a moment longer, sighting nothing of note in particular, "What's the meaning of this?"

—It has occurred to me that I've asked much of you these last several days. Not without good reason, I assure you. But you have assumed great responsibilities, and you have performed admirably. Yet, with little respite or reward. For that, I feel I must apologize—

*Apologize?* He faltered for a moment.

"For what?" he drew several long breaths, "I am nothing. I see that now. I am no more than a whistle in the air, if I am anything at all, and whistles in the air require no pity. Your apology is, therefore, denied." He hadn't truly realized how far he'd fallen until he confessed these things aloud, and he expected to feel the familiar sensation of a drop of discharge fall from both his eyes, down his cheeks. When no such tear was formed, he shuddered. *Of course. Tears are for real people in possession of real emotions, and I am no such being any longer.*

—This is the archipelago where you made landfall on your first operation. You stopped for a moment on the cliffs and stared down at this beach. At that moment, your vital readings stabilized despite exposure at the time to severe circumstances... Do you enjoy the beach, Mister Spurlock?—

He was prepared to lash out at her, to tell her to go to hell for asking a question he certainly could not answer. But something caught his voice and held it in abeyance. In the early morning haze, a gull sang its tune for the sea. The sound of it was carried on the wind, and it sparked something within him. A vision, if only a flash in his mind, of a beach much like this one; of sand between his toes and salt water flowing over his body. What it was, he couldn't exactly say, but it was something deeply embedded; embroidered into the fabric of his soul. So instead of firing back at her, he offered a much simpler response:

"Yes. I believe I do."

—Then you are given this time to do as you wish. I will summon you back to your suit when your return is required. The atmosphere on Deaer will, of course, sustain you without it, but please ensure its utmost safe-keeping until then. You must exercise caution here. But Mr. Spurlock, please… enjoy yourself—

*Enjoy.* He'd almost forgotten the meaning of the word.

He lifted his visor and felt the salt air kiss his face. The smell of the sea, of organic matter—*of life!*—wafted into his nostrils and seemed to swirl around inside his head. The airlock around the helmet's collar leaked open with a command that he whispered into its mouthpiece, and he lifted it off. He closed his eyes and held the helmet out with one hand. He spread open his fingers on the other, fell to his knees in the sand, and tilted his head back to face the spot in the sky where he knew the great Station hung, beyond Deaer's atmosphere. He felt strongly that she was somehow watching him from her place up there. Watching his movements. *I surrender. Whatever you would have of me, it's yours. Whatever I'm meant to do, command me to do it. Whatever fate I'm destined to suffer, lead me toward its end. If you be merciful, or if you be cruel, I bend my knees in acceptance.*

Then he dropped the helmet, which landed with a thud in the sand, and disengaged the suit, letting them both lay where he was. He took himself (in his thermals) down the slope of the beach, and into the water. It was warm and the waves remained active, serving to cleanse him with each rolling pass that crashed into him. He waded deeper, then, and ducked under those waves, allowing himself to be swallowed by their cover, submerged in their depths. He swam for a bit; tentatively at first, not knowing if he'd ever had a knack for it, but he took to it quite naturally.

*There is emotion to be felt in this place, and she's letting me.*

All the while, twinges of familiarity swept through him like spectral visitors to his private frolic. Visions and sensations, they seemed, of a time and place he might somehow recall. So he chased after them with a fierceness that he'd deprived himself of until now. It seemed he was given the proper license this time, permissions to follow the threads that his thoughts dangled in front of him. And now he meant to take advantage of it, finally, for himself.

Swimming parallel to the beach in a vigorous breast stroke, inhaling air in-rhythm, the visions came to him like a picture-show in his mind. The harder he swam, the clearer they became—two hands interlocked, and one of them was his. He could feel the warmth of the other's palm. It was hers, the one from the photo in his solar. They were walking along a beach.

"When we hold hands like this," she said, her curly hair swaying in the wind, "and I squeeze yours three times, it is as if I'm saying to you, 'I… love… you,' like this." And she squeezed his hand in such a manner, three times. "You can squeeze mine back if you want," she suggested, and he gladly complied. "It will be our silent secret that only *we* share."

He looked at her and felt as though he could almost reach out and touch her. He would put his free hand on her cheek, run a few loose strands of her hair around her ear, and he would look into her deep green eyes.

But just as quickly as the vision arrived, it had disappeared, and he was left grasping for it, both in his mind and as he swam through this ocean. So he pushed-on harder still, plunging his arms and gulping the air with desperation, much in the way one tries falling back asleep in hopes of re-entering a pleasant dream, only he was awake and swimming, *swimming, swimming*. Reaching out for the memory. Stroking left and right, cutting through the water, gulping air, and kicking. But the air became less fulfilling to his lungs, his arms were beginning to tire (to burn), and the water filled his ears—combining to return him to his present circumstance.

He began to fail in his efforts, and his body fell limp; enough so that an underlying riptide seized the opportunity to suck him beneath the surface. It drew him down. He felt his shoulders make impact with the sea floor just before a wave surged and rolled him over, pulling him up into its curl for a moment of air, then plunging him back in. It pushed him forward and carried him awhile, then dumped him back onto the sandy floor, robbing him of any breath he had left.

He was coughing and wheezing, breathing by any means he could. But in the effort, he realized he'd been tumbled back onto the beach where the waves lapped harmlessly upon him, merely splashing him a bit while he crawled along. And in time, he eventually laid himself out on his back and had to laugh.

Whether it was at his foolishness or his good fortune in reaping the merciful dictates of the sea's powerful swales, he didn't bother to discern. But he expected it would leave him awfully sore for a number of days to come. *And no telling where I'll be Projected next, to suffer witness of some kind of hysterical scenario. Or to perform one myself. A sore body like this definitely won't help things. But I guess this whirlwind tour will only take turns for the worse from now on, whether my body's prepared to endure them or not.*

Strangely, and for the first time, it all actually started to seem worth the effort. The vision he experienced out there in the water might prove validating enough to continue with this nonsense, after all. And in gratification for this, he dropped his head back and closed his eyes in rest.

\*\*\*

|Planet Deaer, The Archipelago Northern Coastline

Spurlock was lying on the sand after his rigorous attempt to swim his way into the recesses of his memory core had nearly claimed him. At least he finally managed to catch a bit of sincere rest, while the waves slid their way slowly to him and back out. When he sat up, he could hear the shore birds again. But the reminiscence was over. Involuntarily, his thoughts turned again to his Deaerian sources and their varying predicaments, to which he was so (by now) intimately attuned. Try as he may, he couldn't shake them from his mind, even when encouraged by his Operator to do so.

*The little one, who's found the courage to get out in the world a little. Of course all it took was a little perfumed feminine arousal to crack his shell—isn't that always the case? Where would men be without it?... Then the eldest; the heir. So totally full of himself that he can't recognize his own mistakes, even when they bite him right in the rear end. He's smart, though, and his instincts seem pretty dead-on, from what I can tell. And their parents, this Nhyle and Nohnce, who can probably feel the storm brewing, but can't tell where it's coming from or make plans to avoid it... And then the old-salt traveler who just wants to get away from it all.*

Spurlock shook his head.

*Then of course there's the wizard, who's conspiring against everyone. And he'll probably succeed, considering what he's gotten away with so far.*

*Why doesn't she just send me over there to blast the guy?*

On second thought, he sincerely hoped she wouldn't.

These subjects, he knew, were all embroiled in a conflict that might threaten the future of this world he was assigned to study. The volumes of information he'd collected over a mere several days' time clearly suggested as much. Yet, the manner in which the Operator intended to act upon all of this information, to use it to avert disaster—to redirect Deaer's momentum away from war and destruction—remained unclear. *Is this insanity leading to something? If so, I have absolutely no clue what it can possibly have to do with me.*

He sighed.

The effort it took to recite the roles of his sources, alone, left him faint of mind and body. And that was before he even turned a thought toward the two in the mountains; cursed in their love for one another. *Or their disgust; I haven't decided, yet, which it is.* But one thing he *had* decided was that the exile on the mountain's peak was a fool for neglecting the spirited young pilot named Haiyen. She'd become his favorite source to monitor. The only one, in fact, he rather enjoyed listening to in real-time.

The thought inspired him to stand up and make his way back to the place where he'd made landfall; back to his suit. Looking up the beach, he realized he'd swam (and tumbled and drifted) a good distance down the shoreline. But the walk helped him stretch out his aches and pains and allowed him to dry off a bit in the sun. He looked out at the expanse of water and listened again, intently, to the sounds of the sea. And naught but a short while (or so it seemed) had passed before he made his way back.

He bent down and grabbed the helmet, put it on, and said, "Sources." He looked through the menu of names until he found Haiyen Sün, and said, "Select."

A moment later, the young Prima pilot's audio feed was playing in his ears, and he sat down in the sand again with a smile on his face. When he listened, he could imagine the scene in his mind as it transpired. This, he tended to do with all his sources, but most diligently and most vividly of all with her.

"Mum, let me help you with that," said Haiyen. The sound of cups being collected conjured an image of a kitchen, perhaps after the consumption of breakfast, at this (yet early) hour.

"Thank you, dear," more clatter of dishware could be heard. "There goes pa on his morning stroll out to his patch. I thought he might stay around a bit longer, at least to see you away when you leave."

"Oh, let him go. I understand," said Haiyen. "Besides, we had our time together last evening."

"I'm glad for that," said mum, "What did you think of his crops?"

"Amazing... truly. The progress he's made is remarkable. He has a true purpose, and he's dedicated himself to it, thoroughly. It's easy when you have a gift as marvelous he has, I suppose, to march yourself out there and do what you're so skilled at doing. Some may consider it blasphemous to waste such a thing as that."

"How about you? Have you found peace in what you've chosen for yourself in Prima?"

There was a pause, and in it came the sound of water sloshing in a basin. "I'm glad you mention that, actually. I asked pa if he believed you'd found purpose in your days with the Sages; if he believed you felt solidarity with the Rank and with their cause."

"And?"

"And... he said you've both, in some certain ways, found yourselves at odds with the stodgy dictates of Settlement governance, but that, in the end, you would never stand to watch me affiliate myself with an assembly of figures for whom you've developed inexorable distrust."

"Hmm. A reasonable assessment, I suppose. I shall have to commend him for his astuteness."

They seemed to be stacking the table wares now, perhaps as they sorted and dried them.

"But indeed, the Sages in their doings certainly engendered a sense of caution in me," Haiyen's mum continued after giving the matter some thought, "The faint notion there was always something more to Prima than was being disclosed. Have you felt the same? Is this why you ask?"

"I have. And yes, it is."

"Fynian Arynel, the Sage of Judgment. An impressive man, I do not deny. But I always thought his was a particularly pretentious title. Certainly not one appropriate for a man who is interested in passive, altruistic pursuits alone. And he was an old man, even in the years when I served the ranks. We'd conjectured about his age to no ends, those of us in the Ranks, that is. All of the Sages, in fact, seemed such an aged lot. Impossibly so. And yet, they roam the compound, I suspect, to this very day?"

"All four of them, yes."

"And they still maintain their strict regulations?" The voice of Haiyen's mum hardened a tad.

"Of the boundaries, of course," Haiyen was hiding well the fact she'd almost succeeded in breaching that particular regulation just a few days ago, "We dare not pass into the Beyond… to the flatlands."

"And the Heights?"

It seemed Haiyen must have shrugged this question away in confusion before declaring, "The Heights?"

"We were always forbidden from the flatlands, of course," continued her mum, "but in my day, there seemed no greater concern held by the Sages than the prospects of a pilot flying for the Heights, to see how high they might reach. There'd always been legends of a few, long before, who'd sought the surfaces of the Ancillary Moon and had never returned. The Sages prohibited us from testing the story, saying our cabs would freeze solid and shatter, and we'd disintegrate up there."

"Did you ever… try it anyway? Despite their warnings?" Haiyen seemed most intrigued.

"No," there was another pause for a moment or two, "Not *very* seriously, at least."

"*Mum…!*" Haiyen laughed, sounding as if she were a bit scandalized by the vague admission.

"It was for naught. I turned back far before any deep freeze threatened to set in, I assure you. We cannot always bridle our youthful ambitions, I suppose."

"True," said Haiyen, perhaps letting shades of Koryn Naylor infect her thoughts yet again, if for only a passing moment, "I certainly don't blame you for your experimentation, nor your doubting of the Sages. I guess I'm keeping them at an arm's length, too."

"You're right to remain cautious, Haiyen. In all things, and at all times. And you always have a place to come to, whenever you need us. If ever you need refuge… If ever you need a break."

"It's a comfort to know, mum," and with Haiyen's last words, the conversation tapered away to silence.

Spurlock shut the feed down completely, then, but remained seated in the sand.

*That Haiyen certainly is interesting.*

He didn't want to admit it, but his Operator had shown compassion in affording him this respite, and it may have shown she possessed a certain level of interest (perhaps even an investment) in the maintenance of his well-being. But it was a notion for which he still harbored a significant vestige of doubt. *Who's to say, with any confidence at all, her motives aren't entirely selfish?*

—Equip your suit and prepare for Projection at once—

The suddenness and blank tone of her voice severed any connection to emotion he might have been enjoying.

And just like that, his respite was ended, but not (he supposed) without satisfying its intended purpose. He pulled on the suit and sealed the helmet before taking one last look at the sprawling sea and its vastness, which leant to him a true sense of perspective. Similar to the decks of the Station—looking beyond (as he often did) at this mysterious and enormous planet, hanging ominously in space—this coastline impressed upon him his true scale in this universe; humbling and frighteningly small. But the contact with the waves and the sand and the air added a level of intimacy he could not deny and would not soon forget.

*Imagine that…*

Then in moments, he was taken by Projection, and all that was left behind of his visit were his footprints. But even *they* were already starting to wash away under the in-coming tide.

*\*\**

|Planet Deaer, The Archipelago

From the edge of a rocky bluff, overlooking the beach on the northern end of the archipelago's main island, a figure knelt; watching. It witnessed this strangest of occurrences unfold. A man, after shedding a most peculiar form-fitted adornment, had made his recreation in the sea and along the beach, and, in time, had returned to fit himself back into his dressings before flat-out disappearing from existence itself.

This figure (bearing wraith-like qualities in form and movement) watched it all. And when it was through—affected by what had transpired—it raced its way along the cliff sides and farther yet up an incline, climbing and climbing through trees and tropical thickets; whereupon it eventually approached and entered a small, wooden shack. It sat itself down therein and, with a bone-thin hand, scrawled out a message, which it rolled up tightly and fit within a capsule.

And moments after exiting this structure and taking cover in a stand of trees not far away, a fiery streak shot forth like a missile launching; popping, searing, and smoking as it ascended into the sky and then locked itself into its intended course.

*\*\**

|Athynian Countryside

Landfall was made, not back within his solar on the Station as Spurlock had expected, but on an isolated hilltop that overlooked Castle Athyn and its surrounding city limits; the hamlets and scattered cottages along the fringe. The stonework metropolis seemed thrown asunder in a tremendous state of disarray. Black smoke was hemorrhaging from the great castle itself, drifting upwards and darkening the air like a severe storm cloud. He could even smell the burn and the decay at this distance through the helmet's opened vents. People fled to the outer walls and beyond them, to the fields and the city outskirts.

"What's going on down there?"

—This is a departure from my laid plans for you this day. It seems Castle Athyn has been attacked. I have found no evidence in your reporting that you've seen this coming. Have your sources proven enigmatic?—

He could only look upon the scene and gape silently for a moment's time before answering.

"Enigmatic is putting it lightly. I've written about the declaration of war—you must have seen that. And about the deceit of the one named Idris Ansel and his apparent compatriot Salmen Fleurys of Athyn's rival realm, called Maelnlock. And I noted the uncertain motives of these Sages in their mountain Settlement. But those threads, all of them, have remained inconclusive at best of any specific plans for attack."

—It seems we must double our efforts. We simply cannot afford to overlook detection of further cataclysmic atrocities such as this. I can see you will henceforth require my direct oversight in assurance of these goals. Please prepare for Projection—

*She doesn't think she's commanded direct oversight already? So much for restorative respites and supposed well-intentioned investments... I guess I have a real job to do here, after all, and I damn well better do it correctly from now on.*

His helmet's vents sealed themselves, and after holding firm in a kneeling position, he was whisked away from Deaer without further delay.

\*\*\*

|Planet Earth, Washington DC

It was more than four full days removed now from the last message she'd received on her phone from Steven, and—despite the reassurances delivered by his sister Nora, and her own resolutions last evening at the *Cantina* to lighten up over the whole affair—Haley Kenmore was (once again) growing exceedingly impatient. And quite worried, as well.

Haley's boss, the Assistant Secretary, was meeting with top department intelligence officers on this Monday morning, and it was Haley's responsibility to ensure materials were prepared ahead of their arrival. Though she possessed the highest-level security clearance issued by the federal government, attendance at such meetings was quite privileged, and she technically lacked essential 'need to know' status for the bulk of the classified information that would be discussed. Sensitive documents didn't arrive until the analysts did; in Kevlar bags bound by locked, steel-toothed zippers. Only the A/S's appointed subject matter experts would accompany her for these events. Accordingly, she would not attend.

Haley was usually content to avoid these meetings, anyway. She wondered how Steven managed this quandary, to the extent that he did— to walk about in his everyday life, holding such information in his mind everywhere he went without the ability to speak of it.

Her preparatory duties were completed moments prior to the arrival of the visiting interlocutors, and within the conference space, the meeting had worn-on into the mid-morning hours without relent. From her desk, she could distinguish nothing of the conversation within, which was just as well. She couldn't rightly afford distractions. If she let her diligence slip for too long, she'd fall hopelessly behind in her responsibilities. *Never much time at all to catch my breath.* Most days, she worked (out of necessity) straight through the lunch hour and was rendered near lifeless by day's end.

In addition to tall workloads, she'd realized recently that the manner of dialogue passed between herself and the A/S often contributed to her growing levels of angst.

"You're not to attend today's intelligence briefing, Haley," the A/S had said, promptly upon their morning's greeting of one another, "but you'll need to be primed and ready by the door in case I need an errand to be run. Is that going to be a problem?"

Haley had wondered what could have ever given the A/S the idea such requests might pose a *problem*. She'd never so much as batted a lash, furrowed a brow, or squinted an eye at any of the countless such demands made of her, for over a year now.

"Not a problem at all," she'd said, "I'll remain at my desk, just outside the door."

But whether a proper attendee or not, she thought she may actually want to hear the intelligence dialogue of this particular meeting, for once. This was Steven's work. For a brief moment prior to their arrival, she'd wondered if he might appear for the meeting alongside his principals. In the event he had, she didn't know if she'd have hugged him or scowled at him for his recent communication deficiencies. But, of course, he hadn't appeared.

In time, the group finally broke from their meeting, sharing banter as they emerged from the conference room.

"…And like we've said, that particular focus area has garnered a bit of additional high-level interest," said one of the more senior intelligence officers. His name, according to the briefing memo, was Aldan Turner. Haley thought she'd seen him around campus before—perhaps in the cafeteria—and was under the vaguest of understandings that he was positioned in Steven's direct chain of command. Turner bore the look of a man well-attuned to this sort of work; a partial graying of the hair and creases in the face that spoke to a certain level of wisdom, rather than mere age.

Haley listened more attentively while he continued.

"In fact," said Turner, "we're deeply troubled by the recent disappearance of one of our analysts who'd been assigned reporting streams associated with this issue. He has simply gone missing. But that, of course, is close-hold information; we haven't determined anything for a real certainty yet. We only wanted you to be aware of the full scope of what we're dealing with."

"Is that so?" said the A/S in a sort of steely-faced, unfeeling reply, "Of course, I will keep it close-hold."

"If anything should arise outside our scheduled briefing times that requires our assistance, please let us know," Turner nodded his head as he and his group strode toward the exit, "After all, we're only just right across the street." They all chuckled reservedly while parting ways, for the close proximity of their two offices (and the ever-availability to meet with one another) was quite well implied without special say-so.

But Haley Kenmore didn't chuckle. She was left sitting there at her workstation, frozen like an ancient cave crystal.

*Gone missing.* She ran the declaration through her mind again and again. It had wiped away everything else she'd heard, seen, or done throughout the morning, and she expected she'd dwell on it for a good long while throughout the remainder of the day.

*Gone… missing…*

And indeed, she *did* dwell on it.

Quite obsessively so.

### 25 | I Have Seen Something in the Sky

*"We all have a block of stone. And every industrious person thinks that what they are sculpting from their block is the very thing that sits upon the edge of societal progress. If they didn't, they wouldn't have the motivation to crawl back out of bed each day and chip away at it again. A big, raw block of stone, painstakingly chiseled and polished with careful measure. With unyielding passion. And we must always be especially careful to never take that away."*
—excerpt from the personal journal of Steven Spurlock

|Planet Deaer, Castle Athyn

"There you are," said the Nhyle when his son, prospective Heir Prince Ethyn Solis, had finally entered his study. After the explosion, the Nhyle's Inner Circle had assembled at once; that of Perwyn, Master Mossa Zahyle, and High Counsel Idris Ansel.

Ethyn had been the last to arrive, joining the privileged audience with his father. He'd been slowed by his efforts to track down the man who had fled outside South Gate in the midst of the great blast. But the nature of his entrance overshadowed his tardiness as he marched into the room, clanging along with him a cage that held a bird of black and red plumage. He planted himself in front of them with an authoritative posture. All things considered, he was a bit surprised father was willing to extend the invitation to him at all, following the recent scuttlebutt that had occurred between he and the council (and father, himself) at forum. And, although he intended to maintain a calm disposition this time around, he found needs to offer the news of his doings immediately upon his arrival.

"A man is locked up this morning in the dungeons. I apprehended him and his fowl," he held up the cage for the others to see, "he was fleeing our premises moments before the blast and was slowed in the thorns beyond South Gate."

"You believe this man to be our perpetrator?" Mossa Zahyle asked with enthusiasm, "and this, his fowl? What fine work, Ethyn."

"Fine work, indeed," garbled Idris Ansel, without any trace of sincerity in his crackled voice.

"I've no doubt he is," Ethyn replied, still holding up the cage with the bird inside—his evidence. "The bird was meant to deliver these messages; one which I found clipped to its leg and the other hidden inside one of the perpetrator's boots, though I know not for whom they were intended." He produced the tiny scrolls and promptly placed them within Mossa's capable custody.

"They are written in a hand not known to me, but I've no doubt you will find the means to translate it," Ethyn concluded. The Master of Secrets and Whispers (and all other such things) unraveled them with great interest.

"Marvelous," said Zahyle, looking at the writing with enthusiasm. But while her aged eyes scanned the messages, her expression quickly turned troubled, "This hand is unknown to me as well, I'm afraid."

"A truly rare occurrence that is, indeed," muttered Ansel with just a scant twinge of satisfaction, which perhaps only Ethyn could detect, "That a message in your hands should prove too difficult to decipher, my friend."

"Yes," said Zahyle, directing a sideways glance back at Ansel while walking to the windows. She slid a latch free from its holding, and tilted open a leaded pane, whistling softly into the air outside. In a moment's time, a scarlet grosbeak arrived, landing on the narrow sill, and after Mossa fastened the messages securely upon its legs, it was off to the Scholar's Keep, quick as the wind. "But it will not remain a mystery for long."

"Whatever the content of the messages, I expect it will prove ominous in nature," said Ethyn. With all that had occurred, he could not be dissuaded now from his suspicions of foul deeds brewing in the mountains to the south, nor within the archipelago in the west. According to Aryk Frierstag, the wraith at the outpost had screamed of the fires in the sky. *Soon the fire and smoke that lights the sky shall rain down upon the world to burn the oppressors and their cities!* And now that Ethyn had seen the explosive, threatening nature of these warnings firsthand, he was going to make clear his support for the immediate deployment of force to all points and in all directions, "We may be surrounded by the enemy on all sides, even as we speak. We are, by sheer necessity, forced to arms."

"Ethyn, son, please," said Perwyn, drawing his hands down in calming gestures, "it is unwise to force anything upon ourselves. Least of which a call to arms... We need time to convalesce."

"Would that we could, father, but we've no such luxury of time. Can you not see this; even now, after our city has been infiltrated and attacked?" Ethyn looked to the massive windows that stood behind his father and pointed to the destruction of the fallen keep. Its ruin of stone and rubble and wood framings were strewn across East and North Court, "There will be no rest for us; not for a very long time."

"You've done well to apprehend this man of whom you speak—" the tone of Perwyn's commendation was purposefully withdrawn.

"Assassin," Ethyn was blurting his words out now, interrupting; sensing that an order to stand-down would soon be made, and he wanted to get as much of his side of the argument in as he could, "I'd been warned of this treachery, and now it has come true. We must not overlook the significance in this."

"Warned?" asked Mossa Zahyle, "by whom?"

"This tattered wraith figure," Ethyn was drumming the top of the birdcage while he spoke, "from the archipelago in the southwestern seas... I'd tried to elaborate upon this at forum, until I was shone my place."

"Ethyn, as I've suggested, you've displayed valor in these efforts," repeated the Nhyle, "but these are not your rightful duties. You will learn... you *must* learn, son, to leave whisper hunting to the scholars, field combat to the legion, and the apprehension of suspects to the Royal Guard. I'll not have you slinging yourself about the realm with such reckless abandon. It is simply—"

"...Unbecoming of the royal seat," Ethyn said with a snarl, cutting him off again, "yes, I seem to have heard that lecture before."

"Ethyn, I beg you," said his father, "please make yourself comfortable so we may, with all our good senses in order, discuss our plans moving forward."

The prince's stance went limp with exasperation. He could do no more to spell things out for them, and he believed that, perhaps, he ought to simply stop trying. It was only wasting precious time and energy.

Instead, he placed the bird cage down unceremoniously, and leaned defiantly against one of the many bookshelves that lined the great study. This, so that he might find himself in compliance with his father's wishes and hear out what these three figureheads of influence would have to say for themselves.

\*\*\*

The discussion of the Inner Circle had lasted the whole afternoon through, and they all (each in turn) were thoroughly exhausted. Mossa Zahyle paced the length of the king's study so long Ethyn thought the Master of Scholars had likely traveled the equivalent of the Ribbon Road, two times over. Meanwhile, Idris Ansel had hunched himself deep within the cushions of a tall-backed chair, leering precipitously about the room with his beady little eyes. The Nhyle stood in front of the massive windows, looking over Athyn Proper from the lofty vantage point, stroking his beard and tapping the nail of his index finger against the tabac tin hanging from his belt.

As for himself, Ethyn had long-since sat and smoldered in silence, passing in and out of a light sleep, only half listening to the chatter volleyed between the other three principals. He'd figured that, if they weren't going to listen to what *he* had to say, no matter its potential significance, he wasn't going to make the effort to listen to *them*.

Finally, with a certain grogginess, he found himself waking to see the sun was beginning to slide toward evening time, and he was disillusioned by the realization that they'd failed to accomplish anything at all, this whole while, except for jibbing and jabbing over pointless details. *This pontification, this inaction, is enough to unravel the very threads of my patience, and it's bound to get us all killed should it continue. Sitting here idle, debating what's happened to us instead of taking up arms and retaliating against those responsible. We're like the dummy targets in the fletch yard, save only for the absence of bulls'-eyes painted across our tunics. And even one of those isn't very difficult to imagine over old Idris Ansel's chest right about now.*

The Nhyle had called for Commander Thorngrove to join them, but the hairy-faced brute had yet to make his presence felt in the study. *I almost welcome the big man's intrusion into this dialog, however foolish his contributions would prove to be. Even the senseless discord that he is sure to bring with him is preferable to such dreadful inaction as this.*

The image of the fallen and broken keep, of course, still lay ominously in their view outside the windows; a reminder of why they had gathered in the first place, and the strength of the threat they were up against. He wiped a bit of sleep from his eyes. *By gods, the assassin. I wonder if anyone has yet put him to question. Have we yet ordered mobilization against the outlaws in the west? Is that what keeps Thorngrove from joining us? What more must I say or do before they will take heed?*

At long last, Ethyn saw his father run an unsteady hand through his silver-streaked beard, pain reflecting in his eyes from the harrowing sights outside.

"Idris," he asked pointedly, "you say this destruction was the work of Maelnlock, correct?"

"I do, my lord," answered the stargazer as he reclined in his chair. If sighing in the presence of the Nhyle was deemed acceptable, Ansel (or any other person for that matter) would likely have sighed heavily at that moment, as Ethyn had lost count of the times father had asked these two advisors to repeat their views on the current state of affairs. Ansel deftly resisted the urge. Instead, he held a casual air about himself, his voice warbling and cracking in its usual manner, "There can be no greater sensible explanation."

"And Mossa… your thoughts again, please?" asked the Nhyle.

"My lord," Mossa Zahyle continued pacing the floor in contemplative fashion while she offered her response, "we have collected ourselves and we have thought upon all of this for a long while, without distraction. And we've identified elements in this matter, which we hold fast as truths. First, we know Fleurys of Maelnlock has, on behalf of his Emperor, declared war upon us on the basis of an intrusion of deadly assets within their lands. That is what he proclaimed, no?"

"Indeed it is," answered the Nhyle.

Mossa looked over her spectacles at Idris Ansel, as if expecting a corroborative response.

"Indeed," groaned Ansel, "he did."

"Fine, thank you," Mossa said, "and we know we've had naught to do with any such assets, nor their placement in any foreign land whatsoever. Isn't *that* true?"

"That is true," said the Nhyle, looking inquisitively toward his Master of Scholars.

"So the question is, who *did* place the assets there?" Zahyle strode a few more paces before continuing her analysis, "My lord, as you know, we receive messages by fowl from the field in the Scholar's Keep, by the scoreful daily, many of which bear ill tidings from around the world. They are quite troubling. Some are downright unsettling. And though their ties to threats tangible or intangible are most often tentative at best, we must in the very least assess that our surrounding environment stands unstable, perhaps volatile at the present time. This, I have conveyed to you before."

A portion of the setting sun had just moved behind a tall tower in the city at that moment, reducing the bands of light that passed through the windows, and Zahyle paused for effect. But the Nhyle was growing impatient with Mossa's meandering response.

"And so, dear girl," he said, "what exactly are you suggesting?"

"Put simply, my lord, I've therefore—of late—developed mounting suspicions there exists a third-party actor at play, apart from ourselves, of course, and apart from Maelnlock. And that this party, for reasons yet unknown, has placed offensive weapons of some sort upon 'Lockian soil. I cannot make much sense of any other explanation."

"Unless," croaked Ansel, with a hurried manner about himself, sitting up in his chair now, "we might consider Maelnlock has dreamed up the existence of assets to spark conflict."

"Doubtful," Zahyle answered, "Maelnlock has nothing to gain by fabricating a war."

"Yet Fleurys, himself, may," spat Ethyn, entering himself into the conversation, turning the others' heads in his direction as he stood now in the corner. "I've it on good authority from the House of Scholars that Fleurys is a son of our own plains of East Athyn; not Maelnlock, and he'd all but confirmed it by erupting in anger when I made the accusation to his face."

"To his face, Ethyn?" Perwyn pressed.

"Questioning the man's heritage?" blurted Ansel, "Is there any wonder, then, that our assemblage fell to shambles?"

"To his face," Ethyn confirmed, "yes, and I assure you, it made no difference in the outcome of the assemblage. He was primed for the declaration from the moment he requested audience. Of that, I am certain."

The Nhyle gave his son a troubled look before turning to Zahyle, "Has this truly come from your House?"

"From a scholar, yes, though efforts to confirm the integrity of its source have long proven inconclusive. I can as yet, therefore, assess no measure of confidence in the veracity of such information," admitted Zahyle, tilting her head. "The theory that Zahyle began life as an Athynian seems plausible, though I clearly must now devote concerted mind to the mystery anew."

"I think, perhaps, he's forsaken allegiances to both kingdoms," said Ethyn, "and has found a place elsewhere, among powerful allies, about whom we know very little."

"Such an explanation, as you have proposed, is quite preposterous," blurted Ansel, who was practically clawing at his seat cushions now, passing accusative eyes from one person to the next, "What third party would be so foolish as to take on both Athyn and Maelnlock? To deceive us and bring upon war, the world-over? And you think Fleurys—a man sworn to the 'Lock for a two generations—is leading them?"

"These are the things we must determine," Zahyle stopped pacing, "but to outright dismiss any such suspicion at this juncture, no matter how unlikely it may seem, would surely be our greatest folly. We regrettably possess no such luxuries of certainty. I've already set my best scholars upon the task."

"Whoever this third party is," said Ethyn, "they aren't *taking us on*, as you suggest, Ansel. Quite the opposite, truly. They're pitting Athyn and Mealnlock against one another, likely to pull up a seat and watch from the periphery. Theirs is a coward's game we've all been forced to play."

"To what possible benefit?" Ansel begged.

"A leveling of the playing field, perhaps," Zahyle was scratching her chin, "We've no shortage of lesser realms in this world, eager for a slice of Athyn's share; or the 'Lock's for that matter, as well."

"Perhaps I've taken the obvious for granted, but was the timing of this blast we've sustained not a clear enough indication?" Ansel questioned, "We've been attacked immediately in the wake of a 'Lockian declaration of war against us, and you would point your finger elsewhere, to some nameless foe, when our greatest enemy stands before us, waving their flag of aggression?"

"There are stirrings in the west—the archipelago—to which Ethyn has attested at forum," said Zahyle. "If we, together with the 'Lock, can dispel all of this as an unfortunate collection of mere misunderstandings, much bloodshed will be averted. It is at least worth our investigation."

"With our ambassador to Maelnlock already commanded by homing fowl to withdrawal," argued Ansel, "who, exactly, would perform such negotiations, under conditions of war, no less?"

"Naturally, we would order our ambassador to return to the 'Lock, carrying the white banner of peace," suggested Zahyle.

"And if this proves to be no misunderstanding at all," Ansel was standing up from his chair now, "what if we cannot rightly divert the blame for these deadly assets upon some other party; what then? We begin this war with the Maelnlockian execution of an Athynian ambassador."

"This assassin I've thrown in the dungeon is no 'Lockian, of that much I'm sure," said Ethyn. "And I followed Fleurys and his men until they departed the Proper, each one of them. It wasn't they who set the explosives. We must investigate whatever alternative leads we can."

"My lord," Ansel turned again to the Nhyle, the tone of his voice low and intentionally sobering, "in the end, it makes little difference who is to blame. Regardless of fault, we've needs to prepare ourselves for the worst that Maelnlock has to offer, by way of the Central Sea. Reapportionment of focus in any other direction, against any other supposed foe, is tragically ill-advised; you must see this. Great leaders do not risk their men's lives on premonitions. They deal in certainties, and the threat posed by Mealnlock is surely the greatest certainty of all that lay before us this day."

"Are you deaf to words, Ansel?" Ethyn was still hot from the verbal lashings he'd received at forum, and could sense this debate trending in the same direction. "Must you be so dreadfully obtuse at all times? Master Zahyle has just proposed an alternative course. Could we only, by some means, identify a culpable third party, we may yet avoid much needless conflict. But we will have to spread our forces wide," he looked to his father, "pursue our enemies in all directions, not just northward across the Central Sea for Maelnlock."

"I suppose you would have our forces sweep the countryside, then?" Ansel provoked Ethyn with a sarcastic slur, his broken speech seething with pretentiousness. "You'd have the legion ranks turn over stones and toss condor nests for hidden clues? Perhaps a common outlaw from the archipelago, with barely the means to secure his next meal, somehow acquired and placed these assets on 'Lockian soil and devised for us to take the blame. Is that what you believe?"

The sarcasm was taking Ethyn to new heights of anger.

"The south..." he blurted, before he could think better of it. This was a pivotal moment, he knew. He was going to risk looking much like a fool again, but he saw no way around it. "I have seen something," he continued, facing his father now, "in the sky. Not once, but upon several curious occasions now. A scar born of fire painting the atmosphere above the Southspur Mountains; piercing it. I know not what it is, but I sense danger in it. Great danger."

"Fire across the sky?" laughed Ansel, "Come now, Ethyn, you cannot expect your father to send legion soldiers into the mountains, based upon a misshapen cloud catching the sun's glow at dusk."

"Thrice have I seen this," Ethyn answered, "and I assure you it is no common cloud."

"Ethyn, please," said the Nhyle, inserting himself back into the conversation, "you can't even leave *stargazing* to the *astronomer*, can you? When will it end?"

"Comets..." insisted Ansel with a twinge of urgency in his voice now, turning toward the Nhyle, "they are termed comets. Stray fragments from the heavens are what he has seen, my lord. They fly with such speed through the atmosphere that they catch fire, at times. They are natural phenomena. I, too, have seen them; through my looking glasses, of course. We astronomers know of such things. They are real, but they are perfectly harmless." Ansel collected himself with a deep breath and looked again at Ethyn with a forced smile, "Is this where you would mount your search for this third party, Ethyn? Aboard a comet?" And he burst into laughter, in such similar fashion to Ambassador Fleurys' style that Ethyn was forced to cringe with a most sharpened spite.

It took the prince every bit of restraint he could summon to keep himself from striking that laughter straight out of the man's mouth. Perhaps in recognition of this, Ansel's amusement subsided, and his stare shifted, once more, down to Ethyn's tunic where the amber stone hung.

*Again he searches my person for the stone…*

"And what do you know of this?!" Enraged, Ethyn pulled the necklace from beneath his garments and held it up for Ansel to see. The man's face spoke of certain knowledge. And fear. Much like it had when the stone was first revealed at assemblage. Ethyn forced himself upon the older man, grabbing at the scarves about his neck and squeezing them tightly, "Tell me of your interest in this stone. I see your stares. I'll have you confess them, now!"

"Again, you err in your judgments! There is nothing to tell." Ansel summoned all his strength to tear away from the prince and flee back to his chair, digging his feeble body so deeply into the cushions he nearly disappeared between them; mumbling through a few crackled whimpers, "Do you not see his recalcitrance, Lord Nhyle?"

"Ethyn!" the Nhyle's voice was so strained with exasperation, it sounded positively hoarse and broken, nearly as much as Ansel's, "Take your leave of us, this instant. I will have no more…"

He was interrupted by stout poundings on the study door as Commander Thorngrove entered with insistence, his heavy boots thudding on the floor and the joints in his armatures creaking madly as he advanced, "You sent for me with urgency, my lord?"

The Nhyle caught his breath for a moment and turned his attention to the legion commander, calming himself as best as he could in the process.

"I did," he said, clearing his throat, "it pains me to do so, but I must ask. How fares the damage to the keep, commander? The casualties?"

Everyone in the room stood perfectly still to hear the response.

"There are many who deserve the highest commendations for their acts of courage this day," said Thorngrove, taking off his leather cap and casting his gaze to the floor while bowing his head with respect, "folk of all stations have searched the rubble for anyone who might've been trapped or buried. Some've been injured, themselves, in their efforts. The keep's a complete loss, the whole of it; and we've yet confirmed one castellan, two hand maids, and four boys in-training lost to the fallen stone. And head counts stand incomplete; a good number still unaccounted for. Some were tending their duties; others were sleeping in their quarters when the walls were felled. Many more fled during the collapse and sustained injuries; some serious. The soothists and their clerks are overwhelmed with patients."

The room was dead silent; solemn. Each individual's exhaustion doubled over at the grim news, and a length of time trudged by, during which not a word was spoken.

"One more thing, my lord, quite curious indeed," added Thorngrove, finally. "There is rumor passing about the court over the return of one Adrian Thurflyn. That he was observed upon the morn at the very scene of the fallen keep."

"Thurflyn?" Perwyn muttered. "Did anyone make contact with him?"

"Negative, my lord," said Thorngrove, "just rumor of his presence."

Ethyn straightened his stance at this last bit. *It's just like Thurflyn to try and play the hero after being advised to lay low.* In any case, the reality of the situation had become clear enough to Ethyn, who'd considered this attack the absolute tipping point. *This will have to be the moment when Athyn resolves to stand up and strike back. This will be the time for sending a message to all the lands and in all directions; that no one can challenge us like this and get away with it.*

At last, the Nhyle broke another protracted silence by drawing a long, thin breath, "Commander, mobilize the legion at once; the Royal Guard, too. I want rank and file aligned in the court by dawn. Let us make plans to fortify the city. Ours will remain a defensive posture, until we may determine our due course. Send no forces abroad without my leave, but ready them for the worst. And we shall not send further word to our ambassador. Let him and his entourage return to us safely from Maelnlock with haste, as he has been advised to do."

*A defensive posture? He cannot be serious. After all that has occurred.*

"And put an alert out to your men for Thurflyn," added the Nhyle to Thorngrove, "If he's truly returned against my edict, I wish to see him before me at once."

Ethyn could not stifle immediate projection of his feelings of disagreement, which escaped him in the form of a hapless scoff. And in making for the door, he hefted the bird cage violently in hand, turned, and said simply, "Mistake."

He'd quit the room (and all those in it) with a feeling of resoluteness, absent an effort to obtain further response from anyone. *A most contentious convergence of opinions, that was; and again, the most flawed notions prevail. If no others will listen... If no others will act, I suppose I shall rightly take it upon myself to do so. A journey is in order—nay, is far overdue!—and I will be at its lead. I only must now determine where it is we shall go; to the west and its archipelago, or to the Southspur Mountain reaches and their razor-sharp peaks. Or elsewhere, altogether!*

*I only know this. Our foes, who stand out there to be found, will suffer our most merciless wrath, and it will be they who will be forced to assume a posture of stifled defense.*

## 26 | From a Nostalgic Perspective

*"There are, at times, provisions made for the rekindling of a by-gone tradition or muse. I would say, when these opportunities arise, let us seize upon them; welcome them; indulge in them. Because you never know what important part of yourself may also be rekindled in the process."*
—excerpt from the personal journal of Steven Spurlock

|Planet Deaer, Castle Athyn, North Court

Ex-Travel Guildmaster Adrian Thurflyn regretted his visit to the Dapper Duckling tavern. He made his way through the damp underground tunnels that led back to the cellars beneath his old manor house—a satchel full of warm food slung over his shoulder with a lantern and walking stick leading him along—while scolding himself for his own foolhardiness. *What was I thinking, marching into a hive of gossip and rumor, assuming I'd not be recognized? The whole upper city will be tossing my name around tonight, and for all I know, I've still got two more days to go here. I've likely whittled down to nothing the chances they'll pass quietly, and without further incident.*

He continued along, puffing stubbornly at his pipe, shuffling through the darkness, sealing the false walls back tight, and clearing the rest of the spider webs he'd missed earlier in the evening. Suddenly, and with a true measure of force, he heard a great sound from the Manor House, which he feared may have been his visitor, Hattie, with her baby, perhaps in danger. And upon reflex, he extinguished the lantern and hung it with haste so that he might return to the living room to see what (if anything) might be the matter.

"I was able to find us something to eat—" he began to say, pushing his way urgently through the kitchens, taking the satchel strap from his shoulder. He was interrupted by the sight of dozens of people, milling about the house, organizing makeshift workstations and conversing amongst themselves. One woman was kneeling on the floor beside a cot, which Thurflyn took as the source of the loud bang, when they must have set it down, and she was lining up canisters filled with salves and herbs and elixirs beside it. Other folks stood in groups. Some of them appeared visibly upset with tears in their eyes, and some looked relieved, even joyous, as they embraced one another.

It was then that Adrian realized these folks had been many of those he'd seen by the fallen keep in the morning. In fact, he recognized the Head Mistress who'd rejoiced in his saving of her two pupils from the wreckage; and then he'd seen the boys, themselves, as well. They were gathered in a larger group on the grand staircase with others their age, while the mistress took a head count of her pages and maids.

"You're back, m'lord!" called a voice from across the floor. It was Hattie (with tiny Aaryn asleep in the crook of her arm). She was smiling at him while she approached, "I felt the house would serve well as a shelter for everyone, but oh, I just hope you don't mind I've invited all these others. They've nowhere else to go, and you'd said it was really no burden."

Thurflyn was so taken unawares by all the activity bustling around him that he could hardly form a reply. In all honesty, his greatest reaction to all the commotion was one born straight from the heart, which had elicited within him an uncharacteristically emotional response. One he knew not exactly how to handle, but he resolved to do his best.

"Most certainly, my dear," he managed to say, looking across the great living room again, where people were peering in wonder at the rare articles lining the bookshelves and the artifacts hanging on the walls. He saw the children assembled on the grand staircase chittering and chattering. His Manor House of the Travelers Guild had come to life once again, and he could do nothing but crack a deep, soulful smile. "There are dormitories up the stairs, with beds and wardrobes and dressers. They are welcome to use whatever they find. All are welcome. You've done a fine thing, indeed, bringing them here, Hattie. A fine thing."

"Oh, how wonderful!" She put her arms around him, rising upon her toes to kiss his cheek.

"Here, please take this and eat," he said, pulling the wrapped food from his satchel and handing it to her, "you must be starving."

All she did then was smile while accepting his offering, and made for the kitchens, tapping on the shoulders of a few of her friends on the way to invite them to join. And Thurflyn smiled, too. *If my cover wasn't blown in the Dapper Duckling, it certainly is now… I dare say it just may be worth it, though.*

But no sooner had he turned himself around, then did the front door burst open, and standing within its frame was the eldest prince, Ethyn of Athyn, holding a bird cage in his hand and wearing a look of urgency upon his face. Adrian came to his attention immediately, but before he could utter a word, the prince cut in.

"Thurflyn, I can see you're keeping a low profile here." Ethyn looked about the living room at the dozens of guests raising their ruckus.

"My lordship, when tragedies strike, priorities are subject to rapid reassessment."

Thurflyn was unsure whether the prince had heard him or not, because Ethyn had turned on his heel without response and had started up the grand staircase, sternly instructing the guildsman to follow. They stepped over and between the children gathered in their way, and the Head Mistress nearly fainted in her throes of admiration when she saw Ethyn pass.

They climbed one flight and then another, passing more visitors, who were clearly making themselves comfortable in the house. In one bedroom, Thurflyn saw some of the beds were already occupied by folks; fast asleep, no less. Then he and the prince climbed two, and then three flights higher, where they saw more of the same (though many young occupants they saw had taken to play and chatter instead of sleep). *Fortunate thing the manor home was left intact all these seasons, 'else these people would be huddled in the court without any measure of comfort at all.*

"Can I ask you something, Master Traveler?" said Ethyn while they made their ascent.

"Certainly, your lordship," said Thurflyn.

"How is it that you and my father have come to such odds with one another?"

Thurflyn had expected this question would arise eventually, but alas, he'd not yet developed a particularly favored manner of answering it. So he tried his best to deflect. "We'd viewed the world—long ago at certain critical times, I'm afraid—through fundamentally incompatible lenses, which led us to undertake ill deeds of an, admittedly, childish nature against one another. At one point, I suppose, he'd had enough."

"Come now, Thurflyn," said Ethyn, "never has a more vague account of past events ever been delivered upon my ears. You can do better than that, I trust."

"We lack time enough for details, I fear," said Thurflyn, "I'll simply say it was best for all that a deal of distance, at that time, be placed between us."

They continued to climb a few moments further without speaking.

"If I were you," added Ethyn, "I'd expect this inquiry to resurface, and at such time as it does, an adequate explanation shall be required."

Thurflyn simply cringed and nodded his head in understanding.

Two flights later, they found themselves in the attic space where old boxes of supplies and implements were stored and stacked. A balcony ran along the front-facing side of the house, and Ethyn proceeded toward it, opening double glass-paned doors and letting himself out into the evening's fresh air.

The prince set the bird cage down and pulled a message scroll from the pouch at his belt, as well as a quill from an inside pocket of his cloak to make an inscription.

Thurflyn watched, reading in puzzlement as Ethyn wrote.

"Are you truly meaning to send that off somewhere?"

"Truly, I am," answered Ethyn, kneeling down to remove the bird from the cage and affix the scroll within a clip upon its leg.

"May I ask, for whom such a strongly-worded message is intended?"

"I do not know," Ethyn raised his arm high and the bird took off to flight with great, resounding clappings of its wings. "That is what we must find out. And this bird is about to give us our first clue."

They watched with great anticipation while it circled once (then twice) overhead, banking *west,* and it seemed Ethyn had gathered something important from what he saw. Yet just before the prince turned away, the bird climbed in elevation again, almost as if it were acquiring its bearings to establish a more accurate destination point. Finally, it changed its pattern, flapping those beautiful wings to set a new course— due *south,* gaining in speed.

Thurflyn watched the prince turn to face him.

"Prepare your effects and meet me in the stables after dark, Master Traveler," said Ethyn, "We leave for the Southspur Mountains. Tonight. And in the meantime, make yourself good and well hidden. You've the Royal Guard hot on your trail upon orders from my father."

## 27 | Few Spans from the Tattered Flag

*"False starts occur when we are anxious to engage in something we know will require promptness of both thought and action. We must exercise caution in these circumstances, lest we disqualify ourselves from competition before we even begin."*
—excerpt from the personal journal of Steven Spurlock

|Planet Deaer, The Southspur Mountain Settlement

Haiyen Sün had let the day slide into late afternoon before deciding she ought to at least make an attempt to track down Prima pilot Bartyl Gleon. She'd hung around her parents' homestead through midday, seizing the opportunity to connect a bit with her sis, Rhyn; to share some stories and laugh awhile longer. Despite the visit's brevity, she enjoyed the time she'd spent with her family. Then, begrudgingly, she'd returned to the inner Settlement and the Sage's compound to log a report or two, and to meditate upon the many things that clouded her mind. Then finally, when those chores were through, she had begun her search for the generous Prima ranksman, if only half-heartedly.

He was, indeed, her only fellow pilot whom she would ever dare confide in, and she supposed that after their last conversation in the hangar, she'd have to recognize a friendship existed between them; made so in one-fell-swoop by the virtue of the favors he'd so selflessly offered her. The whole business of making friends in this manner didn't sit well with her. She'd much sooner remain utterly friendless than to find herself indebted to anyone, for anything.

No matter how much she tried to deny it, though, the progression toward friendship with Gleon felt good in certain ways; or at least, if nothing else, reassuring. It was something of value to know that someone in this fraternity would support her when the need arose. And in fact, he already *had* offered his support, in pledging to assume her duties provisioning Koryn Naylor's cottage every thirty turns of the silver-clad moon, as had been her unenviable duty for the last two years running. *Yet to think, the embarrassment and the discomfort I suffered in asking this favor of him shall all go for naught.*

In her mind, she replayed Sage Arynel's denial of her request to transfer those awful duties to her new-found friend. It was one of the topics she'd meditated upon as well, but no solution to the conundrum had sprung forth from those mystical sources either. And so, even though there remained a full twenty-eight days that would go by before she'd have to fly back up to Koryn's peak, she already dreaded the chore as if it awaited her, bright and early upon the morrow's first light. And it would loom over her like this, she knew, until all of those days would pass her by. A vicious cycle by all accounts, with which she was painfully all too familiar.

She walked the compound looking for Gleon, her search extending through the gardens, eventually bringing her to the hangar and its broad, open-air gallery that abutted the valley's southern slopes. Gleon was there dressed in his flight suit, engaged in stretching exercises by his lonesome. And suddenly, rather than approach him, Haiyen decided to feign ignorance of his presence and walk her way to the far railing; to lean against it and stare off into the distance as if rapt in a particularly deep mode of contemplation, completely unrelated to the very unsettling topic she was so firmly grappling with inside.

It only took a few moments for Gleon to oblige her charade, "Would you mind a little company?"

She leered at him with a terribly level stare, "I'm beginning to think you enjoy initiating conversations with those who clearly intend to keep to themselves, Gleon. Am I on to something?"

"I only do so when the risk is worth the potential reward," he was folding his sleeves back, bearing well-defined musculature. The Rank's snug flight suits left little of a pilot's form to the imagination as it was, and she was distracted by his posturing, if only for a moment. But he continued without further delay, "And yes, you *are* on to something. I promise, the more we talk, the more you'll learn about me, and maybe you'll find it's not all so bad."

"Well," she softened her expression a bit, "I'll concede that your kindness the other day was a welcome surprise."

"I'm glad for that," his slanted, one-sided smile seemed an effort to coax an even warmer expression out of her, but she chose not to play along. "Speaking of which, and I hope you don't mind my broaching a sensitive topic, but had you a chance to speak with the Sages? About the supply runs to the mountain's peak; taking them for my own duty in your stead?"

*He can really get to the point, can't he? Am I so transparent that he could read the topic written across my face?* She turned a bit sullen now and spoke with a deflated voice, "Indeed, I had."

"I see… It seems they were less than agreeable to the idea, then?"

"Arynel rejected the proposal, outright."

Having delivered the news to him, something halted within her, and she suddenly wanted nothing to do with the situation. Some kind of switch flipped her outlook on things—her direction in all of this—completely around. Those supposed feelings of reassurance born of her nascent friendship with Gleon turned to dust in a wink, and she wanted desperately to be away from him. As odd as it seemed, she wanted to be rid of his willing kindness and his positive energy most of all.

"I'm sorry I even asked this of you from the start," she said, "It was wrong of me."

And lacking ceremony in her manner, she began to depart from the place where they were, deliberately and without much of an expression of emotion. She thought she could feel his eyes on her back while she went, immediate and intense, and considered it a forgone conclusion he would call for her and would plead with her to stay. This, so he could reassure her there'd been no harm in her asking this small—*yet, in reality, not so small at all*—favor of him. But as she continued to distance herself from him, step for step, there came no such plea. Only silence. Silence and, of course, the sound of her own boots on the gallery floor as she marched. And she could make no sense of it.

Finally, she stopped in place, and turned around on her own accord.

"Is that it, then?" she hollered.

He laughed. He'd been watching her walk away the whole while, "Is *what* it? Haiyen, I swear, you're so funny sometimes."

"Funny, you say?"

*Funny? How can any of this be taken remotely for humor?*

They were a good twenty paces apart from one another, and their voices were raised in this exchange, yet she wasn't aware of anyone else around who might hear. And she wasn't sure she would've cared anyway. Maybe she was wrong to think of him as a gentleman. Maybe he was just as cold as the rest. Just as cold as…

"I fail to see what's so *funny* about this, Gleon. This is my *life*."

"No, Haiyen, I meant no offense," his face wore a look of sincerity.

"You've an odd way of showing it…"

"I'll tell you what," he was making his way toward the great hangar doors now, which stood halfway between their respective positions, "I'm set to head out on patrol; I've got rounds this evening. Would you care to join me? It might help take your mind off all this."

Flying always helped clear her mind, true; much more than meditation ever could, anyway. But it didn't necessarily mean Gleon had been especially perceptive in supposing this about her. She was sure he had steam of his own to blow off, from time to time. Everyone has steam. And it was likely that he found flying just as therapeutic as did she. She watched him push the doors open and hold them in a gentlemanly manner, indeed, tilting his head as if to say: *C'mon, it'll be fun!*

Without relaxing the scowl from her face (because she believed she was still quite sore at him), she took it upon herself to march proudly through the doors. Once in the hangar lobby, she turned sharply on her heel again to stare at him straight-on, "I'll come along. But I won't ride with you in that clunky tri-thruster death machine you call a buzzcraft. I'll take my own."

"Who said anything about riding together?" Now it was *his* turn to take broad, confident strides. He passed her by, walking deliberately in a line toward the hangar, "We can't race to the Peninsula riding together in the same craft…"

*Oh, if it's a race he wants, then a race he will most certainly receive!*

\*\*\*

Prima rank pilots Haiyen Sün and Bartyl Gleon hurried to their respective docking bays in the hangar, where each pilot's craft was moored and where a small locker held flight clothes, in case of emergencies. Haiyen was still inside her booth, pulling on her snug flight suit and coat when she heard Gleon's craft roar to life, loud and powerful.

She slipped on her boots and in no time was boarding her own buzzcraft, locking down the cab in preparation for departure.

With each hand, left then right, she grasped the blue stone hanging around her neck and then gripped the throttle to pour the energy of the mystics into the craft's acceleration chambers. The flexor wings started to flicker, to reverberate, and spring into motion. Then she was up from the floor, floating to the center of the open roof when she saw that Gleon was waiting for her to make first clearance. *Chivalrous, indeed. Just as well. He should get used to trailing behind in my turbulence, anyway.*

She made clearance and he followed.

At the outset, they flew conservatively and in perfect tandem to protect against any such chance that a Sage might happen to catch notice of their departure, which (if made at the kind of velocity required of any proper race) would be in serious violation of Prima code. There was, instead, a postern that flew a flag two-dozen spans or so beyond the valley's edge, which marked the beginning of the *safe zone* for the commencement of any such recreational feat of speed, and that was precisely where the contest would begin. But for the moment, Haiyen looked across the space between their crafts into Gleon's cab and saw him turn his head. He raised his eyebrows challengingly, as if to ask: *Do you think you're ready for this?*

*Are you?* She wanted to ask in return. She'd never flown in tandem before, apart from her training. Her mother had once told her it could prove a most exhilarating experience, but again, Haiyen's dismissal of her fellow pilots had, for so long, prohibited her enjoyment of such an arrangement. Until now, of course. And it seemed Gleon was doing everything he could to make her first tandem flight a special one; smiling and hand-gesturing signals, portending good times lay just ahead. *If I weren't firmly sworn off of destructive relationships, I might almost see something more in this awkward Bartyl Gleon character.*

Then, in a moment charged with adrenaline, Haiyen knew they were yet a few spans from the tattered flag, marking the *safe zone*, but she didn't much care. She focused her power into the throttle and blasted her way ahead of him, leaving him behind to suffer the billowing waves of her back-current. The thrust was exhilarating, and she rode it like a supernatural high, taking the buzzcraft down to hug the slopes, using gravity to her advantage. She pushed through a straight-away and a quick turn saw her craft enter a canyon pass; the flexor wings buzzing so fast they were unseen to her naked eye. And her heart was accelerating, too, leaping with each successive sweeping arc.

At the speed she was traveling, there wasn't a moment to spare—to risk a glance in search for her opponent's location, but it was clear that the head start she'd given herself had provided a nice cushioned lead. The landmarks swept by in a blur, and she felt the tilt and sway of the craft with each slight nudge of the yoke she made to avoid them. She knew the lay of the course from the Settlement to the Peninsula well, and it was evident in the way she flew; her zipping along over the rocky terrain.

Suddenly, at the mouth of the canyon when she readied for her emergence from its towering buttes, Bartyl Gleon's craft came out of nowhere, lumbering across her view—with all three thrusters trailing pulse waves like streamers rippling the air—settling down and sliding itself into position directly in front of her.

She took a moment to curse his audacity, then to find the means to draft in his wake, using the power of his own engines to her advantage. The superior aerodynamics of her craft took to the currents perfectly, and she was pushed to his left side, angling herself masterfully until the two crafts became so utterly close to one another, the cabs' shields were almost kissing. She looked at him through their reflective tinting, and they both burst out laughing in the sheer ecstasy of the race; the danger laden within, negotiable only through their expertise as pilots.

With precise maneuverings of the throttle, she arced herself over and around to Gleon's right side before peeling off and finding her way through a chasm and around twists and turns, and dips and dives. He followed and managed to pass her once, then twice, and thrice again. But each time, she regained the lead, and each time, they exchanged glimpses of euphoric laughter from one cab to the other. And they went on like this, in great sport, until the Peninsula—a tall land formation that jutted out into the Arctic South Sea—came into plain view.

They both shot for it, straight as an arrow, passing mere hand widths above the prairie that sprawled over the elevated terrain, blowing tall grasses a-kilter like the parting of a golden sea. It was then that she gripped her blue stone with one hand, and the throttle with the other, and surged her fullest capacity of energy through the craft. She streamed through the air, cutting through it like a molten knife, searing its edgeless form. If the air itself could burn, her speed would have caught the whole world on fire.

And at last, she pulled the craft into a wide-turned approach, decelerated and came to a neatly controlled landing upon a solid shelf of rock on the Peninsula's heights. There was a full five-count before Gleon did the same; touching down just as gingerly, resting his craft side-by-side with hers. She fell back into her seat, exhaling deeply from her extreme efforts, but feeling splendidly victorious all the same.

"Not bad for a tailfin bender like you!" Gleon exclaimed, hopping out of his craft.

"Do you regret helping me fix it now?" she, too, emerged from her craft and joined him on the rock surface, both of them breathing heavily to recover from the time they'd spent holding their breath on the final approach. The Peninsula was a favored place for Prima pilots to stop and seek a bit of rejuvenation while on patrol. Flying was always a draining exercise to be sure, especially at the speeds the two of them had just dared to travel and with the maneuvers they'd pulled. So they were both grateful for the chance to sit down on the cliff's edge, and recover for a moment.

"That last burst of speed…" he sucked in a bit of the cool arctic air that was tossing their hair around in intermittent flits, and then he looked at her necklace. "That must be *some* stone you have there."

"Too proud to admit a girl may have defeated you on her own merits?" she reckoned a figurative punch in the gut was in order, though she quite certainly took his comment for a harmless jape. She held the blue stone by her fingertips and let the sunlight pour into it, "It's the same stone they issued to my mum."

"Quite an appropriate provenance, indeed. It must make you proud to wear it," Gleon was again displaying that genuine quality about him. It seemed he couldn't help it, and she could see no reason to complain this time, or to flee from it in fear. It was nice to see *someone* in the Rank behave as such, and it was nice to be in receipt of such kindness, too. Her switch, it seemed, was flipping back. He continued, "I've always meant to ask you about her. Or, perhaps not *her*, specifically, but your lineage. I've done some digging, and it seems you and I are the only two Prima ranksmen," he coughed to correct himself, "er, ranks *persons*, that is, to bear lineage not tied back, however tenuously, to the Sages themselves. Do you find that peculiar?"

"I had no idea of that," she looked out at the expansive horizon, along which the South Seas turned about in accordance with the tides; the pull of the Ancillary Moon. And farther out, she could see the ice sheets and glaciers, ever set unto their gentle pilgrimage, which some day would find their chunks and bergs floating all the way to the coast, upon which they sat. She spurted a laugh, "But still, it doesn't surprise me to learn our fellow ranksmen have all descended from a long line of judgmental despots."

"A harsh way to describe our leaders, Haiyen."

She looked at him flatly, trying to discern whether she'd crossed a line she shouldn't have, and then asked with a twinge of rebellious indifference, "You're not going to report me for it, are you?"

"Harsh, but extremely appropriate, I would add," his smirk and the candor in his words suggested he had found a comfort level in their newly-assumed mutual trust, "I'm glad to have found someone brave enough to voice that sentiment aloud."

"So you agree the Sages can seem a bit overbearing?"

"Well sure, to a degree," now it was he who was looking out across the horizon, "but I find our possession of such freedom of opinion reassuring; proof that we haven't been completely brainwashed, at least." He laughed.

"Have you ever risked a glimpse of the Beyond, Gleon?" she just blurted it out, realizing she'd phrased it almost exactly as Koryn Naylor had phrased it to her, "I mean, do you ever wonder about the flatlanders and what they're really about? If they even exist?"

"I've put myself to that very question too many times to count," he took his own pendant—a deep green stone with sparkling inclusions—into his hand and looked at it intently, "and I've always come to the same conclusion. That a theoretical non-existence of these flatlander colonies spread across the unknown world, such as the Sages have proposed exist, would assume that a patent and universal dishonesty lies within the Sages themselves; *each* of them. And though I sometimes question their leadership methods and their visions for our Rank, and even the Settlement, too, I cannot in good conscience name them patent liars. I will admit my eyes have strayed in curiosity to the line of peaks that make up our strictest of borders, but I cannot say I've perpetrated the act of flying past them to prove or disprove their version of this storied *Beyond* we've heard so much about. Are you going to tell me you have?"

"No. Though like you, I'll admit to a certain level of curiosity," she fidgeted a little, "enough to have dinged a tailfin on one of those very peaks that you've referenced."

"Oh, I see," He grimaced with understanding, "so this is a new-found curiosity of yours?"

"You could say that."

"Well, if you happen to reach any conclusions, be sure to clue me in," he was looking straight out at the glaciers now, almost as if he were trying to track their movements, which could never actually be seen by the naked eye.

She laughed, peering at him intently, and promised, "I will."

The sun was diving for the horizon in the west smearing horizontal lines of blush and plumb around the curvature of the sky; a natural panorama like no other. Trade winds tossed the hood of her coat and, far above, pushed a few scattered wispy clouds along, much faster than the glaciers would ever move across the sea. And she let her soul rest for a moment. *A quick ride may clear my mind a bit, indeed.*

"By the way," he said after a while, breaking the introspective silence, "I'll do it."

"Do what?"

"I will provision the mountain's peak for you."

"Gleon, did you forget about what I said; that Arynel denied my request? And he didn't just simply say *No*, either. He emphatically, undeniably, unequivocally, and unflinchingly *denied* it, almost before I even finished asking."

"Yes, I remember. But here's the thing, Haiyen," he turned his gaze from the seas around to her; his eyes seeming to penetrate hers with their intense concentration, "I can tell you're ready to leave that part of your life behind, and I want to help you do it. I *need* to help you do it. And besides, I think I've devised a way we can pull it off, to make it seem you're still making the deliveries yourself."

She knew not how to react, except that she felt she must mark this as some kind of affirmation of his feelings for her. The kind of feelings she suspected he may have latently expressed through his acts of kindness in the hangar, before. And surprisingly, yet again, she found herself holding her ground without the sudden urge to flee.

"When did you decide this?"

"Right about the moment I cut you off coming out of the canyon," he cracked a broad grin, while somehow maintaining a look that upheld the earnestness in what he was saying; what he was offering.

"So you perpetrated two decidedly reckless maneuvers at once, then?"

"The canyon? Sure, that probably wasn't the smartest move I made back there. But I won't concede that my offer regarding the mountain peak carries any such similar rash distinction; at least compared against the dangers embedded in your only alternative. What could be more reckless than forcing you to go back up there every thirty days? You must be exhausted from this duty; physically *and* mentally. Can you ever find release from this? Can you ever find release from *him*?"

"I cannot ask this of you, Gleon. I just..." She simply stopped speaking, then, because she had to think about the proposal for a moment. His counterpoints were especially insightful, and they cut to the core in ways he simply had no way of knowing. But her misgivings about all of this were so great, that she scarcely even knew where to start. "If history bears any indication, we know the Sages don't take kindly to betrayal, in any form, and that scares me. I ought to know just as well as anyone the sort of ramifications that can result from wayward deeds like the one you're proposing; deceiving them and defying their orders."

"I hear what you're saying," they were facing each other now, their knees lightly touching, and he reached out and took her hands into his own, holding them tight and secure, and she let him do it, "I just want you to at least think it over. And when you've come to a decision, let me know. I won't force anything upon you. That's not my way." He looked squarely at her a moment longer, then released her hands and stood up.

He smiled warmly, and then slowly began to walk away.

She followed suit, rising and taking one last look at the diving sun—feeling the cool air nip at her cheeks—before climbing into her buzzcraft, and watching him climb into his. But then, he stuck his head out of his cab and said, "Oh and, call me Bart from now on, ok? Gleon seems a bit too... formal."

She gripped the throttle and lifted off from the Peninsula, then shouted out from her cab, "We'll just have to see about that..."

And then she was off, jet-setting a course back to the mountains and the Settlement.

And he was lifting off and following, close behind.

## 28 | A Tempest of Impossible Passion and Fury

*"I suppose we all have secrets; ones we call our own
and those we harbor in trust for others. But I've come
to suspect the universe holds one secret that stands
most volatile of all. One that is too complex for minds
like ours to fully comprehend. And this shortcoming in
understanding just may end up being humanity's saving
grace; or, perforce, its greatest failure. There persists
an ignorance among us for the true manner by which
the fabric of reality is woven. Shall we remain
incapable of deciphering the mechanics of the loom?"*
—excerpt from the personal journal of Steven Spurlock

|Planet Deaer, Castle Athyn

When the Nhyle, Perwyn Solis, retired to the royal bedchambers, he found his Nohnce seated upon an upholstered bench, awaiting his return. Having just commanded a defensive posture in the face of imminent war, and the decision weighing heavily upon his heart, he was in no mood for a single thing that may exacerbate his critical level of emotional distress. And yet, when he saw her face looking upon him, he knew (at once) this would be the outcome of her visitation, and that he would indulge her needs, to any extent that she required.

Theirs had always been an uncommon union. She came to him in near-spectral form, as beautiful females are known to do; at least through the lens of the burgeoning, youthful male's fervent eye. He remembered her appearing before him, like an amorphous mote of dust swirling through fledgling rays of sun as he rode a trail through the wooded Andals, so long ago, when he was but eight years past ten. She seemed as if spliced from a brilliant beam among thousands cast off the horizon, filtered in-between slim trunks and weeping branches, grafted into his world from some kind of fantasy. He'd reared his mount, and she advanced upon him requesting transport to the nearest village, if he may. When he obliged her appeal, no sooner had she climbed into the saddle and seated herself behind him, than he'd felt her warm breath tickle his ear; soft whisperings and incantations as she held firm to his waist and hooked her heels around his boots.

He'd been dispatched from Castle Athyn by his father, the then-Nhyle, to perform delivery of written decrees to lords in the Eastlands, but her sudden presence in the Andals had purged from him all sense of responsibility. From there, through field, forest, and village they would venture; never with a care for time, ever at the expense of duty. He became a sail ship and she the wind, born from a tempest of impossible passion and fury.

Fettered to her at first by primal desires (which they acted upon at the turn of every inn room key), the bond quickly metamorphosed into a cacophony of emotional attachment.

"Like two trees which have grown beside one another," Mailyn once whispered to him during their travels, "whose roots and branches alike have crept, twisted, and locked; pulling the very soil, and crust, and air of the world between them together, cracking and breaking that which might ever keep them apart; unfailingly inseparable... and daringly unafraid."

Eventually they returned to the castle, and he to his duties as the Heir Prince, but she remained beside him—always in lock-step.

The seasons ahead would prove Perwyn held the power of the realm in his hands, and so too, the definitive sway within his and Mailyn's royal covenant, but she was not (in her own right) entirely bereft of command. Looming about them was the fact that she'd never told him from whence she'd come. He only knew that she'd appeared to him one day in the morning, as he passed through the boughs of the Andals, and beyond that, he knew nothing more at all of her beginnings. He'd always perceived in her a dominant presence of Athynian descent, yet her facial features had shone foreign at times (in certain light and at certain angles); emblematic perhaps of some unknown province or some unfamiliar land, he couldn't guess. Yet, when it had all begun, he'd been at a stage in life where none of that quite mattered. Only that she was smart, beautiful, and willing.

Whatever the case, the shroud of mystery surrounding her heritage drove a wedge between Perwyn and his father, the Lord Nhyle Balwyn, who had snarled:

"How might my son have stumbled upon such impenetrable love for a woman who offers no lineage; lacking dowry of value in any form, whatsoever; and offering naught insofar as an account merely of the place in which she began her life?" His father's taste for illustrative sarcasm, at times, dripped from his mouth in a fevered froth, "I'd just as soon bless your betrothal to a scullery maid in the employ of the *Greatlyn's Galley*. At least then the royal seat may stand to receive a pitcher of ale and a roast of mutton in dowry for its trouble."

Yet, despite his father's discontent on the matter, Perwyn never pressed Mailyn, never forced her in any way to divulge the details of her past, for it seemed too painful a topic for her to revisit. And the resultant mystery served to hold him in check through their early period of marriage. Now, all these many seasons later, the matter seemed a decidedly moot point, judged against the grand scheme of things, and thoughts of it seldom ever-more crossed his mind.

"You humble me with your calmness, my love," he said to her, presently, as she sat before him with a placid look on her face, "while I'm a wreck, you manage to project the serenity of a chilled cucumber."

"Seems I've always had a knack for keeping my composure," she answered, "I still hope it might yet rub off on you, my dear. Someday. Even cucumbers and spice-peppers can grow together from the same soil, you know; twist their roots around one another… daringly unafraid…"

*She still remembers all the details as I do, all the whisperings; the fondest of memories we've shared.* He smiled to signal his recognition of her reference to their carefree days long-passed. "I could use some of that calm of yours. We stand against trying times ahead," he despaired, "and I fear they shall require all the composure we can muster."

"I'm glad you're of that mindset," led the Nohnce, "for as we speak, we may already face circumstances which demand a greater discipline of thought than has been exercised of late."

"I sensed you might have something specific on your mind," Perwyn walked to a window and gazed southward, "what exactly is it that can't wait until our heads meet our pillows?"

"The girl," she answered. "I visited the Mystics House and found her room vacant, save for our very distraught Keeper, Almetta."

"The girl is secured in custody," he replied.

"So said Almetta, but what is to become of her? We cannot keep her locked up forever… certainly not without proof of her guilt. I've the impression her alibi is clear. By the mistress' firm account, she was scolding the girl in the garret of the barn when the explosion hit and the damage was inflicted."

"Scolding? What for?"

"Well, in fact, she was missing from her dormitory when came the early morning call in the barn, and the mistress knew not where she was for a time."

"Her whereabouts unaccounted for this morning? And you think this ought to *lessen* my suspicions of the girl? No. She will remain in custody until this madness is worked through."

"She was with Tae all evening last, and all morning through. His motions and nods were emphatic when I questioned him about it. There can be no mistaking her innocence."

"We must suspect all," Perwyn replied.

"The road of warrantless suspicion can lead to perilous ends, Perwyn. We shan't be rash in these times."

"Yet neither can we afford to leave ourselves vulnerable to further harm…" he ran his fingers through his graying hair, "the line between vengeful impulse and obligatory vigilance is *remarkably* fine. I've come to that understanding the hard way, and as such, I'll gladly bruise the egos of a few to secure the safety of the rest."

"But a small girl?"

"I can rule nothing out, Mailyn. Nothing. This girl, she's different; her power is far greater than is necessary to be dangerous. Well-sufficient enough to bring down a tower, according to the accounts I've received of destruction leveraged yesterday—some talk of an energy burst and a demolished garden shed? Could it be a mere coincidence this attack on the Servants' Keep has followed her arrival near-immediately?"

"I looked into her eyes, Perwyn. Yes, I saw great power in her… to an extent that could cause the kind of damage you fear, and maybe more. But I saw not a shred of intent to bring us, nor *anyone*, harm," the Nohnce rose and walked to her Nhyle and kindly began untying his cape for him. "And besides, don't you see? She may well represent the last chance of our ever breaking through to Tae. To *curing* him. I won't deprive him of that. Not after we've come so far and endured so much to reach these ends." She removed the cape and draped it neatly over the back of a chair.

"I supposed this would have something to do with Tae… Why can't we content ourselves with the realization that Tae *is* who he is? That nothing is going to change him?" Perwyn looked at her, "I know that's a difficult proposition for you to confront, but it's his reality. It's *our* reality. We can't force him to do anything. I've allowed that ship to sail long ago. You should, too... The Mystics House; this Order of Wieldlings and their training... It's a fool's trade, and it's haunted me since the day I consented to finance it. This idea you've carried for so long, that someone would someday come along to befriend the boy and show him *the way*."

"To show him his differences aren't so different, yes, I still believe in that dream. And she could be the answer, finally come true." Mailyn was pleading.

Perwyn shook his head, "Tae *is* who he is. He's never going to change, and we should just let him be. We've likely done more damage than good. In fact, I've half a mind, now, to disassemble the Mystics House altogether and bring that ancient barn to the ground, once and for all. It's done us no good," he looked squarely into her eyes. "This experiment has proven a failure. We will end it. And frankly, it will be high time."

"I can't give up on Tae, Perwyn... I won't. His silent accounting of last night's walk-about with the girl was so enthusiastic; I've never seen him so excited before. We would be remiss to think for a moment it had nothing to do with her. They spent all day together walking the court and the districts. All evening as well, Perwyn. All *night*. Who knows what barriers she's begun to break down for him, and I'll not discourage any of it."

The Nhyle paced the length of the floor to allow the conversation to breathe for a moment. *Yes, I don't doubt for an instant this girl has cast all sorts of spells around Tae's head this past turn of the moon. Are young ladies not known for spinning such enchantments? Mailyn should know more about that than anyone. Tae may limp 'round this place beleaguered and mute, but deep down, he's still a red-blooded male. The girl's advances will excite him for a time; but this, like everything else, will come and go, and he will (as always) lull himself back into a state of solitude... I surely cannot forsake the little one, but I won't fool myself either. Why can't she do the same? It's not that we're giving up on him, it's a matter of freeing him from that which ought not to be expected.*

He turned and stood still for a moment, back by the windows. "There is a twist in all of this," he said, finally, "that I've not yet mentioned."

"What twist?" she asked.

"I will not venture to admit it to him directly, but Ethyn—whose behavior has proven most defiant of late, if you hadn't noticed—has adamantly supported a particularly unconventional theory in explanation of the attack, casting suspicion perhaps toward that of a yet unknown third party, apart from us, of course, and apart from Maelnlock, as well. And I'm beginning to actually consider its validity. Even Mossa Zahyle seems in accordance with it, to some degree."

"A third party?"

"Indeed," he looked Mailyn in the eyes again, "Could this girl not be part of some such scheme?"

She took a few moments before replying this time, "I cannot imagine how."

"Ethyn seems to think his theory will be proven by an assassin."

"An assassin; how so?"

"A suspect. Imprisoned in the dungeons. Ethyn spied him fleeing the site of the explosion before it'd even occurred. This man *knew* it was going to happen before it hit. Ethyn even claims to have received hints of this while visiting an outpost prior to the escort. He thinks it all has something to do with outlaws from the archipelago," Perwyn looked out the windows again at the falling evening; the silvery moon, "and comets in the southern sky… Oh, flames and ashes. Who knows *what* to believe?"

"Fleeing a scene makes one suspicious, yes, but fleeing, alone, does not make one guilty. Perhaps this assassin—this man—simply saw the barrels and fuse; saw the flame, too, and ran in fear."

"That explanation has already been considered and disavowed. Ethyn encountered a message fowl beyond South Gate, where the suspect was seized. Curious that the man and bird had arrived at the same place and time, Ethyn searched for and found a message. A message that bore script written in a strange hand. Provided we can translate it, and the content of the message is damning, I may yet find justification for loosening guard over the girl. But, until then, she will be held. In perfect comfort, I assure you, in the Visitor's Keep."

"That is fine…" Mailyn said, exacerbated, "but as I've mentioned, I simply do not believe she's had anything to do with this foulness that has struck upon us with such hateful intent. Certainly, in the least, Maelnlockian agents seem the far likelier perpetrator of an attack, than does a small girl or some third party. Do they not?"

"Such was the sentiment of Idris Ansel, and of course, common sense would suggest it so as well, but again, we can't be too careful. In any case, decisiveness is a virtue which has proven most elusive in all this. Were I to consider Maelnlock, outright, our sole enemy, I might send our legion forces across the Central Sea, leaving us vulnerable to others, whom Ethyn and Zahyle's scholars suspect lurk all around us. If I do as Ethyn would wish, I risk spreading our forces thin—too thin—with orders to roam the world near aimlessly in search for these unknown adversaries. It is a failure, Mailyn, which I perpetrate, no matter which course I take." Perwyn rubbed his forehead, "No, we can afford no undue risks. Especially with strangers we've known for only a day's time; even small girls. Forgetting third parties, who's to say she's no *Maelnlockian* agent, either? It would take little effort for a realm (intent on attacking us) to send forth a destructive package, obscured by such superficial innocence."

"Come now, Perwyn…"

The Nhyle sighed; exhausted by the layers of speculation he'd fussed over the whole day through. "Well, in any case, as soon as one of Mossa Zahyle's scholars can translate the message, we ought to—" the Nhyle paused abruptly, catching his Nohnce staring blankly out the window as he spoke, appearing as if she were in a trance, "Are you listening to me, Mailyn?"

"Yes, I'm sorry, my dear," she said, blinking her eyes hard, "it's nothing at all. I just wanted to know the girl was unharmed."

"I've not the patience tonight," he said.

*She's holding something back… she's always held something back. Ever since climbing aboard my saddle in the wooded Andals that fateful morning. But what can it be? Something from her past, no doubt, and something that haunts her to this very moment. If only I could convince her to confide in me the truth. Yet after all this time, it would hardly seem prudent to try… Hardly at all.*

He followed her gaze again out the window. And that was when he realized she was staring, quite intently, at the wicked peaks that rose from the Southspur Mountain range, cast deep purple and hauntingly ominous.

\*\*\*

After leaving her husband in their bedchamber, the Nohnce of Athyn, Mailyn Solis, had resolved to inform her youngest son of certain details that she'd come to learn about his little friend, Brychen, so that she might calm him a bit and ease his sorrows. Such had always been her routine; at least with Tae, who'd never been capable of achieving a state of calm on his own. It was a necessity, plain and simple. Her boys were the two most important things, the world over, and always would be. So she had sought Tae out and informed him of what she knew, in his chambers without delay.

When it came to real, earnest cause for concern, of course, her energies may have been more appropriately turned toward the dangerously cavalier tendencies exhibited by her eldest son, Ethyn. But she was convinced that her oldest could rightly take care of himself; or at least, to a far greater extent than could Tae. So, while she never intended to remove her power of influence entirely from her eldest Ethyn's life, she knew most of her day-to-day efforts must focus on the littler one, instead. And most would agree it was rightfully so.

Just as she'd expected, the smallish prince had been woefully troubled by the news she provided, but he'd seemed at least pleased to know Brychen was safe. He also seemed content (at least for a while) to hide away in his chambers in response to it all, as was his ritual when things didn't go his way. She was sure he'd get over it. She only hoped that, so too, would the new wieldling girl. After all, involuntary confinement is never a pleasant thing to endure, even if it is made within a luxurious suite in the Visitors' Keep. And Mailyn's interest in Brychen's well-being was, indeed, wrapped within a multitude of varied interests; some of which she kept tightly locked within her own safe-keeping for no one else's perusal.

That is, until now, when she had finally been given a momentary spell of reprieve from the madness of the day's events. She walked through the royal family's private halls and realized just how quiet it had become. Castle folk were still rallying out in the court to the aid of those who'd been injured in the attack on the Servants' Keep, or had locked themselves away in their own private quarters, in safe-keeping from the threat of further danger.

The Nohnce took this rare opportunity, then, to secret herself away to a private place, where no one would see her pass. She needed only step down a few halls and through a few doorways. And having entered a large and open space, she locked a thick wooden door up tight behind her and tip-toed in her flats across the mossy floor of her personal greenhouse, which was cloistered apart from the main keeps altogether.

Many glass panels of the raised clerestory, high above, had been shattered by the jarring reverberations caused by the blast. But here, in this dense and humid Eden, she could hardly be troubled by such superficial concerns, and deftly avoided the fallen shards that littered the ground. In the center of the greenhouse, there was a shallow stand of water, filled from the trickling of many small streams running along the floor into a circular stone pool, and she removed her flats upon reaching it. When she stepped in, the water was warm, and scarcely much deeper than was needed to cover her ankles. She reached out with her senses, then—each of them at once—and noted the distinct absence of any other soul that may bear witness to what she planned to do next.

And when she confirmed this as such—that no one else could see (or even hear) her, or know of her presence in this place at all—she promptly knelt upon one knee in the water, tilted her head down, closed her eyes, held her breath, and very deliberately disappeared entirely from where she had been.

\*\*\*

|Halcyon

Mailyn Solis had taken herself to a place apart from the land of Athyn entirely; or at least, to a place separated from that land (as it was known to those who named themselves Athynians) in certain inalienable ways. She knelt upon one knee, still within a small pool of water, but when she opened her eyes, she was not in her greenhouse. She was not in Castle Athyn at all, in fact. The pool was inset into the ground by a lining of stones, arranged in a circle. That much was the same. But she was surrounded, now, by wide-open skies and sprawling country that was entirely untouched by the hands of men.

She breathed deeply of the purified air, and she gazed with an inner peace at the expanses of land and trees and water and mountain and sky, taking-in the perfect harmony of this place; the perfect nature, and the perfect balance to everything and all. It was as if the conditions of existence were dialed-in upon their utmost precise setting, ideal for promoting the health and strength of each living thing here. It was the land of Athyn, in shape and form, yet unspoiled in each and every regard. The land here contained all of that other world's natural features, yet none of its corruption, waste, or poison. There was, in fact, no city Proper at all. She had, indeed, broken through the barrier to the unspoiled side.

She had broken through to the unsullied, parallel domain of Halcyon.

Not far from the pool (within which she knelt), there stood a weeping willow tree, and a male figure leaned casually against its trunk with longish hair falling down in front of his face—very nearly in the fashion of the tree's branches, themselves—and he wore woven sandals upon his feet.

"Oh," said Mailyn to the figure, "doesn't it feel awfully satisfying to be returned here, Irillio?"

"Indeed, it does," said the glassblower, Irillio Pasca, taking a step now away from the tree trunk and toward her, "though I'll have you know I've been waiting for you here an entire day's time now. I thought you'd forgotten about our plans. Or, perhaps, that you'd changed them without my knowing."

"Surely you've heard of the events that've transpired of late," Mailyn stepped out from the pool; the ring of stones.

"Only when you failed to show upon our agreed time did I trouble myself to return to my boutique and pursue the necessary gossip. It didn't take me long. The great keeps of man don't fall without making a loud noise, as they say."

"I would certainly apologize for my tardiness, had it been a folly of my own making," said Mailyn, "but, as you can imagine, I'd no foresight at all into any such imminent threat as was levied upon my home with such force and destruction this morning."

"You name that palace of man home, then, eh?" challenged Pasca.

Mailyn looked perturbed, "I won't deny I've grown an attachment to it, Irillio. After all this time, I'd be a fool to pretend it isn't so. Athyn is just as much my home as is Halcyon. I'd like to see you spend some twenty years there, raise two children, and love and suffer and scratch and scrape your way through life there, only to attest otherwise."

"Duly noted."

"I should hope by now you've noted at *least* that much," Mailyn had taken her strides over the soft turf and out upon a neat trail that was ideal for walking, and she'd done so at such a pace that ignored Pasca's need to catch up to her from his spot under the willow tree.

"For the record, we had no prior knowledge of the threat, either, of course," said Pasca, taking a few hurried steps to join-in beside her, "Otherwise, we'd certainly have shared it with you."

"Of course," she assured him. She had no reason to think Halcyon had held any prior suspicion Castle Athyn was in danger, and she wanted to make that clear.

They walked for a time, while large-winged butterflies fluttered across their path and a soothing breeze came upon them, easing the effort of their exertions. Then Mailyn spoke again, once her mind triggered something for which she intended to hold Pasca responsible, "You know, all that talk you made in your workshop, in the company of my little Tae and our girl Brychen upon the art of glass-blowing... Do you think you might have bit your tongue against those particular musings? Precisely, your talk of air passing from one *place* into another, and your speculation between the comparative comforts of multiple *worlds*, and all else to which you alluded. It was all a bit precarious, wouldn't you agree?"

"Sure," conceded Pasca, "but only to the point it could've been interpreted or understood for what it was. I, for one, disbelieve that any aspects of the true nature of things fall within the grasp of even the brightest being who names him or herself a denizen to this other place you call home. This *Athyn*, where our very same lands lie in such a tremendously tainted state of disrepute. It is an inferior plane of existence compared to ours, and so are its people; there is no refuting that. You give them too much credit, Mailyn."

"Watch yourself, Irillio. That is my son, whom you disparage with your broad, condemnatory strokes of the tongue. And I'll not have him, or *any* of my family spoken of in such ill terms, simply for calling themselves denizens of Athyn," she scowled at him in disapproval of his prejudiced assertions while they kept at their brisk pace. "So, too, did our own Lord of Halcyon long ago, lest you not forget."

"No, I shall certainly not forget," said Pasca, backing down a bit.

"There is no place for such infected thought nor speech here. You ought to know better."

"Indeed, I do."

"And I'd recommend you engage yourself in a thorough cleansing of your disposition before we venture into the hamlet. You won't last very long there, behaving in such a manner," Mailyn's solemnity could easily be gathered from her tone, which was quite matter-of-fact, indeed, "unless everything has gone completely asunder since last I've made visitation."

Their walk took them through a wooded grove, which was perfect in its natural beauty in every way. Each leaf was of perfect shape and color and texture. Each blade of grass was grown in such even length to one-another and in such fullness that there wasn't a bald patch to be found anywhere; even around the tree roots and in places cast in the deepest shade. And the flowers—*oh, the flowers!*—grew in such abundance and in such brilliant hues, and emitted the most pleasant of perfumes into the air. In short, the environs supported simply the finest conditions, in every conceivable manner, that a person could ever possibly fancy, and it was difficult sometimes for Mailyn to imagine how she could ever leave it behind, for anything.

But then it came to her without having to think very hard at all: *My boys, plain and simple. My boys are what pull me away.*

And yes, they were indeed the chief focus of her life. But even before they had come into being, she'd been given a reason to leave Halcyon and venture into the land of chaos named Athyn. More accurately, she'd been told she *had* to leave, by the Lord of Halcyon, himself.

"Has he changed much since my visit of a season ago?" asked Mailyn when the two of them had emerged from the wooded groves and continued along toward the hamlet, which laid before them in all of its charming tranquility. This world of Halcyon simply had a way of soothing its inhabitants; a way of bringing a calm euphoria to one's mind that was somehow absent any form of complicated distress, to any degree. The place injected within all who dwelt here a sense of childlike whimsy, which was never clouded by greater understandings of evil and nastiness and danger. And so, even though her curiosities surrounding their present circumstances were abundant, Mailyn felt no anxiety or consternation while she awaited Pasca's reply to her question.

"He is the same," said Pasca, "and I mean that in the most literal sense. He looks exactly the same as he always has, he will say the same things he always says, and he will ask the same questions he always asks. And when it comes to you, I'm sure there will be one topic in particular you ought to be expecting him to broach."

"Why it is that I haven't paid more frequent visitation…" offered Mailyn.

Pasca nodded.

The hamlet was a collection of simple dwellings; cottages, mostly, of stone and wood construction and thatched roofs with chimneys releasing puffs of white smoke. Each person they saw either sat leisurely on their porches, or slowly picked vegetables from their gardens, or walked peacefully along with one another, while each of their faces brimmed with contentment in the waning light of the evening. The path they were walking divided this cluster of homes in half and, before long, Mailyn and Pasca turned from the path and made their way to a quaint cottage that stood amongst the others. A neat stone wall stood around its yard, and a sign of welcome hung on the front door.

They stood and looked for a moment at the humble cottage, and then helped themselves in.

It was dimly lit inside, but the place was well-kept. Fastidiously so, in fact. There was a desk for writing, and a single candle set upon it, burning an even-tempered flame. They could see through a doorway into the kitchen, just beyond, where it sounded as if someone was busying himself with a particularly rigorous task. A man's voice came from that direction, quite soon after they'd entered the front door, and they knew (from the sound of it) that it belonged to *him*, the Lord of Halcyon.

"Have a seat, I shall be with you in a moment," said the voice.

A clean-shaven thin man with short white hair came sauntering through the kitchen doorway shortly thereafter to greet them. He was carrying a long-haired fluffy white (and finely-combed) feline, which he set down on the wooden floorboards once his eyes registered the identity of his visitors, and the feline produced a drawn-out *meow*. "The evening wears on, the yardarm swivels subtly upon a gentle breeze, and our fair Mailyn comes to see me at last."

"Where does the time go, my lord?" She spoke with a playfulness that sounded (to her own ear) only subtly forced. It wasn't the question she wanted very desperately to ask—the question, which had prompted her to pass through the Barrier of Worlds to Halcyon in the first place, upon this evening. She wanted to ease slowly into conversation in order to establish a natural pathway to that particular topic, but Pasca spoke up instead, rudely stealing her opportunity.

"My lord, we've wondered, quite intently in fact, upon the purpose of our service, lo these recent years, within our adjacent world. What ends, exactly, have you in mind when you set us upon our curious tasks there? It is our greatest puzzle of all, and we become quite forlorn when we are away from our dearest Halcyon."

This wasn't nearly the question Mailyn wanted to ask, either. In fact, the answer to Pasca's juvenile inquiry seemed awfully obvious to her, and his blurting it out on both of their behalves annoyed her greatly, even through Halcyon's mystical spell of pacifying serenity, which typically seemed to prohibit such negative emotional responses. *I ought to assign him to the repair of every shattered glass panel in my greenhouse in penance for such an ill-conceived commencement to this conversation.*

"Your presence in that other world, that place called Athyn, brings into our possession a most necessary base of knowledge," said the Lord of Halcyon. It was the response Mailyn knew would be given, but she listened-on as the man in white continued. "The time has come, again, when we must become more informed of the intentions swirling about that world, and I'm sure we would all agree the lessons of history justify our naming the city of Athyn Proper a critical place of interest."

"And so," Pasca let a smile break across his face, "you've plans to use us as portals through which whispers may pass, unknown. And this, as a means to secure vital stores of information?"

"Indeed," the Lord of Halcyon's expression remained the same; even-tempered and pleasant, "I believed you both were well aware of this."

"I understand well, my lord," said Pasca. "I only wished to hear it from you again. That I am an important one among the many of us here."

Mailyn rolled her eyes heavily before speaking up for herself.

"Yet we are not the only ones you've sent through the Barrier of Worlds for such purposes," her statement was a weighted one, indeed, and it was not the manner in which she'd hoped to break into the conversation, at all—her *intended* conversation, that is. But she'd been given no choice.

"No, you are not," confirmed the man in white, who (upon hearing her assertion) had decided to take a seat for himself at his desk, shooing the feline from the room.

"You have sent a young female through, in fact, to enchant my dear son," suggested Mailyn.

"Yes, I have," said the man calmly, satisfying Mailyn's suspicions. "Not unlike the manner in which I had sent you, many seasons ago, to enchant your lord husband. I'd intended to inform you of this development, prior to its initiation, yet your prolonged absence from this place has prohibited such preliminary consultations. In time, I was forced to send her along to make acquaintances with your son, short of your knowledge. It could not be helped."

"I am both relieved and concerned by this," continued Mailyn, "as you might expect. He is, after all, a troubled little one, unaccustomed to socialization of any sort; without even the faculty of speech. And while I'm grateful for the new-found energies this girl has stirred within him, I am yet fearful, as would any mother be, over where it all may ultimately lead. I've come to seek your utmost reassurances."

"The manner and traits of which you've spoken," said the man, in continued calmness, "paint an image in my mind of your youngest, which you have called Tae."

"Yes. Tae is of whom I speak."

"I've sent one of our own to enchant your son, yes, and to plant the seeds of influence beyond the Barrier of Worlds to Athyn, where you've spent most of your life these last twenty years. You are well on-track to that extent. But it wasn't unto the attention of the one named Tae that I've sent her. It was unto your eldest. The one named Ethyn, of course. Your heir."

"Unto Ethyn?" Mailyn was perplexed, and she fell silent trying to puzzle the details together.

"Timing was of the essence. He bathed in the waters of the Great Central Sea, and we seized the opportunity to lead him to the amber stone. She will make future visitations to him, as required."

"My Ethyn is in possession of the amber stone?"

This was becoming too much (too fast) for Mailyn to internalize.

"We've received word of your troubles in Athyn Proper; of Maelnlock's ire and of the attack you've sustained, yet you may remain unaware of an equally urgent concern. The ones who mined the stones and took them for their own—from the fissure—the ones who made the intrusion through the pass in the mountains, which we had sealed back up; they are stirring again. They are firing messages to one another. They are preparing a new intrusion. I feel it coming, and it must be stopped. We cannot afford to remain so passive, as we've always vowed we would. Not anymore."

"The highlanders. Does this mean I may finally reveal our knowledge of their mountain Settlement to my husband?" pled Mailyn, "He stands on the precipice of war and knows not what action to follow. If the highlanders should emerge and descend upon Athyn, what do you suppose will happen? And at a time when Maelnlock advances, also, from the north. Please, I ask this permission of you; to make this known to my Nhyle. Surely you, of all people, can understand the burdens he carries."

"And how might you substantiate this information without betraying your connection to the mystics of Halcyon?"

"I will find a way," said Mailyn, "I have no choice. *We* have no choice."

The man dressed in white was silent, closing his eyes in contemplation for long moments. His voice carried a twinge of pain when he finally spoke again, "No. Give me a short while longer."

"We have no such time to spare."

"We must remain ever so cautious of the potential consequences, Mailyn…"

She pressed, "Think of all the lives at stake."

He could only cringe.

"Syrus," said the Nohnce of Athyn, "you're thinking of Syrus, aren't you?"

The Lord of Halcyon looked down in sorrow.

"He could yet be living his life safely in the mountains, or he could be far away after all these years, having pursued a new life. Perhaps a happy life, indeed."

"Or, he could be..." said the thin man seated in front of her, unwilling to verbalize the completion of his thought.

"...Alive and well. Your long lost son could be *alive* and *well;* perhaps able to help us," Mailyn finished. "Perhaps out of all this, we may reunite with him again." She saw the pain in the other's eyes. "Believe me, I know much of worriment for one's own children. I need not expound upon Tae's challenges, and Ethyn... who has grown quite impatient with the world around him. He's seen these firings in the sky you've mentioned. He has seen them over the mountains. He's made note of them to me, in passing, and it seems he will not rest until he has solved their mystery. I believe I've seen them, too."

"He has seen these things because he possesses the *sight* you have given him. You are justified in your worriment. We have secured the amber stone within his custody, yet he lacks the ability to use the power of the stone for himself. He is its ideal caretaker, until such a time comes that it must be used, perhaps by another. But it puts him at great risk."

"So, you have indeed sent a Halcyonen maiden to Ethyn," Mailyn had to repeat the assertion for it to sink in, "and she has put him in possession of the amber stone?"

"It was a measure, which needed to be taken," repeated the man.

Mailyn figured she would have to reconcile herself with these developments, if this was the direction the Lord of Halcyon had decided to take. She also supposed all of this oughtn't have come as a surprise, given Ethyn's station as Heir Prince, and her very own circumstances that'd been arranged, thusly, between her and her lord husband when he occupied the title of Heir Prince, as she'd been reminded. *How should I ever convey all of this without rousing forbidden suspicions? For I simply cannot disclose the existence of this world of Halcyon, nor its calculated machinations, to anyone. Not even to him—the deepest secret a Nohnce has surely ever kept from her Nhyle.*

"May I at least meet her," she asked, "this girl?"

"In time, yes, I assure you," said the Lord of Halcyon, "but not now; not today." At that moment, an elegant figure strode into dim view, through the doorway toward the back—the kitchen—wearing clothes fit for travel and an expression of vast curiosity. The Lord of Halcyon gave Mailyn a bit of an admonishing look when he realized the visual connection had been made, "I wish not to startle her with such an important introduction, absent her means to properly prepare."

"I understand," conceded Mailyn. The girl departed from view, and Mailyn tore her eyes from the kitchen doorway back to the man in white with a deep breath. "Yet, I remain confused in this matter with regards to my youngest, Tae. Have you not sent a Halcyonen maiden to him, as well?"

"I have not."

"Peculiar," she continued, "I ask, only because there has been a young girl, who has made the most improbable arrival to Castle Athyn, in possession of the most advanced aptitudes I've ever known to exist on the obverse side of the Barrier of Worlds. Brychen is her name. I had simply taken it for granted these past few days she'd been sent by your edict. Yet now, you advise she wasn't. Who might she be, if not a child of Halcyon?"

"I will admit I'm forming grave suspicions, as you speak," said the man, "but I may venture to suppose that you, and the rest of us, will want to find out with a most strict expediency. Yes?"

"Yes, indeed," Mailyn said; then added, with an ill-advised shade of consternation in her voice and a bow of her head, "I suppose that I will, Lord Tymian of Halcyon."

*...I suppose that I will.*

## 29 | Under the Veil of the Gathering Night

*"When comes the time for moving on in the story of your life, will you have the courage to take the steps you know are required? I've been, for so long, hesitant to take these steps, for I've feared the possible destinations to which they may lead. But no more. I know now—I think I've always known—that these strands of mine must be allowed to venture forward. They must be given the liberty to branch out where they may. And I can only hope they possess the instinct of the homing fowl, so that they might eventually find their way back where they belong. One and all..."*
—excerpt from the personal journal of Steven Spurlock

|Planet Deaer, Castle Athyn

It was true Tae Solis didn't much relish venturing anywhere outside his own bedchambers, but that was before the girl had shown up. After their morning departure from one another, so abruptly upon Mistress Almetta's lecturing, he'd retired back to his quarters and had paced back and forth about his veranda trying to produce the image of her face in his mind. *Brychen.* He tried to smell her scent in the air, hear her voice in his ears. He tried to remember it all as if she were still sitting right before him in his room, or lying in his bed.

And he'd hoped all the while: *Mistress won't be too hard on her, or give her reason to want to leave, will she?*

Efforts to return to the barn's garret that afternoon had thwarted by the terrible attack that'd caused the Servants' Keep to fall, in pieces, to the ground. The castle had been thrown into mass disorder, and he wanted more desperately than ever to affirm his new friend was unharmed.

Finally, after much fear and anguish over the happenings of the day, his mother had come to bring him comfort in the evening. She had told him softly that Brychen was fine, but that she'd been taken from the

Mystics House to a suite in the Visitor's Keep, and that (for now) she was not permitted company. But *'for now'* had already seemed like an eternity, and before he knew what he was doing, in the deeper depths of night, his feet had carried him down East Hall toward a cluster of suites often patronized by foreign dignitaries on special occasion.

In-so-doing, Tae realized his worriment for her safety had sparked something within him. Something irregular, indeed. *So this time, if I'm able to find her, things are going to be different,* he thought while he walked through a secret, narrow pass. He intended to strengthen his bond with Brychen to some exceptional degree, and there was but only one way he knew how. The only problem was, the mere thought of what he'd decided to do simply frightened him half to death.

A search of the keep's corridors for the girl proved fruitless. Every suite's door was closed and locked. Even rooms he'd relied upon (from time to time) as hiding spots from his royal handlers were tightly secured against intrusion of any sort. He had, in fact, noticed doors had been locked *all over* the castle since the explosion occurred in the morning—a development for which he harbored a profound misliking. It meant his means for escape were severely limited; escape from handlers, escape from mother, and escape from *everything* should the need arise, as it often had.

After a time, and despite the order for all residents of the city to remain indoors, he quit the keep and wandered outside to see if he could find the girl through some other means. The ubiquitous presence of Royal Guard soldiers made skulking about the court undetected no simple task, even in these darkening hours, but thankfully it was a skill in which he was very well-practiced. All his life, he'd worked at perfecting methods aimed at staying out of sight. So, shuffling about unseen, he climbed a tree or two (or three or four or five) and peeked into the windows of the keep, finding all the rooms vacant. This, save for the last; a large suite on the second floor of the Visitor's Keep.

Much to his pleasure, he'd finally found the mysterious girl from the Village of Kyrie, whom he could not extricate from his mind. She was peering through a window, overlooking the court with flowering vines around her that smelled of perfume, all cast in a silver shade produced by the vibrant glow of the risen Ancillary Moon. He'd gathered a few pebbles, and tossed them now lightly at her window.

When she took notice of him (as he clung to a bough in the thick folds of a brambleleaf tree), he saw her rap at the glass and wave her arms in delight. He clambered upon a buckling branch, as far out as he dared, while she opened her window a crack.

"Tae, oh Tae!" She was weeping just a little at the sight of him, "I was hoping you would find me somehow."

He smiled profusely at that.

"Mistress Almetta said that, in the morning, if she can convince the Royal Guard, I could perhaps take a walk about the court. But for now, I must stay here in this room."

Tae frowned to show that he wished she could come out immediately; that they could go somewhere together again.

"The mistress has been so comforting through all of this. She'd just been through her lecture about House rules—which I know I well deserved for returning so late to my room—when the loud bang happened and the ground began to shake. At first, we had no certainty at all for what was happening. We'd both thought the Mystics House, itself, might've begun falling to the ground, and my room along with it... So she and the Masters quickly gathered all the wieldlings together in the Gardens of Grace, and we waited there in confusion. Until, of course, a troupe of soldiers arrived and spoke with the Masters.

"When they tried to take me away, Almetta came to my side saying I was under her care, pleading with them that I was *her* responsibility, no one else's. So they agreed to let her come with me and eventually brought the two of us here to this room. But they didn't let her stay. When they made her leave, she told me she would return to check on me whenever she could. She's been here a few times already to bring me a bit to eat and to tell me whatever news she'd managed to gather. I am so dearly indebted to her." Brychen took a breath and sat back in her chair by the window, "I suppose there was an accident, and a portion of the castle has been damaged. Is that true?"

Tae both nodded and shrugged to convey that her understanding of the terrible happenstance was consistent with his. That even he, himself, didn't know much more than she did.

"I just keep wondering what, exactly, had happened and why they needed to bring me here. This room is beautiful to be certain, and comfortable, too," she said, turning and looking at her surroundings inside, "and I need not complain about a single thing on account of how well I've been treated, but I'd just as soon return to the Mystics House with the mistress. Being locked in here alone just makes me nervous, I suppose… And I can't imagine I'll gather even a bit of sleep tonight."

He wanted so badly to help her escape, yet it seemed an idea that would (more likely than not) result in a worsening of circumstances. He figured she'd been placed in isolation for a reason, and there was no sense in rousing any further suspicion of her. But for the time being, at least, they'd certainly afforded her comfortable arrangements, and were feeding her well; straight from the royal kitchens it seemed, as he spied a monogrammed Solis family saucer lying on a table inside the room. So instead of helping her climb out the window, he meant to (at the very least) comfort her from his perch in the thick-leafed tree. *I just don't know why anyone would ever think she'd have anything to do with an attack on the castle. Perhaps they're protecting her, instead?*

And then his deeper thoughts took over again, turning to the resolution he'd made. The one that would advance their relationship. The resolution that also terrified him more than anything else in life; even more than a great and powerful attack on the castle. *Oh, but the mere thought of it almost makes me sick…*

"Tae, I have to say that I feel we share some sort of connection," she broke in on his internal dialogue, "One that is quite special, indeed."

It was as if she could read his mind and was prompting him to proceed as he had designed. He took her statement as a final sign that what he was about to do was a perfectly natural progression in the pre-ordained course of his life. *Natural…* he kept telling himself, *this is natural…*

But still, he remained stiff as a board.

"Tae?" she asked after a long pause.

Awkwardly, he did nothing. No smile and no gesture. He just sat there, frozen as a statue sitting on the edge of a bulwark. Having brought along with him no object to show her, like another of his glass globes or some kind of other trinket from the collections in his chambers, he lacked the ability to fidget nervously with something in-hand and could do nothing to distract her from his most intense discomfort. And he locked up.

It was discouraging. He thought he'd finally been headed in the right direction; making progress toward an ordinary (healthier) existence, outside the limits of his microscopic comfort zone. She had come into his life and had attracted all of his energy and all of his attention. That is what it took, he realized. That is what mother was always trying to lead him towards: *focus*. Someone to break his shell... but here he was, broken, indeed, and speechless as usual.

Yet how could he *not* focus? He regarded Brychen as some sort of heavenly seraph; without fault and without flaw. He looked at her, then. She exuded all of the qualities everyone always wanted to unearth in *him*. She was a dynamo, a powerfully-magnetic being without even trying.

And so, he hemmed and shuffled on the branch outside her window, stared into space, and almost forgot to breathe. *Ok, here goes nothing...*

And then he spoke:

"I---- h-h-have... a... s-s-s-s-secret... t-t-to... t-tell... y-y-y-you," he managed to slur together the sentence, stuttering and nearly choking on each word; almost shattering his ears to hear himself, it seemed. They were the first words he'd ever spoken to a living soul.

Brychen's jaw dropped open upon hearing his declaration. He could almost sense some kind of ripple in the air about them, a force as great as gravity twisting the fabric of their reality. She stared at him with her enormous eyes, which seemed to absorb all the light of the Ancillary Moon and cast it back upon him with their full force of radiance. Her astonishment would not be masked from him; considering all the time spent together the last two days and the reputation he'd so famously made for himself, a whole lifetime during which he'd not spoken a word. He expected she wouldn't have guessed it possible, and intuited that it left her (at once) shocked and bemused.

"I think you just did," she answered with a bewitching giggle.

\*\*\*

"We have to go," said Brychen, after she and Tae Solis had sat in silence following the unexpected telling of his most highly-guarded secret, "Tae, I hoped not to trouble you with this, but hearing you speak now gives me the courage to do what I must do. You've inspired me!"

The Boy Prince—no longer the Mute Prince he'd once been—cast her a look of puzzlement.

"I don't feel much at ease," she was pushing the window open further, "not at ease one bit. I haven't truly felt at ease since I arrived here, save for the time we've spent together, and I feel like I must leave this place. Immediately." The window was pushed all the way open now. She took a very quick moment to retreat back deeper into the room to fetch the satchel (and the glass globe within it that Tae had given to her). Then she was back at the window in a single breath, throwing a leg over the sill, "Oh, but Tae, I cannot leave without *you*."

"L-L-L-Leave?" he asked with such apprehension.

"Will you come with me? Will you go on an adventure with me? The watchmen will let us through the gates if you ask them to, won't they?" she'd determinedly negotiated her way from the sill to the tree's extended branch with grace. Then she was standing beside him (they were near exactly the same height) and reached out to take one of his hands into her own, "I'm just so unnerved by everything that has happened that I simply cannot stay. You understand, don't you?"

The turn of events was a cataclysmic landslide in Tae's mind, which was prone to over-activity to begin with, and now it simply runneth over. The effect resulted in a whiting out of all reason, and nearly all sensory perception of the physical world, as well. It was as if a concussive blast had numbed his hearing and clouded his vision. He felt her taking his hand, urging him to follow her down the tree to the ground, and he felt the cobblestones of the court beneath his mocks. He sensed his legs moving, taking him in-step with her motions through the East Court gardens, under a cloak of darkness and the veil of the deep, haunted night. They hurried their way through the vine-covered archways and past the flowering bushes. The garden grounds, indeed, seemed to span so terribly far, until—

"Who goes there?" shouted a watchman when they finally approached East Gate, emerging from the shadows of the ornamental trees that stood in lines along the terminus of the gardens. They were greeted by the sharp tip of a spearhead, pointed aggressively in front of their faces.

"Princeling Tae, it's *you*," gasped the man at the gate, when Tae and Brychen stood up straight to be seen in the torchlight. The tone of the gruff voice betrayed its owner's shock, "And the mystics girl we'd seen, just the other night."

The spear was taken back, slowly. Tae, still overcome by a nearly-hallucinogenic numbing of his senses, stepped forward, "O-O-Open p-p-please." He pointed toward the East Gate bypass door and swallowed hard against the pulsing of his nerves.

The man could not hide his astonishment. Tae figured his interactions with this particular watchman must have numbered a scant few at most, as interactions had been scarce, indeed, with nearly every person stationed outside the royal family's private quarters. But he knew his mute reputation had surely spread far enough to have entered into just about every Athynian's general knowledge, the city-over, and that would explain the large man's posture of disbelief.

Alarmingly, Tae realized, many of those subjects throughout the vast city would likely soon enough hear tell of this most gossip-worthy happenstance, which could not be taken back, and which (he found) was now fueling his irrational, seemingly involuntary compliance with Brychen's cues to leave the Proper altogether, under such short notice. So he drew the proverbial bow string a bit more taut, and exclaimed with shocking fervor, "N-N-N-Now!!"

"Certainly, my lord," the guard's acquiescence was voiced slowly; suspiciously, while he surveyed this most impractical situation with a fevered squinting of his eyes. Then, with torch in hand, the man walked to the post that adjoined the gate house, "If you'd be so kind as to make your mark for me, my lordling, for record of your passin' through, I'd be much obliged."

Tae and Brychen followed him to a small table where laid a roll of parchment and he pointed out the place where he'd have the newly-adventurous prince scrawl out his name. Tae took up a feather quill, dipped it into an ink well, and made his mark without much, if any, hesitation. Yet still, the numbing of his cognitive sense of reason persisted. This, even as the watchman gave a discerning look at the inked scratch he'd made, then stared squarely into Tae's eyes, "I mean no disrespect, my Lord Prince, but are you feelin' alright? Do you truly mean to pass through the city-East, this time of night?"

Tae hesitated a moment and continued, "Y-Y-Yes, n-n-now p-p-please..." And he gestured toward the bypass door once again.

When they were allowed through the door, they came to a secured antechamber, then were ushered through two more doors, small and reinforced by iron, before they found themselves on the opposite side, where four more stationed guards watched them pass with faces awash in confusion. The eastern side of the city was not so glamourous as were the northern and the western sides. Few shops and even fewer inns could be found there, but it boasted a bevy of ale houses most unsuitable for a proper lady or a finely-dressed lad. So they passed quickly through the darkened streets. It seemed Brychen intended to make haste no matter the setting, because she'd continued to pull at his hand most vigorously, even once they'd left the city limits; the outer walls, too. And, in time, they'd outdistanced most of the outlying cottages as well; he in his mocks, which were ill-suited for the raw ground.

They found themselves occupants of the main road, which ultimately ran east-bound around forested hills and beyond the lesser villages situated between the Proper and the city of Mawr. Included among them, Tae knew, was the place Brychen had called her home—the village of Kyrie—and he thought it would follow simply that it was there, where she intended to take him. The insects buzzed loudly out here, making one abundantly cognizant of their presence in the trees and shrubs all around. *An adventure, indeed, though we surely ought to have at least secured a mount for ourselves, and proper footwear to ease the travel a bit.*

Surprisingly, the princeling had averted the worst of his habitual neuroses while, instead, finding the open spaces comforting in their absence of people, who so often crowded the narrow halls of the castle. But Tae was growing extremely tired trying to keep pace with his most exuberant companion, even before they'd broken free from the farm lands, which were still considered part and parcel of the greater reaches of Athyn Proper.

\*\*\*

|Planet Deaer, Athynian Countryside

"Here," said Tae Solis' new friend, Brychen, when he was nearly upon the threshold of exhaustion on the east-bound road. She took him by the hand once again and led him from the trample-hardened path into an adjacent wooded expanse known as the Durnbeck Forest. The darkness was exceptional here; the enormous space lit sparingly by flutes of silver light that sliced through the canopy of the lofty trees in thin, diagonal shafts. Brychen tentatively felt her way across the forest floor, looking for something.

By now, Tae's enthusiasm for speaking was expired. He simply followed her, silently, hoping upon hope that they were nearly through with the night's hazardous adventuring. And he'd arrived at a point where he was ready to make a seat for himself on the ground to spell his weariness, when Brychen suddenly quickened her pace.

"This is it," she exclaimed, with notes of relief in her voice. She pulled back heavy limbs and broad leaves to reveal a most peculiar thing to Tae's eyes, and he recoiled from the sight of it. It was a sort of carriage, the likes of which he'd never seen; formed near-completely of glass, or some similar translucent substance. And the surface gleamed with reflective qualities he'd never quite known to exist.

"Climb in!" she said with a sense of enthusiasm that was perhaps infected with a strain of nervousness, as well. There were two small seats within this wheel-less carriage, one forward and one back-mounted, and she gestured toward the one in back.

He was still standing in place, stunned by the sight of this thing, and the bells and whistles of his most powerful inner-hesitancy were blaring inside his head. But he looked at her, and her very presence warmed him from within; reviving him anew. And besides, the prospect of sitting down was tempting, after all the walking (and near-running) they'd done. So he obliged her offer and climbed inside.

She followed, settling herself in the forward seat, and negotiated a switch and a knob (or two) before turning about. He was nestled snugly behind her, without much space to speak of, even for his smallish frame. "Are you alright, Tae?"

He nodded, thinking she intended for them to spend the duration of the night here. That, perhaps, this was some sort of outpost in the forest she'd been accustomed to seeking out as a child; some kind of secret retreat. They were not far from the village center of Kyrie, after all, and no child of Kyrie was a stranger to the Durnbeck Forest. But when she turned to face the front again, and took such a deep breath before exhaling so thoroughly—in a manner that usually precedes the exertion of some considerable amount of effort—he sensed it was not the case at all.

He was right. She took hold of a handle (a throttle) before her, and when she did, the carriage came alive. A sort of film emerged from the body of the craft to cover the opening where they'd entered, and gossamer formations, like insect wings, sprouted forth from the sides. The frame then shook, as did their small bodies where they sat, and he began to feel an apprehension—*an acute panic, in fact*—when the very stifling nature of his confinement within this strange thing brought itself to bear upon him.

Then the craft keeled a bit to the side shifting him in his seat, and he noticed her hair beginning to rise on end as it had when she'd demonstrated her conjuring aptitude for Master Slynth. She was squealing now, high and drawn of voice, and this thing they sat within lurched again while its wings started beating on either side. The leaves on the surrounding trees took hold of the air that was forced against them, bending their branches (and thinner trunks) away as if taken by some kind of mighty storm; the likes of which were known, but rarely, to sweep through this realm.

Then the craft lifted up into the air, and his heart dropped into his stomach. *What is she doing? What is this thing?!*

Too wrapped in panic to speak, he resorted to banging his hands on the back of her seat to catch her attention. She hesitated, but for only a pinch, before doubling her efforts of concentration into the throttle, and this thing (this craft) started rising higher toward the height of the trees, which were swaying and bending away from them with greater force now. Twigs and stones and leaves that were once strewn about the forest floor were cast asunder or caught in one of the many vortexes of swirling air that had formed upon the ground, which was becoming more and more distant as he looked down.

Then they were above the trees, bathed in the light of the Ancillary Moon, as if it were some kind of search light calling them out of hiding. Calling them forth; drawing them up and out of concealment. She seemed to respond to its call with determination while they climbed up, *and up and up*. Tae was caught somewhere between feelings of awe-inspired wonder and horrified exasperation, but his nerves prevailed over his curiosity, and he took to striking her seat again in demands for an explanation. He looked through the translucent cab, then, and saw Castle Athyn in the distance. And even in all its enormity, it seemed to shrink while they continued to climb.

He never dreamed it could look so small.

They were rising into the clouds now; a thin layer of cirrus that'd swept-in overnight from the Central Sea, and then the *whole realm* appeared small through the wispy white traces. The sky looked as if composed of every variant of blue; so deep in places that it'd turned virtually to black, and the stars looked as bright and as large as those silver tiles that spotted the ceiling of his bedroom antechamber.

He was starting to feel faint then, in earnest. Looking down to see that his home had become this spectacular round object that simply hung there without any means to keep itself from falling. Yet it did not fall. Nor did the silver Ancillary Moon, which was before them now, in the distance, shining so brightly. It seemed to grow in size. And he thought that it would eventually become larger than his own world he'd just, so suddenly, left behind.

But the nature of these things would have to wait, in addition to his latest appraisal of this girl—this Brychen—who had simply swept him up and taken him away. For he was really starting to take leave of his senses.

And soon, all was made positively black.

\*\*\*

|The Ancillary Moon

A tall, rail-thin man, wrapped head to toe in robes the shade of coal, stood atop a square platform on the surface of the Moon. Beside him stood another man—a doctor by trade—who wore a fitted felt cap and a tailored jumper the color of sand. They had seen the craft's billowing white wake streaming across the heights as soon as it broke through the synthetic atmosphere, far overhead.

"The boy..." said the tall, thin man in the gray robes. The words were spoken in garbled, strained tones and were framed more like a question than a simple declaration. There was no wind where these men stood, and the gravity pulling them down was just a tad over half the gravitational strength of Planet Deaer. The effect—which at first, long ago, had lent a feeling of such weightlessness to their frames—had worn off almost completely through the generations.

"She's got him," replied the doctor, his manner of speech a bit anxious in tone, "she wouldn't have returned without him."

"Good," said the robed man through his labored voice, "make final preparations for his arrival."

"Certainly," said the doctor, who watched his counterpart turn and walk away in one swift motion with robes swaying in the light air, "I shall do so at once, Alamere."

## 30 | Sense of Authority

*"Mentally preparing oneself for the rigors of life is but the least we can do. For being surprised by unexpected happenstance is forgivable, but being thwarted by the thoroughly probable simply is not."*
—excerpt from the personal journal of Steven Spurlock

|Planet Deaer, Castle Athyn

Old maps were strewn across a table, taken down from the walls and gathered together with haste. Upon a select few of them, lines and arrows (and other such markings) were drawn for plotting an itinerary. Beside them were piled an assortment of personal effects to include a wallet full of gold and silver pieces (stamped with Athynian markings and glittering like the treasures they were). Indeed, Ethyn Solis had wasted not a further moment's time in preparing for the excursion upon which he had resolved to embark, and now he was poised to do so at his very earliest opportunity.

He stood there in his quarters, looking over the plans laid out before him, and he had to admit the very notion of asking his companions to turn tail on a declaration of war (to pursue some unknown intuition that lay leagues upon leagues in the opposite direction) carried with it a certain air of absurdity. But he would not, *could not*, be denied this opportunity to follow his instincts. And he knew the High Council, father included, would only condemn such a journey as rank folly should he formally announce his intentions for everyone to hear.

After all, they'd condemned all else of which he'd spoken.

Earlier in the evening, Balyn Galdur had reported to Ethyn's chambers, just as the prince had bade him to do. At the summons of the heir, the young legion recruit had worn the same expression of naiveté upon his face that he'd exuded upon entering the great castle gates the day prior. But this look faded once Ethyn sent him forth to run an assortment of tasks, nearly in the manner a servant would be sent by his emperor to fetch grapes and pillows and tea. *Not a servant, but an apprentice, or a squire,* thought Ethyn. *Yes, that is what I shall call him; my squire. Though for only a short time, it will be an appointment of substantial privilege for him, no doubt, and he shall be ever grateful for the lessons he's learned by my example.*

At Ethyn's beck and call, Galdur gathered many provisions as would likely prove useful on a journey of unknown distance and length in time, and Ethyn was very much enjoying the sense of authority it transferred upon him as the night had thusly worn on. It felt good; the power to dictate the actions of another. It certainly trumped having to surrender to the desires of some greater authority than he; namely, his father and the council. *To think of how long I craved an invitation to join that assembly, only to be scolded—to be reprimanded and told to sit down. I'll not ask permissions. Not for taking my leave on travel; not for anything.*

*Not ever again.*

Now, looking over the maps strewn about the table and the personal effects piled together (the makings for his final preparations), Ethyn heard young Balyn Galdur knocking at his door once again.

"Are the stable masters prepping the mounts, Balyn?"

"Aye," confirmed Galdur on his way in. They stood in a small den adjacent to Ethyn's bedchambers, and it was here that Galdur had already reported his progress to the prince, thusly, a score-full of times throughout the night.

"And the foodstuffs have been acquired and packed?"

"Aye, the dried fruits and meats, my lord; the cheeses and the breads, too," Galdur was proving himself a useful squire, "and the water skins, two to a man and full to the brim they are, hung on pegs in the stable and ready for the road."

"The arms, boy?" pressed Ethyn, "what of the arms?"

"Them too; your longsword and shield, and your cloaks and helms and greaves," the responses were as natural as could ever be expected from a recruit who'd just set foot inside a castle for his first time, "the metals I took the liberty of spit shining myself. All set about in the stables, as well, awaiting your leave, my lord."

"Good," said Ethyn, who'd picked up an ornamented dagger from the table and started fastening it to his belt, then looked up at the youth with a measure of confusion, "I'm sorry, had you said *spit shining*?"

"Aye, spit shining, my lord."

"Henceforth, no more spit shining; is that understood? You'll forgive me if I'd prefer not to wear your salivic juices about my body as I ride the countryside."

"As you wish, my lord."

"Now, had you a chance to speak with Aryk Frierstag, as I've asked?"

"While in search for him, I was told Legionnaire Frierstag was elsewhere, engaged, but I'd spoken with the older man of the same name, who'd been on escort with us. And I asked if he might be willing to pass along to his nephew word of your interest in his company, down at the stables. Just as you wished."

"Very well," said Ethyn, working his arms into the sleeves of a hooded cloak and pulling on his boots. He rolled up the maps from the table, slid them into a long, narrow leather tube and tossed it to Galdur. Then he took up the coin purse and fastened it to his belt, and slipped a pair of leathern cuffs over his wrists before looking earnestly at Balyn, "This entire affair of travel is, of course, to remain perfectly discreet. I'll have you wait for me here until I send word for you to follow. It shan't take long."

"My lord, I'm expected by the commander and his captains in the yard, and in short order, I'm afraid," looking out the window, Galdur no doubt gauged the approach of dawn laid not terribly far from the horizon; the time the legion planned to take their stock of the localized ranks in North Court.

"No. You will busy yourself no longer with the doings of the legion," insisted Ethyn, making through the doorway to the outer hall while he spoke, "you're *my* man now, not Thorngrove's. Get comfortable with that, and I've no doubt you will do just fine."

And no sooner had the prince finished his statement then he was gone from the room. *Along with Midre Donygal, that makes two officers, now, that I've poached from assigned legion service. Three, if you count Thurflyn. Perhaps I ought to start a running tally.*

\*\*\*

There was, in the southeast corner of the castle's court, a conduit of egress that few persons even knew existed. It was reserved exclusively for the royal seat and High Council and was meant to be used only in times of severe need, when escape from the castle grounds was something of an urgent matter. There was great benefit in taking this conduit, in that it led its occupants away from the city, safely and securely into a rocky riverside crevasse, clear of the city's limits and camouflaged by wilderness. And it was there in the darkness, at the sealed and locked entry to this conduit, that Heir Prince Ethyn Solis and his cloaked companion had led their mounts.

They'd met at the stables and had maintained a code of silence until such a time had come that they could speak aloud to one another without the threat of being overheard. "Had you any trouble on your way to the stables?" Ethyn asked.

"A few passers-by of the Royal Guard, but I found concealment from their piercing eyes," answered Adrian Thurflyn.

"I knew I was right to ignore any and all claims you've lost your cunning," Ethyn looked the former guildmaster straight-on, "And for that reason, I feel that my next question is entirely unnecessary, yet I must ask it. Are you ready for this, Thurflyn?"

"You've selected for us a rather ruthless destination; there's no denying that," Thurflyn's eyes shone bright in the polished silver moonlight, "the question is… are *you*?"

"Actually, the question is…" replied Ethyn with an angled nod of his head, "are *they*?"

Ethyn had sent the Heron Bird to summon Balyn Galdur. The young (recent defector) of the Royal Legion had promptly made his way to the stables and was now reporting to the muster location, just as he was told. And riding closely beside him, quite unexpectedly, was the oversized legionnaire, Othys Frierstag. Aryk role along as well.

The red-haired, mustachioed soldier spoke up for himself when the three of them came within secure earshot, "When the boy had spoken of provisioning my nephew's horse, I seized the opportunity to ready my own, as well."

"Is that so?" Ethyn was intrigued.

"Indeed, there'll be no legion deployments for me, it would seem—figured I'd prefer nearly anything over Thorngrove's muddled foolery at my age; 'specially a treasure hunt, such as you've cooked up for yourselves here," Othys' simplicity was on prime display, "so I've taken for myself a chance to join you all, despite the lack of an invitation. This *is* a treasure hunt we're headed on, is it not?"

Aryk could only shrug his shoulders in apology to Ethyn.

"I've informed you this is *not* a treasure hunt," Balyn Galdur was revealing his youthful impatience with the veteran soldier, which presumably had arisen when they'd met at the stables to retrieve the mounts.

"There will be no legion deployment at all, Othys, not for any of the ranks," answered Ethyn, in a dejected tone, looking over Othys as if appraising his value to the group, "they'll be given orders upon the morning to assume a localized defensive posture."

"*Defensive* posture?" asked Othys in bewilderment, "I'd heard we were heading for war."

"Regardless, it would indeed seem you'll be doing no such thing if you've decided, instead, upon deserting your post and joining us," said Ethyn. His appraisal was complete, and its findings were, unfortunately, less than favorable toward the misshapen, disheveled soldier.

"They've been trying to convince me to abscond from service for a long time; everyone knows it. Wasn't till recently that I've finally faced the truth that they're right; that it's time," Othys was wearing travel gear bearing no association with the legion. "But I refuse to retire, only to sit idle and grow fatter, bored, and useless. I've been lookin' for an excuse to ride off from the legion in style. This seemed as good an opportunity as any I'm likely to get."

"Very well, Othys. Let us have on with it, then," Ethyn doubted the journey would offer much in the way of *style*, but in this scenario, Othys was playing quite the role of the beggar who's not much entitled to a vast array of choices, and Ethyn really hadn't the luxury of casting aside able-bodied (or halfway-able, as it were) contributors to his cause, "We've a long distance to cover and no time at all to waste." *We'll make use of him somehow, I'm sure...* "And I'm very happy to see you've come along, Aryk." The bookish soldier nodded in such a way that conferred he'd not dream of missing an opportunity to assist—in any manner, whatsoever—

his great friend's every endeavor. Unlike his uncle, he'd made the proper arrangements.

"Galdur," Ethyn continued, "You've done a fine job procuring our provisions. I was right to trust in you as well, lad."

Young Galdur smiled broadly.

Othys, in surprise to all, wasted no time proving his value by cranking the counter-weights for the fortified conduit door, allowing them entry before sealing it shut from the inside. The ride through the hidden passage was not a particularly short one, and it proved dark and stale of odor. Thurflyn carried with him his mirrored lantern to guide the way. At the far end, the exit portal was nothing more than a massive rock face, hinged in such a way that it could be nudged open (by force) wide enough to allow a mount and rider to pass, one at a time. Othys, again, was happy to oblige in working the mechanics. When they were all through, the portal was shut closed, and a catch locked it back into place, in perfect camouflage.

In the sky, the moon glowed, and the hour yet felt parcel to the deepest segments of night. They emerged upon the bank of a swiftly-flowing river, and led their mounts to higher ground through a dense wilderness.

"I'd be pleased to assume the point now," Thurflyn's motivation to set upon the road was easily read across his face, "if it suits you, my lordship."

"Indeed, guildmaster," agreed Ethyn, "I've intended for you to lead-on from the start, or at least ever since the latest debate with my father has had time to simmer." The rest gathered around now, in a circle, and the prince shifted in his seat, pulling a long leather tube from Galdur's saddlebags and handing the item promptly to Thurflyn. "Inside, you will find a series of maps, sir, drawn long ago from your own hand, as I told you they've been kept in their proper respect by me these many years. You will see I've marked them in detail to lead their bearer precisely to the source of my greatest hunches and suspicions, and I have every confidence you will find your way into the mountains with care to root them out."

"Ethyn, I'm confused," said Aryk, "are you not coming with us?"

"I wished not to mislead anyone; in fact, there burned within me a sincere desire—nay, an insatiable pull—emanating from those mountains, drawing me to their highest peak, and I've sought ever since to pursue it my very self; there should be little doubt in that. It speaks to the importance of my designs that I, instead, send a company of my finest hosts to investigate on my behalf. For it has been made clear—with an abrupt rudeness of which I sorely disapprove—another destination lies in wait for me, which begs my personal attention with an even greater urgency, all its own."

"You don't intend…" said Aryk, cutting himself short with a hard swallow.

"I send you, friends, away from the politics you so vehemently detest, but toward perhaps an even greater danger, and for that, I must express my deepest regret. I wouldn't do so, you surely understand, if it weren't a matter of the utmost importance," said Ethyn. "I, on the other hand, will venture deeper into the belly of the political serpent than ever before. It simply cannot be helped."

"You mustn't go it alone," said Aryk.

"I shall be alright; I've got the Heron Bird with me." Ethyn looked from Aryk to Thurflyn and to Othys and Balyn Galdur (whose squireship to the prince was very short-lived indeed). He hoped the high regard he held for each of them could be gleaned from his expression in the pale moonlight, "Please, take steadfast care of one another."

"And you, yourself, Ethyn," they echoed, each in their own way.

And so, the company of four found their way to the path—through the wilderness—in a true southerly direction with Thurflyn at the lead. Ethyn, with his longsword strapped across his back, watched them go.

The trees were clad in white bark that reflected the moon's silvery light, in stark contrast to the deep-set backdrop of the darkened woodland depths. Ethyn looked into those depths with prying eyes, as he turned his mount and rode in the opposite direction of his companions. After a time, the amber stone started to pulse against his chest with an energy all its own, while subtle movement seemed to play between the pale trees to either side of the trail.

He paid it no mind.

Further on, when it seemed he may put the strange sensation behind him, there appeared to Ethyn, again, an elegant form gliding from one dark shadow to the next, playing games with his eyes.

And he knew.

*Her. From the lagoon and from his room in the Royal League House of Stief.*

His heart leapt a beat, then his lungs collapsed for a moment, only to fill again with a deep-drawn breath. He could feel a certain presence, and so could the stone. So subtle, yet it wouldn't let go. It *couldn't* let go.

The mount, perhaps spooked by the ethereal presence, picked up a bit of speed, and Ethyn's cloak flapped and rippled in the air. He looked again and believed he saw her there, running alongside him; somehow keeping pace.

"May I ask where you are going?" she whispered softly, though her words came to him ever so clearly, despite the air whipping by his ears. At that moment, he broke free from the trees upon a connector path, which merged into a main conduit, racing northward around Athyn Proper to the distances on the horizon. And there was, revealed to him, a spectacularly unobstructed view of the countryside. This time, he took a moment to notice the expanses of grass, the rolling hills, and the droplets of dew sparkling in the moon's glow.

He glanced back toward the wilderness from which he'd emerged. Then he lifted a hand and pointed ahead north.

Toward the Great Central Sea and beyond.

"That, my dear spirit, is where I am headed! Might you care to follow?"

### 31 | The Knowing Age

*"People ask—what would you tell a younger version of yourself if you were somehow given the opportunity? And I answer like this: Just hold on. Don't stop churning. Don't stop fighting, or building, or charting your course toward something you love. Prepare yourself for the time you might finally be tested to show your worth. Because if you don't, when comes the time for proving yourself—and come, it most certainly will— you'll have sorely wished you had."*
—excerpt from the personal journal of Steven Spurlock

|Planet Deaer, The Southspur Mountains

Koryn Naylor hadn't moved much at all from his position on the mountain's peak since Haiyen had flown away from him. *And why should I? What's left for me if I'm to go on without her?*

At first, he'd remained slumped in the snow, broken and empty. Long enough that icicles had formed in his beard and upon his eye lashes and nose. He'd lost consciousness for a time, but had awakened when a thunderclap had sounded through the blizzards, and it was only then that he finally realized he ought to crawl himself back into the cottage, unless he truly intended to die from the cold.

So crawl, he did. Slowly and pathetically for the shelter of his gloom-ridden domicile, only rising to his knees momentarily to light a fire anew in the fireplace. He lacked the strength to roll the barrels of supplies into the cottage. And, further, he lacked an understanding of the amount of time that'd passed the whole while he'd been out there—*an evening... a day, perhaps?*

There were still a few pieces of smoked venison in the cabinet, and he took to chewing at them for a bit of sustenance. But that was all. His will for survival was nil now, and he had naught but an abundance of time to dwell on his assorted misdeeds. *She was all I ever had in life, and I cast her away. I was so foolish to break the rules; to attempt escape from the Settlement. I should've been content to spend time with her, rather than to long for some kind of escape. I had everything I needed, in her, and never realized it.*

Some few more days had passed, then, and he'd continued to wallow in his misery, finding strength enough only to push the barrels barely within the confines of the cottage, to lower the launching device back down from its raised position, and to close the hatch in the roof to keep the snow from coming in; more than it already had. And it'd been right back to slumping himself on the floor in front of the fire, with nothing but regrets to occupy his mind.

*Bartyl Gleon,* he repeated the name Haiyen had mentioned, lamenting every scrap of memory he could call to mind, *what a tremendous tool he is… always bowing his head to the Sages, if I recall. Always falling in-step with their commands. Doesn't surprise me he's ended up a Prima ranksman. But Haiyen? I don't care if her mum was a pilot, she's got more sense in her than to join Prima, to trust in the dictatorial Sages. But I guess she's getting on together with Gleon. He's probably the one who convinced her to join. I'd like to see him try and amuse her half as much as I always have.*

But it was true that he'd neglected Haiyen. Not only while they were growing up together in the Settlement, but he'd taken her for granted these last two years (or more) as well, and it was sinking-in that he'd only focused on himself all this time—on his own suffering—rather than focusing on the one thing he'd still had left. Her. *She was taking care of me. She was visiting me and investing in me. She was risking her own safety for me, and I've thrown it all away… again. And I suppose Gleon, or someone else, will be there to pick her up; to appreciate her as the ideal companion that she is. To give her the attention she needs… That she deserves.*

*Is this cruel and deranged fate commensurate with the wrongs I've committed?? Oh life, with its many, many pitfalls and with so few truly unfettered indulgences. Were there bliss to be found in the tumultuous throes of the knowing age, once ignorance has turned to understanding, our Sages should have since bestowed to us the secret for reaching it.* He stood up, then, feeling his body ache with the effort, having mostly refrained from erect movement for some days now, and he opened the door to face the blizzard; to walk into it without regard. *But they've passed no such touchstone; no such key to us, those Sages of ours…*

*They've kept it for themselves, whatever it may be, and we're left to suffer. We're left with nothing, except pain and remorse.*

In time, after a bit of traipsing through the snow, he found himself at the mountain's edge, and he grasped the trunk of a tree so that he could peer over at the drop. It was a staggering distance down to the rock below; so far that the snow made it impossible to perceive any true surface or ledge. *Perhaps there is no mountain below at all, only air. Could it be I've already died, and this is the Afterward? Could this be some farcical jape I'm living?*

He was looking down, still, at the depths of the drop.

*There may be but one single way to find out...*

And in that instant, he heard the sound of the copper bell. At least, he *thought* he'd heard it, jingling through the falling snow. He hesitated, looking longingly at the sheer drop once more, then tore himself away from the edge to trudge back to the cottage and have a look. And there, he found that his ears had not deceived him, for there *was* a homing bird there, waiting on its perch.

Koryn sensed immediately that the bird (like he) was in distress. It was the jet black and crimson-feathered one he'd seen once before. Someone unconcerned about the bird's welfare had molested it; that much was clear. But it'd never-the-less made its way, with message in tow, to his meager station. So he took it inside the cottage and unfastened the note.

This time, unlike all the others, a message had arrived when he was ready to discard everything, and his inhibitions were nonexistent. *I don't much care for orders and rules anymore. I'm opening this message and I'm reading what it has to say; the Sages be damned.*

He unfurled the note with hands shaking; his fingers purple and nearly frostbit from exposure. But he found only a short message scrawled across the razor-thin tab—thick black ink blotting and bleeding cruelly into the fibers of the parchment—and he enunciated it in-full:

YOU ARE HEREBY WARNED; WE ARE COMING FOR YOU.
PREPARE TO MEET YOUR DEMISE.

Thereto, he launched himself into a fit of demented laughter. The idea that someone would threaten him in such a way seemed positively absurd. He was at his wit's end. He'd outright *welcome* a confrontation of the sort alluded to in the message.

*Any* confrontation would do, in fact.

This wasn't a message of doom. This was a message of salvation!

Even so, he had to wonder about the origin of the message. From the looks of the bird, he'd already sensed a bit of tampering had occurred; perhaps, as if it'd been intercepted and equipped with a false message. Additionally, the parchment, as a matter of fact, was of an alternate size and substance to those messages he'd yet received.

*It wouldn't make much sense that an agent of the Settlement—Sage or other—would send to me a message such as this*, he considered. *Haiyen would never report ill of me, no matter the degree of my bad behavior. And besides, if they wished me ill tidings, they need only deprive me of my provisions in order to bring me to my end; a much cleaner method for sure, and the Sages have always maintained a perfect cleanliness in all they do. Coming here and attacking me would reach far beyond any notion a Sage might develop to affect my expiration.*

Koryn then considered whether the message was even written for *his* consumption at all. *Indeed, I've been instructed never to read these. But if the message were meant for some other party—the mysterious ones to which the capsules are transmitted by my launching device—there'd be little sense in offering such warning of an attack. Indeed, the message seems more like an imposter; like something someone scrawled in haste and in anger...*

*No, I've every notion this message was intended for me; the derelict on his lonesome, with no shot at mounting a resistance or defense of any significance. And, I suppose, it makes little difference at all, anyway. Perhaps Haiyen was right. Perhaps the flatlanders* do *exist somewhere out there across the great Beyond, and they're coming for me, just like the Sages always warned they might. And perhaps, just so, I'll have my chance to blow off a bit of steam when they do!*

He hefted up the bow that leaned in the corner and walked it out of the cabin; up the hill to a clearing where a stretch of trees stood not far in the distance. The elevation afforded him a wide view of the desolate niche he called home. There seemed to be no movement; no sign of any intruder at all who might challenge him as they threatened they would.

*But when they do...*

He turned, slung the bow string tight, nocked an arrow and pulled to the draw's capacity, then loosed it toward a massive tree. The arrow sunk, dead center, deep into the heart of the trunk, shredding bark and slowly spilling thick strands of sap all over the frozen ground.

Koryn grinned devilishly, and from the depths of his chest, he shouted:

"If you want me, come and *flaming* get me!!!"

## 32 | The SF-86

*"How-so-ever peaceful can the world truly seem, when within the mind there persists a constant buzz concerning some external matter, force, or kerfuffle? I propose it is not until these troubles are tended to in-full that we may breathe as though our chests are unbound and our thoughts are free and clear. Who are these folks who can simply cast aside worry and concern? Who are they to simply care not in the least about the past, about failure, and about the greater darkness? I count myself not among them. For true peace of mind is the hardest-earned bounty of all, and not easily scavenged by the likes of the self-conscious, who tumble life's every speck of minutiae around in their minds. And I do not know or understand any other way. Lo, but when peace is achieved, by any degree, I implore you to hold tight, lock it down, and try never to let it go.*

*Oh, to find something you truly love. Cling to such a thing; nurture it in abundance. Plug into it and feel its energy, its charge. Give yourself over to it—whatever it is, and do not look back. And if you're like me, plagued by ceaseless flotsam and jetsam cluttering the mind, perhaps this thing will help forge a way for you. Perhaps, by devoting your thoughts and your energies to this thing, you can train your mind to ignore the rest—or at least the elements you wish most not to dwell upon—so that you might concentrate more on those that matter; the important things.*

*In this way, I have imagined a place of perfect peace and tranquility. One that is furnished by such tempered discipline of thought. And in this place, there are fields and mountains and lakes, and there are beaches of sand and ocean. There are simple dwellings where live simple peoples, and an abundance of love and life and happiness, and I am one of these peoples. I'm running through a meadow of lavender, lying below a tree whose leaves rustle in a passing breeze, and I'm caring for animals and tending a fresh trickling stream, all of which provide for me food for eating and water for drinking. And above all, I think not a moment upon a single worry in this place, for it is a place—a world— which has within it not one thing that might ever trouble my mind.*

*I figured once to ask for her aid in getting to this place so that I might hasten my transcendence of the mundane; of the immaterial junk that was weighing me down. I asked if she might restore my memory and let me go home. But she refused me, saying it was something I had to accomplish on my own; for myself. And it would take time. It would take patience. She could not help me see the world a certain way, she said. The only thing she could do was guide me through an effort to prevent this Planet Deaer's total self-annihilation, but that it was certainly not time—nor energy—wasted on my part, to seek comfort in the process. She reminded me: Home is a destination reserved only for those who have completed their mission in the new world that they've willingly entered. And if I had somehow taken leave of my senses, she was quick to remind me that this place was wrapped in turmoil that was certain only to grow worse before it improved, rendering my mission yet thoroughly incomplete, indeed.*

*And so we continued, as we had, in our studies of this place; this separate world. And over a short period of time, I believed I might have marked growth while swimming in this world's ocean, if for only a breath or two counts' worth. All the while, wondering... What could possibly be the nature of this place that, even under such duress, I should begin to sense a bit of promise? After all, I doubt I deserve ever being taken for an optimist. There truly is a comic irony to be found in a world where a neurotic, paranoid fool like me might develop a level of comfort within such perilous surroundings as these. Yet I submit, this ounce of deliverance must have surely been furnished by some mystical influence that remains yet illusive, so sorely out of reach, but it is the one thing that keeps me moving forward; that keeps me in wait, with an eager anticipation now, for the rise of a new day. This indefinable component, which allows me to persist in my effort to survive, is indeed real, though I know not how long it may last.*

*I asked if she would help me get there… I begged that she would. That the wait—the mission, surely, as well— would exact no more hardship than I could bear. But she could assure me of so few things, as I've come to learn, and preservation of my well-being, my sanity, was not among them.*

*It comes down to one thing. That there has to be something down there on that blasted planet. Something worth all of this. There simply has to be. Something akin to this concept the human race has oft referred to as… hope."*
—excerpt from the personal journal of Steven Spurlock

|The Station

A long evening in his solar spent reviewing the transcripts of his sources was followed by a late night filled with more of the same. The swim in the ocean had proven somewhat restorative while it lasted. Indeed, his Operator had been generous to grant him such an indulgence. But it was time to get back to work again, and he well knew it. He was looking for clues that might help him determine causality of the events that'd transpired at Castle Athyn (the damage done there), and so he kept returning to the records that had always garnered the greatest of his suspicions—those of the wizard Idris Ansel.

The man didn't speak much. Half of his audio feed found him coaxing the youngest prince, Tae, into helping him along some wild goose chase within the depths of the castle. And nearly the other half placed him amongst fellow High Council members, arguing over theories that could explain the posture of Athyn's varied enemies.

But the bit Spurlock had always kept close at hand—the subdued conversation between Ansel and the foreign ambassador Fleurys—was the one piece that seemed to suggest that, perhaps, the key to the planet's mysteries might lay within reach. The conversation in question (quite convincingly) named Ansel a conspirator, at best, and a murderous traitor at worst. And it was a notion Athynian leaders remained oblivious to, as evidenced by the wizard's continued free run of the castle. *Well, this "Nhyle" is still unaware, at least. But the Heir Prince is another story. His suspicions of this guy Ansel are pretty clear. I think he'd like to throw the old fart into the dungeons and melt down the key.*

*Too bad no one's listing to him...*

He pulled the clip up again on a holoscreen, the conversation between the wizard and his ambassador confidant, and played its translations through. There'd been mention of the launching devices; specifically, those that were hidden in three separate locations, which he'd already taken for the three spots he'd visited during his initial operation—the jungle, the knoll, and the mountain peak.

*But I've already mentioned all that in my reports.*

Then, he noted, there was something *else*. Something he hadn't heard before. Or he *had* heard it, but hadn't quite taken into consideration its potential significance. He played it back again, just to be certain. It was the wizard, Ansel, speaking:

"After all these ages, Alamere has left no stone unturned..."

*How did I miss this?*

He played it back once more, concentrating on the name:

"Alamere has left no stone unturned..."

*I've heard that name before, I'm sure I have. Alamere.* He spent a good measure of time, then, scanning his feeds and the holoscreens for mention of the name, only to confirm his initial claim for truth; that it'd been mentioned by the wraith who led the attack at the outpost; and upon the message retrieved from the assassin, south of the castle after the explosion. *All hail Alamere.* So he marked it down and moved on; more determinedly now with a heightened attention to detail.

*Someone along the way said there is immense wisdom in details. Who was it that said that again?*

It was late, indeed, when he moved on to review more recent dialogue from the evening's feeds. And though he yearned for sleep, he forced himself to at least scan a few transcripts for anything significant.

It didn't take long to find something.

"Lord Tymian of Halcyon," was the detail he'd narrowed-in upon, and it had come from Mailyn's feed, the Nohnce. She seemed to have traveled to a village somewhere, though he couldn't yet decipher where, exactly, and was unable to find it on any of the many maps of Deaer, in his digital atlas. And like Alamere, the name Tymian seemed familiar to him as well.

He queried his feeds for the name, and found it within both the Solis prince's transcripts, as they'd each whispered the name, almost silently to themselves. Tae had whispered the name out on his veranda before taking off for the cellars and disappearing in the catacombs to fetch a wooden practice sword. And Ethyn voiced it in the Nhyle's Court of Castle Athyn, amongst all the grand statues along the promenade, when he'd escaped there after his contentious High Council forum.

Spurlock's research continued, and the systems in his solar hummed steadily along.

He slipped in and out of sleep, propping his chin on a palm. The words became jumbled clusters of letters before his eyes, all melding together, then drifting erratically about the screens while he tried to consider their significance.

And time floated by.

"It lays before you, for the unraveling," said Giza, of a sudden. Spurlock wasn't even aware the unit was powered on, but it continued, "You have the means to decode it all. Even now—the puzzle. Or else you wouldn't have been chosen, as you were."

"What do you mean by that, Giza?" Spurlock's fatigue was really catching up with him. It was almost as if he'd imagined the module's statements altogether. *And maybe I have...*

"Giza?" he said again.

But, after squinting a bit, Spurlock saw that the unit now sat motionless and unlit in the corner, and it did not reply. *If I don't get some sleep, I'll start losing whatever grip on sanity I have left.*

And so, after writing a report containing these potentially vital names—Alamere and Tymian—and after sending it off to his Operator, he half-expected a pronouncement of Projection to commence. But it hadn't.

Immensely relieved, he'd eagerly helped himself to his cot for whatever slice of rest he could muster.

\*\*\*

|Planet Earth, Washington DC

Federal Executive Assistant Haley Kenmore at last put her work away and stood up from her desk in an old building, on the headquarters campus of the U.S. Department of Homeland Security. It had been a tremendously excruciating afternoon, but there was yet a part of her that believed the news delivered earlier by the intelligence officials and Steven's lack of communication (of late) might still prove completely unrelated. Just the same—such hope was quickly withering away.

*Gone missing,* is how the man had put it after his meeting with the Assistance Secretary.

*Gone missing...*

After the jarring anecdote had reached her ears, she'd known immediately what she was going to do after work, and she was setting out to do it now, without further delay.

"You've acted aloof today, Ms. Kenmore," said the A/S, when Haley made her final visit at the executive's door, "Even more so than usual; and that is saying something. Don't think I haven't noticed."

The office was quiet, with most (if not all) of the workforce departed for the evening.

"Aloof, ma'am? If I've seemed aloof, it hasn't been deliberate."

"It rarely is," the A/S looked coldly over the lenses of her reading glasses, as was her habit at times, "I suspect it's related to that intelligence analyst fellow I've seen you bouncing around with. Am I correct?"

*How could she possibly...?* Haley's facial expression and staggered silence seemed to prove confirmation enough.

"You heard Mr. Turner's mention of the analyst today. The one who is missing. I was sure you had, and the look on your face now leaves no doubt," the A/S rose from her chair and sat on the corner of her desk. The woman's demeanor took on an unusually personal manner, and her eyes suddenly looked as if they carried a measure of pain within them. "Spurlock, is it?"

Haley nodded slowly, terrified.

"I thought so," continued the A/S, "I made a few calls… It is him, indeed."

Haley felt her chest cave in.

"Nothing of what I'm about to say leaves this room. Is that understood?"

"Yes, ma'am," Haley was numb. Still crippled by the news. Answering in spoken word, only by sheer reflex.

"Something occurred to me at home this weekend, when I was in my attic. I've got a small box of holiday things. Old things, really, that I've kept for years and years. I began to go through it to see what I might want to get rid of this year, and for the first time, when I pulled out my single lone stocking, it struck me. I've kept that stocking, by itself, for a very long time; my whole adult life. But it hit me hard this year, it really did…"

The A/S adjusted herself on the corner of her desk, took off her reading glasses, and turned slightly away, "Look, Ms. Kenmore. Haley. What I'm trying to say—and I'm not doing a very good job of it; you're probably wondering what in the world this all means. But what I'm saying is this. You're at a crossroads right now." The woman swallowed hard and continued, "I once thought it was the most fatal mistake any young person in this town could make, to mix business with pleasure. I thought, and perhaps rightfully so, that we've got a job to do here, and *feelings* will only get in the way. That this work of ours is too important for all of that. I learned to leave such things behind, entirely. Do you follow what I'm saying?"

"You dismissed your feelings, when you were younger," Haley spoke the words before she'd really had a chance to gauge the appropriateness of their meaning, in context.

"I learned how to suppress them for the sake of my own dignity and professionalism. Weakness doesn't play well in this town, if you haven't noticed."

"But what do we have left, if we give away our feelings?"

"A fighting chance at a meaningful career," snapped the A/S, on instinct, "that's what I believed. In some ways, that's what I've proven, isn't it?"

"At the expense of a fulfilling personal life?" Now Haley was *sure* she'd spoken out of line.

The A/S turned her stare, sharply, back toward Haley, and a palpable silence filled the room.

"Yes well, it appears my point has been made," the A/S stood again and returned to her chair, putting her glasses back on. She sat down. "You should know, the work he's doing is specialized; highly privileged—this friend of yours, that is. Frankly, I'm surprised they've assigned such sensitive threat reporting to a junior analyst. It speaks highly of his talent. But this is a very serious situation best left to the experts. I just want you to realize that." The A/S paused again, perhaps with an introspective gleam, "If you insist on poking around this rabbit hole of his, there is no telling how deep you may fall into it, yourself. I don't want to frighten you, but there's no telling how far away from us he could be, at this very moment. And I don't want the same to happen to you."

Bound by what she'd heard, Haley fastened the last of her coat buttons and tossed her scarf around her neck, staring blankly ahead.

"It is well after six," the older woman lowered her eyes back to the papers on her desk, "You may be excused."

"Thank you, ma'am," managed Haley, "for your advice. I appreciate it."

Wondering how much damage she may have done to her relationship with the A/S, Haley left the office and made her way to the circle at the front entrance of campus, where the shuttle busses sat idling. It was, indeed, that time of year on the east coast when the evening turned to darkness early; and as quickly as the sun dropped, so too did the temperatures. She made double-haste to catch the earliest departure she could. And she wondered if the numbness she felt was more a result of the cold, or of the completely unexpected conversation she'd just had, which she was trying desperately to understand. She didn't know if she and the A/S might become closer for having it, or drift even farther apart.

She found her fellow shuttle riders were more inclined to bundle themselves up and turn themselves over to silent introspection this time of year. This, she knew, stood in stark comparison to the summer-time gab fests folks enjoyed over warmer periods, and, settling into her seat, she was grateful for the quiet.

Down the Rock Creek Parkway they motored, to the edge of the Potomac River and around the Lincoln Memorial to Independence Drive, where they were suddenly flanked by the Tidal Basin on their right and the Washington Monument on their left. The great stone obelisk floated past her window like a shadow, the red lights near its peak glowing dully, on and off in the dark like slowly blinking, watchful eyes. Haley half-expected it might begin speaking to her, in her present daze.

She found she couldn't help but wonder how the uncomfortable talk with her A/S—strangely personal as it was—would affect their working relationship going forward. Her boss' assertions certainly rang true, though. Indeed, it seemed many of the most successful people around this town had sacrificed a great deal in their lives to get to the top. She wondered if she could ever do the same. If her immediate reaction to Steven's (now confirmed) disappearance were any indication, it didn't seem likely. But the conversation held more within it than a mere commentary on personal relationships. It spoke to a very clear and fearful warning of danger, as well.

When they'd made their stop at L'Enfant Plaza, she stepped back into the cold evening air. Car horns blared and helicopter blades buzzed urgently from somewhere above—ever-present elements of the fray in the District. It had begun to rain, and the slickness of the streets reflected all the lights of the city like over-saturated brush strokes of watercolor running across the walkways and streets. And she was careful in finding her way. The stresses of the day had lit her like a candle at both ends, and she imagined the wind and rain might extinguish the flames before they burned the last of her waxy existence in splatters on the ground.

But time was of the essence, and she hurried along so that she might catch the next train, bound for Virginia.

\*\*\*

|The Station

Nighttime on the Station was creeping along when Spurlock was awoken, not by his audible feeds, nor by his Operator's voice this time, but by a strange sensation; the faint feeling of air tickling his earlobe. His breaking from sleep, in this manner, was a gradual process. He held his head up and rubbed sleep-sealed eyelids apart with one hand, while the other groped clumsily around in an effort to detect the source of the current. And shortly, he'd found that air was leaking, quite liberally, from the loose-fitted cover to his receptor chute; the console from which he'd retrieved his meals each morning and evening.

He stood up out of bed to complete a more thorough appraisal.

*If the chute malfunctions, how am I supposed to get my food?*

It was certainly a viable concern.

"Fear is a tricky one, isn't it?" Giza's voice again surprised Spurlock, who had no idea the unit was powered up.

"Giza?" Spurlock turned around, still quite dreary, "Is that you?"

"It is one of the more particularly harmful emotions, isn't it? Fear."

Spurlock pressed, "What are you trying to tell me, Giza?"

"You have a choice," said the module, "you can turn yourself over to fear at a time like this, thinking you may be left to go hungry…"

"Or what?"

"Or, you could search for a practical solution."

Spurlock was dressed in his snug-fitting thermals, leaning now over the receptor chute like a crooked tree looming over a mailbox. He lifted the lid and peered inside while a surge of air hit him in the face, tossing his hair asunder, and it was made immediately clear he'd find no way to repair the thing from inside his solar.

He turned toward the module, "Now what?"

"You're not going to give up that easily, are you?" Giza's blue light illumined brighter than ever before, "I process billions of terabytes of data before I declare a problem unsolvable. Now is when you *persist*."

Spurlock grunted and toed his way to the door, hitting the lit button to open it up. He found his tract enveloped in the deep grays of the simulated night.

Lightyears beyond the great Station's oracular dome, millions of stars twinkled and pulsed brilliantly; most of them appearing to burn off an ethereal, swirling whiteness, but a few bore tints of blue, yellow, green, and red. Toward the Station's bow, Spurlock saw Planet Deaer hanging in space like a jewel. Then he saw the planet's moon, held captive in Deaer's revolutionary path, shining half in sparkling silver and half-redacted in pitch darkness. And for a moment, he wondered if Projection could place him on moons just as well as it could on planets.

*I think I'd rather not find out. I'm sure it's got its own brand of insanity, needing to be untangled.*

"Fine," Spurlock called back to Giza, who was hovering just inside the solar doorway, "I'll see what I can do."

The receptor chute was mounted on the wall opposite his door, necessitating his passing around the back-end of the solar; a detour he had not taken often—*only once out of curiosity a few days past, and only to have a peek*. Dense vegetation prohibitive of easy access grew there, but if anything could be done to repair the chute, it would most likely involve something along this rear side. So he continued forth.

*Stupid little robot. What's so bad about fear, anyway? At least it's an evil I can understand, and it keeps me out of trouble. Not like this automated, duty-driven mumbo jumbo he's trying to jam down my throat. Him and this Operator of mine.* Spurlock wasn't yet prepared to admit the demonstrative duo's methods had already, indeed, helped him solve a problem or two. Likely because they had also pressed him into precarious, uncomfortable positions, time and time again.

With deliberate movements, he fought through the brush against the solar's outer casing; a labored process, really, and he hadn't even a notion of what he might be searching for—*A service hatch of some kind?* Yet, he could find no such access point at all. Stepping farther along, however, he saw the floor panels closest to the solar appeared compromised, structurally. It looked like an especially invasive species of vine had threaded itself around the perimeter of one panel and had penetrated its edges; had even begun pulling the panel up and away from the rest of the tract floor, bending and twisting its form in a most intriguing way.

One corner rivet of the panel had already been pulled free, and a longer edge had given way for the thickness of the plant to intrude into the open space below. As a result, a gap in the floor was made in evidence to him.

*Could I possibly fit through there?*

The debate in his mind—waged between leaving well enough alone and pressing forward—was short-lived.

*I guess now is when I'm supposed to persist.*

*...Stupid robot.*

He slipped through the gap, feet first, having no expectation for the size of the space he might encounter below, and if it be cavernous, he felt he'd rather land hard on his feet than hard on his head. But soon, he felt his bare toes brush against a solid surface, and dared to drop all the way down inside.

\*\*\*

|Planet Earth, Washington DC

Haley Kenmore took a long escalator ride into the bowels of L'Enfant Station, only a few blocks south of the National Mall. She had no particular affection for the DC metro system. There was a sort of filthiness down in those depths that seemed to wrap itself around her and bind her in gloom. She much preferred her seven-minute, above-ground bus ride to campus over this drab foolery, which felt more like a mining expedition than a sensible option for one's daily commute. Walkways and tunnels down below were lined with enormous, rectangular cement forms that looked to her like the cellular structure of some enormous beast. It made her feel as if she were walking through a great worm's insides, laid dormant under the capitol city.

It was all very *science fiction*—not her favorite genre of storytelling, in the least.

The marquee on the platform showed the next train—Yellow Line—would arrive in six minutes, and people were already gathering like cattle to be amongst the first to board. Shuffling within the fray, she managed (but only with concerted effort) to keep a solid footing in her heels and longed desperately for a pair of her athletic shoes, with their air-infused soles and gel-padded interiors.

She knew Steven cared no more for the metro than she did, and she couldn't help but ponder a plea she'd made to him with more frequency over the past month or so now. *If he'd show any interest at all in moving closer to work, I can think of someone who wouldn't mind accepting him as a roommate. Then neither of us would have to deal with this madness down here anymore!*

Shattering her thoughts, a man on the platform turned abruptly to her, clumsily dragging an elbow against her arm.

She looked at him with a frown.

"You *must* find him," said the man, staring straight at her, hauntingly.

Her heart skipped. *Who could possibly know to say such a thing?*

Alarmed, she saw the older gentleman peering down at her from the concealment of a heavy coat; collars raised, casting deep shadows across his face. His cool, gray-tinted eyes, the likes of which she felt she'd never quite seen before, looked deep within her, nearly glowing.

"Excuse me?" she replied.

It was then that the train had arrived in the station. Its squealing breaks echoing through the great tunnels, combining with the din of the milling crowd to further obfuscate any kind of exchange with the strange person that might have continued. A current of fetid air blew into all their waiting faces. When the cluster of bodies squeezed together, she thought she heard a reply from the man, which she might have taken for a foreign language, this time. But when the man shuffled ahead without further interaction—*could I even call that a conversation?*—it seemed (more and more) to have been a strange misunderstanding than anything else.

She finally stepped aboard, one of the last few to make it onto the train. People were smashed together like sardines in their tin can, standing and grasping for a hand rail wherever one could be found. The man was nowhere to be seen, and the doors slid shut on a disgruntled crowd of folks left standing on the platform, who'd have to wait for the arrival of the next train to continue their miserable trek home for the evening.

A gray darkness consumed the metro despite the muted and flickering interior lights, and the lit signals that rushed past windows as they picked up speed through the tunnel. Moments later, they emerged from the underground into the gloom-ridden evening, out over a bridge spanning the Potomac River with its choppy freezing waters sloshing erratically below. And ahead, she saw the banks of Virginia.

*Virginia...*

Haley tightened her grip on the hand rail and hardened her resolve while the train forged ahead.

\*\*\*

|The Station

The space below Spurlock's tract resembled a sort of subterranean byway system, much akin to something he couldn't put his mind to, but something he felt strongly he'd known well, or had frequented often at some time in his life. The sensation of familiarity (however vague) made the act of venturing farther down a bit more tolerable. Yet all the while, he made assurances his ability to return from whence he'd come was retained, in full; careful not to drop any distances—from one ledge to another—that he couldn't then turn around and climb back up again.

There was a robust system of ducts and piping that (he figured) sourced the utilities in his solar, for they ran along the underside of its approximate location. He identified a particular duct as the one responsible for servicing his meal receptor, aligning quite precisely with the location of the chute above. Along its form, indeed, he saw a piece of casing was hanging askew, as if left unfastened or broken, which might have accounted for the chute's malfunction.

It was then that he'd truly felt the formidable strength of the wind current in this tunnel, taking it, therefore, as no surprise that such a healthy gust of air might've made its way into his solar through the means of this duct. It seemed a simple fix, really, upon cursory inspection. The loose casing hung well within reach. He needed only proceed a very short distance along an adjoining platform to make the necessary repair. *Maybe there's something to this robotic, persistence thing, after all.*

But his efforts were suddenly delayed by a certain tentativeness.

Presently, he heard a sound he could not place; something like static-electric shocks, discharged in short, intermittent fragments almost too faint to hear, and he felt as though they came from a sort of track that ran down the center of the tunnel. The track continued from his location toward the stern end of the Station and disappeared around a darkened curve, beyond which nothing further could be seen. By instinct, he grew wary of this sound, as if it were a prelude to danger. So he doubled back, finding a shadowed recess in which to hide, until it might pass.

Moments later a pod arrived, suspended so gracefully in the air over the track and coming to a stop with such fluidity that he couldn't possibly conceive of the power under which it must have been moving, to exhibit such control. Colorless, its surface reflected nothing and had shone no seams nor blemishes whatsoever, until its two sides sliced free from the core of its body and peeled upward to create two openings.

Out of the pod stepped two beings, the sight of which made Spurlock's heart skip two beats, for they were so positively surreal in form; tall, slender, and nearly featureless. Their bodies seemed not to be bodies at all, but instead, mere gatherings of white smoke, floating like clouds in an upright, yet frighteningly abstract, state of animation. Remarkably, they wore distinguishable faces where their smoky forms gathered with greater definition, marked by distinctive silver-gray eyes. He thought he might choke on his breath in shock while he watched from his hiding place.

The being closest to him drifted to the duct that fed his receptor chute, carrying with it a tray, which could only be his morning meal. And once it slid the tray into place, it repaired the broken duct casing without a hint of trouble at all, and turned around with such graceful movements that nary a single remote comparison in the natural world could've ever come to mind. It made an indistinguishable, yet pleasant, sound for its companion as it transitioned from the platform back into the pod.

The companion had entered a door on the opposite side of the track and was, itself, now returning to the pod as well. But in the course of its duties, it seemed to have dropped something, which lay there on the ground, unnoticed by either of them. Then the sides of the pod melded back into its core while it turned a half rotation and whisked itself fluidly back in the direction from which it had come, along the track and around the darkened corner and away.

In the space where the pod had been, there hung a denseness in the air. In fact, the air seemed altered throughout the tunnel, as if it still contained a trace of those beings' makeup, some strain of their chemical composition, or perhaps whatever element (or combination thereof) that might have powered their pod. And he suddenly realized he'd scarcely drawn a single breath the entire time he spent witnessing this unbelievable display.

He slowly, cautiously, emerged from his hiding spot back out onto the platform. There was no reason left to tinker with the duct leading to the receptor chute. One swift glance confirmed it was, indeed, flawlessly repaired. But instead, his attentions turned to the opposite platform where one of the strange beings had dropped something, and he made his way there, cautiously following a walkway that curved around the end of the track, connecting the two sides of the platform seamlessly. And there on the metal-mesh surface laid a document, comprised of many pages and bound with a staple. He bent and lifted it up to read the heading printed at the top:

*Standard Form 86*

He paged through eagerly to find, in black and white, the data points of his life.

He saw his first name, and recited it to himself. *Steven.*

Then he thumbed through every address where he'd ever lived. All of his travel destinations, and the dates he'd visited them. Every educational institution he'd attended. Every place where he'd ever been employed. Persons who knew him best of all, and where and how they might be reached. All his relatives with like information, and nearly every other detail that might define his personal past, in whole.

He looked at the words on the pages, and at the titles—the names, the streets, the cities—and realized that, while they must have represented a great deal of the information he so desperately sought to regain, they brought no distinct images to his mind, clear or vague. They were, after all, just names and numbers and words. Yet his possession of them made him feel something. Like he had something of his past he could hold in his very hands; something he could study.

*Just, something...*

Standing there, he wondered precisely what else lay behind the door that stood on this side of the platform. A plate mounted above it bore engraved characters that seemed to label the room for its purpose, but the characters were alien, and offered no clue.

Around his neck, he felt the presence of the string that held his key (one of his only two personal possessions) in place beneath his thermal top, and his thoughts turned to the possibility he might have found the very portal it was meant to open. But he saw no such lock that might be released with a key. And there seemed to be a lack of compatibility in form and size between the two objects; the key seeming far too small for the size of this rather large door.

The track, then, suddenly began spitting its tiny electric shocks again, pulling urgently at his attention once more.

In all the world—in all the *universe* for that matter—he thought he would least of all like to remain present in this place, if and when those beings returned. So he tucked the document into his waistband, raced back to the other side of the track, and made for the ledges he'd come down upon; reaching and climbing, pulling himself up. *This isn't fear driving me away from these things,* he told himself, *it's calculated conflict resolution... obviously.*

The shock sounds continued to snap and sizzle behind while he reached deep within for the strength to make himself scarce from the place. And with great effort, he finally pulled himself back up into the tangle of brush again behind his solar, scrambling and crawling his way through; pushing and sliding past dense growth on the tract floor. And then he was free from it, making his return to the entry door of his living space.

This, while the simulated night continued to bathe the Station in its gray-tinted palette of gloom.

\*\*\*

|Planet Earth, Washington DC

The Yellow Line metro car's brakes were engaged on its approach to the Pentagon, forcing Haley Kenmore forward in momentum, then back again at its abrupt halt. She disembarked, twisting and bending and leaning her way through the crowded train and out onto the platform. Up and over the tracks and back down she hurried to the other side where, fortuitously, a Blue Line train waited; and she filed onboard with a score of others.

The doors closed, and the new train took off, just as packed as the last, with a stop at Arlington Cemetery and, finally, then to her destination point—Rosslyn.

Riding the escalators up and out of the stuffy underground was a welcomed (if only short-lived) relief, hampered by the reality of her present troubles; the darkness, the wind, and the cold as well. Raindrops fell on the display of her phone while she pulled up Steven's name from her contact list and placed a call. If she was going to storm his apartment unannounced, she figured she ought to at least make one last effort to confirm his whereabouts by conventional means. After all, he may just be laid-up sick in bed for all she knew. *Please let that be the case.*

But after seven rings, she figured he wasn't going to answer, and she ended the call with a sigh.

*Just like all my other attempts...*

His building was a well-kept (if a bit dated) box of brick and glass, but its value was in the view, raised up on a hill just south of Arlington Boulevard overlooking the Potomac River and aligned with the National Mall, sprawling eastward beyond. The automatic doors slid open when she made her approach to the front entrance, and she was glad to be out of the rain.

"Excuse me," she said in her natural tone of politeness. The woman seated at the front desk acknowledged her with a smile as Haley continued, "I'm in a bit of a bind. I need to get into my boyfriend's apartment, but I don't have a key."

Half-way through, she realized how suspicious her predicament may have sounded.

"Oh," remarked the woman, who wore a silk scarf around her neck and, still, a reassuring smile on her face, "Mr. Spurlock, correct? Yes, I've seen you before... with him. You look awfully nice together, the two of you."

"Oh," said Haley, blushing; both (she supposed) from the compliment and the awkward confession of voyeurism.

"May I help you?" A building manager had overheard the exchange from his office, and came out to assist, holding a tablet in his hand. He looked up when she didn't immediately respond, "Your last name, Miss...?"

"Kenmore," said Haley.

He tapped a few times on the screen and came to Steven's profile, which indeed listed Haley as an authorized visitant. "Okay. Come along, then, Miss Kenmore."

They rode the elevator to Steven's floor—eleven—and proceeded to the end of the hall. The manager had taken a master key out of his pocket just as, to Haley's surprise, they saw the door to Steven's unit standing ajar.

"Looks like you didn't need me after all. He must've left it open for you," a slight hint of vexation tinted the manager's voice, and he turned on his heel, quickly in return back down the hall toward the elevators, before Haley could venture a reply or an expression of gratitude for his assistance.

She took a deep breath. The door pushed open easily.

The apartment's small kitchenette was revealed inside to her left; dark and vacant. Straight ahead were the large bank of windows, which revealed streams of rain coming down even harder now than before. Windows of tall apartment buildings across the expressway in Rosslyn loomed outside like lit boxes, floating in the darkness.

She hit the lights.

It was a one-room studio unit, five-hundred square feet or so, with a tight (nearly closet-like) bathroom wedged in the corner. His desk was pushed up against the wall to the right. Hard-bound philosophy texts were neatly organized beside various reference books. A few lay open. *The Geographic History of the Middle East*. And various language texts were there, as well; Hebrew and Latin among them.

It wasn't unusual to see such items in his place, but several of the texts were laid open and strewn about, which was a tad irregular, indeed.

His bed was small—much to her discomfort those nights when she'd stayed over till morning—but it was made up immaculately, as per Steven's meticulous nature. She took a few long steps into the room, and everything else seemed in place. Yet, she sensed something was amiss; even apart from the door having been left suspiciously ajar.

*A certain scent, perhaps, that I haven't ever noticed here before? Stale and mineral.*

Opening his wardrobe revealed a row of his dress shirts and suits, neatly hung, but she had no way to presume whether they were all accounted for—whether or not he'd possibly packed a few into a suitcase, and had taken them on travel somewhere, as was Nora's suggestion. A modestly-sized luggage case was stored atop the wardrobe, but he might have had another, for all she knew. She certainly couldn't rule his sister's hypothesis out entirely. *But if he were traveling for work, why would his principals declare him missing?*

That's what kept her from dialing Nora up, or searching online for Steven's parents' number to tell of his disappearance. Or calling her *own* parents for advice; or the police for that matter, as well.

She didn't know what kind of damage such actions might cause—how they might compromise any chance of finding him, or how they might endanger those contacted. *There must be a reason the department hasn't reached out to Nora and the rest of his family. There must be some sort of danger in all of this, like the A/S warned.*

Wandering over to his dresser, she pulled out a lower drawer and found his sweats—drawstring pants she could pull tight to fit her slim waist and a hooded top with its *Phillies* script sewn across the chest. If any article of clothing spoke to Steven's very persona, it was that sweatshirt. That's why she liked it so much. There was positively no way she was going to endure several metro transfers to get back to her own place tonight. She'd hunker down here until morning; needing rest to process all of this, and she just wanted to feel close to him in the meantime. She threw down her hand bag, pulled off her stuffy work clothes and stockings and heels, put on the acquired comfort wear, and turned up the heat in his ice-cold apartment.

She often thought he seemed secluded here. Outside the District limits, up in a tall building, confined to this box-like dwelling. When they spent time together, it'd been at her place more often than not; so close to work, and a good deal more spacious and comfortable. She took pity on him, though, visiting whenever she found the patience; bringing him care packages once in a while to stock his cupboards for him. It was a nurturing instinct of hers, for which she was now quite grateful. There was a bag of instant popcorn left over that she'd once brought to him, and she had grown a bit hungry (for all the later in the evening it had so quickly become).

The microwave door hung slightly off its hinge, but she shut it secure enough with a bit of finagling, and in minutes, was enjoying a salty, buttery bowlful. Whatever the source of the odd smell she'd sensed, it wasn't in the kitchen; nor the bathroom, to which she paid an express visit. And now, the popcorn had made the place smell like a movie theater, instead.

From a small armchair in front of the windows, she indulged herself in the view, glad to have a seat for herself. Passenger planes filed in from the skies one after another, descending along the trajectory of the river to land at Reagan International Airport. Against the ink-blue backdrop of night, they looked more like enormous shadows of planes decorated with blinking lights that somehow glided their way to the ground with grace. She could see over the green areas below, of the memorials there, across their sloping hills, down to the river's edge, and across the Roosevelt Bridge to the Lincoln Memorial. Surprisingly robust clusters of trees were tucked-in here and there, and (of course) beyond it all, rose the capitol dome, lit up like a beacon in the night's landscape.

For all that Nora had said about the faults of this city and for all the fuss that Haley made over the metro, there were a great many things to appreciate here, too. There were experiences here that weren't possible anywhere else. This was the epicenter of the nation for a great many things, and for that, she held a deep sense of pride in the place where she lived.

Nestling down into the chair, she'd browsed on her phone awhile and texted a friend or two—nothing about Steven, she ensured—and time continued to pass quickly.

She'd just about dozed off, when a subtle creaking sound disturbed her calm.

*Did I forget to shut the door?*

When she turned to look, she saw the man standing there; an invader in the apartment, and she was stricken with horror. Her heart leapt into her throat; she stood up and backed herself against the windows, popcorn falling to the floor. She recognized him. *The man from the metro who spoke that gibberish to me.* Tall, but aged, he still wore his heavy raincoat with the turned-up collars.

He reached his hands out as if to dispel her alarm.

"Hello," he said, in the voice she recognized from earlier, "I didn't mean to distress you."

"What are you doing here?"

"I live in the apartment next door," he said calmly, "and I've seen this door left open the past several days, which seemed strange enough. But I've just now returned home to see that it's been opened wider, and the light has been turned on, that's all. My curiosity overcame me, and I only hoped to make sure everything was alright here."

"I don't need any help," she said. There were only two things Haley was certain of regarding this man—that, first, despite his overtures of innocence, his presence still felt threatening; and second, that this was (indeed) most assuredly the same man she'd seen on the metro platform while she waited to board the Yellow Line train.

"Well, that's a good thing," replied the man. She saw that his coat (despite the downpour outside) was, strangely, quite dry when he turned away to leave, "I'll be on my way, then, and hope that you have a pleasant night. I'm sorry to have startled you."

She exhaled deeply in response to his motions for retreat, and took a moment, standing against the windows to collect herself after he'd left. But soon, she made for the door in pursuit, "Hey, I'd like to ask you something. I want to know what you meant when you spoke to me on the platform at L'Enfant Plaza. I know it was you."

But when she peered down the hallway, she saw nothing except the closed doors of all the units nearby, and the man with the gray eyes did not re-emerge from any one of them to continue the conversation. She furrowed her brow. The feeling his presence had produced within her— the aura of danger that'd entered the space between them when he stood there in trespass—was severely unwelcome. *So it's probably just as well that he's gone.*

Back into Steven's apartment, Haley closed the door tightly and locked and bolted it shut. She crossed the room to pick up the fallen popcorn, and put away the bowl in the sink. And then, overrun by her thoughts and with the exhaustion that all the day's events had caused, she flicked off the lights and climbed warily into Steven's bed. She hoped that sleep would come, and on its heels, a new day that might prove more sensible than the one she'd just experienced.

It was then that she noticed something was missing from Steven's night stand—the photograph he'd snapped of her at the Tidal Basin in the spring; the Cherry Blossom Festival. She'd kept a picture of him in her own bedroom as well, taken that same day, and they'd exchanged them as gifts upon their six-month anniversary. But now, his photo seemed gone, missing.

*Gone missing.* She could still hear the words ringing in her ears.

*But where could he have gone, and why?*

Beginning tomorrow, she would set out on her quest, in earnest, to find out.

***

|The Station

Spurlock took the stapled document—the Standard Form 86—and creased it hard, opening his solar's wardrobe panel. The suit and helmet hung solemnly within. He shoved the papers deep into a corner of the upper shelf, and (after pausing for a moment) pulled his helmet from its peg and took it tightly into his hands. Then he closed the wardrobe panel securely so that he might not have to entertain thoughts of the papers, nor the information captured within them, until he could better prepare himself for all the implications they surely carried.

But entertain those thoughts he did, while he sat down upon his chair holding the helmet in his lap. Alongside those thoughts were considerations aplenty for the open space he now knew sprawled below him, and for the beings he'd observed down there. *The beings.* Their images, particularly, were vivid constructions, which he would not soon—or likely ever—find the means to forget.

"Giza," he said, quietly.

The module, which had since returned to its silent state, powered up gracefully in the corner and hovered slightly, "I am at your service. What do you need?"

"Just… watch the door, ok? And, perhaps a little light, if you can manage it."

"Sensors set for motion detection," said Giza, "And will this do?" The unit produced a soft blue glow that barely spread to the ceiling and walls.

"That will do nicely, thank you."

And so Spurlock sat there for a while, staring blankly at the helmet in his hands. Thinking upon his mission and his subjects on Planet Deaer, and about… himself.

"Giza," he said at last.

The unit pivoted its apex in his direction.

"I persisted, like you told me to."

Giza replied, "And what did it gain you?"

"Information," blue light was cast across Steven's face as he looked over at the module.

"And what do you intend to do with that information?"

"Process it. Analyze it. Use it to my advantage," said Spurlock, "Tell me something, Giza. Would you begrudge me for attempting to imitate your methods; your protocols?"

"To the contrary, I would welcome such attempts," the module stopped and hummed for a moment, "you must do what you feel necessary without hindrance."

Spurlock set the helmet on his desk.

"You see, this girl Haiyen," at his beckoning, the holoscreens came alive, and he opened two particular feed logs, "she pilots some kind of craft that sounds like—this."

He tapped his touchpad to navigate through a number of logs. Suddenly, the audiblers played the sounds of Haiyen's buzzcraft, captured during several flights the Prima pilot had made over the last few days. A whirring and swooping mechanic atop a sonic baseline combined to inspire a very unique waveform, which Spurlock displayed on one of the screens.

"And the boy, Tae," Steven continued, "He was taken somewhere by his new friend."

Spurlock played Tae's feed in real-time, and indeed, the sounds of Brychen's craft—its depth and fidelity in waveform—closely resembled Haiyen's. "And it seems they are still in flight, right now."

The sounds played for a few moments longer while their waveforms displayed clearly on the screens, side-by-side. Spurlock looked at them intently, then stood and walked outside alone, carrying the helmet, "Hold tight, Giza"

At the prow-end of his tract, he stood, facing the brilliant orb of Deaer.

He put the helmet on.

"Filters," he said, "Optical Zoom."

Zooming as far as the visor would allow, he could only just make out some of the features of Deaer's surface. Cloud accumulation blocked a good deal of the landforms and most of the seas, and he searched them in vain. After long moments, he finally saw something of interest. An arcing plume of smoke so faint, but highlighted nicely once he applied the Light Inversion and Thermal Imaging filters.

The plume streaked across the deep blue depths of space, and he followed it as best he could.

*There. It's a craft, alright. Heading straight for… Deaer's moon.*

Spurlock squinted his eyes; thinking. He'd spent a lot of time listening to these subjects of his; following their movements and interpreting their motives—surmising their significance. It was no wonder he felt a connection to them.

*Poor little Tae,* he thought.

"Filters off," he said, and the visor's filter effects disappeared.

He stood there, again, thinking. Pondering this mission he'd been given. This game he was being made to play. He still wore the helmet.

"Menu," he said on impulse. Nothing happened.

"Options," he said, and still, nothing happened.

"Manual override," he said, and this time (much to his astonishment) a menu appeared in the visor with a handful of new features. He didn't recognize any of them, except for the last—*Projection.*

He looked toward it and said, "Select."

A blinking rectangular cursor then appeared below the words:

INPUT COORDINATES:

*Did I just hack into this thing? Can I just, go ahead and Project myself somewhere on my own?*

But without proper Coordinates—and the protection of the rest of the suit, of course—it seemed he'd be headed nowhere. So he walked himself swiftly back into the solar, took off the helmet, and turned to Giza with urgency.

"Let's talk about Coordinates."

"Coordinates?" The module rotated a pinch, "Yes, my codex contains instruction for the use of Coordinates."

"Let's see what it says," Spurlock urged, seating himself on the edge of his cot, tapping on the helmet with anticipation. But the unit didn't seem to be in a very cooperative mood.

"The information will be ready for you in the morning," said Giza.

"The morning?" Spurlock frowned, "No, I want it now. You always ask me what I need, and now I'm telling you. I need *Coordinates*."

"You need rest. Even robots need to rest and recharge."

Though his instinct was to rebel, Spurlock could not deny his weariness, cracking a yawn, long and loud. "Okay, Giza. But I want to know everything there is to know about Coordinates, first thing tomorrow."

"I will ready my codex," said the module.

"And I'm not a robot," insisted Steven, "you said so once, yourself."

"Indeed," said Giza, and then the module settled in the corner, dimming his blue light to a soothing level of luminescence.

Spurlock stored away his helmet in the wardrobe, then returned to draw down the sheets on his bed. In so doing, the framed photograph caught his eye from its ledge, and he looked at it. Deeply. More resolutely than before.

*I'm going to find a way back to you.*

She was a sight for the sorest of eyes, and he devoured her image with his own, which were quite sore indeed, and watering now a bit, too. Because among the dozens upon dozens of names (and titles and numbers) he'd read over so hastily. Of all the information he'd seen, scanning those papers acquired down in the space below his tract, one name had inexorably stuck with him.

*Haley Kenmore.*

He looked at her face, thusly, while he laid himself down on the cot. Though the image was just that, only a photo, he thought he could almost see the smile on her face broaden ever so faintly at him. And his fear of the mission—of the insanity of Planet Deaer, and even of the unreal beings skulking about the Station's depths—melted away. An image came to him: he walked with her beneath those blossoming trees in the picture, squeezing her hand three times as they went.

He lay as still as he could. *Our silent secret...*

A calm and relative peace overcame him, then, if only for a moment.

And he breathed deeply.

—You have had an eventful evening, Mr. Spurlock—

The Operator's voice froze him solid in place. She had been, for once, the farthest thing from his mind. He figured, then, she'd somehow become aware of his escapade in the underside of the Station and his meddling with his helmet; that she might send those ethereal beings to extract him from his solar; to take him some place on the Station where they deal with those who do not cooperate, who do not follow the rules.

But she did none of those things.

She said this instead:

—The findings in your latest report have proven especially insightful. Please get some rest, now. You will need to prepare yourself for a most active slate of days to come—

There was a pause filled with nothing but the sound of his breathing, which had hurried itself a bit at the sound of her voice, but had already begun returning to normal.

—Please. Do try and get some rest—

With her words, his head eased back down upon the pillow.

*Oh yes, the days ahead will most definitely be active,* he thought.

And the machine grinded on.

And on. And on.

And on...

...Here ends The Psyop System, Book One: Lights in the Sky.
Please look for Book Two of the series, when the stories of these characters will pick up where they left off, to continue the saga of Steven Spurlock and his subjects on Planet Deaer.

Please visit www.everett-hall.com for updates and more.

www.ingramcontent.com/pod-product-compliance
Lightning Source LLC
Chambersburg PA
CBHW032132190626
46814CB00005BA/1661